PENGUIN BOOKS

Faking Friends

Jane Fallon is the multi-award-winning television producer behind shows such as *This Life*, *Teachers* and *20 Things to Do before You're 30*. Her books include *Getting Rid of Matthew*, *Got You Back*, *Foursome*, *The Ugly Sister*, *Skeletons*, *Strictly Between Us* and *My Sweet Revenge*.

Faking Friends

JANE FALLON

PENGUIN BOOKS

PENGUIN BOOKS

UK | USA | Canada | Ireland | Australia
India | New Zealand | South Africa

Penguin Books is part of the Penguin Random House group of companies
whose addresses can be found at global.penguinrandomhouse.com.

First published in Penguin Books 2018
001

Set in 12.5/14.75 pt Garamond MT Std
Typeset by Jouve (UK), Milton Keynes
Printed in Great Britain by Clays Ltd, St Ives plc

A CIP catalogue record for this book is available from the British Library

ISBN: 978–1–405–93309–4

www.greenpenguin.co.uk

Penguin Random House is committed to a
sustainable future for our business, our readers
and our planet. This book is made from Forest
Stewardship Council® certified paper.

Prologue

'Why are you ringing me at half past five in the morning? Is everything okay?'

I can hear the concern in his voice. Even though he's three years younger than me, my brother's always been the protective one.

'I'm not in New York. I'm in London, remember?'

Thankfully, he does. 'Of course! The big surprise. How is it? Are you having a lovely time?'

'Not really,' I say. I don't know how to begin to tell him that I'm currently sitting on my bed looking at a suitcase full of another woman's clothes. That I found unfamiliar toiletries in my bathroom. That a week ago I had both a job and a boyfriend that I loved and now I don't seem to have either.

'What's up?'

I lie back on the – *my* – bed, in the bedroom I painted myself, on the duvet cover Jack and I chose together, and stare at the ceiling.

'You still there, Amy?'

*

Later, I type a text.

Guess what??? I'm coming home for the weekend!! I arrive late tonight. Flight gets in about half eight. Don't tell Mel. Big surprise!!!! Call you later. Love you xxx

I press send before I can change my mind.

PART ONE

I

The second my plane hit the runway I was already beginning to wonder if I'd done the right thing. Didn't surprise visits always end in disaster? But, up until the moment the flight took off, a big part of me had been worried that I would have to cancel at the last minute, that work would call and say they'd rejigged things again and they needed me after all, so it had seemed safer not to tell anyone. No expectations, no disappointment: that was my rationale. And, besides, I thought it would be fun.

Not to mention the fact that I needed a bit of home comfort. I was still reeling from my big news. It felt, to be honest, a bit like the world was about to end, but I knew deep down that I was overreacting. I had always known it was a possibility. I had watched as many others had suffered the same fate. I just hadn't been expecting it to be so sudden.

I'd been living in New York for seven and a half months. In two weeks, I'd be home for good.

And I thought that breaking the news to Jack face to face would help. Because sad though he'd be for me that I was losing my job, I was pretty sure his main reaction would be happiness: that I was coming home, that we could get on with setting a date for the wedding we'd announced before I'd left, that we'd be back to being a normal couple who lived together rather than more than three thousand miles apart. And I knew that would rub off on me. I needed a bit of perspective.

My heart was kicking up a storm as I approached our road, sweaty and overtired with the jet lag that was kicking in already. I have never done anything like this – flown halfway round the world on a whim. Over and over again, I'd been imagining Jack's face when he found me at home – shock, but I had no doubt it would be quickly followed by sheer delight. I knew, of course, that he would already have left for work by the time I arrived, but there was always a chance he'd have taken the day off sick or as a random holiday. Not that I have ever known him to do either of those things. He loves his job. Or, at least, he loves his work – which is in advertising. He's finding his actual job a bit frustrating. He's impatient to move on and up.

I had spent the whole flight trying to decide what I would do – should I hide and jump out on him? (Might give him a heart attack.) Stand proudly beside a lovingly cooked meal with a serving spoon in my hand? (Too *Stepford Wives*.) Or be lounging on the sofa wearing nothing but a basque? (He'd probably laugh. Also, the slight hitch that I don't own a basque, wouldn't know where to buy one if you paid me. I barely know what one is.) In the end, I decided that booze was the way to go. Wine bottle in one hand, glasses in the other. Don't tell me I don't know the way to a man's heart. Or a woman's, for that matter. I was already planning a trip to the offy around the corner.

I lugged my – way too big for a weekend – suitcase up the stairs. I was transporting as much of my crap home as I could manage before the big move: another reason why this trip made sense. I smiled when I saw that Jack must have been watering the rubber plant on the landing that is my pride and joy, because it looked so healthy and shiny. He might even have polished the leaves, too. That would be a first. This, I realize in retrospect, is when I should have known. Thirty-eight-year-old men do not suddenly start buffing up the leaves of houseplants for no reason. I let myself in, calling out his name, crossing my fingers that today might be the day he had decided to go in late. It was still only a quarter past nine but deep down I knew he'd already be at his desk. He wouldn't be home till half six, quarter to seven at the earliest. And I hadn't even dared think about the fact that he might go out straight from the office. When I spoke to him last night – just before I boarded the plane, although he didn't know that – he didn't mention any plans, but these things change.

The moment I opened the door I knew something wasn't right. The flat looked tidy, for a start. And there was a smell I didn't recognize. Just a hint of it, mixed in with Jack's earthy blend of coconut shower gel, takeaway curries and laundry with a hint of unwashed gym

5

kit. I sniffed loudly, trying to work out what I was finding so unsettling. Could it be me, a faint trace left in my possessions, even though I hadn't been back since Christmas, over three months ago?

I ditched my case and my computer bag and snuffled my way around the flat like a bloodhound. There was more evidence of extreme tidiness – the dishwasher was empty and everything put away, papers were stacked neatly on the coffee table; even the remotes were in a straight line. Maybe he'd invited his mum up, it occurred to me. I should have checked with her, let her in on my secret. He probably wants to show her how well he's coping without me. I know how concerned she was when she heard work was taking me to New York. Maybe she was here already and she'd just gone out for the day, leaving a lingering, unidentifiable but most definitely female scent behind her.

I jumped as Oscar, our portly black cat, appeared out of nowhere and ran towards me. Grateful that he remembered me, I picked him up and made a fuss of him, but I was distracted. I looked in the fridge for his food.

Hummus? Jack thinks the only thing hummus is good for is grouting the bathroom. He thinks it tastes like old sofa cushions, although when he's ever tasted those I have no idea. I shut the fridge door, plonked a handful of Dreamies down for Oscar, who looked at me, disappointed.

I checked in the spare bedroom for signs of life. The bed was stripped and piled up with junk, like it always is. Most of it has been there since the day I moved in four and a half years ago. Pictures we'd never got around to hanging, two tennis racquets we'd used once on holiday, a lamp neither of us liked. No visiting mother, then. I went back out and along the windowless hall. In the bathroom, I stopped short. There was a little cluster of girly toiletries on the windowsill. None of it belonged to me. Shampoo for fine hair. Toner for combination skin. I suddenly felt light-headed. Put out a hand to steady myself on the sink.

In the bedroom, the bed was made. I don't think I've ever known Jack to make the bed in the five years we've been together. Not because he's lazy, he just doesn't see the point. He's only going to get back in and mess it up again. There was an unfamiliar suitcase on my side. I flung it open, riffled through the clothes inside. She was a size eight, whoever she was. In the wardrobe, a row of dresses, blouses and skirts edged my own stuff to the far corner. Some of them looked familiar, but I couldn't work out why. The labels revealed they were from Zara, Top Shop, Maje. Half my friends probably have the same things.

I resisted the urge to phone Jack to demand answers. He didn't even know I was in the country. I retrieved my bags and made sure I'd left no trace behind. Then I exited the flat and headed down to the street. I went straight to the park across the road and sat on a bench. I needed time to think.

2

My name is Amy Jane Forrester. Actually, strictly speaking, it's Aimee Jayne. I was born in the 1970s, when, apparently, it was essential to spell names using random extra letters wherever possible. 1977, to be exact. I gave up correcting people when they spelt it wrongly years ago and started using the simplified version. Life's too short. Average height (five foot five), average size (twelve on a good day), middle child of three (Nichola, forty-one, and thirty-six-year-old Christopher. The extra-letter thing only applied to girls, it seems), auntie to Nichola's two boys.

In New York, I've been filming a new series that has just made its prime-time network TV debut. My big break after years of 'Second prostitute' or 'Woman at station'. Sometimes even just 'Woman'. I've made a living, don't get me wrong. Sort of. Most of it working in actor-friendly call centres, to be completely honest. When I say 'big break', I mean I am a properly named character who appears in every episode. In this, the first season, at least. Not that I am one of the stars. I am part of the ensemble. I bear an uncanny resemblance to the English actress who plays the lead, which led to the happy stroke of good fortune that was me being cast to play her big sister. Actually 'bear an uncanny resemblance' is a bit of an overstatement. By that, I mean we both have near-black, shiny hair, brown eyes and a roundish face. We're close enough, and the English accent swung it.

I say I appear in every episode. I should add 'up till now'. Because the big sister of the hero English detective is about to get bumped off by the very serial killer the detective is hunting for. And I only found out the day before yesterday, when the latest script was issued and there I was being strangled on page thirty-six.

The first thing I did was try to phone Jack. There was no reply. So I went out for a few drinks with sympathetic castmate friends instead, and that's when my plan for a surprise visit home was born.

I live – when in London – with Jack. There was no question that he would be able to relocate with me. We thought about it. He was tempted by the idea of living it large in the Big Apple, until we realized that there's only so large you can live it without a job and an income. And it wasn't as if I was going for ever. We both knew that my adventure would only be temporary.

His response had been to get down on one knee when we were halfway through a Thai curry and an episode of *House of Cards* one evening a couple of days before I left and produce a blue Tiffany box from somewhere under the sofa. Inside was a ring pull from a beer can and a note: 'IOU one engagement ring'. He'd pushed the ring pull on to my third finger. It was so sweet and unexpected that I'd cried, and so had he, and then we'd laughed about what idiots we were and how everything was going to be okay.

We both studiously avoided discussing what would happen if the programme was such a success that it ran and ran, or if my small turn got noticed and I suddenly found myself with a flourishing US career. The odds on either of those things happening were so low, they weren't even worth planning for. He visits when he can get the time off, and I've managed to get home three times, when the filming schedule has allowed. We're making it work. Or so I thought.

The deciding factor about this week's visit, though — the thing that made it worth it, even though I'll be home for good in a couple of weeks' time — was my best friend Melissa. Mel. It's her fortieth birthday tomorrow, and she's organized a party, even though she didn't feel up to celebrating in the slightest because she's been having a really shit time of it. Her marriage fell apart without her even noticing. The first she knew of it was her husband, Sam, telling her he didn't love her any more, he actually loved a woman called Camilla, and that he was off. To say that I felt bad for not being there while my closest mate tried to piece her life back together — well, you can imagine. Or maybe you can't. But trust me, it was awful.

She made no secret of the fact that she was gutted when I said I couldn't get the time off for her party. Even though she knows that my time is never really my own these days, and that it's a long way to fly just to get pissed and sing 'Happy Birthday'. I promised I'd make it up to her when I came home for good. Spend a whole weekend in a spa, being pampered and catching up.

So, as soon as I heard that my fate was sealed, my first thought – actually, my third, after *Oh, shit, what am I going to do with my life now?* and *Which way is the writers' room? I'm going to kill them all slowly and painfully* – was *Sod it, I'll go home, celebrate Mel's birthday with her, have a blast and fuck them all.*

I thought it would be fun to keep my visit a surprise. I spent days fantasizing about how happy both Jack and Mel would be to see me. How they would never expect in a million years that I would come halfway across the world just for a birthday party. And it seems, in Jack's case, I was right.

I find my mobile and call Mel. She'll know what to do. It goes straight through to voicemail. She's probably on the Tube, on her way to work. I'm about to leave a message when I realize I can't do that to her. She's been focusing on this birthday party as if it was going to be the thing that saved her life. I know she's been working out extra hard and half starving herself in an effort to 'show Sam what he's missing'. Even though he won't be there (obviously), she's counting on the fact that they still share a lot of friends who might post pictures of the birthday girl on social media. I know, because she's told me a hundred times, that she's booked a facial tonight and that tomorrow is a blur of waxing, blow-drying and Shellac manicuring. It's not that she wants him back, she just wants him to notice.

I can't put a damper on her night. Even though she's been the first person I've turned to ever since I was eleven years old, it'll have to wait.

I try to channel what she might say to me instead. I can imagine the incredulous look on her face. Big green eyes wide. Mouth a perfect O. Mel has a very expressive face. Sometimes it's like watching an over-enthusiastic mime. And I know exactly what the first thing she'd ask me would be: 'Who the fuck is she?'

That's a very good question.

It hits me that this might be my only chance to find out who this woman is. If – when – I confront Jack, he might shut down and refuse to tell me. He might decide he cares about her so much that protecting her is more important than appeasing me. And for some reason, it's imperative that I know. I'm sure Sun Tzu must have something to say about situations like this. 'Before you can defeat your enemy, you must know who they are' or 'Don't let that bitch get away scot-free.' Something along those lines.

Before I know what I'm doing, I'm back on my feet and heading over the road towards my home again, giant suitcase dragging behind me like a reluctant dog, oversized handbag drooping off my shoulder. The unidentifiable smell is still there. I look through the (neat) piles of magazines and papers on the coffee table, searching for anything with a name attached. There's nothing,

12

which makes me think that, whoever she is, she might not have moved herself in completely.

I open the unfamiliar suitcase again and start flinging stuff out, not caring about the mess I'm making. It's mostly underwear and definitely not the kind that's gone grey through being washed too many times. It feels weird to examine it too closely so I pile it all up on one side. There are a couple of T-shirts and a pair of jeans, none of which give much away. A few brightly coloured tops. I start going through the pockets of the case. Keys, a novel, a few old receipts, a tissue, a few hairgrips, a comb. I examine the comb for stray hairs. None. I pick the receipts up again. They're all for things paid for with cash – a sandwich from Pret, some Lemsip, a coffee. I'm none the wiser. Apart from the fact she's a woman with a cold who likes ham.

I kick the case in frustration.

I can't just sit here and wait for one or other of them to come home. What if she arrives first and she's a psycho? What if they turn up with friends in tow? (Some of our coupley friends, even? It doesn't bear thinking about. Does everyone know? Am I a laughing stock?) I'm not sure I can face the humiliation. And, besides, I don't want my own drama to overshadow the reason I'm here. To make sure my best friend has the night of her life.

I decide to phone my brother, Chris. He always knows what to do in any kind of sticky situation. Not to mention the fact that I'm confident he's one person who won't already be talking about my errant boyfriend behind my back.

'Hey, Sis,' he says when he picks up. He always calls me Sis. It started as a joke because we were both watching the same awful drama on TV years ago and got obsessed with the way the writers would keep trying to remind us of everyone's relationships through the dialogue. My favourite line – 'You know your older brother, Martin, the one who's an estate agent down in Dorking and lives with his wife, Sue, in Reigate?' We started mimicking it whenever we spoke – 'Could you ask our mum, Margaret, who's married to our dad, Graham . . .' 'Hello, younger brother, Chris, have you seen our older sister, Nichola, or her husband, Mark, lately?' You had to be there really, but it made us laugh at the time. Anyway, 'Sis' stuck.

'Why are you ringing me at half past five in the morning? Is everything okay?'

'I'm not in New York. I'm in London, remember?'

'Of course! The big surprise. How is it? Are you having a lovely time?'

'Not really,' I say. I lie back on the bed, stare at the ceiling.

'What's up? . . . You still there, Amy?'

I bring him up to date as succinctly as I can. When I get to the part about the suitcase of clothes, I hear him say, 'What the fuck?' so loudly that his partner, Lewis, appears in the background, asking if everything's all right. Chris puts me on speaker.

14

'I know,' I say. 'I have no idea either. Hi, Lew.'

'You're up late. Or early. One or the other.'

I listen as Chris tries to fill him in.

'There has to be a logical explanation,' Lewis says, once he's up to speed. 'Something obvious that we're all missing.'

'He's having an affair,' I say morosely.

'Some other explanation, I mean. His sister?'

'He doesn't have a sister.'

'I don't know . . . cousin or something?' Chris tries. 'Old friend?'

'Then why wouldn't he have told me?'

'Maybe he hasn't had a chance. Maybe she only showed up last night and it was some kind of emergency.'

'No one's slept in the spare bed.'

'I'll kill him,' Lew says helpfully.

I hear myself sigh.

'Don't. He won't.' Chris says.

'No, you can. Really.'

'Do you have any idea who it might be?' Chris again.

'None. I need to find out.'

'Does it matter?'

'Yes! Jesus. What if it's someone I know? Someone he works with. I can't just suspect every woman he's ever been in contact with. I mean, how will I ever know who I can trust?'

'Or it could just as well be someone you've never met –' Lew says.

Chris interrupts him. '– And it was only meant to be

a fling – not that that excuses either of them – but it got a bit more serious . . .'

'. . . But they're still intending to end it all before . . . you know . . .'

'. . . And, in their minds, what you don't know can't hurt you . . .'

'. . . Or he's been desperate to tell you, eaten up with the guilt, but he knew he had to do it face to face . . .'

'. . . Yes! He'll probably confess everything tonight. Not that that . . . well, you know, it's still awful . . .'

I listen to them talking over each other for a moment. What they're saying does make sense.

'What are you going to do?' Chris asks finally.

'I have no idea. That's why I'm calling you. I mean, if I'm here when he gets home from work, he's going to know I've found out, obviously.'

'So you'll get your answers.'

'But then I'll never know if he would have told me if I hadn't outed him. And what if he just refuses to tell me who she is? And then we've got to get through Mel's party as if nothing's wrong.'

There's silence for a moment.

'How long are you here for?'

'A week. I don't know how I'm going to get through it, though.'

'Here's what I think,' Chris says. I can hear a seagull shrieking and I wonder if they're out in their little sunny Devon garden. I can picture them sitting at the wooden table by their back door, Chris's dark-brown head and

16

Lew's tanned bald one leaning over the phone. Chris has the same habit as me of worrying at his earlobes when he's concentrating, and I imagine him doing it now. 'Text him and tell him you're coming home tonight. Then get out of the flat and watch to see what happens. Chances are, whoever she is, she'll turn up to retrieve her stuff. At least then you'll get a look at her. If he makes a big confession tonight, then you'll just have to go to the party on your own and tell Mel he's ill. You're a good actress, you can do it. And if he doesn't, then pretend everything's fine. Let Mel have her big night. Then hit him with it on Sunday. Or . . . does he know how long you're staying?'

'He doesn't even know I'm here yet, remember.'

'Perfect,' Chris says. 'Tell him you're leaving on Sunday morning. Then you can go to Mel's, cry on her shoulder for a few days and forget about Jack altogether.'

'What? Not even try and work it out?'

'What's to work out?' Lew chips in. 'Whether he 'fesses up or not, he's been seeing someone on the side.'

'Shit.'

'Or you could come and spend the week down here?' Chris says.

It's tempting. Chris has almost Jedi-like powers in terms of making people feel calm and rested. I always thought he should train as a therapist. He preferred to have a job he could leave behind on a Friday night, he said. He knew that he'd end up carrying people's problems with him all weekend. Phoning them up and offering them free sessions so he could help them feel better. But it still became his unofficial role in life. Whenever any of his friends is having a crisis, the first thing they do is call him.

It doesn't make sense for me to hide down there now, though. I need Mel's 'fuck 'em all' take on things if I'm going to get through this.

'No. Thanks, though. I'll be fine. It's a plan. Oh, and there's another thing, I'm getting killed off.'

'No! Damn, I'm sorry.'

'It's okay. I don't think it's any reflection on me, it just makes for a good storyline. Don't tell Mum and Dad yet, though, I can't face it. Or anyone else. It's top secret till it airs.'

'Of course not. So what are you going to do?'

'Well, until just now, I was going to move home, start planning my wedding and get on with my life. Now, I have no idea.'

'Okay, maybe I *will* kill him,' Lew says.

Chris chips in. 'Come down when you get back. You can hide down here and lick your wounds for as long as you want.'

I promise to ring them again as soon as I have any more intel. Then I lean back against the pillows, feeling as if the bottom has gone out of my world. I always wondered what people meant when they said that, but now I know. I feel as if a huge chasm has opened up underneath me and I need to grasp on to something tightly to stop myself from falling into oblivion. Oscar slinks in and jumps up next to me, curling into my side. I sink my fingers into the soft fur on his tummy. Try not to think about some random woman attempting to ingratiate herself with him by sneaking him bits of his favourite cheese.

I have an overwhelming urge to crawl under the covers and sleep. I think it's a version of 'If I close my eyes, the monster isn't there'. But then I look at (my) crisp white pillows and (my) cheerful butter-yellow duvet cover and imagine Jack and God knows who doing God knows what all over them and the urge passes. Besides, I would probably still be there, comatose, when one or the other of them got home and I'm not sure that's a good idea. Not yet.

If I'm going to let Jack know that I'm coming home this evening, I need to get out of the way. But I can't wander the streets with my giant case. In the end – after carefully rearranging my rival's stuff so she won't realize anyone's been examining it – I drag my case to the hotel diagonally opposite our house and book myself into a single room. That's how posh a hotel it is. It has single rooms with single beds. With hairdryers that are wired into the wall to stop you from stealing them. I think it's aimed at lone travellers from struggling businesses. Or prostitutes and their clients renting by the hour. But it's clean. If you don't examine things too closely. Then I crawl into the small but comfy bed, drag the duvet over my face and, despite everything, I manage to cry myself to sleep.

3

I wake bleary-eyed I don't know how much later. The first thing I notice is a folded-up ironing board screwed into the wall at the foot of the bed. I can't remember installing that in my state-of-the-art Manhattan apartment. I look around, taking in the tiny TV (screwed to the wall), the kettle (wired in) radio alarm (ditto), and it all comes crashing back. I check the time on my phone. Twenty-five past twelve. I've slept for about an hour and a half.

I make myself a tinny-tasting coffee from a complimentary sachet (only two provided) with a sliver of milk from one of three tiny plastic capsules. Then I lie back down on the bed and try to process what's going on. Jack is having an affair? Could that really be happening? We FaceTime practically every night, unless one of our work schedules makes the time difference a nightmare. I think back over the past few nights and try to remember if there were any tell-tale signs. Nothing. We've never been the type to be all lovey-dovey over the phone. Or in real life, for that matter. We both find that stuff a bit cringy. By which I don't mean we don't tell each other we love each other. We do. Always. We just say it in plain English, and in normal voices. Not like we're suddenly five years old. Anyway, there's been nothing that rang any alarm bells. Nothing that felt different. No stage whispers, no accidental eye flicks to whoever else was in the room. No abrupt ending of calls.

Before I can think too much about what I'm doing, I send Jack a text.

Guess what??? I'm coming home for the weekend!! I arrive late tonight. Flight gets in about half eight. Don't tell Mel. Big surprise!!!! Call you later. Love you xxx

Almost immediately my phone rings with the distinctive FaceTime tone. I can't answer, obviously, because he might wonder why I've suddenly got an ironing board mounted on my wall. I let it time out and then I call him back, audio only.

'Sorry. Terrible reception.'

'You're really coming today? That's fantastic!'

'Yes!' I say, in what I hope is my happiest voice. 'I'm at the airport now, actually. We should board in a few minutes.' I get up and force open the mud-spotted window of my room and traffic noise blasts in.

'Do you want me to come and meet you?'

Shit. I should have thought this through. Jack likes to meet me at Heathrow. The first time, it didn't even occur to me that he would be there, so I was halfway to the train before I noticed him huffing along beside me, half swamped by a mountain of flowers and balloons. We both cried, I remember. Me with happiness at seeing him, him probably because of exhaustion.

'No! You know what I'd really like? I'll jump in a cab and, if I ring you when I'm on my way, you could order an Indian. I've been fantasizing about mushroom balti and pilau rice.'

Jack laughs. He sounds like his usual relaxed self, not like I've sent him into a major panic. 'You're not pregnant, are you?'

I try to laugh along, but it comes out a bit like a strangled cat. 'No!'

'I can't wait to see you.'

'You, too.'

'I'd better . . . I'm about to go into a meeting. What time did you say your flight gets in again?'

'Eight thirty. So I should get home for tennish. Half ten.' I mentally curse myself for picking such a late flight, but I was trying to go for authenticity.

'Result,' he says.

'You didn't . . .' I say, making an effort not to sound as if I'm asking a loaded question. 'You hadn't made plans, had you?'

'Are you kidding? Like I wouldn't cancel them. But no, this lonely saddo had no plans. Beyond a quick after-work drink. And now I've had a much better offer.'

I ring off, promising to call him as soon as I land. It's so confusing. He sounded genuinely excited at the prospect of seeing me. Maybe I have this whole thing wrong. Maybe there really is an innocent explanation.

I'm suddenly starving. It seems ridiculous to go and

buy something to eat when there's a flat full of food that, by rights, should be mine across the road, but I don't want to risk going back in there now. Jack will have got straight on the phone to *her* and I'm pretty sure she won't be spending her lunch hour eating a sandwich at her desk now, not when she has tracks she needs to cover. I have a quick shower to wake me up and then walk up the road to Tesco Metro. By five past one I'm back sitting on a bench in the park opposite my flat, eating a tuna baguette. I'm far enough away and obscured by enough trees that no one would see me unless they were looking, but I still put a baseball cap over my dark (not to mention dirty) hair, just in case. Air travel does that to me. I get on a plane looking like a Silvikrin advert but by the time I get off you could stand a fork up in the grease. It's a mystery.

It's turned into a beautiful early-spring day and I share a crumb with a couple of mangy-looking pigeons, which turns out to be a mistake, because now they think we're friends for life and they're making me feel guilty about not just tossing them the whole thing. Eventually I do, just to get rid of them, but all that does is cause them to fight among themselves.

Of course, whoever she is, she could decide to come after work rather than in her lunch hour, although if it were me – not that it ever would be – I would want to get it over with as soon as I possibly could. Just to be on the safe side. Or she might not even have a job, or work shifts – that would mean she could show up at any point between now and half ten this evening. I have nothing better to do, though, I tell myself. I may as well sit here as anywhere.

At twenty-five past, just as I'm resigning myself to the fact that it might be a long wait, a taxi pulls up outside our door. I actually gasp out loud and fling my hand over my mouth, like an overacting heroine in a silent movie. I find myself looking around to check no one has heard me. Thankfully, everyone else is concentrating on eating their lunch or walking their dog, relieved to be away from their workplace for an hour's fresh air.

I hold my breath, waiting for her to emerge. I have no idea what I'm going to do. Run over and accuse her? Demand that she gives me answers? Sing the chorus of 'Jolene' right in her face? Punch her and run away? All of the above?

The door opens. I can hear my heart beating. There's a second's pause and Jack climbs out. For some reason, I hadn't even considered this an option. That he might be the one to hide the evidence. He looks so . . . Jack. Not like a man who has been living some kind of secret life. He's never been what you would call classically good-looking, but a happy accident of individually imperfect features resulted in something very attractive. I've always thought so, anyway. His nose is a bit too long, his eyes a smidge too close together, his lips a little thin. The combination – along with the violet blue of his irises and the dark brown of his hair – gives him a kind of wolf-like quality. A sort of better-looking Baldwin brother. Without the anger-management issues.

He's obviously told the driver to wait because the cab doesn't move, engine ticking over, meter running up. Jack runs up the steps to our front door. I pull my hat down over my face and allow myself to look at the upstairs window. From here, I can see the living-room bay and the spare bedroom. There are flat white sheers over both to preserve our privacy but I think I see one of them flap in a Jack-created draught as he – I imagine – runs around like a whirlwind, gathering up anything incriminating.

I know he can't have long. He's never been one for extended lunch breaks. He likes to be seen to be conscientious while all his colleagues are sinking glasses of red at the local bistro. Sure enough, the front door slams open and there he is again, suitcase in one hand, two carrier bags in another and half a dozen girly outfits on hangers slung over his shoulder. The taxi driver chooses just that moment to examine something fascinating on his fingernail, so Jack staggers down the steps alone, goes back up to pick up something he's dropped, then wrestles with the car-door handle. I can practically hear him huffing with frustration. Safe in the knowledge that he's not going to be expected to carry anything, the taxi driver springs to life and gets out and opens the door for him, and he half tumbles in, throwing the suitcase in front of him.

Despite everything, my overwhelming urge is to call out to him, to let him know I'm here. To hurtle across the street and throw myself into his arms.

It hits me like a ton of bricks that that is never going to happen again.

4

One. Two. Three.

I take a deep breath to steady my nerves and fling open the flat door.

I've spent the whole afternoon imagining this moment. I kept veering between wanting to be the reasonable one, to hear what he has to say without interruption and then tell him he needs to leave, at least until after the weekend, or to go in all guns blazing, pull the floor out from under him and not give him a chance to get his story straight. I want to know the truth. How it happened. When. Where. Above all, who.

In the end, I decide that I'm going to keep my cool. Give him the chance to come clean. I plaster a smile on my face. It's just possible I look like Jack Nicholson in *The Shining*. Hi, honey, I'm home.

'Hey!' He pops his head out from the kitchen, arms wide. He looks so pleased to see me I almost forget what's been going on. He swoops me up in a hug.

'Mmm, you smell amazing,' he says, burying his nose in my hair. Shit, I knew I shouldn't have had another shower. Usually, I arrive after a long flight smelling of old food and other people's fetid breath, with skin the colour and consistency of a radish. You might have

27

picked up that I'm not a good traveller. I once caught chickenpox travelling on the train from Reading to London.

I mumble something into his chest that I hope sounds like an endearment.

'Curry'll be here any minute,' he says, holding me at arm's length. I struggle to make eye contact. 'I can't believe you're here!'

'Me neither.'

'Mel's going to be beside herself.'

I take my jacket off. 'You haven't mentioned it to her, have you?'

''Course not, you told me not to. I haven't spoken to her for ages anyhow.'

'Right.' I don't know what to say next so I try, 'It's looking very clean in here. Have you had the Hoover out?' just to see what his reaction is.

He has the gall to look smug. 'Couldn't have you coming home to a dirty flat.'

Luckily, the doorbell rings so I'm saved from having to respond. Jack hotfoots it down the stairs to retrieve the curry, giving me a chance to have a look around. In the bathroom, all trace of the woman's bits and pieces has gone and he's made the effort to spread his own stuff out to fill the gaps and even got a few of my toiletries out from wherever he had hidden them away.

The bedroom is, of course, clear of her belongings. I have a look to see if Jack has changed the sheets, and I'm relieved to see he has. Even the duvet cover, which must be a first. The dryer contains the warm softness of the discarded ones.

I hear him thumping back up the stairs and I root around in the fridge and find a bottle of Prosecco.

'One mushroom balti coming up,' he announces as he comes back in. While I open the fizz and he heaps the hot food on to plates, I have a sneaky look at him. He looks tired – well, no surprise there.

He catches me staring. Smiles.

'What?' he says.

I feel tears rush to my eyes. Blink them back. Gulp like a frog swallowing a fly.

'Nothing. Just great to see you, that's all.'

'You big softy. Come here.' He pulls me in for a hug, kisses the top of my head.

Curry over, we polish off the rest of the Prosecco and I wait. Jet lag is making me sweaty and nauseous. I move from 'I'm a little bit tired' to 'I'm going to fall asleep face first in my leftover pilau rice' in the space of about two minutes. I'm desperate to go to bed, to sleep off my fug, to give my brain the chance to work out what exactly is going on. But I'm too scared to say so, in case he thinks it's a proposition. And the thing about living so far apart from your partner is that you pretty much do have sex every time you see each other, so he's bound to be thinking it's a done deal. I consider allowing myself to pass out on the sofa. That might be the way to go.

'Do you want a nightcap?' he says now, and snakes an arm around my shoulders. I ignore the comment, which I know he thinks is flirty foreplay, and indulge myself in a big, gaping yawn.

'God, sorry. It's because I didn't get any sleep last night.'

'Last night? What were you up to?'

Shit, yes, he has no idea I came in overnight on the red-eye, that I've been hanging around in a hotel all day. 'Just because I had to get up so early to get to the airport, you know. I ended up hardly sleeping because I was so afraid I'd sleep through my alarm.'

'I know a way to wake you up,' he says, nuzzling into my hair. I sit there rigid. Has he always talked in such horrendous clichés?

'I think I might be too far gone,' I say, moving away as gently as I can.

'You can just lie there, let me have my wicked way.' He laughs at how witty this is and I try to join in. I want to shout at him, hurl accusations, but my head is foggy and I know I need to keep my cool.

'Sleep,' I say, hoping Jack will get the message.

'Come on, let's get you into bed,' he says, and then he laughs. 'And I don't mean that how it sounds.'

5

In the end, I sleep badly but I do sleep. At one point, I wake up and find I'm wrapped around Jack's back like a loved-up clam, and then I remember what's happened and I shove him away, not caring if he wakes or not, although he's dead to the world.

I wake up again only when Jack nudges me, cup of tea in hand, at what turns out to be eleven o'clock. All I want is to get through the day, get through the party without ruining Mel's night, and face whatever comes my way tomorrow. Jack, however, has other ideas.

'So, I thought we could go into the West End and have lunch somewhere. Oh, and I need to get some new jeans, so maybe Selfridges?'

I take the mug of tea gratefully. My mouth feels like I've been eating sandpaper.

Usually, I realize now, I just go along with whatever he wants to do on my visits home. Such is my guilt at being the one who upped and left to go and work abroad. Funnily enough, I don't feel so bad about that now.

'I can't face the West End. You go if you want. To be honest, I could just sleep all day.'

'Well, I won't go if you don't want to come,' he says petulantly. 'I just thought it would be nice. We could

get your ring resized. You're always saying it's too big.'
A few days after Jack's proposal, we'd chosen a ring
together. Simple. Understated. A tiny pink diamond
embedded into a plain gold band. I had no interest in a
big rock. I'd have been happy sticking with the ring
pull. In fact, I think I still have it somewhere, nestled in
its light blue box.

I know I have to make a bit more of an effort if I
don't want him to realize I've sussed him before tonight,
so I reach a hand out and rub his arm. 'Tell you what,
let's go for a walk later. I just need to sleep it off some
more.'

He sits down next to me and pulls me towards him.

'Shall I wake you again in an hour or so?'

'Mmm . . .' I say. It's the best I can come up with at
short notice.

In the end, we potter about locally, buying treats for
tomorrow's breakfast and browsing in the bookshop,
sampling smelly cheese in the little deli. Ordinarily,
this is exactly what I love to do whenever I'm home.
The mundane stuff. The everyday normality that most
people find boring. It's what I miss. Today, I go through
the motions.

I just want this day to be over.

6

Mel's fortieth is being held in a room above a pub in Shoreditch. But it's a pub that's far more Parmesan crisps and flat whites than beer and peanuts. We've often spent the evening here, surrounded by fairy lights in the small, fragrant patio garden, if I've gone to meet Mel from work. I always check it's just going to be the two of us before I venture down here, though. I find it a bit uncomfortable watching the version of Mel that she presents to her work colleagues, not that I would ever want her to know that. We all do it, over-exaggerate our past to the people who didn't know us then, make ourselves sound more working or upper class, or cooler/nerdier/sportier. As if it's not enough just to have been a normal, average child with a functional upbringing. But, for Mel, it's an extreme sport. To hear her talk, you would think she had been a star in a previous life, or at least a professional. That her achievements weren't just confined to our village, that it wasn't all over by the time she was twenty. And no one ever questions it because, why would they?

She's always dropping little references into her conversations with people who haven't known her as long as I have. The odd 'when I was modelling' or 'in my acting days', as if she's an old Hollywood legend sharing her past with her adoring fans. It's just Mel. She can't help herself. I don't think she even realizes she's doing it.

She hates her job, which is doing something incomprehensively dull-sounding in an insurance office, and is about as far as it gets from the glamorous life she – and we all – envisioned for herself when she was young. I'll be honest, I've sometimes envied her the regular hours, the security and the absolute lack of any requirement to think about work between home time and nine-thirty the next morning, but I have never wanted to swap places with her.

If St Augustine's School for Girls had been the kind of place to indulge in these things, then Melissa Moynahan would almost certainly have been voted 'Most Likely to be a Star' in 1993. In the five years we had been at the school, she had taken the lead in every end-of-term play. Willowy, flame-haired and head-turningly pretty, she was every mother's idea of the perfect daughter. She acted, she sang, she danced, all to perfection. Barely a week went by when the local paper didn't list one of her achievements on its inside pages. (Thinking about it, though, it was a small place and they had about twenty sides to fill with news, so someone passing their tap exam with distinction or achieving their BAGA Grade 1 gymnastics was as good a scoop as anything.) She was also well turned out and polite and in the top third of the class in every subject. 'Why can't you be more like Melissa?' was a lament heard by most of the girls in my year at some point or other, either from parents or teachers. Or, in my case, both.

She should have been easy to hate but, somehow, she wasn't. She was sharp and funny and had just the right amount of eye-rolling disdain for the constant praise she received. And she could be badly behaved, too, something I always loved about her. Although she somehow got away with it, because no one could believe she would be capable of being anything other than perfect.

I was in awe of her, I'm not going to lie. She seemed to breeze through life without a care in the world, everything she touched turning to stardust. She lived in one of the neat three-bedroom houses on the neat estate on the edge of town, with weeping willows in the front gardens and dads washing their cars on the drives at weekends. She was an only child and had her own pink bedroom, I discovered when we became friends. With white furniture, and her own armchair, covered in a Laura Ashley floral. I shared a room with Nichola in our damp old cottage, painted magnolia as a compromise between our two contrasting tastes and therefore pleasing no one, the two beds practically touching. If we reached out, we could hold hands – not that we ever did. Nichola and I have never been close.

I have no idea how Mel and I became friends. One minute, I was admiring her from afar, quite content with my small circle of pals but convinced there was a soulmate out there for me somewhere, and the next she had turned the full force of her beam on me and I was being invited round for tea one Saturday afternoon. Later, as we stuffed in mini chicken kievs and pizza bites from Iceland (everything in my house was lovingly made from scratch and contained absolutely no E-numbers, so this in itself was a major treat for me), she told me it was because she wanted to rescue me from my circle of goody-goody friends, which should have been insulting but which I took as a huge compliment. She could tell I was different, she said.

After that, I would spend every spare moment in her pink-and-white bedroom or watching while she twirled or tapped or acted her way through her charmed life. I was her chief cheerleader. And I knew that was my role. I cheered, while she soaked up admiration from all sides. I worked steadily, while she effortlessly shone. It sounds one-sided. It wasn't. What she gave me back was fun and friendship. Where I had the tendency to see the glass as half empty, she was the only person who could convince me it was overflowing.

Physically, we were polar opposites. Me dark-haired, brown-eyed, honey-skinned and sporty; her red-haired, green-eyed, skin a luminous white that was almost blue, and fragile-looking, although that belied her tough interior. We used to spend hours comparing our differences, as if we could only really see ourselves in the ways we contrasted with each other. Beside her, I felt ordinary. As if my own looks were ten a penny while everything about hers stood out from the norm.

Soon we had our futures mapped out. She was going to be a star. I had no such ambitions for myself. I had no desire to be in the spotlight. I was going to be successful at something boring but lucrative, I just hadn't quite worked out what yet. Something that would leave me with enough time off so that I could travel around the world with her, having fabulous adventures.

I know from our many FaceTime conversations on the subject that tonight there are about a hundred people expected, that there will be a DJ playing mainly nineties hits, and that the pub are laying on staff to serve drinks from the small corner bar. Melissa has hired a catering company to provide a selection of mouthwatering-sounding canapés, along with two roving waiters. My contribution — because, obviously, she has no idea that I'm going to be there in person and neither did I when she first started planning it — has been to provide the cake.

'It's too sad if I have to choose my own cake,' she had said to me one night. She was in the living room of the beautiful flat in Kingston that she and Sam had shared until a couple of months before. He was trying to pressure her into selling so that they could split the profits and both start again, and I knew that this, above all, was tearing her up. She loved that flat. They'd lived in it since before they were married — eight years — and she had decorated every inch several times and chosen pretty much every piece of furniture, too, because Sam had no interest in that kind of thing. He just stumped up the cash. That was Sam's solution to everything, by the way.

'I mean, what kind of tragic loser has no one to organize a surprise fortieth-birthday cake for her?' Mel has always been obsessed with ageing, and her fortieth had taken on the significance of a religious festival. My own was coming up in a couple of months, and I wasn't really bothered.

'Maybe someone has but you don't know about it. Because it's a surprise.'

'No. No one cares enough except you.'

I laughed, because she was being typically melodramatic. Everything is a performance with Mel. 'Why don't I do it?'

'Oh my God, would you?' she said, cheering up in an instant. She swept her hair up in both hands and pulled it back off her face. I could tell she was checking out how it looked on her phone. 'Use the Hummingbird Bakery and get one with little flowers on. Or one of those topsy-turvy ones . . .'

'If I do it, I'm picking everything. I don't want any instructions.'

'Okay. With raspberries . . .'

'Shut up, or I'm not getting involved. The whole fun is that I get to choose. One more word and I'm not doing it.'

'I wish you could come,' she'd said, as she did pretty much every time we talked.

'Me, too.'

'I would, literally, uninvite everyone else if it meant you could be there.'

I'd checked on the cake yesterday and the small West End company I'd chosen had sent a photo of the finished product: one layer salted caramel and raspberry, Mel's go-to flavour option on any dessert menu, and the other a sticky combination of chocolate, almonds and marshmallows in honour of rocky-road ice cream, her favourite during our long, hot, teenage summers. I have no idea if it all goes together but I know she'll love the sentiment. The top was decorated with a flame-red-haired figure lounging on a chaise longue, champagne glass in her manicured hand. Piped around her were the words 'Forty and fucking fabulous beatches', which I knew would make her laugh. I had spent an unhealthy amount of time discussing the spelling of the word 'beatches' with the woman on the other end of the phone when I placed the order. She kept thinking that I was trying to say beaches and that the chaise longue should be a sun lounger. She asked me if I wanted a palm tree at least three times. I had to explain to her what it means but she was still getting over the fact I wanted the word 'fucking' on there so she didn't really take it in.

'I don't think I'll be putting this one on our website,' she'd said huffily as she wrote down my credit-card number.

Anyway, the wording looks perfect in the photo. I can't wait for Mel's reaction.

I know she'll be feeling nervous setting everything up – I think she roped in a couple of work friends to help her with the finishing touches so, while I'm getting ready, I send her a text – 'Hope all going okay. SO sad I'm not going to be there but you'll have a blast. Don't wake up anywhere you shouldn't! Call you tomorrow xxx' – and I'm rewarded almost immediately with a reply: 'Won't be the same without you! Xxx'

The sounds of 'Parklife' by Blur greet us as we head up the stairs to the function room. I remember dancing to this with Mel the first time she came to visit me at uni in London. Even though I was having the time of my life, and I loved all my new friends already, I'd missed her so much I felt as if I'd had a part of me removed.

Jack edges in ahead of me, hiding me behind him. The room is packed, a testament to Mel's popularity. But it's not oppressive. I know pretty much everyone and they all greet me like a returning explorer they thought they might never see again. Jack makes an elaborate show of *sshh*ing them, and propels me along to find Mel. I want her to see me before she hears a rumour that I'm there.

And then I spot her. Red hair, bright orange top, skinny jeans and towering heels. She's laughing heartily at something someone has just said to her, head back, perfect teeth gleaming white.

'Hey, Mel,' Jack says, and she looks over and greets him warmly with a peck on the cheek. She hasn't noticed me yet.

'Jack! Hi! Thanks for coming.'

'Happy birthday,' he says. 'You're looking well.'

'For a forty-year-old,' she says with a scowl. 'For the rest of my life now, I'll have to add a coda whenever anyone gives me a compliment.'

I pop my head out from behind his back. It takes a moment for her to register what she's seeing but just as Jack is saying, 'Oh, look who I brought . . .' Mel lets out a piercing squeal.

'Oh my God!! You're here!!' She grabs me into a hug, half crushing the life out of me. The familiar, safe touch of her is so comforting I want to blurt out my secrets right away, even with Jack standing there, but I remind myself that this is her night and I'm not going to spoil it. 'How on earth?'

I hold her at arm's length. 'Last-minute madness. I couldn't bear to miss it.'

'I can't fucking believe it.'

Someone thrusts a glass of Prosecco into my hand. I remind myself that drinking too much would not be a good idea but then I down it anyway. It's not every day your best friend turns forty. We try and snatch bits of conversation in between the hordes of people flinging themselves at Mel to wish her a happy birthday. I don't care. I know I'll have her all to myself tomorrow. I wonder if I should check whether she's going to be at home, but I don't want to give myself away in front of Jack. Although my guess is she'll be lying in bed moaning about her hangover for most of the day anyway.

Around ten, the party thins out a bit as our friends who have little ones start to drift off to relieve babysitters. I see Mel roll her eyes at the retreating back of one couple. Party-pooping is a bit of a sin in her book. I'm exhausted from chatting to all her friends – most of whom I haven't seen since I left for the States. Everyone asks how the show is going and I have to smile and say, 'Great,' because it's written in blood in my contract that I don't let slip plot lines to anyone. What they're all going to think when I suddenly move home, tail between my legs, in two weeks' time, I have no idea. Except that, of course, I no longer seem to have a home. Shit, I realize, I need to start thinking about where I'm going to live. Maybe Mel and I could look for somewhere together. Two sad fortyish singles back to sharing rented accommodation. Actually, that doesn't sound so bad.

'I have about five lines an episode,' I say, over and over again, trying to manage expectations that I'm suddenly a big star, but I know I'll still be in for a barrage of 'You weren't in it much' comments when it eventually airs over here.

'Lucky for you there's a free bar, or the drinks would definitely be on you,' Shaz, Mel's best work friend and someone I've always found more than a little brash and irritating, crows. She leans in too close, swaying slightly, eyes glassy from too much booze. 'Bringing in the big bucks!'

I don't tell her that, even though this is the most I have ever earned on an acting job, it's still just a wage. No one is paying me extra because mine is a name they simply have to have associated with their show. The trade-off for them casting an unknown from the UK was that I had to pay all my own relocation expenses and any travel back and forth. (Thankfully, my rent was taken care of by the production company, otherwise I would have been taking home negative amounts. I get – got – to live in a smart block on the far reaches of the Upper East Side, in spitting distance of the studios across the bridge in Queens.) I've managed to save a bit, but it's hardly a life-changing amount. Especially now there won't be any more.

I take refuge at an empty table for a second, down a big glass of water. Past experience tells me too much alcohol and jet lag don't mix so I'm trying to apply the 'soft drink between each hard drink' rule, which just means I have to keep running to the loo. Mel is on the dance floor – I say 'dance floor', it's actually a small space in the middle of the room where a few people are half-heartedly breaking moves. Not Mel. Dancing is one thing she is never half-hearted about. She's a blur of bright colours in a sea of blacks and browns. Not for the first time I marvel at my friend's confidence.

I look around to see where Jack is – I've been monitoring his interactions with women, looking for clues – but he seems to be on his best behaviour. I catch sight of him chatting happily to one of Mel's work colleagues – John, I think his name is – so I head back towards the bar. No such luck. Mel has me in her sights and she reaches out to grab me as I pass. I'm a horrible dancer. Awful. I'm way too aware of what I'm doing, how ridiculous we all look jigging about together, arms and legs flapping like a floor full of chickens. And as soon as I think that, I'm lost. I'm out of time with myself, let alone the music. She won't let me go, though. One of Mel's favourite things has always been to force me on to a dance floor and watch me suffer.

'This is my best birthday present ever,' she says.

'What? Watching me make a prat of myself?'

'You being here,' she laughs.

'I wouldn't have missed it for the world.'

'Yes, you would. You'd have missed it if you were filming.'

'Well, yes, there is that. But otherwise . . .'

She laughs again. 'You've made an old woman very happy.'

The music stops abruptly. We dancers stumble to a halt. The door opens and in walk two waiters, carrying Mel's cake, candles lit. They parade it in front of her while everyone sings 'Happy Birthday', and her face lights up when she sees it. She squeals when she reads the writing.

'That is brilliant.' She throws her arms around me. 'Have you got any idea how much I love you?'

Despite everything, I'm so happy I'm here.

*

44

Later – it must be one in the morning – I look around for Jack and can't see him. I'm tempted to leave without him. Let him find his own way home and discover me fast asleep. I'm knackered, and the last time I saw Mel she was ranting about going on to a club. Safe in the knowledge she has enough friends who will indulge her in her desire to dance till dawn, I have every intention of sneaking out without saying goodbye. She's so happily drunk she won't even remember whether I was there at the death or not. I wander around the periphery of the room, scouting who's still there. The pub staff are wanting to close up and everyone – apart from the hard core – is starting to hunt for their coats.

I find him eventually, coming out of the gents. He's more than a little drunk, grinning wolfishly, hair standing up on one side.

'Are you ready to go? They're closing up, I think.'

'Definitely,' he slurs. 'Are we Ubering?'

I fish my phone out. 'Okay. I was going to try and sneak out without Mel noticing. Otherwise she's going to try and force us to go to –'

'You're not leaving?'

Too late. Mel is making a beeline for us. She's staggering on her vertiginous heels.

'Busted. Are you sure you're okay to go out? Do you have people to go with?'

She flings her arms around me. 'Loads. But it won't be the same without you.'

'I'll ring you tomorrow. Make sure you get home safe.'

'Yes, Mum.'

She finally lets me go and then throws her arms round Jack, too. I find myself thinking that's probably the last time she'll do that. Not once she knows the truth about him. Jack pats her on the back like he's burping a baby. He's never been any good at hugs. Public ones, at least.

He pulls away and, as he does, as I turn around to wrestle my other arm into my coat, that's when I see it. Their hands interlinked as they separate. Fingers moving reluctantly apart, making contact until the last minute.

And then I remember where I've seen that orange top before. The one that Mel's wearing. It was in the suitcase. In my bedroom.

I lean back in to hug Mel again. Just to check. That's it. That's the smell I caught a hint of in my flat. Melissa's Diptyque perfume.

7

You'd think I would cry. Fall to the floor in a heap and bawl my eyes out. My boyfriend and my best friend. Him, I can get over. Her, never. But actually my over-riding emotion is anger. I'm furious. Absofuckinglutely incandescent with rage. I want to hurt them. I want to make them suffer.

Jack is too pissed to notice my mood as we wait in the street for the car and then, the minute we're in, he falls asleep. Head back, mouth open. At the other end, the Uber driver helps me get him out – I assume because he wants him gone from his car, not because he wants to win Driver of the Year. In fact, the second we've got Jack into a standing position, he lets go of his side and I'm left with the whole lolloping weight of him. I manage to half drag him up the steps – even in this mood I'm not mean enough to leave him on the street – but once we're through the front door there is no way I'm killing myself by dragging him up to the first floor. I let go of him and he *thunks* to the hallway carpet. Then I head up the stairs, slamming the flat door behind me. I can only hope our downstairs neighbours are already home and won't have to negotiate six foot one of drunk, semi-conscious bastard on their doorstep any time soon.

Once in the flat, I get ready for bed. I'm tempted to call Chris again but I know he'll have been asleep for hours. I check my phone anyway. It's always possible the production have been trying to get hold of me, telling me they're changing the schedule again. Because I only appear in four scenes in my final episode, they have been able to schedule them all for the second week. I think they felt sorry for me. But it's not out of the question that something could cause them to re-arrange the shooting order. I'm not supposed to leave the country without permission but, on this occasion, I thought, *Sod it*. What were they going to do if they suddenly called me in for tomorrow and I had to tell them I'm halfway across the world? Fire me?

Instead, I have three missed calls from Kat. Kat is a friend, but one of those friends that, every time you see them, you pretty much wish you hadn't made the effort. Actually, that's too harsh. She means well. She just has a tendency to be a bit blunt. She shared a house with Mel and me in Finsbury Park when I first left uni and Mel moved up to try and hit the big time. I found Kat in a *Time Out* ad, along with another girl called Liz, who none of us ever really saw in the three years we lived together. Basically, we just needed numbers to make renting a whole house on next to no money feasible. We would have teamed up with anyone who wasn't a serial killer. Although the jury is still out on Liz. Anyway, Kat and I became friends. She's spiky, and that can come across as mean, but she can be kind with it, which is what sealed the deal for me. She and Mel were too much like argumentative cats to ever get on, although, to give her credit, Kat tried. But Mel loathed her. Referred to her as Katty. Put her down whenever she got the opportunity.

Kat found Mel's self-belief baffling. And I know she got more than a little satisfaction from watching as Mel's dreams failed to materialize and she finally had to admit defeat. Still, once we all went our separate ways — Kat to a job in Birmingham, Mel and I to a tiny flat in Bounds Green and Liz to God knows where, none of us ever asked — we kept in touch, she and me as friends, Mel as a reluctant occasional third wheel. I haven't seen her in months. More than a year, I realize guiltily.

I know she will be calling because someone will have posted pictures of the party already and she'll be demanding to know why she wasn't invited. And, to be fair, I don't blame her. She and Mel are 'friends', they're just not very friendly. If Mel's celebration had been an intimate dinner for eight, she wouldn't have expected to be there. But a party for a hundred? I can't face appeasing her now, even though the last call was only ten minutes ago so I'm pretty sure she's still up. But then it occurs to me that, if one person might appreciate what I'm going through, it would be her. If there's one person who would indulge me in a bit of bitching about Mel . . .

I listen, and there's no sound coming from the hallway. Jack must be sound asleep on the floor. I made sure he was in a safe position before I left him (the only thing I can remember from a weekend first-aid course about twenty years ago is the recovery position, and I'm gratified that it's finally come in handy) so I have no qualms about leaving him there. I hit Kat's number. I know I shouldn't, that she's in no way impartial, but I desperately feel the need to offload on someone who'll indulge me. She answers almost immediately. I can picture her sitting in her stylish living room, which is like a museum of the sixties and seventies, lips pursed tight, her poor husband, Greg, trying but failing to convince her that it must have been an oversight.

'Unbelievable!' she says, before I can get a word in. 'I invited her to my wedding. My fucking *wedding*! And she had the gall to come and then not invite me to her fortieth!'

'Your wedding was four years ago. You probably saw more of each other then.'

'That's what Greg says,' she says, in a tone of voice that implies agreeing with Greg in this instance is not the correct thing to do.

'Well, she's probably just being a bitch.' That takes the wind out of her sails. Never in the eighteen years I've known Kat have I slagged off Mel in front of her.

'Well . . . are you okay?'

Here goes nothing. 'I think Mel and Jack might be having an affair. Kat, you mustn't tell anyone. I'm trusting you.'

'Greg, why don't you go to bed, love? I'm going to be a while.'

I hear him mumble his assent, probably grateful to be off the hook. 'Night, Amy,' he calls as he goes. I love Greg – in an entirely appropriate friend-of-his-wife kind of way – he's the calm, unrufflable opposite that buffs away Kat's hard edges.

'I won't. Shit. Where's this come from?'

I tell her what I saw. We get sidetracked at around the point where she realizes I was at the party too.

'You're in England? Since when?'

'Yesterday. Well, technically, the day before, as it's Sunday now. It was a last-minute thing.'

She huffs but she lets it go.

'And you're really sure it's her? I mean, far be it from me to want to defend her, but you couldn't have misinterpreted? Like you said, they were both plastered.'

'No. The perfume sealed it. I knew I recognized that smell.'

'She could have popped round to see him, though. I mean, they're friends . . .'

'He said he hadn't spoken to her. Why would he lie? And, anyway, the top. It was there in the case. That was her stuff.'

'Fuck.'

'That's an understatement.'

'It makes sense. You know how jealous she's always been of you, right?'

I let out an involuntary snort. 'Hardly.'

'Blatantly.'

There's a crash as – I assume – Jack stumbles up the

stairs, obviously having woken from his floor bed. 'Shit, I'd better go. Jack's coming and I don't want to have to deal with him now.'

He fumbles around, trying to get his key in the lock. Burps loudly. I have no intention of going to help him.

'Okay. Listen, come to us tomorrow. You can hide out here till you go back. We'll be in all morning. Come as early as you like.'

'Thanks, Kat. You can tell Greg, by the way. Just no one else. Not yet.'

'Oh, I was going to. You tell me, you tell us both, them's the rules.'

I actually laugh as I say goodnight. Then I put out the light and pull the covers over my head just as Jack manages to get the door open. He falls over the coffee table, swearing loudly. I leave him to it.

When I wake up in the morning, he's found his way to bed. A quick check under the covers reveals he still has all his clothes on, including his shoes. It's already nearly eleven so, by the time I've had a shower, dressed and eaten something, it's time to go: my fictional flight is just after four. I pack my case quietly. I don't want to disturb him if I can help it. He doesn't deserve a fair hearing. He doesn't deserve for us to sort this out like adults. He's forfeited that right. At five to twelve I write him a note: 'Didn't want to wake you, you looked so peaceful :) Waited as long as I could but I didn't want to risk missing the plane! Talk later xxx,' and leave it by the kettle.

On the way to the Tube my phone pings with a message. Mel. 'Jesus, head like a sick buffalo! Why did you let me drink that much!! How fun was that, though?? Wanted to wish you bon voyage, now back to bed (on my own, before you ask!!!!) with an Alka Seltzer! Love you xxx'

I resist the urge to tell her to go fuck herself. Send her a non-committal smiley face instead.

8

Kat and Greg live in a brutalist ex-council block near Russell Square in a beautiful two-bedroom flat with a tiny north-facing balcony. It cost them a small fortune, but it perfectly suits their retro aesthetic.

She's standing in the open doorway when I get out of the lift. Black, fringed bob shining, thick-framed glasses, a slash of red lipstick. She greets me with a quick hug.

'Jesus, you look terrible,' she says as we pull apart, and I manage a weak smile. It's such a Kat comment. In fact, I remember much of Mel's problem with her stemmed from the time she came into our shared kitchen dressed for a party and asked her usual question, 'How do I look?'

We all do it. Mel more than most. And we all just expect platitudes in response, not a full critique. Kat, it turned out, had never understood why someone would ask if they just wanted a compliment regardless.

'That length's not great on you. It cuts you off at the knees and makes your legs look short. Which they definitely aren't.'

I'd laughed, but Mel had looked as if she was going to explode.

'Thanks for your advice, Mrs Super-stylish. Remind me to take you with me next time I'm clothes shopping.'

Kat had shrugged. 'You asked. I was just trying to say you have great legs so why not show them off to their best advantage?'

Mel had huffed out of the room, but when she stuck her head around my door ten minutes later to say good-bye I noticed she was wearing something different.

'Thanks,' I say now.

'Greg's cooking lunch.' Now she mentions it, I notice there's a nutty, garlicky aroma wafting from the kitchen that, on any other day, would have me salivating.

'I don't have much of an appetite, to be honest.'

'Tough luck. There'll be no getting down from the table until you've finished what's on your plate.'

She takes my case from me and stashes it in a corner. 'Come and have a cup of tea at least.'

I allow myself to be led into the living room, stopping on the way to say hi to Greg. From the sympathetic expression on his face, I know Kat's filled him in on all the gory details.

'So what happened this morning?' she asks, pouring tea from a floral teapot into a waiting cup as I perch on the mustard G-plan sofa. Only Kat would still be using loose tea and china cups and saucers.

'Nothing. I left before he woke up.'

She opens her perfectly batwing-lined eyes wide.

'So they still don't know you know?'

I shake my head. 'I couldn't face it. I don't know . . . what's the point?'

'To get it out of your system?'

'I'd have killed him.'

She shrugs as if to say, 'And . . . ?'

'And as for Mel . . . Jesus. She gave me such a hard time about my not being able to come to the party. And then she acted so surprised to see me there, but she must have known. No way would Jack not have told her. He managed to get her top back to her somehow, so he must have seen her at some point.'

Kat purses her lips. 'I've known Mel long enough to know that she comes first and sod everyone else.'

I find myself reaching for my default defence. I've never let anyone get away with badmouthing Mel. I check myself, though. 'Maybe.'

'No "maybe" about it.'

'How could she do this to me? I mean, it's one thing being a bit self-obsessed . . .'

'I told you, she's jealous of you, always has been. Well, I don't know about when you were kids . . .'

'As if . . .'

She sits back and looks at me. 'What? You don't think she'd like to be doing what you're doing?'

I've thought about this over the years, of course I have. But the reality of my career hardly matches up to Mel's former ambitions. 'Playing a bit part?'

'Making a living from acting. Working in New York. Rubbing shoulders with the rich and famous. While she works in an insurance office.'

'So you think she deliberately set out to seduce my boyfriend? Come on, Kat, that's a bit far-fetched.'

'Maybe not, but I think, when it happened, she didn't spend too much time worrying about you.'

'She's my best friend.'

'She's got a fucking weird way of showing it.'

I rub my eyes with the heels of my hands. 'I'm moving back here in two weeks.'

Kat says, 'What?' just as Greg pops his head out of the kitchen and says, 'Great! I mean . . . it is, isn't it . . . or . . . ?'

'I suppose. I need to find somewhere to live.'

They both bombard me with questions and I answer as many as I can, repeating my mantra that this remain between us. I don't know why I'm being so loyal to the production that's just fired me. Fear, I think. As if they might have a team of lawyers scouring the globe for the source of any plot leaks.

'You can't just let Jack keep the flat,' Kat says once I've finished.

'I don't have any choice. It's his.'

'But . . .' she splutters. 'It's in your name, too, right?'

I'm tempted not to tell her, because I know exactly how she'll react. Here goes. 'We never got around to it. I pay half the mortgage and the idea always was that we'd go and see the bank and have me added . . .'

'You are kidding me.'

'I know. It just didn't feel like a priority. And then we were talking about selling up next year and buying somewhere together anyway . . .'

She's looking at me like you might look at your

sixty-five-year-old aunt who's trying to convince you the twenty-year-old local boy she met on her holiday really is in love with her, just as she signs over her life savings to him.

'How long had he lived there before you moved in?'

I look at the floor. 'A couple of months. He was in the process of buying it when I met him.' I feel a lump come up in my throat. 'I helped him choose everything. I even painted all the walls. I grouted the fucking bathroom.'

'So you've basically paid half the mortgage the whole time he's had the flat?'

'Pretty much.'

'Shit, Amy. Maybe he'll do the decent thing and sell up and split the profits with you anyway.'

It would be fair, but I know it won't happen. 'He won't. I know what he's like. The minute I accuse him, he'll go on the defensive. He hates being backed into a corner.'

'This is so fucked up.'

'Tell me about it.'

We sit there in silence for a moment.

'Okay.' She snaps into business mode. 'You need somewhere to live before you tell him you're on to him. That way, you can make a clean break. I'll help you find somewhere this week.' Kat is an estate agent. How she ended up doing this and not curating a museum of sixties art or running a diner escapes me. It always seems so unlikely. It comes back to me now that, these days, she's a property consultant, which means she helps rich people find houses and steers them through the tricky negotiations for a percentage of the value.

'I can't afford you,' I say, in an attempt to make a joke, and she rolls her eyes at me. 'Anyway, I was going to try and change my ticket to go home tomorrow.'

'You have way too much to sort out.'

'I genuinely can't afford much, actually.' I've been hiding my head in the sand about my loss of income. It didn't really matter when I had a roof over my head and a boyfriend who could afford to cover the mortgage while I readjusted. God knows when I'll get another acting job, and call-centre wages aren't going to cover my rent for long. 'Oh, Jesus, I'm too old to flat-share with random strangers.'

'You won't have to. We'll find something. You're going to have to confront Jack at some point, though, you know that. Even if you decide never to speak to Mel again – and who would blame you? – you have to disentangle your life from his. Take what's yours.'

'Damn. I should have taken my file with all my personal stuff in. I have some money in an ISA I could take out . . .'

Kat looks at me intently. 'You still have the keys, don't you?'

Which is how we find ourselves on Monday morning, Kat and I, sneaking into my flat like a pair of burglars who just happen to have keys. I'm afraid one of the neighbours will see me and unthinkingly mention something to Jack, but Kat is all for brazening it out. Last night, once I worked out that my plane should have landed at JFK and I could feasibly be through Customs and heading for Manhattan, I sent him a text. Luckily, the fact that it was nearly 1 a.m. in London meant he wouldn't be expecting a call, not to mention that he was probably already getting down to it with Mel. In my bed. I kept it to the basics: 'Just landed. Call you tomorrow xx'

When I got up this morning there was a reply: 'Later xx'.

Bastard.

Oscar heads out of the bedroom as we let ourselves in, happy but confused at company arriving so early in the day.

'Oskie!' Kat shrieks, and makes a grab for him. She loves him. It's mutual.

'Mel hates cats,' I say. 'She'd better be being fucking nice to him.'

A quick glance tells me that Mel and her case are back. I'm tempted to open it and leave it open, because Oscar has a tendency to find a soft surface much more appealing than his litter tray when nature calls. It would be too much of a giveaway, though. Mel is a neat freak and I know she wouldn't leave for work in the morning without checking everything was in perfect order first. Plus, she might shout at him and I really can't bear to think of that happening.

I head for the large wooden chest where both Jack and I keep all the important stuff: chequebooks, bank statements, birth certificates. I start rooting through, sorting out my stuff from his.

'It's so annoying that most of my savings are in our joint account. I don't want to take them out yet because he'll wonder why.' I look around as I say this. 'What the hell are you doing?'

Kat has Jack's laptop open and is calmly browsing through. 'Nothing. Just looking. You never know. Don't you want questions answered? Like when they got together or who else knows?'

'Kat! No. I mean . . . yes, but, no. I can't believe he'd be stupid enough to email her, anyway.'

She barely breaks her stride. 'No, they've been using direct messages on Twitter, look.'

I stomp over, meaning to stop her in her tracks, when she says, 'Eew!' so, of course, I say, 'What?' and she slams down the lid and says, 'It just got rather phone-sexy.'

'Let me see.' I try to grab the laptop but she pulls it back, and it all gets a bit Laurel and Hardy while we wrestle back and forth.

'I don't think you should read it.'

'Jesus Christ, Kat!' I shout. 'Give it to me.'

Shocked by my raised voice, she hands it over and I flop on to the sofa. She's right, I probably shouldn't look. I mean, really, who wants to read anyone's tweet sex, let alone their boyfriend's with their best friend?

Mel, Jack and I all joined Twitter at the same time, but none of us – I thought – were that into using it. Now I look at Jack (@jack_inthebox666) and Melissa

(@redhairdontcare77) going back and forth on the screen about who wants to do what to who and with what part of their own body and I feel as if I don't know these people. Written down, it seems laughable rather than erotic, but then I guess it's all about being in the moment.

I scroll back in time and see arrangements to meet up, random declarations of lust. The earliest missive was just before Christmas, but it doesn't feel like the beginning.

'I'll be wishing I was with you the whole time,' Jack had written. And Mel had replied, 'Me, too.'

That was the day I was due home – production had closed for just over a week. The day Jack and I had a tearful reunion (on both parts, I should add). The day before we went hunting for the perfect tree and I spent hours choosing a top in Sandro that I knew Mel would love, to go with the sunglasses I'd picked out for her in Barneys on Madison Avenue. The day before she and I got tipsy on mulled wine and she cried when she talked about how much she missed Sam and speculated about where he was and who with. I remember telling her he must have been insane to choose someone else over her. That any man should be so lucky.

Kat is sitting across from me, Oscar purring contentedly on her lap, looking as if she wishes she'd never started this. I feel bad for snapping at her.

'It's good,' I say, wiping away a tear. 'I needed to know that it was real.'

Relief washes over her. I see a hint of a smile. 'Did you know she called her vag her minky?'

'Definitely not.'

Kat snorts and I start to laugh. And then I can't stop and neither can she. It's as if someone has turned a tap on. So now I'm laughing and crying at the same time. I imagine it's a good look.

'Also, I'd like to make it clear that he and I have never done that whole, you know, smearing-on-the-face thing . . . not deliberately, anyway. Just in case you were wondering.'

'Who has?'

'Although I did once read it was meant to be good for your skin.'

She shrieks. 'Eew!'

Eventually, we laugh ourselves out. I feel better. Well, not so much better as stronger. There is nothing left to salvage in either of these relationships. There's nothing to mourn the loss of, because they weren't the people I thought they were. I don't need to mope around missing them, I can focus on hating them, and that feels like progress.

'You should take a photo of those DMs,' Kat is saying. 'You never know when you might have access to them again.'

'Good idea.' I fish my phone out of my pocket, snap away. It takes nine pictures to capture the whole lot. I don't know why I feel the need to preserve the evidence. Just because, one day, I might throw it in their faces and say, 'See, I know everything.'

I click out of Twitter. 'Let's see what else we can find on here.'

9

It turns out it's way too easy to feel at home in what, essentially, is your own home, even though you really shouldn't be there. By lunchtime, Kat and I have had two coffees each, the first time assiduously washing and drying the mugs afterwards and stashing them in the cupboard before getting them out again and repeating the process. I have eaten a cereal bar I found in the cupboard – after convincing myself that neither Jack nor Mel would have counted how many were left – and then crawled around on my hands and knees, checking for giveaway crumbs. Kat has her feet up on the coffee table as she browses through Jack's laptop, hunting for we don't know what.

'What if he checks his history?' I ask, panicked, at one point, way too late to do anything about it if he did.

Kat shrugs. 'He'll think it was Mel. You're in New York, remember? And then he might accuse her and she'll deny it, but he'll think she's lying and that she doesn't trust him.'

She's right. 'You're right.'

I carry on rummaging through the wardrobe, looking for anything that's precious to me but that he won't notice has been removed. I already have a bag full of all my important personal stuff.

'What are you looking for, anyway?'

She peers over the laptop at me, cats'-eye glasses perched on the end of her nose. 'I don't know. Anything. You never know when things might come in handy.'

'Well, we can't stay too much longer. What if one of them decides to take the rest of the day off?'

'I'm just amusing myself till you finish. Anyway, we have two flats to look at this afternoon.'

'We do?'

'Don't get too excited. You were right when you said you couldn't afford much.'

'Don't you have work to do? Rich clients waiting for you impatiently?'

'Today, you're my client. I just won't earn anything.'

'Okay. Well, I think I'm done.' I check through my bag again.

'You can always come back again if you desperately need something.'

I roll my eyes at her. 'I'm not making a habit of this. Once I'm back for good and I have somewhere to go I'm telling him it's over, and we can sort the rest out like adults.'

'Good luck with that.' Kat, I have always suspected, has never been Jack's greatest fan. Not that she's ever really said anything to me but, once, when she'd had a few drinks, she did start quizzing me about whether or not I thought he was good enough for me. I got the impression she thought he was a bit full of himself. Which he is, but in a way I always put down to confidence, not arrogance. He has swagger, but not cockiness.

And most of it is a front, anyway. I always liked the fact that he had – or, at least, I thought he had – a soft centre under there somewhere.

I ignore her comment. Take a last look around to make sure everything is as we found it.

'Can you remember what was up on the screen when you first opened it?'

'Of course.' The computer pings. 'Ooh, hello . . .'

Kat is looking at something intently.

'What?'

She hits a couple of keys and the printer starts whirring.

'He just got an email. Did you know he'd applied for a job at Colby Sachs? Senior account director?'

'Yes. He was quite hopeful.'

Kat smiles. 'Well, he got it.'

'Right.' I feel a stab of jealousy. Jack has been desperate to get some kind of a promotion, feels he's stuck in a rut at the advertising agency where he works. But it won't be me he's celebrating with.

'Shame he won't know that.'

She sits back and looks at me triumphantly.

'Kat, what have you done?'

She raises a finely plucked brow. She looks excited and terrified at the same time. 'I just deleted the email.'

'No, you didn't. We need to try and get it back.'

'Too late. There's no chance he'll know because I did it almost as soon as it arrived. Unless he was hovering over his phone . . .'

'Shit. Well, they'll just contact him again in a few days when they don't hear from him. Or . . . I know . . . we could ring them and tell them what happened and ask them to resend.'

'Or' – Kat says as she retrieves a piece of paper from the printer – 'I could make Greg ring them and say he's Jack. That he's sorry but he doesn't want the job any more because he's decided to stay where he is. I have all the details here . . .'

'No. Absolutely not.' I snatch the paper out of her hand. Skim-read the letter. 'Jesus, that's a good salary. He's not earning anything like that at the moment.'

'Mel'll be thrilled. He'll be able to keep her in the style she's always thought she deserved.'

'We can't, can we?'

'Why not? After all, you're in America, so it can't have been anything to do with you, even if he does ever find out. Not that he will.'

I feel an adrenaline rush like I did the first time I did a bungee jump. Teetering on the lip of a bridge in Croatia, knowing that if I took even a tiny step forward there would be no return. That I'd be plunged into the unknown with no way of stopping myself. And, afterwards, feeling like the queen of the world, as if I could do anything. Invincible.

I take a long breath in, try to exhale slowly.

'Sod it. Let's do it.'

10

Surprisingly Greg isn't as keen to break the law by impersonating someone else on the phone and turning down a job on their behalf as you might imagine. At least, I assume it must be breaking the law. If it isn't, it should be. And it's not even because he has such a strong moral compass that he thinks what we're doing is wrong. Jack deserves everything he gets, Greg believes. He's just scared of getting caught.

'What if I give myself away?' We're sitting on their balcony, drinking wine under a patio heater, after a long day.

'You can't,' Kat insists for the third time. 'I mean, you can give away that you're not Jack, but not who you really are. Not unless you announce yourself, and why would you do that?'

'And you're sure our number won't come up?'

'We're ex-directory. And anyway, why would they be making a note of the number that someone rings them from?'

She's putting way too much pressure on him. I chip in. 'You really don't have to do it, Greg. We can just forget about it and, eventually, they'll probably contact him again and everyone'll assume the first email got lost in the ether somewhere.'

'I want to. I mean, I don't want him swanning around with some flash new job after what he's done to you.'

He looks at Kat imploringly. 'Can't you do it and say you're my assistant? That I'm away or something?'

'No! Why would his assistant even know he'd been applying for other jobs? Why do you think the offer letter went to his home email? Because he doesn't want people at work to know.'

'And you're sure he won't have picked it up on his phone?'

Kat rolls her eyes exaggeratedly. 'I told you. I printed it and deleted it within about a millisecond of it arriving. He'd have to have been standing there looking at his inbox –'

'He had a big presentation today. He would have been in that.' I'd felt much better when I'd remembered this. I knew that a randomly beeping phone was a big no-no when pitching to a client, so Jack's would have been turned off. Or, at least, he wouldn't have been looking at it.

Greg runs his fingers through his neat quiff. 'Jesus. Give it here.' He snatches the letter out of her hand, heads inside towards the hallway.

'Rob Sanders, please . . . Jack Carmichael here . . . sorry . . .' he mutters as he goes off, rehearsing his role. 'Many apologies . . . no . . . I appreciate it, but I'm afraid my circumstances have changed . . .'

'Let's go in the kitchen and shut the door,' I say, pulling Kat's arm. 'I can't bear to listen in.'

*

Earlier this afternoon, Kat and I visited two of the most soul-destroying flats known to man. One in King's Cross, which, in itself, isn't a bad thing but, in this instance, what the listing described as a flat was actually a damp-infested room with a manky old cooker in one corner and a shower and toilet behind a curtain in the other. One sink for both brushing your teeth and doing the dishes.

'Jesus, this is awful,' Kat said to the man showing us around. I'd like to call him an estate agent but he was more like someone you'd find lurking around a girls' school at home time with his hand in his tracksuit pocket. 'How can you justify charging this much for this? It says "studio flat with bathroom and kitchen" in the ad.'

The man waved his arm sulkily at the en suite facilities. Kat propelled me towards the door.

'We're leaving. This is a disgrace. I should report you.'

'Report him to who?' I said when we were back out on York Place.

'I don't know. Fucking idiot.'

The second, five minutes up the road, was marginally better, in that the toilet was behind a door. Well, half a door. One of those ones you see a horse peering over in a stable. Clearly to shell out for the top section would have been prohibitively expensive. The shower was still in the main room, though, next to the cooking area, which would be handy if you ever fancied a snack while lathering up. Or felt in need of a swift electric shock. Once again, we walked in and more or less straight out again, Kat a ball of fury on my behalf.

'Honestly. I had no idea places like this even existed on the market.'

I laughed. 'I thought you worked in property.'

'Well, clearly none of my clients is looking in this price range.'

'Sorry for not being rich,' I said tetchily, and then felt bad because she had taken a whole day out of her real life to help me. Thankfully, she ignored my barb. I didn't want to get into a fight with her.

'I'll have to do more research upfront. And you might have to up your budget a bit.'

I felt a wave of panic. 'I don't know if I can. What if I don't get work –'

'You'll get something. You just need to get over the hump of paying a month's deposit and a month upfront and you'll be fine. And you'll be able to get your savings out soon.'

'You're right. If I'm careful, I might be able to manage. Just about.'

'Let me talk to a few people,' Kat said. 'You never know.'

While we're waiting in the kitchen, gin and tonics poured, for Greg to reappear, my mobile rings.

'Shit. It's him. Jack.'

Her eyebrows shoot upwards. 'Don't answer it.'

'If I'm going to keep up the pretence everything's fine, I have to talk to him sometime.'

'Okay. Back to the balcony.'

I let his request for a video chat ring out, and then I call back.

'Hi!' I keep the phone pressed against my ear as hard as I can, in the hope that it will cut out the ambient noise.

'Hey,' he says. 'All okay in the Big Apple?'

It's freezing out here. I stand there shivering. 'Sure. We got a bit delayed last night so I didn't dare try you when we got in –'

'Listen, Ames, sorry I got so wasted on Saturday. You really should have woken me up to say goodbye. I felt awful that I'd missed you.'

'It's all right. It was fun, though, wasn't it? The party. I wonder if Mel got home okay.'

I wait for a giveaway pause but he doesn't miss a beat.

'God knows. Someone's home probably, even if not hers.'

'She's bound to call me later. Give me all the gory details.'

He laughs, and I think how satisfying it would be to land a punch square on the end of his long nose. 'Where are you? It sounds windy.'

'We're filming by the river. I don't have much time, actually, they broke early for lunch.'

Through the glass patio door I can see a silent film of Kat telling Greg to shush, pointing at me out in the cold, trying to make sure he doesn't say anything loud enough that Jack might hear.

'Shit, I see the third assistant. We must be back. If I get off early enough, I'll try you later, but I'm in every scene from now on. Are you going out?'

'God, no. I'm still recovering from Saturday. Early night.'

'Right. Well, maybe later, then.'

'Love you,' he says as I hang up.

The firm of Colby Sachs, so Greg tells us when I go back in, is sorry that Jack won't be joining them but have asked that he keep them apprised of his movements in the future.

'They asked if it was to do with the money, as if they might offer more if I said yes. I was tempted to ask them how much they'd go to.'

'You didn't, though, did you?' Kat asks with a frown.

'Of course not. They obviously really wanted him, though.'

'Shit,' I say. 'Now I feel guilty. Have we done a terrible thing?'

'Well, yes . . .' Greg says. 'But he's done much worse. Anyway, it's only a job. If he's that in demand, he'll be offered something else sooner or later.'

'Oh my God, what if he calls them to find out why he hasn't heard?' Why this has only just occurred to me I have no idea. But you would, wouldn't you? If you'd applied for something you really thought you were in with a chance of getting and they never replied.

73

Kat shrugs. 'He might, but who cares? Although I don't think I would –'

'Me neither,' Greg says. 'I mean, you'd just assume they didn't want you and you wouldn't want to humiliate yourself by calling.'

'And they'll probably have offered it to someone else by then, that's the beauty of it.'

She's right. Whatever way you look at it, we've almost certainly lost him the job.

I think about how happy I would have been for him in our old life when he told me his good news. How proud I would have felt. How we would have planned a celebration, maybe thought again about moving to a bigger and better flat. Set a date for the wedding.

But that's the problem with living in blissful ignorance. At some point, you might just find out the truth.

At a few minutes before nine, just as I'm about to announce I'm off to have a bath, my phone rings again. Mel wanting to video chat, as she does maybe three or four times a week. Usually, I can't wait to grab up the phone to catch up on what I'm missing. I do a quick mental calculation. It's nearly four in the afternoon in New York. Even though I'm sure she's not studying the relative sunset times, I'm pretty sure the lack of daylight would give me away. I could happily ignore the call and she'd just assume I was filming, but I want to speak to her. I want to hear her voice as she tries to pretend that everything is fine with us.

I wait for the ringing to stop.

'I'm going to call her back. Keep it down a bit.'

I head for the spare bedroom and shut myself in. I put some music on the iPod by the bed in case Greg or Kat forget their instructions and suddenly say something loud. Then I double check that I'm making an audio call. I sit on the bed to try to steady my nerves. She picks up almost immediately.

'Hi! I just tried you.'

'I know. I'm at the studio, so not enough reception for video, I think. How's it going?'

She launches into a story I have no interest in about her boss, John, and the way he's been flirting with her. Melissa always thinks everyone is flirting with her. I've teased her about it before but now it feels like proof of how self-obsessed she is. As she prattles on, I suddenly remember a night years ago when the two of us had gone to a club with a group of her work colleagues. She was already with Sam but he was away, and I was single, yet to meet Jack. A bloke had come over and started chatting to me. A good-looking bloke, I remember that much. Andy, I think his name was. He was with a big, mixed group of friends, and I remember he made me laugh, telling me that he was the only single saddo. All his friends were feeling loved up and he was starting to feel left out.

'I just love how guys are always too intimidated to approach me directly,' Mel had said when he went off to the loo at one point. 'It's so funny the way he's chatting to you but he keeps giving me little looks to check I'm listening.'

Or he could just be being polite. 'He seems nice,' I said, because he did. Not love-of-my-life material but fun for the evening and possibly a bit longer.

'I'm married,' she said, rolling her eyes.

I should have said, 'I don't think he's interested in you, I think it's me he likes, actually,' but, as usual, I didn't. I fell back into my role as her chief cheerleader.

'Well, you can't blame him for trying.'

When Andy came back I notched my own flirtation down and watched as she turned hers up to eleven. At first he looked a bit confused. He kept trying to reignite the little spark he and I had had, but I retreated into monosyllabic monotone. In the end he gave up and, no doubt flattered by Mel's attentions, allowed himself to bask in her attention. Of course, when he asked for her number at the end of the night she said no. Looked at him like he was a speck of dirt on her Jimmy Choos. But she'd won.

And I knew, I've always known, that that's what she was like. But I used to defend her to other people by saying things like, 'That's just Mel, she can't help her-self' or 'She's totally unaware she's doing it.' And I believed that, too. I never would have thought she'd have done anything to hurt me.

I realize the topic's moved on when she says some-thing about Saturday night. I wonder where she is at the moment. Back in her own place, or still at mine?

76

Has she effectively moved in, or does she flit between the two? Is Jack lurking in the other room, or is she alone in her flat and in need of an audience?

I suddenly can't be bothered to listen to her any more.

'I think we're about to rehearse the next scene,' I say when she's halfway through a sentence. 'Gotta go.'

'Speak soon,' she says, as I cut her off.

I never had any doubts that I was going to stay on in the sixth form. I had no idea what I wanted to do with my life but I knew I needed to get some qualifications – *any* qualifications – in order to enable me to do something. I had no obvious talent, no calling. I was good at random things like netball, French and art. Nothing that screamed out for me to make it my career. But I was happy to be the tortoise, to plod along slowly and let things unravel at their own pace.

Mel, though, couldn't wait to leave school. It was all the teachers could do to persuade her to stay long enough to take some GCSEs. And then she only agreed because we were doing an end-of-year production of *The Boyfriend* (I was in charge of lighting, which basically meant I flicked a couple of switches. But I got to miss a few lessons and hang out with Mel during rehearsals) and she couldn't bear the idea of someone else taking the lead. All that singing and dancing and praise and applause.

By then her parents had found a local agent to take her on. She mostly looked after children and didn't seem to do much else beyond getting them work in the local amateur panto, but Mel couldn't have been more excited. 'My agent . . .' she would say at any opportunity. 'Sylvia . . . she's my agent.' And, to be honest, I was excited for her, too. Obviously, I didn't know then what I know now, which is that the fact Sylvia charged a (small) regular fee to represent her clients, as well as her fifteen per cent should they ever get any work, was a dead giveaway that she was a bit of a charlatan. Not a crook, really, but someone clueless. Someone who had basically come to terms with the fact she was never going to deliver the goods so she needed to cover her costs.

So Mel left school, steadfastly refusing to apply for college, even to do drama. Why waste time? was her rationale. Why not get a head start on all those other young hopefuls who were going to lose precious years training to do what she could already do instinctively? She was teetering on the brink of stardom and she didn't want to miss her moment.

That summer solidified our friendship even more, if that were possible. She was a ball of energy. Sylvia arranged for her to have her head shots taken in a variety of costumes (such a no-no, I realized later. No producer has ever asked to see an actress because they were wearing a cowgirl outfit in a photo. Even if they are making a Western). I helped her do her make-up and went to the shoot with her because she was nervous. Sylvia was there in a floaty scarf and even floatier, tent-like dress over her large frame, shouting, 'Eyes and teeth!' at every opportunity. She had me pile a bit more eyeshadow on Mel and borrowed another client's hair tongs (there were five other girls and one boy there also having their pictures done. All clients of Sylvia's. She had obviously got a group discount with the photographer) and curled her hair into ringlets.

'You're not worried you don't quite look like you?' I asked hesitantly at one point. I had recently watched *Just William* one rainy afternoon with my mum and let's just say there were alarm bells.

Mel had looked at me with a slight eye-roll. 'It's stage make-up.'

'Ah, okay,' I said, feeling stupid. What did I know? Maybe she was right.

That night I was staying at hers, as I often did. I loved sleeping in her family's spare bedroom. The crisp pale yellow sheets always smelled of flowers and the sun-coloured walls and blue floral curtains defied you to be anything less than cheerful. I remember there was a thunderstorm. Lightning flashing across the sky. Thunder roaring. I eventually managed to fall asleep – we'd had our tea in front of the TV after the photo shoot and then sat up way too late in Mel's room, chatting about everything and nothing – but I was woken in the early hours by someone crawling in beside me. I knew immediately it was Mel.

'Are you okay?' I said, only half awake.

'I'm scared,' she answered, snuggling down under the duvet. I had never known Mel to be scared of anything.

I turned over to look at her in the half-light. 'Of the thunder?'

'Yep. Stupid, right?'

There was another loud crack and she squeaked, grabbing on to my arm.

'It's nothing to worry about,' I said. 'It's miles away.'

'It was okay today, the photo shoot, wasn't it? I didn't look like an idiot?'

What could I say? I would never have wanted her to know the truth. 'Of course not. It was great. You looked gorge. Obvs.'

'So long as you think so. I mean, obviously Sylvia knows better than anyone, but I really trust your opinion. I've decided. You're going to be the person who keeps me grounded when I'm a huge star.'

I laughed, but the idea that Mel was thinking we'd still be best friends when she hit the big time made me feel warm inside.

'Go to sleep,' I said. 'That's me keeping you grounded. I'm making sure you get your beauty sleep.'

'I'll be okay now I'm with you,' she said sleepily. 'You make me feel safe. You always do.'

It was the first time I had ever seen her vulnerable. I lay there, listening to her breathing slowing down, glowing with the thought that she needed me.

11

'It's a bit quiet out there, to be honest. There are a couple of things gearing up but they're only going for star casting at the moment. It'll probably be a few weeks before they start on the lower tier. Not the best time of year to suddenly find yourself out of work.'

My agent, Sara, ladies and gentlemen. Also known as the prophet of doom.

'Yes, sorry about that.'

She shuffles a few bits of paper around on her desk. I have no doubt that when I got offered the job on *Murder in Manhattan* and had to sign the watertight option (on their part only) for a further six seasons, her first thought was relief that she could forget about me for the foreseeable future while her fifteen per cent commission on my fee rolled steadily in. Me being written out was probably as big a blow to her as to me. After all, it's not as if I really earned her anything significant in the five years she'd represented me before that. I like her, though. She's straightforward. She tells it like it is. And that's a positive in this industry, where so much of what you hear is bullshit.

'Hardly your fault,' she says, laughing. 'Just bad timing. How long can you survive?'

'Not that long. Just put me up for everything, I don't care.'

'I always do,' she says, which hardly fills me with confidence.

Before I leave I ask her to pay my final cheque from the show into a solo account I set up at the bank this morning. She doesn't ask me why, and I'm grateful.

Bizarrely, as I'm walking down Rosebery Avenue, having left her office basically saying I'd do anything in the short term, including cleaning her house, if it'd earn me a bit of money (she refused), two American women – I assume tourists – accost me.

'You're Yvon!' one of them squeaks. I can't help it, I'm flattered. This has happened a few times on the New York streets since the series started airing. Yvon is my character's name, in case you hadn't guessed.

She's got me by the arm so I have to stop. 'I am,' I say, blushing. It hasn't happened often enough that I'm in any way blasé about it.

'Oh my God, we love you,' the other one says. 'It's our favourite show, we're obsessed.'

'Is it Michael?' the first one chips in. 'You can tell us.' People are forever speculating on who the killer might be. There are whole forums dedicated to different theories.

'I really can't,' I say. And I don't just mean I'm not allowed. I don't know. No one does. Well, except for the producers and, I assume, the actor playing the role. Maybe not even them yet. Cast parties inevitably descend into 'Is it you? Go on, you can tell me,' when we've all had a few drinks. It suddenly occurs to me that I'll find out next week when I go back to film my demise. Mine will be the first murder that will happen on screen. All the rest have been shown through the eyes of whoever discovers the body, killer long gone. It hits me that it's quite a big deal. The forums will go nuts.

The ladies grab a selfie with me and go off happy. I feel a bit better knowing my death will be a landmark event for the show, a watercooler moment. It makes me hopeful that I'll stand out more as an actress because of it. People will remember my character, at least.

I'm brought swiftly down to earth by the first of three more flats Kat has lined up for me to see. This one is in Camden, in one of the less salubrious streets, and I arrive to find her standing outside, clutching her bag to her chest as if she thinks it might be wrestled from her by a passer-by at any moment. We climb over a comatose youth who is using the front bin area as a bed. It's a slight improvement on yesterday, though – as evidenced by the higher rent – but it's still, well, how can I put this . . . an absolute shit hole.

'We're going to have to go further out,' Kat says as we leave, barely three minutes after we've arrived. 'Much, much further out.'

'I suppose so,' I say reluctantly. I had been clinging on to the hope that I would be able to find something that would still allow me to walk to the West End on a nice day. It was something I did whenever I could from our flat in Gospel Oak, even though it took the best part of an hour. Losing that freedom would feel like moving out of London.

'Let's just look at these others, anyway, as we have the appointments. They're close to each other and I'll be interested to see what you think of the last one.'

'If I can just find something that doesn't have the toilet in the living room, I'll be happy.'

'You should have said. That's been my main requirement, the need to be able to open the fridge while you're sat on the loo. That and a crackhead sitting on the front step.'

'Very funny.'

Kat treats us to a taxi north to our next destination, off the Finchley Road. While we idle in traffic she takes a phone call that puts into perspective how grateful I should be that she's taking time away from her paid work to help me.

'The point is they're cash buyers with no need to sell their current home,' she says, her accent going up two notches on the poshness scale. 'So we feel twelve point five is a fair and appropriate offer. Okay . . . okay . . . Yes. I'm showing them something on Winnington Road this afternoon, so a swift response would be much appreciated.'

'Twelve point five . . . that's twelve and a half million, right?' I know I'm sitting there with my mouth open, but I can't help it. How did my snippy friend become someone who works for people who have twelve and a half million pounds lying around they can pay cash for a house with?

She nods. 'Right.'

'And, if they buy it you get . . . what?'

She pushes her glasses up her nose. 'One per cent.'

'Unreal.'

'But it can take months to find them the right thing. Or they can change their mind and decide they're not moving after all, or they're emigrating or something.'

'And then you get nothing.'

'Exactly.'

'Crazy.'

Flat number two might be the worst we've seen yet. There's cardboard on one of the windows and it's furnished with what I can only describe as the 'bad jumble sale from the eighties range'. And it smells. What of, I couldn't tell you, but none of it pleasant. It's also the cheapest we've seen, so I'm tempted, just to have a roof over my head.

'I assume you'll replace the window?' Kat says to the shady-looking man showing us around.

He shrugs. 'Not my problem.'

'Jesus Christ,' she snarls as we leave, her kitten heels click-clacking on the pavement.

'Can we get a coffee before we see the next one?' I'm knackered, and I know I'm dragging my feet like a toddler.

'No time.'

I follow her back on to the main road and we turn

right, moving further away from the Tube. We walk for what seems like for ever. And then we get on a bus.

'Are we still in London?' I say facetiously at one point, and she just scowls at me. Once we reach our stop, we start walking again. Eventually, after God knows how long, she stops short outside some kind of rundown haberdashery store. She consults her phone.

'Here.'

'This is a shop.'

'Upstairs. Obviously.'

I follow her in. I've always loved fabric shops. It feels as if there's a world of possibilities in all the different colourways and textures. Not that I've ever made anything in my life. But there's something quite romantic about the idea. Not so much in here, though, which is like an assault course of brightly coloured chaos. There's a tiny old woman hidden among the rolls at the back and a younger one – mid-thirties, I'd guess – at her side.

The younger woman approaches us with a smile on her face. It's the first time anyone at any of the properties has done anything but scowl so I'm immediately suspicious.

'Kat?' she says, and extends a hand. 'Fiona Sheridan.'

She tells us the tiny woman owns the building but barely speaks any English so she's going to show us around. She's a lettings agent for a local firm and I can tell she's in a hurry because she has bigger fish to fry than anything I can afford.

We exit out into the street again and in through another door. Kat and Fiona make polite conversation as we pick our way through the narrow hall that doubles as some kind of stockroom and up some creaky wooden stairs.

'How long has the shop been here?'

'Since the forties,' Fiona says. 'Mrs Lam and her husband started the business, but he's not around any more. Obviously, if they hadn't bought the building, then they never would have been able to –'

She interrupts herself as we round the first landing. 'This is another flat. There's a young couple live there. We're up one. It's too much for her, really, so she's going to sell up at some point . . . right . . .'

We all come to a stop on the top landing as she wrestles with the lock. 'It's a bit run-down but . . . you know . . . that's reflected in the price . . .'

To say the place is a tip would be an insult to the refuse industry. It clearly hasn't been redecorated since the seventies and there's junk everywhere. Fiona has the good grace to look embarrassed.

'The last tenant lived here for ever, but she never really looked after the place. She's gone into a care home and her family were meant to be clearing everything out, but they just took all the good stuff. It just needs taking to the dump . . .'

I can see there's more than one room, though, which is a first. On closer examination, there's a bedroom at the back with just enough room for a bed and not much else, a largish living-room-stroke-kitchen at the front and a bathroom crammed with an old bath and toilet in-between. In terms of volume, it's a palace, compared to anything else we've seen.

Fiona seems keen to offload the place. I imagine she's ticking up the commission she would earn in her head and trying to work out if it's worth her time being here at all. 'Mrs Lam just wants someone nice in. Someone who won't give her any trouble.'

'I'm nice,' I say. 'How long's the lease?'

'Six months. Like I said, she might sell up, so no guarantees of any longer, but if she doesn't . . .'

'I should take it, shouldn't I?' I ask, turning to Kat.

You would think Kat would be relieved. We could tie this up and she could get back to her million-pound mansions. Instead, she just looks a bit furtive and guilty.

'Do you mind if we just have a quick chat?' she says to Fiona.

'No problem. I'll wait downstairs.'

'What?' I say, once I think she's out of earshot. 'This is by far the best thing we've seen and, given we don't have much time —'

She interrupts me. 'It's way over what you want to pay.'

'What? Why did you bring me here, then?'

'I wanted to prove a point. I thought you still wouldn't think it was good enough and then, when I told you you couldn't even afford this, you'd agree you had to completely rethink the areas you were looking in. I wasn't expecting you to want to take it.'

'We're so far up the fucking Finchley Road I'll need a Sherpa to find the Tube. How can I not even be able to afford to live here?'

'That's why most people share. Or move out to places the Tube doesn't even go to. That brings the cost right down.'

'I *was* sharing!' I realize I'm shouting, but I can't stop myself. 'I was sharing with my boyfriend. I had a beautiful flat in a lovely part of London and now I can't even afford . . . this . . . ? Is that what you're telling me?'

Kat blinks. 'I guess so. It's only a blip, though, Amy. You just need time to get your next big break and then things'll turn around again.'

I sit down on a fusty-smelling chair. 'I'm never going to get another break. Do you have any idea how many out-of-work actresses there are? Most of them, that's how many.'

'Sorry, I shouldn't have brought you here. I just thought it'd be educational.'

'How much over my budget is it?'

'A hundred,' she says, trying to sound casual.

'A month?'

'Um . . . a week.'

'Fuck's sake.'

'I suppose your ISA would cover the deposit and the first couple of months . . .'

'But that's all I've got!'

'If you work in the call centre until some acting work comes up, would that pay the rent? Just until you can get your hands on your joint savings?'

I put my head in my hands. 'Just about. If I did every shift I could get. And didn't eat. Fuck.'

'You can come and eat with us. Any time you want.'

'Thanks. You're going to regret saying that.'

'What do you want me to say to her?'

I go back to New York in three days and, when I return, I'm going to need somewhere to run to once I've dropped my bombshell on Jack and Mel. I don't have time for this.

'Tell her I'll take it.' Shit.

'You know what really pisses me off?' I say to Kat on the long trek back down towards the Tube. Fiona has agreed to accept me so long as I can come back with the deposit tomorrow and some kind of a reference. I'm pretty sure I'll have to turn around as soon as I get home to get back here on time. At least I didn't have to fight for the place, because Kat, with her estate-agent contacts, had heard about it before a listing had actually been posted anywhere. After a bit of a kerfuffle, while I stood on the pavement like a spare part and Fiona, Kat and Mrs Lam huddled in the shop, Kat told me she had negotiated £25 a week off.

'So long as you take the place as is.'

'What does that mean?'

'They won't clear the crap out. That'll be up to you.'

'Fine.' I knew I should be sounding more grateful. Left to my own devices, I probably would have ended up having to move down to Wiltshire, tail between my legs, into my mum and dad's spare bedroom, the oldest teenager in town.

'And thanks, by the way.'

'It was nothing. I wouldn't have wanted to leave you trailing around on your own.'

I felt bad. Now I came to think about it, I couldn't remember Mel ever taking time out of her own life to make sure everything was okay in mine.

'I mean it,' I said to Kat. 'I really appreciate it.'

Kat huffed, and I remembered she never could deal with praise.

'Whatever,' she said, with all the sophistication of a sulky fourteen-year-old. 'Like I said, it was nothing.'

'What?' she says now. She's out of breath, trying to keep up with me in her clicky heels. I slow my pace down.

'All the stuff I bought that I'm going to have to buy again. Duvet covers and towels and all that crap. Saucepans. I mean, if I just walk away, I'll have nothing.'

'Once you tell him you're leaving, you can negotiate all that stuff, can't you?'

'Once I walk out, that's it. I don't want anything to do with either of them ever again. I'll just take what I can carry. My clothes and stuff.'

She looks at me as if I'm crazy. Before Kat met Greg she had already been divorced. She and her first husband worked out a very civilized division of all their chattels, right down to the teaspoons. I remember being impressed and horrified in equal parts.

'Do you have the key on you?' she says, as she spots a cab and flaps her arm out.

'Yes, why? Oh . . . no . . .'

'Gospel Oak, please,' I hear her say to the driver.

She piles in and I follow, grateful to sit down. 'We can't.'

She looks at her watch. 'They'll both be at work, right?'

'Yes . . . but . . .'

She leans forward and gives the driver the name of the road. 'You shouldn't make this any more difficult for yourself than you have to. If you're going to be struggling financially for a while, then at least take what's yours. We'll just get a starter kit.'

This time, I make Kat ring on the doorbell while I hide behind a bush over the road. If, for any reason, either Jack or Mel is there, she can claim to have been in the area and thought it might be nice to check how he was doing in my absence. They'd think it was a bit odd, given that neither of them is particularly fond of her (Jack always referred to her as 'your arsey friend'), but they wouldn't think it was suspicious.

Safe in the knowledge the flat is empty, I leave my hiding place and follow her in. Oscar saunters over, more blasé about seeing me now, and I break off a tiny piece of Cheddar from a lump I find in the fridge.

'That's not good for him, you know,' Kat says. She's headed straight for Jack's laptop again.

92

'It's not as if Mel's going to be feeding him any treats,' I say, stroking his head. 'Why are you on there again?'

'Just checking Colby Sachs haven't been back in touch. I want to know if we got away with it.'

'Now I'm here, I don't know what to take.' I look around. There are so many things we bought over the years. So many memories. The Warholesque painting of a cat that was the first real piece of art either of us had ever owned (we used to walk around the Affordable Art Fair in Hampstead every year, moaning about how un-Affordable it all was), and which reminded us so much of Oscar we had to have it; the huge grey vase that we only splashed out on because Jack managed to chip a chunk off the base in the shop and we felt so guilty we thought we'd better buy it, both nearly crying with laughter at the counter; the collection of neon-haired trolls haunting our bookshelves, added to whenever we could find one in a vintage shop because they reminded us both of being kids.

'Just the basics,' Kat says. 'The things you'll need to live but you don't want to have to go out and buy all over again. The things that are obviously yours you can sort out with him later. I hardly think he's going to argue about a framed photo of your mum and dad. Today is all about setting up your bolthole with the boring but costly stuff.'

I open the trunk at the end of our bed where we keep the clean covers and start rooting through.

'"Come back, all is forgiven,"' Kat says from the other room. I have no idea what she's on about, so I peer around the door. She's reading something aloud off Jack's laptop.

'"Haha! I have a stinking hangover. Be over when I can face getting up," smiley face.' She looks up and sees me looking. 'Twitter.'

'Let me see.'

'There's only two more. Both from Sunday. Her again: "On my way. Everything was okay, wasn't it? Sure A. not suspicious? I have big memory gap . . ."'

And then him: "All fine. Did sleep through her leaving though!"' She pushes her glasses up her nose. 'That's it.'

'Fuckers.'

I root out a teal-coloured duvet cover with a cute pattern of white birds and trees on it. I remember it cost a fortune but, when I put it on the first time, Jack said it gave him nightmares when he half-woke up in the early morning and wondered what was crawling over him – so we never used it again. I know he won't miss it. I have no idea how well Mel has acquainted herself with my stuff, so there's a chance she might, but I decide it's so unlikely it's a risk worth taking. I add a couple of plain white sheets and pillowcases, not that I have anything to put them on. And a big bath towel.

'What else?'

Kat is still engrossed, Oscar purring on her lap. 'I don't know. Mugs?'

'You can buy four mugs for about two pounds fifty. I'm not that desperate.'

I hunt about in the drawer under the hob and take out a Le Creuset saucepan and frying pan. Neither Jack nor Mel ever cooks, beyond heating up a can of beans. I rearrange the drawer a bit so it's not obvious anything's missing. Luckily, Mel's tidiness obsession hasn't yet extended to the insides of my storage units.

I look longingly at the beautiful Alessi kettle I bought a couple of years ago. I know I can't get away with it but then I remember that I stuck the old one – which was still functional, but ugly – at the back of one of the kitchen cupboards so I help myself to that. I add the tin opener just for fun, check that they're still feeding Oscar his favourite pouches so it won't affect him. And the corkscrew. Let's hope for their sake they buy a screw-top bottle next time they want to share a cosy drink.

My mobile rings, making us both jump. 'Shit, it's Mel.'

'You can't answer it. Not now.'

'I know that.'

We both stand there, listening to it ring. When it stops, I realize I've been holding my breath. A minute later, just as we're about to leave, it pings to tell me I have a message.

'Let me just listen to this.'

Kat waves: be my guest.

'Oh God, where are you? I'm so bored.' Mel often rings me from work when she can get away with it. It always used to be a welcome distraction. A taste of home.

'John's given me half of Mick's outstanding approvals to do because he's so fucking slow . . .'

She rambles on about work. I'm fascinated by how routine the message is, how so exactly like her normal self she sounds. No hint that she might be feeling guilty or anxious that I might one day find out what she's doing.

'. . . so now I've got twice as much work, which means, what am I doing? Calling you, obvs! Do you think I should try and seduce him at the next office party? John? He might go a bit easier on me then. Only as a means to an end. He's hideous. Well, you've seen him. Oh Christ, I'm losing it. Call me back when you can. Save me from terminal boredom. Or terminal slut-dom. One or the other.'

The thing is, I have always felt bad for Mel that her job is so dull. I know her life didn't turn out like she thought it would, but that's largely because she sat around waiting to be handed everything on a plate, waiting for the future she felt was rightfully hers. I've spent years listening to her complain about how hard done by she is. And I've never once said what I really think, which is *Do something about it, then*. Because she was my best friend.

*

Mel's mum started buying *The Stage* every week, and we would scour the pages for news of any upcoming productions she might be able to audition for. The local theatre in Windsor put the word out that they needed an actress who could convincingly be thirteen so we got a copy of the play out of the library and Mel studied it in her sunny garden and rehearsed the scenes out loud. (I read all the other parts. Badly, I should add. Although, who knows? Maybe the experience helped me get better in the long run.) I tested her on her two audition pieces – one tragic, one comic – that Sylvia had told her to have 'camera ready' at all times. When she heard she had got an audition I practically took out an ad in the local paper I was so proud.

On the big day, we curled her hair and did her make-up. I went with her to keep her mum company while she waited.

'I wonder what Sylvia's told them about me,' Mel said as we got off the bus. 'Maybe they've seen me in something.'

'Probably *The Sound of Music*,' I said. Mel had played Liesl in a recent production by the Pentagram Players, our local am-dram group, in the village hall.

'Remember to smile,' her mum chipped in. Sylvia was very keen on her protégés smiling.

When we got there, I thought I'd come to the wrong place. The queue was round the block and further. Hundreds of girls aged anywhere from eleven to twenty, some of whom I recognized as other locals Sylvia represented (they were easily spotted, with their ringlets and blue eyeshadow. Blue eyeshadow, Sylvia always said, made the eyes pop from the stage).

'This can't be right,' Mel said, in a smaller voice than usual, as we lined up at the back.

'You two wait here. I'll find Sylvia,' her mum said, wandering off towards the stage door, where the line snaked inside.

I desperately wanted to cheer Mel up. 'They're probably here for all sorts of different parts,' I said, and she snapped, 'Then I should be up for those parts, too.' So I shut up and concentrated on picking off a hangnail.

'She says not to worry,' Mel's mum said reassuringly when she returned. 'It's always like this, but half these girls won't have any experience at all.'

It took two hours to move to the front of the queue. They were seeing girls in batches, and we all held our breath when it was Mel's turn to go in with the next group of ten. Her mum and I hotfooted it round to the other side of the theatre, where, we had been told, the girls would exit. The whole process, a woman with a clipboard who had walked up and down the line had told us, could take anything up to three hours, as there would be a series of cuts and recalls. Mrs Moynahan and I found a spot on a low wall and she got chatting to a couple of other mothers while I dug in my bag for my book. Thankfully, it was a warm day, and I leaned back, happy to be there for the long haul.

It couldn't have been five minutes later that a

red-faced Melissa stormed out of the exit, trailed by four other devastated-looking girls.

'Too tall,' she snapped, tears brimming at the corners of her eyes, blue eyeshadow smudged.

Her mum tried to give her a hug, but she wasn't having it. 'It's still good experience. What did they say about your pieces?'

'I didn't get to do them, did I? I don't want to talk about it.'

That was a fun bus ride home.

Before Kat and I leave, I go in the bathroom, prop the toilet seat up and squirt a bit of toothpaste in the sink. If Mel gets back before Jack, she'll go spare. I remember she once had a blazing row with Sam when the four of us went on holiday together because he'd failed to clean the bath tub the second he'd got out of it. Mel has always been a clean freak. That alone should have given the game away when I saw how tidy my flat was.

I get a little warm glow, imagining her and Jack fighting over who used the bathroom last. I can picture Mel, cheeks flushed, getting righteously angry. She's never been one to let things go. 'It must have been you. Why would I ever put the seat up in the first place? I'm a woman!'

It's as easy as that.

12

Kat has to go back to her real life on Wednesday, leaving me to trek to the frozen north of London to sign the contract on my new pied-à-terre alone. I've closed down my ISA and withdrawn the cash for the deposit and the first month's rent, and it's burning a hole in my pocket as I traipse up the road from the bus stop. *Murder in Manhattan* have emailed a reference in which they've somehow managed to imply that I'm good for the rent and not mention they've just sacked me. I asked Morgan, the production secretary, to provide it and, being a good friend, she helped me compose something that served my purposes but didn't leave her too exposed, should Fiona uncover my fate. The truth is, so long as I produce the money from somewhere each month I don't think she'll give me a second thought.

Once I have the key in my hand, I know I should go and take another look at what I've let myself in for, but I can't quite face it so I take a walk round the block to get to know my new area.

There's a hardware store that I imagine might come in handy at some point, a little newsagent's and a few shops selling specialist things I can't imagine I'll ever need, like bathroom fittings and carpets. I get myself a watery coffee from a café on the corner and decide to brave the horror.

Last night, I was trying to convince myself that, maybe, there would be some kind of hidden treasure among the previous tenant's stuff. Authentic seventies pieces that I could clean up and use to furnish the place. Maybe even a couple of bits I could sell on eBay. Of course, the reality is very different. It's just a pile of crap. Old newspapers and heaps of fusty old-lady clothes. A sofa that not only smells of wee but looks as if it might collapse if you so much as breathed on it. A cheap divan bed that has lost two wheels. I can't even look at the mattress. I know no one's naked mattress holds up to close scrutiny, but this one could probably be used to cultivate new antibiotics. I want to sink to the floor and cry but no way am I touching that thing without a bio-hazard suit on, so I just do it standing up, coffee in hand.

I try to make myself feel better by replaying last night's phone conversation with Jack in my head. I'd called him from the safety of Kat and Greg's spare room, hoping that it would go to voicemail – he would probably be sitting with Mel and wouldn't feel able to pull off the deception. This has been my ploy every evening: ring when I'm pretty sure he won't answer and then leave a loving message saying I'm probably not going to be available for him to call back for some reason or another, but that I'll try him again next day. I imagine he's as relieved as I am. This time, though, he picked up, so I can only assume Mel was having a night out, or in her own place. Hopefully, she'd stomped off for the evening after Toiletseatgate.

'Hi, babe,' he said and, despite everything, I felt a bit melty.

I rambled on a bit about things I might conceivably be up to, just trying to fill the silence. 'How's work?' I said finally, when I'd run out of steam.

'I didn't get the Colby Sachs job,' he said with a sigh. My heart started to race. How did he know?

'Oh, no. Did they call you?'

'No. Because Dave fucking Sharp got it.' Dave fucking Sharp is Jack's main rival at work. He and Dave fucking Sharp started at the same time, as junior account managers, and Jack has measured his own success against Dave's also stellar progress ever since. I fight to subdue the smile that has crept over my face. He'll hear it in my voice. I can't wait to get off the phone and tell Kat and Greg.

'Shit. Bad luck, babe.'

'I mean, what the fuck could they have seen in him that they didn't see ten times over in me?'

'Maybe he asked for less money?'

'It can't be about the money. They're rolling in the stuff.'

'Well, they're idiots, then. Something else will come up.'

He huffed. 'That was the one I really wanted, though. They're the most prestigious –'

'I know. But it's not like you really hate it where you are.'

'He's really fucking gloating, too.'

'Ignore him.'

'I mean, why would they ever pick him over me? I'm not being funny . . .'

I leaned back against the pillows. 'You just have to let it go. They'll soon realize they've made a mistake.'

'I miss you,' he said after a moment.

'Me, too,' I said, after a too long pause.

13

As the taxi edges up Third Avenue, I feel as if I'm seeing New York for the first time. Before, when I've got back from a trip home to England, I've felt out of sorts, uprooted all over again, anxious about what I've left behind, my heart firmly in London. Now that I'm about to leave, I wonder if I've appreciated it enough. If I actually realized how lucky I was as it was happening.

I surprised myself by managing to sleep for most of the flight, my head wedged against my jacket. I woke with a stiff neck, just as they announced twenty minutes to landing, grateful that I'd managed not to spend the whole journey fretting about my mess of a life.

We turn right and head towards the Hudson River. The doormen at my building greet me like an old friend, carrying my bag, handing me a small pile of post, holding the lift. Up on the fourth floor, I shut the door behind me and almost burst into tears at the sight of my tiny but perfectly formed apartment. The shiny dark wood floors that I'd never be able to afford at home. The sleek miniature kitchen like something from a space capsule. The production company have long-term leases on several apartments in the building and I know that, in a week or so, some other member of the cast will be moving in, sitting on my beautiful cream sectional sofa and gazing out of the window at the sliver of Manhattan skyline that's visible beyond the surrounding buildings.

It'll be someone with a smallish role, because the more important members of cast have bigger apartments on higher floors, while the stars are housed in another, plusher building altogether. I've never cared. It's a little slice of heaven and, for the past seven and a half months, it's been mine.

It's still light outside so I grab my phone, a book and some dollars and head downstairs again without even taking off my coat. There's a table free outside my favourite neighbourhood café on the corner. Of course there is, it's barely April. The overhead heaters are on, though, so I take my usual seat, order a glass of white wine and settle down to people-watch. I brush away the offer of a menu – even though my flat, like most flats in Manhattan, has a kitchen so small it's more for show than practicality because no one here really cooks, I am going to have to start. In London, I used to make dinner every night. It was my favourite way to relax. But once I got here it never seemed worth shelling out on pots and pans when there was no one to share the meal. I blush when I consider the amount I've spent on takeout deliveries. It doesn't bear thinking about.

When I got off the plane, I noticed I had two missed calls from Jack. Of course, he has no idea that I've been in the air most of the day but, luckily, the nature of my job means it's not an issue if he can't raise me for hours or even days on end. I check my watch. It's almost midnight at home. I can at least show willing. As predicted, it rings and rings. I'm relieved.

I spend most of Saturday and Sunday sorting out my stuff and trying to work out how I'm going to get it all home. You can accumulate a lot of crap in seven and a half months. On Saturday afternoon, I take a box of potentially useful things that it makes no sense to take halfway across the world with me – a digital radio, a make-up mirror, hair tongs – up to floor six, where my friend and fellow cast member Mary has an apartment that's about six inches bigger than mine, because she plays a regular in the police precinct where our heroine works and therefore has, maybe, two minutes more air time than me each week.

'You're back!' she squeals when she opens the door. Because so many of us know each other in the building (and because of the two burly doormen, not to mention the concierge at the front desk, who screen all strangers twenty-four-seven), no one bats an eyelid at unannounced visitors.

She's dressed for a workout. But then, Mary is pretty much always dressed for a workout when she's not in costume, so it's difficult to know if I've disturbed her or not.

'Shit, sorry, are you on your way to the gym?'

She looks down at herself, confused. 'What? Oh, no. Come in. How was it?'

She makes coffee while I fill her in. Oohs and aahs in

all the right places. Swears a few times when I get to the juicy bits.

'Do you want any of this?' I say, handing over the box. 'It's a bit random.'

She falls on it like a fox on a bin bag. Mary has always had a much better sense than me of how temporary this whole thing is. She was in a big network show about ten years ago but it got axed halfway through the season because the ratings weren't high enough. She was partway through buying a new apartment and she'd had to pull out. For years after, she was back to one line here and there and a lot of off-off-off-off-Broadway theatre (i.e. in a room above a bar) and precious little else. She kept herself going by waitressing. So she has no shame about accepting freebies.

'Definitely. I can't believe you're going back. Hey, why don't you stay? Now you've . . . well . . .'

'Got nothing to go home for?'

She shrugs sheepishly. Don't get me wrong, I'd be lying if I said I hadn't considered it the past few days. Not being in the same city as Jack and Mel definitely has its appeal. But, truthfully, being jobless in London feels less scary than being jobless in New York. Not to mention the fact that I'd have to work illegally if I worked here at all. My visa was very specifically for one job and one job only.

'Let's go to the flea market on Sixty-seventh,' I say, standing up. 'It's a beautiful day.'

*

My death scene is scheduled to be shot on Monday night but there's a freak rainstorm so, after many hours of hanging around hoping it will pass, it's postponed until Tuesday. Despite the fact I was psyched up to get it over with, I'm relieved I won't have to lie for hours in a freezing puddle while lightning bounces off the pavement beside me.

They finally send us all home around three in the morning, so I FaceTime Jack from the cab on the way. This time he answers, so either Mel didn't stay over last night or she's gone home before she goes to work. No way would she have left for her office at 8 a.m. She always leaves it to the last minute, postponing the misery for long as she can. Of course, she might just be hiding in the other room, tiptoeing around so as not to give herself away.

Jack is sitting at the kitchen table, work clothes on.

'You're up late,' he says, as soon as we connect.

'It would have been later but they had to stand down.' I aim my phone out of the window just as there's a thunder crack that makes the taxi windows rattle.

'Jesus.'

'Rescheduled for tomorrow.' I can't, of course, tell him exactly what we were supposed to be filming. 'How was work yesterday? Dave still showing off?'

'I was thinking about calling their HR department,' he says, brandishing a piece of toast. 'Just to ask what it came down to. So, you know, I know what not to do next time.'

My heart stops for a second. 'I wouldn't. It might make you seem a bit defensive. I'd just wait for them to realize they've made a terrible mistake hiring Dave. It's bound to happen.'

There's a crash from another room. Jack looks momentarily startled.

'What was that?'

'No idea,' he says, regaining his composure. 'Oscar must have knocked something over.'

'Give him a big kiss from me,' I say, not letting him know that I don't believe him for a second.

'Will do,' he says. I imagine he just wants to end the call and tell Mel she nearly gave the game away. 'Sleep well.'

On Tuesday night, I am strangled fourteen times, from three different camera angles, in a very smelly alley next door to the studios. I'm worn out with screaming and fighting off Ryan, the actor who, it turns out, is playing the killer. When the call sheet was issued I imagine a collective gasp went up among the cast and crew because Ryan's character, Peterson, is the head of our fictional police precinct, boss of my fictional sister. You couldn't make it up. Or rather you could, but why would you? Because he's twice my size and not a little clumsy, I'm battered and bruised by the end, and several takes are ruined by him suddenly stepping out of character to say, 'Oh God, I'm so sorry' or 'Did I hurt you? I hurt you, didn't I?' before doing it all over again.

On Wednesday, I film a scene in a bar that immediately precedes my doomed walk home. And then all that's left are two street shots in Midtown on Thursday night, following my journey from the exterior of the bar to the place where I'm dragged off the pavement and into the alley. Filming is a bit like assembling a jigsaw. Consecutive scenes are shot days and miles apart. You turn a corner on Forty-third Street in Manhattan and end up in an alleyway next to Silvercup Studios in Queens. You exit a bar that's a permanent set in the studio and walk out on to Fifty-first Street. It's a miracle anything ever cuts together but it somehow does, for the most part.

When we finish on Thursday, at two in the morning, the first assistant shouts, 'And that's a wrap on the series for Amy!' and everyone breaks out into applause, as is the custom whenever someone leaves the show. I stand there, embarrassed and tearful. Because it's such a late finish, there is no celebratory drink or cake. I hug as many of the crew as I can, vowing to keep in touch, although we all know that never happens.

Between filming and sleeping I carry on packing up my things, keeping only what I can cram into my two remaining cases. Later, I take all my half-drunk bottles of alcohol up to Mary, along with the contents of my freezer and some of my toiletries. She insists on taking me for dinner at our neighbourhood Italian on the Friday night – I have to leave for the airport at around three on the Saturday – and when I get there I'm so touched to see a bunch of our fellow actors, along with Morgan, one of the producers, Liam, and the costume designer, Linda, that I burst into tears. Something I seem to be doing a lot lately. They ply me with drink, insist that I'll be missed, present me with a beautiful cashmere cardigan from Katherine, the star of the show, and a pair of the cutest PJs I've ever seen – pink gingham shorts with a white lace trim and a pink vest top – and a soft grey throw from the rest of them.

'I told them we had to get you something you could fit in your case,' Mary says as she hands them over.

Then they all accompany me back to my apartment and Mary has to go up to hers to retrieve all the alcohol so we can have a final toast. It's a perfect night and one that I know I'll treasure.

Once they've all gone, I stand at the window with all the lights out and savour my view for the last time.

14

Kat and Greg have offered to put me up for a couple more days while I try and get my new flat straight. Or, at least, while I attempt to decontaminate it just enough so that what's left in there won't kill me. I don't want to take advantage, though, so, when I arrive at their place just after eight on Sunday morning, having tossed and turned in my uncomfortable aeroplane seat all night, and find Chris and Lewis sitting in their front room, I'm so grateful I almost forget how tired I am.

'What are you doing here?' I hug my brother and his other half in turn.

'Chris and Lew have hired a van,' Kat says, before either of them can get a word in. 'They came up last night.'

'What she said,' Chris says, laughing.

'How long are you here for?'

'We have to go back this afternoon. We're both working tomorrow. So we figured, shove as much stuff in the van as we can, do a couple of trips to the tip and then drive back.'

'That's . . .' I start to say, and then I don't manage to say any more because I break into noisy tears yet again. It's so sweet of them to organize this behind my back, of Chris and Lew to give up their weekend, of Kat and Greg to put them up. Plus, I'm tired and clammy and befuddled from the overnight flight.

'I told you she wouldn't want to see us,' Lew says, and that makes me laugh, so now there are tears and snot and God knows what else everywhere.

Chris steers me to the sofa and Greg plonks a cup of tea in front of me. 'Drink this, give us the keys and go to bed,' he says. 'We'll get going. I doubt we're going to be able to clear it all, but we can take the big stuff.'

I stand up. Sit down again. Stand up. 'No, I want to come. I can't let you come all this way and then leave you to it.'

It's only then that I notice Kat is wearing dungarees and a polka-dotted scarf tied around her head with a big knot in the front. 'Oh God, you look so cute!' I say, and that starts me off all over again.

'Well, now you can really see the mould,' Lew says when we've filled the van for the first time. 'So that's nice.' I've been to the café on the corner and bought coffees, although Chris insisted on paying.

I always thought rooms were supposed to look bigger without clutter, but the living-room-stroke-kitchen almost seems smaller without the sofa, Formica-covered kitchen table, four rickety chairs and an upright cooker coated in God knows what – I made Chris and Greg put on some rubber gloves I'd cleverly thought to stuff in my bag at the last minute, promising Kat I'd replace them – before they touched it. Behind the cooker there was what can only be described as a slightly smaller model of the iceberg that sunk the *Titanic* made of grease. I can't even look at it without heaving. I had thought about trying to save the fridge – I really can't afford to buy a new one – but, when we opened it up it was such a mess of old food and rust I decided it would be too much of a health hazard even to think about cleaning it out. Also gone are an MDF cupboard, an ancient TV and its stand, an armchair and, finally, the carpet, which we rolled up, capturing all sorts of other detritus inside. I think it had a pattern on it. I couldn't swear on it in court. It might just have been dirty.

'Looks better already,' Chris says, ever cheerful. Nobody has it in them to answer.

The euphoric mood that overtook us all as we hurtled up the Finchley Road in the van – Kat, Greg and I bouncing around in the back, squealing at every bump – and which was still going strong as we parked up conveniently right outside, had dissipated as soon as I opened the door to the flat. The fusty, sulphury, mouldy smell was overwhelming. I imagine nice Fiona the agent must have got up there early and let some air in the other day, as it had definitely not been so bad then. Because the sun isn't out today, the place looked dingy and dark. The fact that the windows have been practically rendered opaque by years of grime from the traffic outside didn't help.

'Right. Big stuff first. Come on.' Kat had grabbed

one end of the sofa, galvanizing us all into action as we stood there speechless, taking it in.

Now we all stand around drinking our coffee because, even though we're knackered, we're all too scared to sit on the floor. I'd love to be able to say we found a stunning wooden floor under the carpet, just waiting to be sanded back and polished up but, sadly, what we found were nailed down sheets of grubby hardboard, so that's what I'm left with.

Because only two people can fit in the van now it's loaded, Lew and Greg head for the nearest tip, leaving the rest of us to start moving stuff around in the bedroom.

'When are you moving in?' Chris says as we flip the mattress on its side and attempt to shift it out into the hall, touching as little of it as we can. It weighs a ton.

'I don't know,' I say. 'I need to get a bed. But I don't want to impose on Kat and Greg for any longer than I have to.'

'You're not imposing,' Kat says. I'd almost forgotten she was there. All I can see is the knot of a polka-dot scarf above the rim of the mattress.

By the time Lew and Greg get back, we've moved all the large items through to the hall and they're stacked up in a line leading to the top of the stairs. Bed, wardrobe, chest of drawers, bedside table and another carpet. When the van is loaded, there's still space so we all run up and down the stairs, picking up anything we can and throwing it in. By the time it's full to the roof, the flat is still a long way off empty. I force the four of them to let me buy them a sandwich lunch (after we've all doused ourselves in the antibac hand gel Kat produces from the depths of her huge bag) and then Chris and Lew are on their way home via a second visit to the tip, leaving the three of us to stagger to the bus stop.

'Have you got any idea how much I love the pair of you?' I say as I hug them goodbye.

'Looking good, babe.'

We're FaceTiming. I've decided I'm not going to be able to get away with pretending I don't have enough reception for pictures every time, so today I organized a tiny area of Kat and Greg's spare room so that it looks like my New York bedroom, if you don't look very hard. It's basically white pillows against a white wall, but I've added Mr T, my battered old teddy, who made the journey across the Atlantic both ways with me. (On the way out, Mel – who, by the way, has no sentimentality where possessions are concerned because, being the sole focus of her parents' life, she basically got nice new things whenever she asked for them, which was often – had said, 'You could fit another pair of jeans and a couple of tops in the space that thing is taking up in your case.' She was helping me pack, and I was trying to keep a lid on my nervous excitement. Partly because I was scared I might bottle out at the last minute but also because I didn't want to rub my good fortune in her face. She'd insisted on it just being me and her, a girls' night in. Because she wanted to spend as much time with me as she could before I left. Or so I had thought. Maybe she just wanted to make sure I really did go.) I've also propped up a small cushion that Chris and Lew sent me for my birthday last year – with a cute London skyline embroidered in white on a pink background –which I always kept on my bed.

The bed frame isn't the same, of course, so before I call I make sure the pillows are propped up high behind me and, in any case, they aren't a million miles apart, both pale wood, so if he does see a tiny bit I don't think it's a deal breaker. I have to keep the picture tight, obviously. If he suddenly asks me to pan round the room for some reason, I'm screwed.

It's eight in the morning in New York, lunchtime in London, so light in both places. Kat is so paranoid about me giving myself away that she's set a small digital alarm clock to Eastern Time and propped up a big note behind it that says 'USA'. I laughed at her when she did it but, actually, I'm so nervous I find myself looking across the room at it several times as we speak.

Before I called I got back into my PJs – not the new ones, I thought I should go for something he'd recognize, so I went for the cute light grey T-shirt top with a pattern of orange and white foxes. For authenticity, I also put on the matching bottoms, not that he'll see them. Thankfully, I hadn't yet got round to putting any make-up on so I just rubbed a bit of mascara under my eyes as if I'd been sleeping (I always wake up with panda eyes. Mel, on the other hand has always been one of those women who wakes up fresh as a daisy, her pale complexion pristine), piled my hair up on top of my head and then pulled a few handfuls of it down again, and I was ready. Kat and Greg were both out at work so I knew I had the place to myself.

I checked the picture as I waited for him to pick up. Me, pillows, Mr T's right eye and ear, London skyline cushion nestled behind me. To say the whole thing was a palaver would be to do the word a disservice, but I've decided I need to do this only once or twice a week, and then he won't question the times I claim to have bad reception and we have to make do with voice-only calls. And I texted him earlier to check he would be around, so I knew I hadn't done all this for nothing. I'd replaced the US mobile the production company had kindly provided for me with another registered to Mary's address before I left: I was terrified that, otherwise, the ringtone would give away the fact that I wasn't in New York. It's a stupid extra expense and one I'll ditch as soon as all this is over.

Jack is outside a café. He's looks as if he's pleased to see me but, thankfully, the warzone noise levels on the street mean we can't talk about anything much beyond the 'Are you okay?'s and 'How's work?'s.

'Not going in till late today?' he shouts as a bus rumbles past.

I screw my face up. 'Split day.' He knows I hate those days that are neither day shoot or night shoot but somewhere in between, meaning you don't get either a whole morning or a whole evening to yourself.

'Bad luck.'

There's a hiatus where neither of us speaks. I wrack my brain for an interesting anecdote and come up pitifully short. It's strange. I used to look forward to our conversations – however rushed, however banal, however frustrating because of bad reception or interruptions – all day. They were a tiny connection with my real life, the one I couldn't wait to return to, eventually. Now I feel as if I'm talking to an acquaintance. And one I don't even like that much. I can't believe we ever had so little to say to one another.

'I might get another hour's sleep in before I get up.'

'You do that, beautiful,' he says, and I wait to see if the suggestive tone of his voice sparks anything in me. Nothing.

'Oh,' I say, before we hang up. I want to test his reaction. 'Have you spoken to Mel? I haven't heard from her for a few days.'

I watch him closely to see if he gives anything away. Not a flicker. He's missed his calling. There must be a way you can turn 'highly skilled at lying' into a career.

'No. But then I rarely do. She's probably busy at work, or getting the flat ready to sell. They're putting it on the market this week, aren't they?'

Are they? I know that Sam wants her out, wants them to be able to split the profits and move on as soon as possible but, last time I spoke to her, she was holding out.

'Are they? When did she tell you that?'

And there it is. The tiniest flinch. 'Must have been at the party. That was the last time I spoke to her.'

'That's odd, because I talk to her all the time, and she hasn't said anything. Maybe you heard her wrong.'

'Probably,' he says, looking shifty. 'I was probably too overexcited that you were home to listen properly.'

I spend the afternoon trying and failing to find Mel's flat for sale online.

'I've got a great idea,' I say to Kat when she gets home from showing a client round what, to all intents and purposes, sounds like an actual palace. I've spent the afternoon painting their bathroom walls as a surprise, because she had showed me the paint they'd bought weeks ago but hadn't had the chance to use, and I thought I could at least try to repay them for their kindness. Luckily, it's tiny. And more than half of it is tiled.

'You are kidding,' she says when I tell her what it is. I showed her the bathroom first as a softener and it worked, because she almost shed a tear. With happiness, I should add. Not because my cutting in is so appalling.

'Not really.'

'Shit.'

She looks confused. 'Aren't you just going to confront them both now you've got somewhere to move into?'

I've been thinking about this a lot. Originally, all I wanted was somewhere to run to. I could drop my bomb and leave. Now, though, it doesn't feel like enough. I can't bear the thought of Mel looking at my life – jobless, boyfriendless, living in a dump – and feeling smug. As if she's won.

'Not yet. I need to sort myself out a bit more first. I don't want to give her the satisfaction of thinking my life's shit —'

'Hardly . . .' Kat interrupts. But I'm on a roll.

'And if I can fuck her about a bit in the meantime . . .'

Kat smiles. 'Sounds good to me.'

Which is how come we're back outside the flat the next morning, hiding in the bushes in the park across the road, waiting for Jack and Mel to leave for work. I had to make Kat change before we left home because she was hardly going to blend into the foliage in her white-spotted skirt with a bright red bow in her black hair, looking for all the world like Minnie Mouse's angry sister. So now she's channelling Secret Squirrel in a chic brown mac with the collar turned up and sunglasses, and we're trying to look inconspicuous drinking our takeaway coffees while lurking in the drizzle.

We've been there for the best part of forty-five minutes, and I'm considering sitting down on the damp grass, my back is hurting so much, when we see the front door open. Kat digs her nails into my arm so hard I let out a yelp, and I see Melissa's red head whip round like that girl in *The Exorcist*, but then Jack says something to her and her focus is back on him. I watch as they walk towards the Tube, him laughing at something she's saying. If I didn't know better, I'd say they made a good couple.

We wait a few more minutes just to make sure

neither of them suddenly remembers something they've forgotten. We're about to cross the road when the front door opens again and my downstairs neighbours, Bev and Julian, emerge.

'Hold on,' I say, turning my back on the house.

'Okay, they're getting in their car' – Kat gives me a running commentary – 'and . . . they've gone.'

Inside, I make a fuss of Oscar while Kat settles down in front of Mel's laptop. She clicks through her emails.

'Ooh, look, she's been talking to Sam.' She leans in and concentrates. Even with her glasses on, Kat always reads everything from about an inch away. 'Blah blah, she's getting defensive saying, yes, she is organizing the sale, and he's basically accusing her of dragging her heels.'

She goes back to concentrating while I riffle through a neat pile of mail on the desk. Nothing out of the ordinary.

'So . . .' Kat says eventually. 'She's made contact with two agents, Barkers and Goldborne Friedman, asking them to come and give her a valuation. The first one is on Saturday.'

'Great,' I say. 'We can get in there first.'

Kat peers at me over the top of the laptop. 'We?'

'You.'

'Jesus,' she says, slamming it shut. Then she takes a long breath in, pushes her glasses up her nose. 'Okay. Fuck it. Bring it on.'

15

I pretend I'm not listening in as Kat makes the call, busy myself trying to find a jacket I particularly like in the cramped corner of the wardrobe my clothes once again occupy now Mel is back, but Kat has that small-human, big-voice thing going on, as if she had to shout to be heard from a young age.

I know she's calling on the office number because, if her name came up on Mel's mobile, no way would she answer, and we both know Mel's not senior enough at work to have anyone screening her calls.

'Mel! Hi! It's Kat.'

There's silence, where I assume Mel says something like 'I'm too busy to talk to you', because Kat launches straight into her rehearsed spiel.

'I'll only be a second. Listen, I heard on the grapevine from a friend of mine at Goldborne Friedman that you were selling your flat and I just wanted to check whether you'd signed any kind of exclusivity deal with them yet, because I have a couple of people who might be interested. It would save you having to pay fees, which, you know, can end up being a fortune . . .'

She pauses for a reaction and I find myself standing statue-like, holding my breath. Oscar looks up at me and meows loudly, so I pick him up and flip him on to his back and he starts purring like a steam train.

'Exactly . . .' Kat says. 'And, if you're looking to buy somewhere else, that money's going to come in handy. Are you looking to buy somewhere else?'

Even though I'm curious to hear the answer, I just want Kat to stick to the script and achieve her objective.

'Right . . . yes, I know what you mean . . . and do you know what you're putting it on for? . . . No . . . right . . .'

It's like listening to half a radio play and all the important stuff is happening off air.

'Well, assuming you haven't made any drastic alterations since I was last there, I'd say you must be looking at late eight hundreds, maybe even nine. I'd have to have another look, though, because it's been years . . . Okay, good plan. I'll pop round tonight. And then if neither of the couples I have in mind think it's right for them, you can still go ahead and put it on with an agent and you won't have lost anything . . . Great . . . See you then. Bye, Mel.'

I wait until I'm sure she's ended the call. 'Well done. Jesus. I couldn't have pulled that off.'

'I'm going over there later. Luckily, she's so uninterested in me that she's never cottoned on to the fact I only do the really high-end stuff these days.'

I hadn't really thought beyond the fact that having Kat spend time with Mel might be enlightening, but now another thought pops into my head.

'Make sure you get her spare keys.'

Kat rolls her eyes as if this is the most obvious thing anyone has ever said.

'Obviously. I'm going to tell her my clients can only view on weekdays because they go away every weekend. And they have kids, so they don't want to do evenings, so unless she wants to keep taking the day off work and having to spend more time with me she'll have to give them to me.'

I spend half the afternoon in Homebase on Finchley Road, stocking up on industrial-strength cleaning products and a couple of pots of paint (a chalky white and a light sagey green which, if Farrow and Ball made it, would probably be called Ear Wax or Toe Jam), some brushes, a roller-and-paint-tray set and some tape. I add bin bags, rubber gloves and then sandpaper, because I have this big idea that I'm going to repaint the woodwork. Then I drag it all on to the bus, already regretting that I picked up so much in one trip before I even make it out of the car park.

It's only the second time I've been to the flat on my own. When we left after taking out all the furniture, I'd propped two windows open, one at the front and one at the back, figuring it didn't really matter at this point if someone broke in, so the smell is a little less intense than it was. There's still a mountain of crap in here, lying about everywhere you look, so I set down the takeaway coffee I bought in the corner café, having first dumped my booty in the hallway, don the rubber gloves and start loading everything into bin bags.

I'm loading up my fifth when my mobile rings. It's such an event that my agent rings me that I almost rip the gloves trying to pull them off so I don't miss her.

'Hi!'

'Amy! How are you doing?'

'I've been better,' I say, and then I think I don't want her to start dreading calling me because she's going to have to listen to a litany of my woes every time, so I add, 'Things are turning round, though. I'm just decorating my new flat.'

She asks me for the address and I give it to her, but mostly I'm just thinking, *Get to the point: why have you phoned?*

'So,' she says eventually, 'are you free tomorrow morning for an audition?'

'Definitely.' More than anything, I want to be able to hold off going back to the call centre. 'What is it?'

'Don't get excited. It's one scene. *Death by Numbers.* Filming in Brighton the week after next.'

'What's the part?' I say, clinging on to the hope that this might be some kind of a break.

'Woman in Park. Thirty-five. That's all it says.'

I try not to let my disappointment sound in my voice. 'I can do that.'

'It's for Sky, so the money's not bad.'

'Great.'

'It'll get better after *Murder in Manhattan* starts airing here,' she says. 'I'll be able to flog you to death while it's on.'

*

I realized I wanted to act almost as soon as I tried it for the first time. It was pure chance. A boy I had my eye on at uni was a dedicated member of the Drama Society so I decided to go along to see if they needed help with lighting or set building – but really so that I could bask in his intoxicating presence. I wasn't a natural joiner but I had made a rule for myself when I went to college that I was going to force myself out of my comfort zone. Make friends on my own instead of hiding behind Mel, nodding and smiling while she effortlessly won people over.

Mel was shocked at first that I wasn't coming home every weekend but I knew that, if I was going to fit in, I had to throw myself headlong into everything. She had an open invitation to come and stay in my room in halls whenever she wanted, and she often did, but she never really liked any of my new friends. She said she felt uncomfortable around them because they all thought she must be some kind of thicko because she left school at sixteen. I couldn't see it but, whenever she came up, we increasingly just hung out together. Above all, I didn't want her to stop coming.

So far, I had tried the Photography Society, the Fine Art Club and the Literary Society, looking for a tribe I could join. Even though I'd met some fun people, I didn't feel entirely at home anywhere. But I couldn't conjure up a passion where there was none. So, when I found out Kieron spent all his time in the little college theatre space the Drama Society called home I decided to give it a try.

There's nothing quite so intimidating as walking into a self-proclaimed exclusive club unannounced. It's not that I was shy, I just wasn't one of those 'Look at me, aren't I fabulous?' people like Mel. I tended to lurk, feeling out the possibilities rather than tap-dancing into the spotlight. That day, I walked into the centre of a heated row. Five people – three men (one of them Kieron) and two women – were standing in the centre of the room, shouting at each other. I was about to turn around and walk straight out again when they all stopped arguing and turned and looked at me.

'Can I help you?' one of the women said. It sounded more unfriendly than I think it was meant to.

I stood there blushing, uncomfortable with five pairs of eyes focused on me.

'Um . . . I was . . . well, I was wondering if you needed any help but, I mean, I can see this isn't a good time . . .'

'She looks just like Lucy,' one of the others said, and that made me blush more, even though I had no idea what they were on about.

'Do you act?' This from Kieron.

'I was thinking more sets or lighting or something –'

'We don't need that,' he snapped. 'What we need is someone to replace Lucy in the play. She's decided it's more important to go home on the weekend we open because it's her parents' anniversary.'

'I keep telling you, it's their twenty-fifth . . .' wailed a girl I assumed was Lucy. And, actually, she did look a bit like me. In that we were both dark and female.

'So you shouldn't have taken the part then.' I was starting to realize Kieron was in fact a bit arsey, but in a way that my eighteen-year-old self found strangely appealing.

'I didn't know they'd have the party that weekend, did I? I thought it'd be the one before, because that's nearer the actual date . . .'

I stood there while they all fired off again.

'Well, you should have checked . . .'

'I'll be back for the Sunday night, anyway . . .'

'No way. You can't miss the opening night and then expect to still be in it . . .' This from the other girl. Tiny, dark-haired, sallow-skinned and stunning.

'And don't tell me you only just found out now, with a week and a half to go,' one of the other boys chipped in. A tall, skinny, floppy-haired fop.

I began to edge back towards the door. Kieron spotted me.

'Wait. So, do you act or not? It's hardly a difficult question.'

I looked at the floor. 'I don't know. I've never tried.'

'Jesus,' Floppy-haired fop said.

Kieron strode over and took my arm. My knees and everything else went a bit weak. 'You'd really be helping us out. Just give it a go. You never know, you might be brilliant. And if you're not, we'll just have to set up more auditions. And that'll lose us another few days, even assuming we find someone. So, no pressure.'

I laughed, and I was gratified to see he did, too. 'No, no pressure.'

'Give her your script, Lucy.'

Lucy more or less hurled a sheaf of paper in my direction, turned on her heels and flounced out.

Anyway, to cut a long story short, they gave me the script and let me look at it for about thirty seconds before they asked me to read aloud. I can't even remember what the play was. Some godawful thing written by one of our fellow students who thought they were a playwright. Overwrought and self-indulgent. By this point, I just wanted to get out of there. I'd never have to speak to any of these people again so long as I kept my eyes peeled and turned a corner if I ever spotted one of them coming.

The first time I read it, with the stunning dark-haired girl, Pia, reading the other parts, I stumbled and stuttered. Floppy-haired fop, who turned out to be called Alistair, actually gave me a few quite helpful pointers, and in a calm and supportive tone that helped soothe my nerves. By the third read, they had all convinced themselves I was the one.

Kieron beamed at me. 'Thank God you walked in when you did.'

'I don't know if I can do it,' I said, not wanting to break the moment but equally not wanting to put myself in a position where I'd make a massive arse of myself.

He'd put his arm around me. 'Of course you can. You'll be brilliant.'

Obviously, I agreed, and I threw myself into the best few weeks I'd ever had in my life. I loved every single second of every part of it, even including the vomiting with nerves backstage on the first night of the play's one-week run. At the risk of sounding like a pretentious twat, I'd found my calling.

For some reason, I didn't tell Mel. I just, I don't know, felt as if she might think I was trying to muscle into her chosen niche or something. That she would think it was ridiculous, the whole idea of me performing. That wasn't who I was. And this was in the days before social media, thankfully – I don't think I'd ever even met anyone who had a mobile phone at this point – so I didn't have to worry about her spotting photos of me strutting my stuff. I remember she did wonder why I told her she couldn't come and visit two weekends in a row, but I just claimed I had too much coursework. I felt bad. In so far as I knew, we had never kept a secret from one another. But I also knew it was better for me to keep it to myself. And because I'd probably make such a fool of myself, it would never happen again, so I told myself, what's the harm?

But I had a new passion, one that I never in a million years would have imagined I'd have. From that point on, all my spare time was spent in the dusty little theatre, or sitting in Pia's tiny room in halls, eating Pot Noodles with Kieron, Alistair and Tom, a lanky, puppyish-looking boy, the other witness to my impromptu audition, reading through plays, hunting for our next project. And laughing. When I think of those times, I remember a lot of laughing.

Of course, Kieron turned out to be gay, as did half the boys I fancied at college. In the end, I was glad. I needed like-minded friends much more than I needed a boyfriend.

The auditions are being held in an old church on Tottenham Court Road that has a warren of rooms they let out for rehearsals and castings. I'm used to the drill. 'Woman in Park' doesn't give much away in terms of the image I should present, so I go for neutral. A cute summer dress with boots and a denim jacket. In my head, I look like Stevie Nicks but I'm probably giving off something more like 'got dressed in the dark and couldn't find her shoes'. I wear my hair down and minimal make-up.

I've met the casting director, Angie, a few times over the years and her assistant, Sally, recognizes me when I walk in. There are two other women waiting (mid-forties, short hair, plump; and early thirties, blonde ponytail, skinny, so obviously no one really knows or cares what Woman in Park looks like).

'Hi!' Sally greets me with a smile as she ticks my name off a list. I can see there are at least ten other potential Women in Parks on there, because each actor has the name of the character they're reading for next to their name. 'How have you been?'

Rule number one of casting club: never give them

the idea there are any problems in your life that might get in the way of you doing a good job.

'Great, thanks. Just got back from the States.'

'Oh, yes!'

We chat for a second and I can see Blonde Ponytail looking me over surreptitiously as she hears about my big-time US job. Always good to rattle the competition.

'Here's your sides,' Sally says eventually. 'They're running about five minutes late.'

I take the pages from the script she hands me and sit next to Plump Short Hair, who smiles as she moves her bag out of the way. We all sit there in silence, studying the highlighted lines. Woman in Park, it seems, has witnessed some kind of crime and she's nervously reporting what she saw to the police, clutching her five-year-old child close. It's the kind of procedural dialogue that merely requires you not to fuck up and to make sure the audience pick up any relevant information. Less is more, as they say. It's not exactly Lady Macbeth.

Plump Short Hair goes in and comes out less than five minutes later. That doesn't signify anything. When the part has only nine lines, there's not much to say. They call Blonde Ponytail next, just as someone else arrives – I assume for a different part, because it's an elderly man. Or else Woman in Park has hidden depths I'm unaware of.

Four or so minutes later, it's my turn. Same old same old. Angie greets me warmly, introduces me to the director and producer, neither of whom I've met before, tells them briefly about my recent work, and then I'm reading for them, Angie playing all the other parts.

It's over in a flash. Joanne, the director, asks me to read it a second time (this is par for the course and means nothing, I've learned). There are no notes, from which I deduce either I was absolutely perfect and couldn't be improved upon (unlikely), so bad there's no point (again, I feel, unlikely) or the part is so small their hearts aren't really in it and pretty much anyone who vaguely fits the bill and who can walk and talk at the same time will do (bingo!).

And that's it. I walk out into the spring sunshine. With most of these small roles, you don't even hear if you haven't got it. You just wait and wait until eventually your agent picks up on the grapevine that an offer has gone out to someone else. I've learned to forget about them the minute the audition is over. Not that I don't care, I do. I really want this job, and not just for the money. I want to be working, I want to keep reminding people – casting directors, producers, directors, writers – that I'm out there. More than anything, I want to spend a day acting, because it's what I love doing.

On the way to the Tube I call Kat, who, since I've been staying with her, seems to have taken on the role of anxious stage mother. She insisted I let her know how the audition had gone, even though I explained a hundred times that it wasn't a big deal. She's probably feeling guilty that she's found me a flat I might not be able to afford to live in for long.

As it happens, when she answers, she has other fish to fry.

'I'm at the key-cutting place,' she says in a stage whisper, although I have no idea who she's afraid of being overheard by.

Yesterday evening, she'd headed down to Mel's flat in Kingston, friendly bottle of wine in hand. Mel, she told me, when she got home at around nine, was looking good, if a bit thin. Acted pleased to see her, which Kat knew immediately was put on. They'd sat at the kitchen island and Mel had opened the wine. Kat told me gleefully that one of the first things she'd asked was how I was.

'Good,' Mel had said. 'She came over the other week but only for a flying visit.'

'Oh,' Kat had said. 'She didn't tell me.' She'd waited for Mel to mention the birthday party but, of course, she didn't, because then she would have had to make some excuse as to why Kat and Greg hadn't been invited.

'Like I say, she was only here for forty-eight hours.'

'It's incredible, isn't it?' Kat had apparently said, twisting the knife. 'To think of her over there, part of some big new TV show. She must be having the time of her life.'

I snorted when she told me this bit, knowing how much Mel must have hated having to play along.

'Ha! What did she say to that?'

Kat crossed her legs and held the top of her wine glass loosely between her fingers in a very Mel-like way. 'Mmmm . . . shame it's such a small part.'

I nearly choked on my Gavi di Gavi. 'She really said that?'

Kat nodded. 'So I said, "Still, it's an amazing experience, though," and she was all "Oh, God, yes, incredible," like that's what she'd been going to say all along. Of course, she knows she won't get anywhere bitching about you to me. It's not as if we've ever bonded like that before. I'll have to work on her.'

'She's going to let you have a go at selling it, then?'

She reached into her bag, which was propped up next to the sofa, and pulled out a key-ring with two keys attached. Rattled them at me. 'She is. And actually, it's a lovely flat so – who knows? – I might even come across someone who'd want it. I'd forgotten how big it was.'

'Did she say anything about where she's moving to?' The last conversation Mel and I had had about this, she said she hadn't made up her mind because she had no intention of selling up and leaving. She was still intending to fight Sam tooth and nail to keep it. He could afford it, she'd snapped. And it was him who'd upped and left.

Kat pulled a face. 'She said maybe north. Nearer you.'

'Jesus. Do you think they're planning on carrying on after we get married? I mean, assuming we ever did get married, which, obviously, now, we won't.'

'In all honesty, yes. Her, anyway. I wouldn't put it past her.'

I leaned back in my chair. 'Christ, she might be even more of a bitch than I thought.'

*

136

'You'll never guess who came over last night!'

I'm back in my pillow nest with Mr T and the pink cushion. No PJs, though, because it's midnight in the UK so only seven in New York. For authenticity, I have a work document of Greg's face down on my lap that could pass for a script.

Mel is in her own bed, at least. She's a bit pissed – she tells me she's had a night in the pub with people from work, including John, her boss, the one she told me she was thinking of seducing for career-enhancement opportunities. She's looking scrubbed and shiny, her hair falling in waves around her face. Mel is always scrupulous about taking her make-up off, protecting her pale, delicate skin. I, on the other hand, have pillows that resemble a dirty protest because I can't be arsed to do anything more than run a wet wipe over my face before I fall asleep.

'Who?'

'Katty Mackenzie!' She pulls a 'yuk' face. Even though she knows I've stayed friends with Kat she never bothers to temper her dislike for her in front of me.

'Really? How on earth did that happen?'

'I've decided to sell the flat. I'm sick of fighting with Sam about it.'

'Right, gosh, well, it's probably the best thing to do in the long run. Otherwise, you'll never have a clean break.'

'I just don't see why I should lose my home because he went off with some tart, that's all.'

Oh, the irony. I almost laugh. 'I know. But don't cut off your nose to spite your face, and all that.'

'I hate that expression. Who's cutting off their nose?'

'Anyway, what's Kat got to do with it?'

'She popped up out of nowhere and said she'd heard I was selling and she might have a buyer for me. You know she does that thing where she helps people find houses or something . . .'

'Great. I assume her fee would come from them and not you, so you'd save a fortune.'

'Exactly. Anyway, she clicked around here last night in her stupid little kitten heels. Who in God's name wears kitten heels? Oh, I told her you came home last week. Sorry!'

I shrug. 'Doesn't matter. I hardly ever hear from her these days, anyway.'

'She reckons we could get as much as nine two five.'

'Amazing. Are you looking for a new place yet?'

She yawns and stretches. 'Not yet. I can't decide where to go. Besides, I need you here to look at things with me.'

'Well, that might not happen for a while. Email me pictures. Or we can FaceTime when you go and look at places.'

'When are you coming over again?'

'No idea. Not for ages. Oh,' I say, remembering Kat's theory about Mel envying my life, 'did I tell you? They're bumping up my part. Apparently, Yvon's proving quite popular.'

For a split second, Mel's expression is like the one a baby makes when it eats something unexpectedly bitter. I try to keep the smirk off mine.

'Oh,' she says. 'Right.'

I shrug and try to look casual. 'It's no big deal. It just means I'll get less time off.' I feign a yawn, stretch luxuriously.

'Great . . . Well done . . .'

'I'd better go. I'm going out. Some of the cast are meeting up at the 21 Club for dinner.'

Mel's face is a picture. The one time she visited me – for a long weekend a couple of weeks before Sam dropped his bombshell and she no longer felt she could splash out on flights to New York – she'd been obsessed with wanting to go to '21', as she'd called it, thinking it made her sound like a local. Along with the top of the Empire State, walking across Brooklyn Bridge and skating in Central Park. Basically, all the things she'd seen in movies and that tourists want to cross off their lists. I'd been no different when I'd first arrived, although my castmates had soon persuaded me that there were better, more authentic, not to mention cheaper, icons to visit. But for Mel's sake, I'd tried – and failed – to get us a table. I'd even taken her to look at the little statues of jockeys that line the street outside.

She can't even bring herself to comment. 'I'll talk to you soon, in that case.'

'Love you,' I say, trying not to laugh as I hang up.

16

By the weekend, I'm ready to move in. By which I mean the whole flat has been scrubbed to within an inch of its life, had a coat of paint (woodwork cleaned but not painted. Life, I decided, is too short) and I have taken delivery of a cheap bed, microwave and fridge from Argos. My final-episode fee has come through so I've splashed out on a tiny two-seater oatmeal-coloured sofa (being delivered on Monday) and a Netflix subscription. There's still nothing on the floors, or in the greasy, gaping hole in the kitchen where the cooker once was, or covering the windows. Apart from grime. But I'm very conscious that I don't want to outstay my welcome at Kat and Greg's.

On Sunday morning, we pile my cases and the scavenged booty that is all I have to show for a five-year relationship into their car. On our way through chichi St John's Wood, Kat spots a skip outside a posh house that is being refurbished and insists we stop for a rummage. I'd forgotten how much she loves a skip. When we lived together, she was forever dragging in some bit of mid-century modern tat that she would lovingly restore to its former glory. She still has some of it, now I come to think about it. A fifties side table, a sixties magazine rack, a seventies floor lamp.

This one contains mostly builders' rubble but, with her practised eye, Kat spots what turns out to be a small, battered wooden table buried among it. I only realize what it is after Kat has made Greg jump in and dig it out. From the way he throws himself straight in there, I assume this is a regular occurrence. He comes out holding it above his head like a weightlifter with a barbell, quiff askew.

'Sand that back and paint it and it'll be lovely in your kitchen,' Kat says as we help Greg out.

'Excuse me, are you throwing stuff in my skip?' The three of us jump guiltily as a man appears – early forties, I would say, with paint-speckled hair that I identify only too well with at the moment.

Kat gives him her best, most confident grin. 'Taking it out. So now you'll have more room.'

Thankfully, the man smiles. 'Really? That's not very St John's Wood.'

'No, well, neither are we,' I say. 'This table's going to live up by the North Circular.'

'I think there were some chairs that went with it,' the man says, looking around. 'I mean, if you're in the market for other stuff.'

'We can't pay you, though, that's the thing,' Kat says, and I feel myself blushing. Apparently, this is a perfectly acceptable statement, because the man doesn't bat an eyelid.

'God, no, that's fine. To be honest, anything I can offload means more space in the skip. And this is our

141

eighth skip on this job so far, so you can imagine . . . It's costing a fortune.'

'Is this your house?' I can't imagine someone who lives in a mansion like this worrying about the price of the odd skip.

'No. God, no. I'm in charge of the refit. Simon Rigby.' He sticks out a hand and shakes each of ours.

'Is it for sale?' Kat says. She probably knows five people who could afford it and would be interested in looking round. I can see the pound signs ticking up in her eyes.

'Not so far as I know.' While we've been talking, he's been edging back towards the drive and we've been edging along behind him. We follow him through the gates and there's another pile of cast-offs.

'Help yourself. It's only stuff out of the maid's quarters, but you're welcome . . .'

I feel as if I've entered a parallel universe. 'They have a maid? With her own flat? They don't need a new one, do they, because I need a job.'

Simon Rigby flashes a smile at me. It lights up his face and transforms his features into something altogether more interesting. 'I don't think so, but I can ask.'

For some reason, I don't want him to think I'm a saddo who goes around scrounging furniture off the street and begging for live-in domestic work. 'It's okay. I'm an actress, really. I'd be very unreliable. They'd be waiting for their breakfast and I'd be off auditioning for a toilet-roll commercial.'

I wait for him to say that most annoying thing any-one can say to an actor but seems to be half the population's response to finding out what I do: 'What might I have seen you in?' I've never understood it. If I hear someone's a nanny, I don't say, 'What children do you look after that I might know?' or, if someone works in IT, 'What computers have you programmed that I might have come across?' To give him credit, he doesn't, he just laughs.

'Can we have these?' Kat and Greg are ferreting through the pile of cast-offs and have put two kitchen chairs and a low, tiled coffee table to one side.

'Be my guest,' Simon says.

'We honestly don't usually go rummaging through people's shit,' I say. I don't know why I feel the need to apologize for our behaviour but, for some reason, I do.

'Speak for yourself,' Kat says. 'That's where I find all my best things. I'll have the coffee table if you don't want it.'

'It's fine,' I say. I may be proud but I need a coffee table and even I have to admit this one has a kind of retro charm.

'Is this a cooker?' Greg says out of nowhere. And I mean, really out of nowhere, because I can't see him in the midst of all the crap.

'Probably,' Simon says. 'I think there was one in there. It's not exactly state of the art.'

'It works, though, right?' We've all found Greg now, and he's sniffing about an old free-standing cooker

with four rings on top, what looks like a grill underneath and a tiny oven.

'No idea, but I don't see why not.'

'I think we've got enough stuff for now,' I say, eager
to get out of there. God knows what Simon must think
of us.

'It's clean, too, Amy, look.' Greg holds open the oven
door like one of those women displaying the prizes in an
old TV game show. All he needs is a bikini and high heels.

'We could take it inside and plug it in to see . . .'

'No!' I almost shout at Kat's suggestion. 'Let's just
take the other things and get out of Simon's way.'

Simon seems to be fairly amused by the whole thing.
'You're welcome to do that if you want.'

'I'm not sure we're going to be able to get everything
in the car as it is. What with all your cases and the stuff
that's in there already,' Greg says helpfully. 'We might
have to do two journeys.'

I feel as if I want the earth to swallow me up. How
did my life come to this? At the age of nearly forty, I'm
scrabbling around in other people's rubbish piles.

'Let's just get what we can in,' I say. 'We really don't
want to disturb Simon more than we have to.'

Simon shrugs. 'You can just come back and help
yourselves. Like I said, anything I can get rid of is a
bonus for me.'

'Thanks, mate,' Greg says. I don't think I've ever
heard him call anyone mate before. It's such an un-
Greg thing to say.

We manage to cram the kitchen table into the boot – which won't now close – by taking the legs off, and the coffee table fits in the back seat alongside me.

'I really think we should come back later for the chairs,' Kat says. 'I mean, what's the problem? You need them.'

'Tell you what,' Simon says. 'If you come back for the chairs, I'll have a couple of the guys take the cooker inside and plug it in in the meantime. See what happens. If I'm not going to be here when you get back, I'll leave a note on it letting you know. How's that?'

I mumble my thanks, looking at the floor. I'm now officially a charity case.

'And I'll get them to have a scout around, see if there's anything else interesting we were just going to throw out.'

'God, that was so embarrassing,' I say sulkily once we're in the car.

Kat turns around and looks at me wide-eyed, like an owl with glasses. 'Why? He wants to get rid of that stuff, you need it, we can take it off his hands. Everyone benefits.'

'Scrounging someone else's thrown-away furniture. Not even their furniture, their *maid's* furniture. I'm scrabbling about for things that aren't even deemed good enough for the maid!'

'Stop being such a snob,' Kat says. I know she's right. I have no idea why I'm reacting like this.

'And Simon totally liked the look of you, by the way,' she adds.

My blush, which seems to have been hovering just underneath the surface for the past ten minutes, bursts though. I have no idea why. I'm just grateful that I'm sitting in the back, where they can't scrutinize me too much. 'Don't be stupid.'

'A hundred per cent. Back me up, Greg.'

'Ninety-nine point eight per cent.'

'Why else do you think he's going to all the trouble of testing out the cooker for you?'

'Because he's a nice guy?'

'Yeah, right. He'd put himself out like that for anyone.'

'You don't even know him!'

'Amy and Simon sitting in a tree . . .' Greg chips in, which is so childish I can't help but laugh.

We lug all the stuff up the two flights of stairs and then Kat disappears to get coffees from the café on the corner and comes back with some questionable looking pastries, too.

'You two go back for the rest of the things, and I'll get going on the table,' she says.

'No way. You and Greg go. I'm not having the pair of you trying to matchmake between me and some bloke I met in the street for five minutes.'

'He wasn't in the street. He was in a very posh house on Avenue Road. And he wasn't wearing a wedding ring. Just saying.'

'Stop it, Kat. It's too soon.'

She pushes her glasses up her nose. 'I'm only teasing you. Sorry.'

I back down immediately. I don't know why I'm getting so defensive in the first place.

'I know. I've got a bit of a sense-of-humour failure at the moment.'

'Nothing a quick fumble with a random man you've only just met wouldn't cure,' she says, and waggles her eyebrows in such a ridiculously exaggerated way I laugh.

'Well, I can't do it on my own,' Greg says. He's brandishing a piece of card on which he's marked the size of the gap left by the old cooker.

'Come on, then,' Kat says, obviously sensing that I'm still reluctant. 'We can take our coffees with us.'

Once they've gone, I dither about a bit, not sure what to do first. There's no point unpacking most of the contents of my cases because there's nowhere to put anything, so I just empty the box of pans and things that I got from the flat and then make up the bed. I dig out Mr T and my pink skyline cushion and nestle them among the pillows. I'll have to remember to hide my bird-adorned duvet cover when I FaceTime with either Jack or Mel, and I'll just have to hope they don't notice my bed has lost its headboard.

I'm sanding down the top of the kitchen table (I started with a leg but the turned ridges made it too frustrating so I gave up) and am actually feeling quite content because the sun has come out and it's streaming through the kitchen-stroke-living-room window – actually, that's a lie. There's one thin shaft of it that hits the window at an oblique angle, causing a thirty-centimetre-square patch of sunlight in which I'm now standing – when the bell rings, announcing that Kat and Greg are back. I run down the two flights of stairs to find them not only with the cooker and two chairs but proudly brandishing quite a nice wooden floor lamp, too.

'It needs a new shade, but those things cost nothing,' Kat says.

'Brilliant.'

'And the cooker seems to work perfectly,' Greg adds. 'At least, Simon had plugged it in and it heated up. Plus, it'll fit into that space exactly.'

'He had one of his blokes giving it another clean-out when we got there.'

I help Greg lug it up the stairs, cursing myself for agreeing to live on the second floor. Kat manages to get both chairs and the lamp up in the time it takes us, skipping past us as we pause for breath on the landings. At one point, two people – presumably the couple who live there – come out of the first-floor flat and tut loudly at the chaos.

'Sorry. I'm just moving in upstairs,' I say to the woman, who I would guess is in her mid-thirties. Face like a provoked piranha.

'It's Sunday,' she says snappily.

'I know. Like I said, sorry. We're pretty much done now.'

She stomps off, followed by the man – also mid-thirties and stringy. In a film, his part would be played by a weasel.

'Well, they seem nice,' Greg says once we've heard the front door slam.

'That's a point,' I say. 'How come Simon has all his crew working on a Sunday?'

'Rich people don't acknowledge weekends,' Kat says. 'If you want the job, then you agree to be on site every day until it's done.'

'Sounds like Dickensian times,' I say, bending down to pick up my end of the cooker.

'Except they're probably all being paid a small fortune. Oh . . . I gave him your number, by the way.'

I drop the cooker again. Greg yelps.

'You did what?'

Kat shrugs. 'He seemed disappointed that you hadn't come back with us, so . . . It's no big deal. What's the worst that can happen?'

17

'I'm going to get Oscar.'

Kat and I are talking on the phone on Monday morning. Last night, I slept only fitfully, partly because I was in a new place with strange noises and downstairs neighbours who, I decided at 3 a.m., were actually marginally more scary than any stranger who might break in. Eventually, I gave in and did what every other person unintentionally awake at that time would do and ran through everything in my life that's gone wrong in glorious Technicolor. Despite Kat and Greg's kindness and generosity, I felt achingly lonely.

Inevitably, I indulged in a bit of self-pity, but then I started to get angry. How could they do this to me? How could Mel, above all? Not that I think Jack is any less to blame, but she was the one who had known me most of my life. She knew more about my vulnerabilities and weaknesses than anyone else in the world. She's the person I always thought would have my back if everyone else on earth turned against me. And now she was shagging my boyfriend, in my home, and playing Mum to my cat. And she doesn't even fucking like cats.

So now here I am, with a plan to wrestle my furry

friend from her grasp and cause a bit of trouble in paradise, too.

Kat gasps. 'Not really?'

'Why not? He's mine, I had him before I moved in with Jack. There's no way Mel's being nice to him.'

'Oh, yeah, she hates cats, doesn't she?'

When we were all sharing a house, a local stray had tried to adopt us. Kat and I used to leave food in the tiny back garden for him and built an elaborate shelter out of old bits of wood so he could hide from the elements. We'd been all for the idea of inviting him to move in. Even Liz had been up for it. But Mel had vetoed the idea without a second thought. I think I even remember her uttering the phrase, 'Cats are evil,' although my memory might be embellishing. I do recall that she used to kick out at him if he came within a few feet of her. When we went our separate ways, Kat had managed to wrestle him into a carrier and take him to Birmingham with her, although he'd subsequently run away, been found by the local RSPCA, scanned and discovered to have a microchip announcing that he actually belonged to our old next-door neighbours in Finsbury Park. Not so stray, after all. I did use to wonder why he was a bit on the chubby side.

'Exactly,' I say. 'Remember Fat Albert?'

'You're really going to go in and just take him?'

I take a long sip of my coffee. I'm sitting at my sanded-but-not-painted table on one of my salvaged chairs, drinking out of one of yesterday's polystyrene cups because I forgot to buy any mugs. 'Well . . . we both are. I need you to help me.'

'I'm on my way to meet a client.'

'That's okay. I'm waiting in for the sofa this morning. This afternoon.'

'Isn't Jack going to realize something's up? I mean, cats don't just let themselves out.'

'Here's the genius part. I'm going to open the bathroom window a bit. He'll think it's Mel's fault. He must know she couldn't give a shit about Oscar.'

'Oh my God. And then he'll have to tell you he's gone missing! I can't wait to see how he explains that one away. Why do you need me there, though?'

'Moral support. I can't do it on my own. Please, Kat, I know I'm asking you way too many favours at the moment –'

'Of course!' she says, and I find myself thinking, not for the first time in the past couple of weeks, how I misjudged her. 'I could get there by half two.'

'Perfect.'

The sofa arrives on time, which I take as a good omen. It looks oddly out of place, all shiny and new on the bare hardboard floors and next to the tiled coffee table that I haven't had time to clean up yet. I pop down to the hardware shop and the convenience store and get a carrier, a litter tray and a bag of litter, along with a couple of tins of food. They don't have Oscar's favourite but I figure I can help myself to a couple of sachets from the flat and keep these for emergencies.

I wait in the park for Kat. I'm early, so there's time to sit and look at my former home. It's nothing special. A flat in a Victorian terraced house with a tiny paved front garden, mostly taken up by bins, but I remember thinking, when I moved in, that it was perfect. I couldn't imagine there being anywhere Jack and I could be happier. I'm pleased to realize I feel detached from it now. As if my emotional ties have been severed.

Kat does her trick of ringing the doorbell while I stay hidden. This time, we don't wait around looking through Jack's laptop or scouring for useful things they won't miss (although I do stuff two old mugs into my bag, because I'm still using the same manky polysty-rene cup. 'See, I told you to take mugs,' Kat says smugly when she sees me. And I add one cereal bowl for me and a little china dish from the depths of a cupboard for Oscar.)

He's pleased to see me, of course, but with some kind of super cat sense he recognizes the carrier for what it is and scoots under the bed.

'Oh God,' I say, half crawling under after him. He backs out the other way, right into Kat's grasp. A glint of something catches my eye. I reach my hand out and my fingers close around a necklace. A gold-coloured chain with a delicate gold daisy dangling from it.

'Unbefuckinglievable.' I crawl out and show it to

Kat. 'I gave her that for her thirty-fifth. She used to wear it all the time.'

'Let's take it,' Kat says. She's managed to wrangle Oscar into the box and he's yowling in protest. 'She clearly won't realize, and you never know when it might come in handy.'

I can't imagine how but I don't argue and stuff it into my pocket. I take a couple of sachets of posh cat food and I pick out one toy from Oscar's little pile because I want him to have something familiar.

'Okay, let's get out of here.'

'Did you open the window?'

'Shit, no.'

I prop open the top bathroom window just enough so that's it's feasible a cat could worm his way out if he really tried. Jack and I were always a bit obsessive about making sure all the windows were closed. Oscar is very much an indoor cat and we knew that if he found his way outside there'd be precious little chance of him finding his way home again.

We're out of there ten minutes after we arrived.

I try to picture the scenario that will unfold later. In my mind, Jack arrives home first. Maybe he thinks it's odd that Oscar doesn't come running as he usually does when he hears the door. Maybe he's had a hard day and he just doesn't notice anything as he fixes himself a beer and then wonders why there's a draught. He locates the open window. Realizes with heart-stopping terror that he hasn't laid eyes on his pet since he arrived home.

Slams the window shut. Scours the flat, increasingly panicked. Looks under the beds and then in the cupboards, hoping against hope that he accidentally shut him in somewhere before he left for work. Or that Mel did, because she usually leaves ten minutes later than him. He tries to remember back to this morning. Did they leave together? Did she go into the bathroom after him? Shit. The cat is nowhere to be found. He must have somehow got through the open window. He could be anywhere by now. Or have hurt himself scrambling down from the first-floor ledge. He could have been run over hours ago. Jack has lectured Mel on the importance of never leaving a window or door open countless times. How could she be so stupid? Because she hates cats, that's why. Because she didn't care.

And then with a crashing weight: *Amy. Oh my God. I'm going to have to tell Amy her beloved pet is gone.*

18

Except that he doesn't.

He FaceTimes me in the evening, so I assume Mel is at her own place, wiping down her already pristine surfaces because Kat has told her she's taking the first of her interested parties for a viewing in the morning.

Or, even more likely, they've had a huge fight because she apparently let the cat out and now he's missing, possibly never to be seen again. Perhaps she's out knocking on neighbours' doors and putting up flyers. Crawling around the park on her hands and knees, calling his name. Not that he would come to her, anyway.

I'm at home but unprepared when he calls, so I let it ring out, rush around plumping up my pillows and positioning myself in my anonymous space, double check that it's late enough to be dark in both countries, and then I FaceTime him back. If he wonders why I seem to be lounging on my bed all the time these days, he doesn't say so. Jack is lying down, shirt off. This is a clear indication he's feeling horny. I pretend not to have noticed. 'Evening, gorgeous,' he says, in what he thinks is his sexy voice. I can't believe that, until a couple of weeks ago, it still had the power to make me go weak at the knees. Now I just think it sounds like a cliché. Something he's learned from movies.

'Evening.'

He runs his hand down his bare chest and stares into the camera. I know exactly where this is leading. I want to laugh. Or cry. Or both at the same time. Mostly, I want to derail this particular train before it reaches the station.

'We filmed a scene outside the new World Trade Center today,' I say blithely. I zip my hoody up higher as I say it, a silent signal that my clothes are staying firmly on.

'Right.' He can't even feign interest. His hand traces a path lower, thankfully, thus far, off screen. 'I've been thinking about you a lot today.'

'It was chaos because there's this big memorial there and, of course, now the show's going out people started recognizing us. Even me. Can you imagine?' I witter on, trying to break the moment he seems to think we're having. 'I signed two autographs!'

'Wow,' he says unenthusiastically, and I know I've killed the passion successfully. 'That's amazing.'

'How's Oskie?' I often ask Jack to go and find the cat and hold him up in front of the camera while we're FaceTiming. I'm hoping he won't be able to hear the plaintive meows coming from behind my closed living-room door. I couldn't risk Oscar deciding he wanted to sit on my head halfway through our chat. I watch carefully to see if Jack gives himself away and I think I see the tiniest flash of panic.

'He's fine. Fast asleep in his bed last time I saw him.'

'Aww! Show me.' I almost give myself away by laughing as I say this.

He fakes a big yawn. 'Can't be bothered to get up. Actually, babe, I'd better go. It's really late. Early start and all that.'

Once he's gone, I let Oscar into the bedroom and he snuggles down next to me. I have the best night's sleep I've had in ages.

When my mobile rings and I don't recognize the number I almost don't answer it, but a quick check of the time tells me I could be up and about in either time zone, so I risk it. I find it almost impossible to ignore a ringing phone. What if it's an opportunity that could change my life, and not just a bloke asking if I have PPI?

'Hello.'

'Amy? It's Simon.'

It takes me a moment, then, just as it's all coming back to me, he says, 'From the house on Avenue Road . . . the skip . . .'

Damn Kat and her matchmaking.

'Yes, Simon. How are you?'

I'm on my way to meet Kat at Mel's, sitting on the lower deck of the 113 bus as it shudders down Finchley Road.

'Your friend gave me your number, did she tell you? In case I came across anything else you might like.' Ah, so that was her angle.

'Right. Yes.' I always do this, go monosyllabic when I feel put on the spot. Luckily, Simon doesn't seem to notice.

'Anyway, we found this carpet in the attic. Well, a rug, really. But huge. And Kat was saying you had nothing on your floors . . . It's nice. Seventies, I'd guess. Geometric. Orangey.'

I stop myself from saying, 'Was it the maid's?' It's very nice of him to bother, and I really would like to be walking on something other than hardboard. All I manage to come out with, though, is, 'Orangey?'

'I know, I'm not selling it well. It's sort of orange and brown . . .'

I scoff. 'You're not making it sound any better.'

Thankfully, he laughs, too, so I don't have to beat myself up for sounding rude and ungrateful. 'I know. But it actually is quite cool.'

'How big did you say it was?'

He gives me the dimensions and I'm pretty sure it would fit in the living room, taking up most of the space, which would be a good thing, so long as it's not hideous.

'Okay, well, thanks. I'll see if I can get Kat and Greg to swing by in the car at the weekend, if you'll be there. Will it fit in the car?'

'It might be a squeeze. Listen, I was thinking I could get one of the guys to drop it off in the van. You're up near the North Circular, didn't you say?'

'Oh, no . . . I mean, I couldn't . . .'

'Really, Amy, you'd be doing me a favour . . .'

'Okay, so, this time, I know that's not true. I'm sure you have better things for your team to do than deliver rugs to far north London.'

'Okay, you've got me. I was planning on coming with them. I wanted an excuse to see you again.'

I'm so taken aback I don't know what to say. So I just say, 'Um . . .'

'Is that creepy?' he says. 'It is, it's creepy, isn't it?'

I laugh again. 'Well, maybe just a bit . . .'

'I am so out of practice at this.'

'Well, I'm not exactly an expert.'

'Kat told me you'd recently split with your boyfriend.' Did she? They were only gone about twenty minutes and they somehow managed to drive to St John's Wood and back and give a complete stranger my life history?

'Oh. What else did she say?' I can't keep the irritation out of my voice. I've become very fond of Kat, but she does have a tendency to meddle.

'Nothing. To be fair, I asked if you were attached. I didn't really give her much option. Please don't be cross with her.'

'I'm not. It's just . . . it's a bit soon.'

'Of course!' he says. 'Listen. Why don't we drop the rug off, anyway? You might take one look at me and think, *Actually, I feel ready to meet a man for a drink again.*'

'Ha! Or I might think, *That's it, I'm off men for life.*'

'Sadly, more likely that one. But what's the worst that can happen?'

'Okay, you've worn me down,' I say. 'This had better be one good rug.'

Kat is sitting on the low wall outside the modern block where Mel has her flat on the fifth floor. There are eight floors in total, about fifty flats. It's not the most beautiful building in the world from the outside but its purpose-built, boxy proportions make for well-laid-out interiors. Mel's place has floor-to-ceiling windows in the living room and a large terrace overlooking the beautifully landscaped communal gardens. I couldn't even begin to count the number of evenings she and I have sat out there with a bottle of wine and put the world to rights.

'You been here long? It took me about a week to get here from my place.'

Kat shakes her head no. 'I've been in and checked that the coast is clear, though.'

We let ourselves in and walk up the stairs. Just as Kat is putting the key in the door of Flat 55, a woman emerges from next door, small child in tow, harassed-looking. I jump, blush, start to sweat, but Kat is as cool as anything.

'Oh. Hi,' the woman says with a quizzical look.

'Hello.' Kat holds out her hand and the woman has to juggle the child, her keys and a stroller to shake it. 'Kat Mackenzie. I'm handling the sale of Miss Moynahan's apartment. This is Julia Pembridge. I'm hoping to persuade her she wants to buy it.' She laughs a big old fake laugh. Luckily, I've never met Mel's neighbour. I don't think she's lived there long.

'Nice to meet you,' the woman says, moving off, any suspicions gone. I shove Kat through Mel's door.

'Jesus!'

'Right, Ms Pembridge, what would you like to see first?'

'Oh, God, what are we doing?'

'It's fine. If she says anything to Mel, it'll be that she saw an estate agent showing a woman the flat. Perfect.'

The front door leads on to a hallway and then the big, airy living room, which smells of polish and lilies. Surfaces gleam. Nothing that shouldn't be on display is on display.

'For Christ's sake, don't touch anything you don't have to.' On autopilot, I bend down and take my shoes off. Mel hates people wearing shoes indoors.

I know exactly where Mel keeps all her personal stuff, so I head straight for it after Kat has double-locked the door. I don't know what I'd do if Mel suddenly decided to come home and meet whoever was viewing her place. Hide under the bed? Jump off the balcony? Feign amnesia? On balance, jumping seems like the best bet.

I riffle through her desk, no idea what I'm looking for. I want to find a way to mess with her life the way she's messed with mine, if I'm being honest. Because she's Mel, everything is tidy and in place. Unpaid bills on one side, a pile with a Post-it note on saying 'Filing' on the other, already in alphabetical order. An ornate box containing her passport, various loyalty and membership cards, and the paper part of her driver's licence. There's nothing interesting, nothing that stands out. While I scour through her files – all orange box files arranged in a row on a shelf by the desk, labelled things like 'Bank' 'and 'Insurance' – Kat mooches around, trying not to make a mess.

She presses a key on Mel's ancient desktop computer and it springs into life. 'Might as well catch up on Twitter.'

'Remember exactly what was on there,' I say as I come through. My search has turned up precisely nothing of any interest. 'Exactly.'

Like everyone else, Mel leaves her computer unsecured at home. It's plugged in, turned on and happy to fill in any necessary passwords. It's quickly apparent there have been no new DMs since the last time we looked. We open her mail. There are two unread messages at the top of her inbox.

'Don't touch those,' I say, and Kat looks at me in a way I can only describe as 'Do you think I'm an idiot?'

She scrolls down. 'What shall I look for?'

'I don't know. Search "Jack".'

There are a few emails back and forth to his work address, but they're anodyne. Nothing his assistant would find odd. And we know that they do most of their communicating privately on Twitter.

'This is pointless. Look up that cow she works with. Shaz. Carpenter.'

'What's her real name?'

'I don't know. Sharon, I guess.'

Kat enters 'Sharon' and comes up with an email address that contains the same company name as Mel's.

We scroll through, skim-reading, looking for anything that catches our eye. The latest thread – 'Oh Jesus, I think I let the fucking cat out' – makes my blood boil.

Oh, shit. Haha!

No, I really think I might have. It's gone, anyway, and Jack is totally blaming me for leaving the window open. I can't even remember opening the fucking thing in the first place. And even if I did, you wouldn't think it would be stupid enough to fling itself out there.

Does A know???

No, God, she'd go crazy. J out posting flyers and asking the neighbours.

We move back through inane stuff about their work colleagues, weekends, families.

All boring and routine. Something catches my eye further down the list.

Fuck Fuck Fuck!!!!!

'Go to that one,' I say, pointing. Kat pushes her

164

glasses up her nose and clicks on it. The first thing we see is Shaz's response, dated three days after Mel's party.

> Whoa! That came out of nowhere (no pun intended!!!). John as in . . . JOHN WELLER??? You fucked him???? I need you to tell me all. Ring me NOW!!!

And before that, Mel's message.

> It just happened! Me and John!! Shit, what have I done?? Goes without saying, don't tell ANYONE!!!

'Who's John?' Kat says.

'Her boss. Jesus, she's cheated on Jack already. This is priceless.'

'Wow. What if I just accidentally forwarded this on to Jack?' Her finger hovers over the key.

'No! She'd know it was you. She knows you're here today, remember.'

'Does this John have a girlfriend?'

I feel myself grimace. 'A wife, I think. Mel's been going on for ages about whether to seduce him to stop him giving her a hard time at work. I thought she was joking.'

'I'll print them off, then. You never know.'

Mel has always been the kind of person who takes what she wants. Lip gloss from Boots, because she didn't see why she should pay for it; other people's homework to copy, because she couldn't be bothered to do it herself;

other people's husbands ... just because she could. Over the years, there have been several married men. It always ends in tears, although usually not hers.

Eventually, after trying and getting nowhere for more than two years, being supported by her indulgent mum and dad, attending casting calls and chasing after modelling jobs she was never going to be tall enough to get and auditions for girl bands she was already too old to appeal to, Mel had reluctantly decided to apply to drama school. She still viewed it as a waste of her time but I think she was starting to panic that her reign was running out. She was losing her title of star of our little town.

I helped her fill in the forms in my room in halls. By now, I was convinced that I knew what I wanted to do with the rest of my life. I had no idea how I was going to go about it or why anyone would ever be interested in hiring me but I didn't really care. Unlike Mel, my dream wasn't to be a star, it was to act. All I needed was to get by just enough so that I could keep on doing it and not have to be swallowed up by another, all-consuming, career. I kept my secret to myself, though. I decided that, once Mel had been accepted by somewhere fabulous like RADA, I'd come clean.

Except that she never was. She tried them all, working her way down the list from the prestigious to the downright dodgy-sounding. Most of them gave her an audition. I tried to suggest that maybe she should drop her over-perfected pieces chosen by Sylvia and do something more contemporary, more natural, but of course she just told me I had no idea what I was talking about. She was the one with the agent.

It was painful to watch. By the time the academic year was over, she had been rejected by every one. I don't think any of them had even suggested she try again next year. I remember she wanted to come up for a few days, but I had the leading role in our end-of-year production, *The Deep Blue Sea*, and I was spending every waking moment rehearsing, so I had to keep putting her off, telling her I was revising for exams. Which, to be fair, I was. Occasionally.

But it was hard, because I so wanted to be there for her. Even though she wouldn't admit it, she was devastated by all the rejection, I could tell. She covered it by saying that she'd been right all along about drama school being for people who had no experience. Her version of the truth, the one she chose to present to the world, was that they clearly thought she was too advanced already, that there would be nothing they could teach her.

In the end, one night when I called her from the payphone in halls, she asked me outright why I was avoiding her. Her mum and dad had bought her a mobile by this time, a big, bricky thing with an aerial that could take someone's eye out. She was the only person I knew who had one. I decided I couldn't lie completely so I told her I'd been roped in to help out with a play and that it was proving more time-consuming than I'd anticipated. And then, of course, I'd felt bad that I wasn't telling her the whole truth, so I did.

'Actually, Mel, don't laugh . . . but I'm in it.'

'In what?' Already I could hear a note of panic in her voice.

'The play. I don't know, they must have been desperate.'

'You're acting? I thought standing up in front of people was your worst nightmare?'

'It was. I mean, it still is . . . just . . . not so much like this . . . I enjoy it, how weird is that?'

'What? Has it already started?'

So then, of course, I had to tell her I'd already appeared in a couple of things, but I hadn't wanted to mention them because it was all a bit embarrassing and I thought she might laugh (I didn't, I thought she'd be pissed off with me and, as it turned out, I was right. She didn't actually say that acting was her thing, not mine, but I could feel the statement hanging out there, waiting to be said).

'Wow,' she said, unconvincingly enthusiastic. 'That's amazing. Well, I'll have to come up and see it. When did you say it opened?'

'We only do about six performances and it's in a tiny little space . . .' I said, but even as the words came out of my mouth I knew there was no putting her off. I could have tried to interpret it as her being supportive but I knew it was more about her feeling threatened and wanting to try to derail my newfound ambitions.

'That's okay. God, it's not as if I'm doing much else at the moment and, besides, I haven't seen you for ages.'

So that was that.

She showed up on the second night of the run — thankfully, not the first. I had lied and said we were all sold out that night because, even though I'd found my confidence, I still wasn't sure I could get through my largest role yet with Mel's critical eyes boring into me. Anyway, she was polite but uneffusive about my performance, got quite drunk afterwards, insulted Pia and Kieron and ended up going back with my on-stage husband, Will, who she knew I was mad keen on and who I knew, or thought I knew, liked me, but who I had decided to give a wide berth to until the run was over. I had had big plans for the last-night party, which was going to be held in Kieron's shared house in Streatham. I'd confided in Mel just after I introduced her to him.

Afterwards, I put it down to her feeling a bit out of place among my new friends. She couldn't have under-stood what I'd told her about my feelings for him (not in the slightest bit romantic, luckily. Pure lust) because, if she had, she would never have made a play for him herself. I made excuses in my head for the way she behaved and I made myself believe them, even though there was no evidence being presented in her favour.

After we find out about Mel and John, Kat and I are at a bit of a loss what to do next.

'What are we doing here again?' she asks.

'Looking for ammunition,' is all I can come up with.

19

I don't tell Kat that Simon is going to bring the rug round. I don't know why. Well, I do: because she would be unbearably smug about having given him my number in the first place and then she'd want to have a blow-by-blow re-enactment of everything that was said. For some reason, I do put some make-up on and change out of my scruffy, baggy cut-offs and into a reasonably decent pair of jeans. I know I'm being ridiculous. I know it's way too soon for me to even be thinking about hooking up with someone else. I tell myself I'm just being polite but, deep down, I also know I want him to like what he sees. Because I could do with the ego boost – nothing else, just to be clear. I can barely even remember what he looks like.

He arrives right on time and I'm a bit disappointed to see he's brought one of his team with him. Of course he has, because even with two of them they struggle to get the giant slab of carpet up the stairs, while I fuss around making coffee and shouting encouragement.

'This is so kind of you,' I say, for the hundredth time when they appear on the top landing.

The other bloke, Martin, who is clearly there only under duress, gives me a forced grin. More of a grimace.

A random spring heatwave has just started and it must be eighty degrees in the windowless hallway. No wonder he hates me. I would, too.

'Do you want milk and sugar?' I say, waving a mug at him.

'Have you got anything cold?' he says grumpily.

'Only water, I'm afraid. Tap water . . . Sorry . . .'

'Tap water would be lovely.' Thankfully, Simon and his end of the rug have appeared in the room. 'And coffee after for me, if that's okay?'

'Great,' I say, fussing around. I don't know why I'm acting so twittery. I tell myself to calm down. It doesn't work. 'The thing is,' I go on, 'I don't have any glasses yet. And I only have two mugs and I've just put coffee in them.'

This pitiful statement seems to thaw Martin out a bit and he cracks a smile.

'Been here long?'

'A week or so,' I say, pulling an apologetic face. 'Tell you what, I'll nip downstairs and get some bottles of water.'

By the time I get back, they have moved what little furniture I have out of the way, laid the rug down and are in the process of moving everything back. The place certainly looks more homely, if a little like a seventies film set.

'Brilliant.' I hand them each a bottle. 'Thank you both so much.'

Martin takes a long swig from his. 'I'm going to get back, boss.'

Simon nods, and I feel a bit awkward because they've clearly prearranged this, that Martin would take the van and Simon would find his own way back. I should be annoyed that he's just assumed I would be amenable to that. But, on the other hand, I am, so I guess I haven't really got a case.

'I'll see you in a bit. I mean, if that's all right with you, Amy? I was just going to stay and drink that coffee.'

'Of course,' I say. 'I'm not doing anything.'

Part of me wonders if he's going to try and seduce me, right here and now, on my new brown-and-orange rug that I'm planning on shampooing as soon as I can borrow a machine. Who knows where it's been? I'm hoping he doesn't because, even though he seems nice and he's definitely quite attractive, I've never really been a sex-on-impulse person. I like the build-up, the anticipation. That's half the point, as far as I'm concerned.

I'm thinking about the best way to let him down gently when I hear my name and realize I've been staring into space for what must be a good few minutes. Simon is sitting at the kitchen table – not on the more seduction-friendly sofa – looking at me quizzically.

'Sorry, I was miles away.' I go and sit opposite him.

'The table looks good,' he says, running his hand over the sanded surface. In so far as I'm aware, no one has ever used discussing furniture upcycling as a come-on.

'I just need to paint it. I already feel as if it's one of those things that I'm never going to get around to.'

'I could get one of the guys –'

'No!' I interrupt, a bit more forcefully than I mean to. 'You've done enough, really. Did you want milk in that, by the way? Or even a fresh one? It's a bit cold now.'

'Lovely, thanks.'

I distract myself by making more coffee and Simon proves surprisingly easy to talk to.

'So, how did you end up here? With no furniture?'

I tell him about Jack and Mel and how I've had to start again from next to nothing, leaving out the bit about them not knowing I know yet and my quest to hit them where it hurts. I know that, by omission, I'm allowing him to think that Jack and I have had a clean break but I don't want to sound like a psycho on our first date. If this *is* a date. I don't really know what the rules are any more. 'That's rough,' he says. 'Your fiancé and your best friend. Jesus.'

'And my job.' I feel as if I can confide in him. Maybe because he's so far removed from everyone who knows me I don't have to worry about it getting back. And he hardly seems the type to spend his time on Twitter or calling the tabloids, leaking plot secrets.

'No wonder you were in my skip. Not that there's anything wrong with that. I mean ... Sorry, I was attempting a joke. I'm crap at jokes. You might as well know that now.'

I laugh. He's obviously nervous, too. Why hadn't it even occurred to me that he might be? He's the one making all the moves, so he's much more exposed than I am.

'Would you like to go and have lunch somewhere?' he says after a while. 'We might both relax a bit more on neutral ground.'

'I'd love to. Although there is literally nowhere to go around here. I mean . . . there's the café downstairs, but that's, like, a health hazard . . .'

'It's a lovely day. Is there a bench or something we could go and sit on?' He's right, it is. The spring sun is warm, and even my little flat is looking cheerier.

'I have no idea.'

'There must be something. Come on.'

We buy lavash bread, hummus and olives from the convenience store, along with some dodgy-looking blue cheese, a bag of little tomatoes and two bottles of Diet Sprite. Then we walk away from the main road and eventually find a patch of green that looks as if it doesn't belong to anyone in particular and set up camp on the grass. It actually feels way more intimate than sitting down in a restaurant together would.

'How did you get into doing up rich people's houses?' I ask as we pass the olive tub back and forth.

He tells me he trained as a set designer but then the first job he was able to get out of college was as a runner working for an interior-design company.

'I realized I was good at it. And I loved it, too. It took me years to get enough experience to set up on my own though, obviously.'

'You should team up with Kat. Did she tell you she's a property-finder?'

He nods. 'We've exchanged cards. You never know. I often hear about properties that are being done up to sell, so it'd work both ways.'

He tells me he's divorced. All a bit acrimonious, but he has his kid (a girl, Ruby, twelve) most weekends, so that's all that matters. He doesn't offer up the story of what went wrong with his marriage, and I don't ask. God knows, I don't want him quizzing me too much about the finer details of my own situation.

We talk about my acting and following your passion for its own sake rather than the potential rewards, and about our childhoods (like me, he was the middle child of three; like me, he was a watcher not a doer) and our small-town upbringings. I'm amazed by the similarities between us.

By the time he says he has to go back to work I feel as if I've known him for years, and I think he feels the same because as we say goodbye he asks if I'd like to go for a proper meal sometime – one with tables and waiters, not dandelions and ants – and I don't even hesitate before I say yes. As I say goodbye to him at the bus stop and walk back in the direction of my flat, I can hardly keep the smile off my face.

20

'The thing is, Ames. It's Oscar . . .'

Jack and I are talking. I'm at the place I now call home, getting ready for Kat and Greg to come over. It's the first time I will have cooked anything other than toast on my reclaimed cooker, but I want to do something to repay them for everything they've done for me. Plus, they're dropping off their Vax, so it's win–win. I haven't quite worked out where we can all sit yet, but I figure we'll sort it out when they get here. I have, though, been out and bought a set of four wine glasses and another two mugs, along with four plates (no more eating out of cereal bowls) and three more knives and forks. I almost went crazy and splashed out on a set of four but, as Woman in Park seems to have gone to some other lucky person, I forced myself to be frugal.

Yesterday, I called the supervisor at the call centre and said I might be up for doing a few shifts and, because they have a policy of pretty much only employing out-of-work actors (I assume because they think we have nice voices and can convincingly pretend to be enthusiastic about the possibilities of purchasing a subscription to *Garden Pond Weekly*. Plus, most of us are desperate. And broke) and so are used to people coming and going at little or no notice, she just said fine and wrote down the times I said I was available without asking any questions. So, on Tuesday, I'll be back on the phones. It could be worse. It could be cold-calling rather than following up on an interest someone has foolishly owned up to in a survey somewhere. Of course, the pay is terrible, but who else is going to put up with me wanting to work only when it suits me, and the flexibility to cancel at the last moment?

Now, I try to imagine how I would react if what Jack was telling me was a surprise, if there wasn't a black, purring bundle asleep on my bed in the other room right now. Panic.

'What? Is he ill?'

'It's . . . shit, I'm just going to say it . . . he's gone missing.'

'What do you mean? When? How did he get out? Oh my God!'

'A couple of days ago. I was hoping he'd turn up . . .'

I manage to resist saying, 'Actually, Jack, it's been over a week.' I force a sob. 'A couple of days? Jesus. Have you asked around the neighbours?'

'Of course. And I've put up flyers and called a load of shelters and all the local vets. Everyone's looking out for him.'

'I don't understand. How did he get out?'

He ignores that question for a second time. 'I don't know what else to do. I'm sorry, Amy.'

'Poor baby. He could be anywhere by now. He could

have been run over! Or picked up by one of those dog-fighting gangs as bait . . .' Even *I* think I might be laying it on a bit too thick as I say this.

'You mustn't think like that. He's probably hiding somewhere or something, scared to come out.'

'You're supposed to put his litter tray outside and then he might recognize the smell. I read that somewhere. Oh God, Jack, this is awful. What if he's hurt himself?'

'You hear about missing cats turning up all the time –'

'Do you? I don't understand though, how did he get out?'

Third time lucky. 'He must have slipped through my feet when I had the door open and I didn't notice. I feel awful.'

'What? And the street door was open, too? What're the chances of that?'

'Or, maybe, I opened the bathroom window a bit – really, no more than a crack, and only for a second –'

'You didn't let him in there while it was open?'

'Maybe. I don't know.'

'For fuck's sake.'

'I didn't do it deliberately, obviously,' he says petulantly.

I realize I have to tone it down a bit. I don't want a full-scale row, I just want him to be eaten up with guilt.

'Oh God, I can't bear it. Where do you think he is now?'

'I'll find him. I promise. Maybe I shouldn't have told

you . . . when all you can do is worry, thousands of miles away, I mean.'

'No, you were right to. Otherwise, how would I ever trust that things were okay in the future? You need to always tell me exactly what's going on, however bad.'

'Of course,' he says, without a hint of irony. 'I promise.'

'Oh,' he says a couple of minutes later. I'm thinking I can duck out of the call early, citing being upset about Oscar, but he has suddenly remembered something he meant to say just as I'm about to hang up. 'Guess what? I have to go to Reykjavik at the weekend. We have a client who wants to meet there.'

Jack and I always talked about going to Reykjavik. He knows it's my dream destination. So it strikes me as a little bit of a coincidence. Plus, although work has taken him abroad a few times over the years, it's hardly a regular occurrence. And a weekend? Really? I start with that.

'Oh my God, really? On a weekend, though?'

'That's the only time they can do, apparently. I feel bad though, babe, going without you . . .'

Yes, of course he does.

'I'm not even going to pretend I'm not jealous. Reykjavik?'

'I know! I'll try and keep my eyes on the floor. Not see anything until we get a chance to go together.' He laughs to show me he's joking, in a caring, sweet, thoughtful boyfriend kind of way.

'And so soon? This weekend?'

'Yep. I leave Friday afternoon and get back late Sunday night. So it's not as if I'll really get any time there.'

'No but . . . still amazing. Who's the client?'

'Some yoghurt-type product. They're launching over here. Well, obviously . . .'

'And they're all going in on a Saturday just to meet you?'

'Seems so. Just so I can pitch for it, you know. I imagine they're meeting other agencies, too.'

'But they're paying to fly you out? That must be good, right?'

He gives a little self-deprecating laugh. 'I guess so.'

'Wow. Well, you'd better start doing your homework. "Buy some yoghurt-type product" isn't going to cut it, I imagine.'

After he's ended the call, I ring Mel. I'm pretty sure they're not together because Jack seemed very relaxed and happy to talk to me.

'Hello!' I say when she answers. 'I'm literally just calling to say that and then go. I realized I haven't talked to you for ages — my schedule's been insane — so I thought I'd ring and say let's put aside a time on the weekend and really catch up . . .'

I leave it hanging out there. Wait for her excuse.

'Shit, I'm having a spa weekend. Chewton Glen.'

I stop myself from saying, 'On your own?' or 'How can you afford that?' Mel hates going anywhere on her own. She needs an audience. And I know she's broke until the flat is sold.

'Oh! Well, not to worry. Next week, maybe. Have a lovely time . . .'

'Can't we chat now?'

'No. They've just called me, I'm actually walking to set. I've got this huge two-hander scene. Five pages. They've given my character a love interest now and built a whole new set for my apartment and everything.'

Clearly, Mel does not want to engage with this potentially career-boosting piece of good news.

'Okay, well, talk to you soon.'

'I miss you,' I say, happy that I've rattled her.

Kat and Greg have been to an early-evening screening of *Barbarella* at some too-cool-for-school cinema club in Shoreditch. Afterwards, they arrive at mine in a taxi, clutching a bottle of Prosecco and a huge, ribbon-tied box.

'Housewarming present,' Kat says, thrusting it into my hands.

'What? No. You already got me most of my furniture, technically.'

'Honestly, it's less impressive than it looks. Wow, nice rug by the way.'

'Simon,' I say, rolling my eyes and going red at the same time, thus giving away that something is going on.

'You're blushing,' Kat says gleefully. 'Why are you blushing?'

'I'm not,' is all I can manage. I turn my attention to the box, pull off the wrapping. Inside is an oatmeal-coloured lampshade that perfectly matches the sofa, with a taupe geometric motif around the rim.

'It's gorgeous,' I say, balancing it on top of the wooden standard lamp. 'And it's the perfect size.'

Kat beams. 'We went for neutrals because we weren't sure –'

'I love it. You know you shouldn't have, but thanks.'

I fiddle around, fixing it to the wooden stand, while Greg pours the Prosecco.

'He's taking her to Reykjavik for the weekend.'

Kat gasps. She knows me well enough to know how much that must hurt. 'Are you sure?'

'Yep. He says he's going for work but –'

'Could he be?' Greg says. 'I mean, he's had to go away before, right? When the two of you went to Copenhagen, wasn't that because he had some pitch to do?'

'Yes. I mean, it's possible. Either way, he's taking Mel. Well, that's what he's planning, anyway . . .'

'Oh shit,' Greg says, putting down the bottle. 'What are you going to do?'

21

I assume that stealing someone's passport is illegal. Even if they are your soon-to-be-ex fiancé who is taking your best friend away for a romantic weekend in your dream destination. Even if you're intending to return it again in a few days. So I don't. I just let myself in (after watching them leave for work one after another, and then making myself wait an agonizing fifteen minutes just in case. I amuse myself by looking for Lost Cat posters with Oscar's face on and am gratified to spot three. I pull one down and stuff it in my pocket to show him later) and hide the passport somewhere he will never think to look. Which is under the bath. Pushed right to the back, behind the pipes.

It's just possible he might discover it if he has enough time and he takes the flat apart piece by piece. But I know Jack. He leaves everything to the last minute. He likes to give off the impression he's a seasoned traveller just breezing out the door, no big deal.

First, though, I go through his emails and ascertain that, surprisingly, this trip is indeed work-related. He has a meeting scheduled on the Saturday afternoon at three at the headquarters of Volcano Skyr. There are notes attached reminding him of the virtues of the product – fat free, all natural, blah blah. Other than that, his time is his own. He's staying at the Hotel Borg, which, if I remember rightly, is the smart hotel he and I selected when we planned a fantasy trip once. In fact, we'd decided to save the trip for our honeymoon. Even though we hadn't even started planning the wedding, we had the itinerary for the two weeks after it worked out in detail. Five days in Iceland, five in the north of Sweden and four in Stockholm. It occurs to me that, now my stint in New York is over, we could have set the date. That was what had always held us back, not knowing when I might have enough free time to plan it, let alone actually do it.

Kat, meanwhile, is at Mel's, where, she texts to tell me, there is a confirmation for a flight to Iceland sitting tucked into Mel's passport on top of her desk. Her clothes are laid out neatly on the bed and the smaller of her two suitcases is on the floor next to them. The icing on the cake, she tells me, is a guide book – *Iceland's Top 10* – lined up neatly with her magazines on the coffee table.

'Are you sure you want to do this?' she texts when I respond.

'Definitely.'

I check my secret hiding place once more. There's nothing more I need to do.

Except that just before I leave I have a flash of inspiration. I call Kat back and she tells me she's already left Mel's.

184

'I just wanted to get out of there. It's scary doing it on your own.'

'Tell me about it,' I say. 'Can I do this? I don't know if I can –'

'What?'

'You've given her her keys back, right?'

'Yes, and I told her neither of my buyers is interested. She was quite pissed off with me. You have to tell me what you're up to.'

'So there's no reason she would think it was you –'

'What? Think *what* was me?'

'Did she even have Facebook on her desktop? I mean, bookmarked or whatever?'

'Not obviously, no. I didn't see it . . .'

'Great. So no suspicion as far as you're concerned. She probably just uses her laptop, which is here, or her phone. When she uses it at all, because she hates Facebook. I remember her saying that every time she went on there she felt this overwhelming wave of doom, worrying about which person she'd been happily avoiding for twenty years was going to pop up with a friend request next . . .'

Kat interrupts me. 'Amy Forrester, just tell me what the hell you're planning! The suspense is practically killing me.'

'Shit, sorry. Okay. What if I changed her Facebook status? Just . . . I don't know . . . I was thinking of something like, "Sleeping with my boss".'

I type it in, just to try it for size, as I wait for her

reaction. My finger hovers over the 'Save changes' key but I make myself wait. I need to be sure it's foolproof.

Kat gasps. 'Won't someone just tell her?'

'Yes, but that means whoever it is will have seen it. And God knows who else, too. Most people would probably just send a funny comment or something, or even a message saying, "Have you been hacked?" and the beauty of that is she won't see those either.'

'Are you sure she doesn't get notifications?'

'No way. Actually, shit, I'm going to check.'

I scrabble around and find her settings. Notifications are most definitely off.

'This might be genius,' Kat says when I tell her. 'Or the worst idea ever. I can't work it out.'

'Shall I just do it? Fuck the consequences.'

There's a pause. 'Do it.'

'Oh my God, really? I thought you might talk me out of it.'

'Well, don't do it, then. I don't want this to be on me.'

'No, I can't. It's too . . .'

My heart leaps up to my ears and crashes back down again. There's a noise. Someone is coming up the stairs.

'Shit! Fuck! Kat, someone's coming. I've gotta go. Don't call me back.'

'Jesus . . .' I hear her say as I hang up.

I slam the laptop shut and then think I should have exited the page first, but there's no time now because I can hear a key in the door. I grab my cardigan, which I'd draped over the back of the chair, and run into the bedroom. Thankfully, I know that I can fit under the bed because of retrieving Mel's necklace the other day, so I shove myself under there, huddle back against the wall, and wait.

Jack is whistling to himself as he comes through the door. I hold my breath. Flick my phone on to silent just in case.

I catch a flash of him as he passes the bedroom door, hear the fridge open and close and a ring pull being pulled. I look at my phone – five past three. Why on earth would he be home at this time? He's not acting like he's sick. He wanders into the bathroom, still whistling as he pees. Lets out a loud fart. I hear the taps start to run. He's having a bath. So long as he doesn't leave the door wide open, I should be able to make it out while he's splashing around in there. Jack in the bath is like an angry shark in a tank at the aquarium. He's a one-man tsunami. I allow myself to breathe again and then the noise of running water stops as suddenly as it started. There's no way, with our dodgy plumbing, that the bath is even a fifth full yet.

I see a pair of bare feet walking towards me. Close my eyes as if that might help. There's a creak as he flings himself back on to the bed. The struts under the mattress groan and I congratulate myself for insisting that we bought an expensive frame, otherwise I'd have been flattened by now.

'Melissa Moynahan, please.'

He's on the phone.

'Thanks.'

I can't help it, I'm interested to hear how they speak to each other. I mean, obviously, I've witnessed them speaking to each other thousands of times, but never, by definition, when no one else has been around. A few seconds later, and I'm not so interested. I'm in danger of chucking up my lunch.

'Hey,' he says when she answers. 'How's it going? . . . At home. Bill wants me to go and sweet-talk this client with him over dinner so I came home to change . . . the Dorchester . . . I know . . . I know . . . I was about to have a bath but then I started thinking about this morning and I got a bit horny . . .'

Yes, my dear friends, this is where this is going. I'll spare you the details. The gist seems to be that he's called her on her office phone rather than her mobile because it turns him on to think she's sat there surrounded by her unsuspecting colleagues while he 'gets her wet' by burbling sub-porn clichés at her.

'I want to lick your minky,' he groans at one point. I have to stop myself from laughing out loud, but then I remember it's been a very long time since he suggested that doing that to me – using any word at all – would be a huge turn-on.

At least it doesn't take him long. I imagine Mel is sitting there filing her nails or drinking a cup of tea like a bored sex-chat-line worker. Or maybe this is the kind of thing she likes. Who knows? I certainly don't want to.

As soon as it's over, he makes his excuses and leaves. That is, he tells her he won't be home till late and that he needs to get ready quickly and get out of the door. The bed groans again, the bare feet pad away, the taps fire up again. I lie there motionless.

When the water stops running and the splashing starts I summon up every ounce of courage in my body and crawl out from under my hiding place. It's almost comical to imagine what his reaction would be if he caught me. I doubt his brain would even know where to start. I creep to the door and risk peeping out. The bathroom door is pulled to. Not fully closed, but enough so that he won't see me.

I know I have to deal with Mel's laptop on the way out. I open it gingerly. The 'Edit settings' page is still up. My tentative status change still beckons enticingly. I go to exit Facebook and then I think, *Fuck it.*

I hit 'Save changes', exit back to the home screen and then, just for luck, I click on 'Delete history'.

And then I get out of there.

'Where's my fucking passport?'

Jack's eyes are wide, panic written all over his face.

'What? In the box, isn't it?'

'No! It's not there. Fuck.'

'It must be there somewhere.'

The picture swings around as he flings everything out of the box. I strain to catch a glimpse of red hair cowering in the background.

'Calm down. If it's not in the box, it'll be on the desk somewhere. It'll be wherever you put it last time you used it.'

'You didn't see it when you were home?'

'No. If I had, I would have put it in the box. Is there any news of Oscar, by the way? What if he comes home when you're away?'

'No. Bev and Julian'll look out for him. Shit! I have to go.'

'Let me know –' I start to say, but he's gone.

I try not to think about what might be happening with Jack and Mel as I get ready for my big date, because I'm finding it hard to get excited about having dinner with Simon when my mind keeps veering between fear of being caught, smug satisfaction and guilt (to be fair, the guilt pangs are few and far between). In the end, I break off from my preening and call Kat, who puts me on speakerphone so I can relay the whole exchange to both her and Greg.

'Have I done a terrible thing?' I say before I hang up.

'Which one?' she says, and she has a point. It's been hours since I changed Mel's status and my alteration is still there.

'Jack's passport.'

'No! Well, and yes . . . it depends how you look at it.'

'Oh God, I feel sick.'

'Enjoy it,' Greg pipes up. 'Nothing you can do about

it now, anyway. There's no way Jack's leaving the country today.'

'I can't worry about it now. I have to get ready.'

'Have a nice date!' Kat shouts out in the background.

'It's not a date. We're just having dinner.'

'Yeah, right. Tell him that.'

'Bye, Kat. Bye, Greg.'

'Ring me tomorrow. I want details.'

Simon is already sitting at the shiny black bar when I get to the restaurant. I'm glad. It gives me a moment to compose myself, but not so long that I work myself up into a panic about what I'm getting into. I watch him for a second through the glass door. He's not as striking as Jack, whose face is all angles and drama, not by a long shot – Simon has fairish hair that has a habit of flopping into his eyes, muddy, blue-grey eyes, an undefined jaw that he's made the most of by cultivating permastubble – but he's still a good-looking bloke. Plus, he looks kind. And that's a big bonus in my book.

The doorman sees me hovering and must think I'm standing there waiting for him to do the honours. Too posh to push. So he pulls as I shove and I sort of fall through the doorway like a drunk leaving a club. I manage to right myself by grabbing on to him, so the first thing Simon sees when he turns around is me in a clinch with a stranger. A big smile lights up his face.

'I thought you said you'd never been here before,' he

says as he comes over. 'Or are you always like this with people the first time you meet them?'

'Entirely my fault, madam,' the doorman says.

'God, no, it was mine. Sorry. I haven't even had a drink yet.'

At my request, we're at The Cardinal. Somewhere Jack and I always wanted to try but the waiting list is about a century long. I figured that if he can take Mel to the city we always intended to visit together (or actually not. I got another hysterical call from him just before I left the house, saying he had had to cancel the trip because his 'stupid fucking passport' had still not materialized. He'd even tried phoning Iceland Air to ask if there was any way he might be able to board without it and, unsurprisingly, they'd said a flat-out no. I was dying to know where Mel was, whether she'd stormed off, furious at his lack of organization, or whether she was waiting at the check-in desk, wondering why he hadn't showed up. I wondered if she'd go ahead without him. I couldn't imagine she would. It might be a bit awkward explaining to Jack's replacement what she was doing in his hotel room), then the least I can do is meet another man at our dream dinner destination. It turned out Simon has some kind of connection through a house he did up once, so getting a table wasn't a problem. Paying for the meal might be, though, because I'm insisting we go half each in an effort to pretend to myself that this really isn't a date and a quick look on the website menu before I left home put me in a cold sweat of financial angst.

The waiter comes over to tell us our table is ready and we're led to a little booth by the window. We sit there in silence for a moment, suddenly awkward in each other's company, all the easy back and forth from the day of the picnic evaporated.

'So . . .' he says, while I'm still scraping the edges of my brain for an interesting anecdote. 'How's the rug?'

'Good. It sends its love.'

'That was a terrible conversation opener, right? I'm a bit nervous. Is that ridiculous?'

'No! So am I. I've got out of the habit of . . . you know . . . whatever this is . . .'

His mouth curls up at the edges, a cute half-smile. 'Talking?'

'No. You know . . .'

'Eating?'

'Don't make me say it! Going on dates . . . if that's . . . I mean . . .'

'Are we on a date? I hope so. I had a shower specially.'

'Me, too. I put on make-up and everything.'

He waits while our drinks arrive – vodka and tonic for me, a Manhattan for him.

'If it makes you feel more at ease, I don't do this very often either.'

He tells me that, since he and his wife split up four years ago, he's only had one real relationship and that lasted about eight months. He's been on a few dates here and there, but it doesn't come naturally.

'Well, put me down as zero. This is my first first date for over five years. I have literally no skills to call on.'

He sighs theatrically. 'Well, this is going to be a long evening.'

'Ha! I thought you said you were no good at jokes?'

He grins, bearing even, white teeth. 'Who said I was joking?'

I ask about his daughter, and the way his expression softens when he talks about her speaks volumes about what he's like as a person. It's obvious he's cut up about her staying with him only at the weekends but, from the sound of it, he attends every school event, every sports day and end-of-term play.

'She'd love you,' he tells me. 'She wants to be an actress. Well, this week, anyway.'

'Oh God, try and put her off,' I say with a fake grimace. 'Or at least tell her to learn another skill as well. My life would be so much easier if I could do something else on the side.'

'You never wanted kids?' he says later, as our main courses arrive – sea bream with a tomato and caper sauce for me and an elaborate-looking beef dish for him. I have to admit I always find it odd that people just ask this outright. They have no idea of what personal tragedies might lie behind the truth. Thankfully, in my case, there are none. Just that life got in the way and, now, suddenly, I'm single and nearly forty.

'Yes. I mean, in theory. Jack and I talked about it and we always said we would one day but then neither of us ever came out and said the time was right. That must say something about our relationship, right?'

'Sorry. That was an insensitive question.'

'No . . . not at all . . . it's something I'll probably regret, but it's not as if it's blighted my life –'

'I do have a tendency to ask the wrong things. My wife used to say I had a skill for sniffing out awkwardness and drawing everyone's attention to it. Accidentally, I think she meant. I hope so, anyway.'

'Honestly, it's not a big deal. My friend Mel used to say that if I really wanted them it would have just happened and sod the consequences . . .' I tail off, realizing this is the first time I've mentioned Mel since her party and not been overwhelmed by a feeling of nausea. 'She's the one . . . you know . . .'

He reaches over and plucks the wine bottle out of the ice bucket next to our table. Two waiters both jolt into action, as if he's about to pull the pin from a hand grenade. He gestures to them that he's happy pouring for himself and they back off sulkily.

'Well, she's probably right, not that I'm inclined to agree with anything she says, given what you've told me.'

'Yes, I'm kind of revisiting all the advice she gave me over the years and trying to work out what was in it for her each time. It's weird not knowing if she ever really cared about me or not.'

'She must have done. That, or she's just too phenomenally lazy to have bothered to try and find a new best friend.'

I shrug. I don't want to let Mel spoil this experience. 'Anyway, let's not talk about her.'

'You know what they say. The best revenge is living well.'

'Let me see: tiny, rented – not to mention damp and mouldy – flat in the back of beyond; unemployed; single. Yes, I'm doing well.'

'You know what I mean,' he says. 'At the risk of sounding like some kind of new-age idiot, just concentrate on you.'

He reaches over and puts his hand over mine. I actually jump, it's such a surprise, and I nearly pull my own away before relaxing into it. 'It sounds like Kat is right. It sounds like she's eaten up with jealousy. She just wants what you have. I imagine she's the kind of person who couldn't bear it if no one was talking about her, so I agree, let's not.'

We stay like that for a moment, his hand on top of mine, and then I turn mine over and intertwine my fingers with his.

22

When it became obvious there were no other options left, Mel's mum and dad had stumped up the money for her to do a three-year course at a drama school in Maidenhead that didn't seem to require auditions, just cash.

I could tell she was a bit battered by the whole experience but, in typical Mel fashion, she added a tubload of gloss on top and made it sound to anyone who'd listen like she'd been shortlisted for an Oscar. Even me.

'It's so much better than going to one of those snobby London ones where they all sit around contemplating their motivation,' she said, as we sat in deckchairs on her parents' manicured lawn.

I had come home for the summer holidays after my first year and I had no plans beyond getting both a tan and a part-time job so I could pay my way. I'd agreed to share a house with Pia, Kieron, Alistair and Tom in year two, when halls weren't available, and we had already agreed to take over the place some friends of Kieron's from the year above me were vacating at the end of August. It had all been surprisingly smooth, given the horror stories that were always bandied around about the lack of affordable rentals in London. Yes, we knew there was mould and a mouse problem and you had to run from the night-bus stop after dark to avoid getting into a fight, but we'd all reasoned that we could travel in a pack for safety.

'That's brilliant!' I said. I was genuinely pleased for her. Even though everything she said about the place sounded worse than the thing before, I just wanted her to be happy, not to feel as if all her ambitions had been crushed. I had bought into the myth of Mel the star as much as anyone else, and I couldn't imagine what else she would do with her life if it was taken away from her.

'It's all practical,' she said now, taking a long draw on the straw in her Diet Coke. She was sitting in the shade of an umbrella, her fair skin luminous in her tiny red bikini. Mel has always worn bright colours, preferably those that know-it-alls would like to tell her clashed with her hair. Sometimes it's like going out with a traffic light. 'There are classes all day – singing, tap, acting. They make sure you're good all round so you can go anywhere, you know?'

It was all sounding more like an old-fashioned stage school than somewhere where you might pick up some serious acting skills. And it turned out it was run by a friend of Sylvia's so I couldn't help imagining rows of ringleted girls in blue eyeshadow gurning away. Overgrown Violet Elizabeth Botts.

'And you can still live here? That's a bonus.' It wasn't in my book. Even though she'd save a shedload of money because, of course, her parents wouldn't even consider charging her for her keep, that didn't compensate for the lack of freedom that living in halls or a shared flat would have given her. But she had no choice. There was no chance of her getting a grant for her fee-paying, non-accredited college.

'Exactly,' she said. 'And it means I'll be able to dedicate myself to training and not have to worry about getting a part-time job.' She knew that I already had two in London – shifts in a local café (although it was debatable whether this would still be available to me in September, I knew they would definitely take me back if and when they needed anyone) and a couple of lunch-time stints in one of the college cafeterias. I didn't care. It was just what you had to do to get by.

'I'm so glad it's all worked out.'

Actually – if I'm being completely truthful – I had begun to get a bit nervous about the prospect of Mel moving to London. I knew she would expect we'd move in together – and, a year before, that would have been a no-brainer for me. But I had a gang now. I belonged. Okay, none of them was ever going to be as close to me individually as Mel was – although Pia and I were almost inseparable now, so much so that we were phoning each other most evenings during the holiday to catch up – but I didn't need that. And I knew that Mel would never have consented to sharing a place with my Dram Soc friends. She'd made that very clear. So a small part of me had felt relieved when her plans had had to change. I wasn't proud of that fact. But it was true.

She peered at me over her sunglasses. 'You will come and see me in stuff, won't you?'

'God, yes. Of course.'

After the night she'd watched me in *The Deep Blue Sea*, Mel had never mentioned it again, or even alluded to the fact that I might ever want to repeat the experience. Even when I'd mentioned my soon-to-be housemates she'd just screwed her face up and said nothing. So I hadn't felt I could talk about it either. And the more the days went on, the less likely it became that I would feel I could just drop it into our conversations. She had effectively built a barrier and she had no intention of taking it down.

23

From Jack, I hear that, when his trip to Reykjavik had to be cancelled, one of his colleagues had had to step in and go in his place, totally unprepared for the pitch. That Jack is in the doghouse at work and the account has almost certainly been lost.

'They're never going to fucking trust me again. I mean, for fuck's sake.'

'They must understand it was an honest mistake . . .'

He groans. 'What idiot of a grown man can't find his own passport?'

'It must be there somewhere. You shouldn't have left it to the last minute.'

'I know that. Jesus. That's not helping, Amy.'

'Sorry, I know. I didn't mean it like that –'

'I mean, where the fuck is it? It's always in the box, right?'

'I thought so. I definitely wouldn't have put it anywhere else.'

'I'm going to lose my job.' This comes out as almost a howl. I reach inside me for the *Schadenfreude* I was so looking forward to feeling. Can't locate it.

'You're not going to lose your job,' I say, as convincingly as I can. But maybe he will. Stranger things have happened.

'Even if I don't, I'll never get promoted now. Shit. Why couldn't I have got Colby Sachs?'

'There'll be other jobs to apply for.'

'You know this story's gone round like wildfire, don't you? What a fuckwit Jack Carmichael is because he lost an account because he couldn't find his own passport. I'm a fucking joke. No one's going to take me seriously.'

'They'll forget about it in a few days.'

'This was a big contract, Amy. Don't you get it?'

I do. I'm actually feeling a bit bad. A bit grubby. It's as if I don't care enough about Jack any more to take any pleasure in hurting him.

'I know,' I say. 'It sucks.'

From Mel, a couple of days later, I hear that Chewton Glen was 'fine' and 'uneventful'.

'You sound fed up,' I say. Actually, what she sounds is angry, although of course she would have no way of telling me the reason why.

'Oh, and guess what?' she says, her voice going up at the end, as it always does when she's getting worked up. 'Someone hacked my fucking Facebook page.'

'Really? How?'

'Fuck knows. They must have guessed my password. They changed my relationship status.' She tells me what it said. 'And I only know because Bella from work saw it and realized that, obviously, I would never have put that up myself.'

'But . . .' I say, summoning my best thespian skills. 'How . . . I mean . . . is it true?'

'That I'm sleeping with John? Yes. Well, I have a couple of times. Anyway, that's not the point –'

'Why didn't you tell me?'

'Amy! Are you not listening to what I'm telling you? Someone went into *my* Facebook account and changed *my* status so everyone knows about it. I mean, who . . . ?'

'Well, whoever they are, they clearly know about you and John. It can't have been a lucky guess. I thought you couldn't stand him?'

'I can't. Not really. The only person I told was Shaz and I never thought she'd tell anyone, because they all know about his wife . . .'

'Oh God, Mel.'

'It must have been her. That's the only explanation that makes any sense.'

'Do you think she'd do that? Really?' I feel a bit bad that Shaz seems to have been found guilty without trial but, on the other hand, she's always been a bit of a bitch to me so maybe this whole thing is karma.

'No one else knew. Literally, no one.'

'Is it going to get you into trouble at work? I mean . . . if everyone finds out and he's meant to be your boss –'

'Of course it will. Plus, he'll go spare. I don't think he even knows yet. I just got told this morning, and God knows how long it's been up there.'

I leave a meaningful pause. 'Don't you feel bad about his wife?'

'Jesus, I don't need a lecture. And do you know what? No. He's the one cheating on her, not me.'

'I'm just thinking about you. Don't get in a mess.'

'I won't. Oh, and don't tell anyone about this, will you? Anyone who doesn't know already. Don't tell Jack.'

Ha! 'Of course I won't. But why do you care if Jack knows? He's the least of your worries, I would have thought.'

'I know. I just wouldn't want him to think badly of me. People get very judgemental about this kind of thing.'

'I won't tell anyone. Let me know how it goes at work tomorrow.'

'Oh shit. I might just call in sick.'

'Brazen it out. Way fewer people will have seen it than you imagine.'

'Love you,' she says, as she always does.

'Yep,' I say.

When I sneak back in to the flat on Monday to retrieve Jack's passport – I hide it in a messy pile of papers on the desk, somewhere he will probably have checked a hundred times during his search – I check Mel's laptop. Of course, she will have changed her Facebook password but, of course, she will have saved it on the computer because otherwise she'd never remember what it was. Her relationship status has been changed back to 'Single'. I can't help myself. I go back to the edit page, delete 'Single' and write 'Fucking one of my supervisors at Safeguard Insurance, even though he has a wife'. I press save before I can talk myself out of it. Go back to the home screen. Delete history.

A couple of hours later, Mel FaceTimes me in tears.

'Oh, thank God you're there,' she says when she sees me nestled in my pillows and the pink cushion.

'Day off,' I say. 'Are you okay? Are you crying?'

'Someone's really got it in for me. They did it again – the Facebook thing. And it can't have been Shaz because I was with her all afternoon. What's John going to think? There's no way someone won't tell him now. He's going to hate me.'

'Do you really care?'

'I was only shagging him in the first place to get him to go easy on me at work! This'll probably make him even meaner.'

'Didn't you change the password?'

'Of course I did! That's what's so strange. I mean, how could they know?'

'God knows. I'd just disable your page, if I were you. Then forget about it. It's just someone playing a stupid joke.'

'No. No one would risk me losing my job for a stupid joke.'

'You won't lose your job. Does it even say which one of the bosses it's supposed to be?' – I know there are several. Probably all male and mostly married – 'And it's not as if there's any proof, even if they could sack you for that, which I'm sure they can't. Just brazen it out.'

'Someone's properly out to get me.'

She lets out a wail. Mel has never been anything other than the most popular girl in the room. Even though there have been plenty of people who couldn't stand her over the years, they've always somehow managed to do it without her having the slightest idea. Despite everything, the sight of her in tears gets to me. I can't help myself.

'It'll all blow over. Just tell John you were hacked. No one's out to get you, Mel. It'll be okay.'

She sniffs loudly. 'Do you really think so? Because I couldn't stand it if, you know, someone really hated me.'

'Just ride it out.'

After she hangs up, I call Kat.

'I'm done.'

'What? Really? Hold on, I'm putting you on speaker.'

'Really. I've given them both a miserable few weeks, but I haven't ruined their lives irrevocably. And that's a good thing. I get to be the bigger person.'

'Good move,' Greg says.

'Are you sure?' Kat says, and I can tell she's a bit disappointed. I think, in her fantasy, we were going to reduce Mel to an unconfident quivering wreck – and in mine, too, when this all started, if I'm being honest. I don't have it in me, though.

'They don't deserve the attention. Fuck 'em.'

Greg echoes me. 'Fuck 'em. To moving on.'

'Exactly,' I say. 'To moving on.'

'So are you going to tell them you know?'

'Not yet. Not while my life is still such a mess. I may not care any more but I care enough not to want the pair of them to think I'm a failure.'

'You're a million miles from being a failure,' Greg says, which is a lie, but I love him for saying it anyway.

'I'm keeping the copies of her keys, though,' Kat says grumpily. 'Just in case.'

PART TWO

24

'Hello, is that Paul Hatfield? . . . This is Anna Freeman and I'm calling from Huntley Media Marketing. You expressed an interest in a subscription to *Motorcycle Monthly . . .*'

Guess where I am.

Nothing has changed, only the people. That's the one good thing about Huntley Media Marketing (well, apart from the flexibility and the freedom to let them down at a moment's notice with no penalty, that is), the turnover is so rapid and no one works regular hours so you can often go days without coming across anyone you know. Which means I don't have to face a barrage of questions about why I'm back and what happened. Plus, because, like I said, they pretty much only employ actors, everyone understands how temporary success can be. Laughably, none of us uses our real names on the phones because we're all convinced that, one day, those names will mean something. And for maybe 0.01 per cent of us that could be true.

During the thirty-minute lunch break the talk is all of who is auditioning for what. Considering the competitive nature of the business, most people are pleasingly generous with their intel. There's a big new touring production of *Blood Brothers* that's about to start casting (no use to me, I can't sing a note), *Emmerdale* are looking for a new family (but the mum, the only one for whom I am age appropriate, is Asian), the BBC have just announced they're doing an adaptation of *Middlemarch* (but not until next year). Still, it's fun to talk shop, even if that shop is empty.

By five thirty I'm exhausted from doing a proper day's work, hoarse from talking so much and my brain is fried from repeating myself: only the names and the titles of the publications ever change. My soul is a little bit destroyed. I am, however, grateful to have survived the regular lunchtime cull, when anyone who hasn't hit their target is let go for the day. I personally have achieved the princely total of three sales – two this morning, which kept me my spot, and a measly one this afternoon. I head down in the lift and out to the street towards the Tube, turning my phone on for the first time since lunchtime. It beeps with a message. Sara.

Amy. Are you around for a casting tomorrow? Couple of scenes in *EastEnders*. I have to let them know by six so call me when you can.

I can't help myself, I get a buzz of excitement. I always do when I know I might be going for an audition, it doesn't matter how small the part. I hit Sara's number and turn on my heels to walk back to the call centre. If I'm not going to be free tomorrow after all, I need to let them know now.

'Is Sara there? It's Amy Forrester.'

I wait while Alexis, the assistant, relays the information.

'Amy! Hi!' Sara always booms a greeting, as if you're just the person she's been wanting to talk to each day. I've learned that it means nothing. She'd adopt the same tone of voice if Spielberg wanted to see me as if I had a shot at being seen for an ad for cream to clear up thrush. I hold the phone away from my ear.

'Right . . . now, where is it . . . Okay, so, *EastEnders*, two days the week after next. But they're scenes for two different episodes, so that's good, because you get paid extra. They're seeing people tomorrow – they've got ten fifteen, ten twenty-five or twelve twenty left, or they did when they called me. Auditions are in Elstree. Interested?'

'Of course. What's the part?'

I wait while she scans the information she's been given. 'Woman in Pub.'

'That's all you have?'

'That's all I have. Well, the breakdown says thirty-five to forty-five.'

'Well, that's me, I suppose. Any of those times is fine, just let me know.'

Even though I know my chances are slim, I allow myself to indulge in a tiny fantasy. Mel watching *EastEnders*, her favourite show, enjoying a glass of wine, getting caught up in whatever drama is going on in the pub. And then suddenly up I pop. Priceless.

*

Sara books me the ten twenty-five slot. She has found out a few more details, Alexis tells me, when she rings to confirm the time.

'You witness a fight in the pub between two of the main characters. There's two scenes in there, one at the end of one episode, so the big boom-boom-boom moment, and then the next episode picks up just after. The reason there's a second day is because you'd be in an exterior of the pub, leaving with everyone else before the police arrive.'

'Right. Any lines?'

'Three,' she says.

I try to keep the sigh out of my voice. 'Great. Thanks.'

'Have you noticed how you're always a witness to something?' Kat asks when I tell her later. 'It must say something about you.'

'It says I'm good at being a woman with no specific qualities other than her approximate age.'

If I had a car, I could do the drive in about a third of the time it takes me to get a bus to the station, the train to Elstree and walk up to the studios. I arrive red-faced and puffing. I announce myself to the guard on the gate, who checks me on a list and then tells me to wait with an assorted bunch of other actors until a runner comes down to collect us. I meet two other Woman in Pubs, three Man in Pubs (also potential witnesses, but only one line) and two Lens. I assume the Lens are more important than the rest of us because the character actually has a name, but one of them tells me it's only a one-episode part, although, as it's the cousin of Kathy Beale, he's hopeful there could be a possibility of more.

After about fifteen minutes and with two new arrivals (I would guess two more Lens), we're shepherded across the car park and inside.

Eleven minutes later, I'm walking back out, having read my lines several times with the casting director. Apparently, roles this small don't necessitate the director or producer being involved.

'Vodka and tonic and . . . what you having?' I say over and over again. 'Hey, watch yourself!'

I assume that's when the fight breaks out, although I am only given the page with my two lines on, to avoid leaks to the press.

'Come on, let's get out of here.' This is from the second episode. By the third time of repeating it, the words no longer have any meaning.

'Thanks, Amy. We'll be in touch,' the casting director says, effectively dismissing me.

And that's it.

One day's work missed, fifteen pounds spent on fares, self-esteem at an all-time low.

'There's a serial killer haunting the streets of New York. Detective Sienna Coburn is leading the hunt to find him. But will he catch up with her first?'

Kat, Greg and I sit there open-mouthed, staring at the TV. 'Oh my God, is this it?' Kat says finally.

'Shit. Yes.'

We're eating a paella cooked by Greg, sitting in their living room, waiting for the first episode of a new Scandi drama that caught our eye. A montage of shots from *Murder in Manhattan* whips by. I knew it was airing in the UK at some point, because that had been part of my original fee, but, up until now, I had no idea when.

'That was you!' Kat squeaks, as an image that lasts no longer than a millisecond of me and 'sister' Sienna touching beer bottles flashes up. It's almost subliminal. If you didn't know it was me, then you would never know it was me, if you get my meaning. But I do, and it is.

'The hit US drama everyone is talking about. Coming soon to Channel 4,' the booming voice says ominously.

As Kat scrabbles for the remote to rewind so we can watch again, it hits me that this means two things.

I am going to be on prime-time TV every week for eleven weeks, casting directors will see me, directors, producers, my mum and dad. People I haven't seen for years will pause and say, 'Isn't that Amy Forrester?'

And then, in the twelfth week, it will no longer be a secret that my contract is over. I'll no longer be able to pretend to be living on the other side of the world. Jack and Mel will want to know where I am.

I have just three months to get my life together.

25

Woman in Pub eludes me, just as Woman in Park did. Maybe I'm just not cut out to play a generic woman. Maybe casting people take one look at me and think, *I just don't believe that woman would ever be in a park. Or a pub. Or anywhere else, for that matter.* There's something intrinsically wrong with my womanness. My very womanosity. It's just not womanish enough.

I pester Sara enough so that she puts a bit of effort in and manages to get me two more auditions: Nancy in a touring production of *Steaming* which will be playing the smaller community venues rather than the prestigious Theatre Royals, and 'Mum' in an advert for washing powder. I attack them both with the enthusiasm of a child on Christmas morning, but it's to no avail. I actually get a call back for the commercial but, in the end, it's a no. Still, I tell myself, that's two more directors I've met, two more people who might remember me in the future.

Simon calls me a few days after our date. The end of the evening had been both awkward and surprising. I had just assumed we'd end up somewhere together. I'd even tidied up in case he wanted to come back to mine, although his place in Barnes sounds infinitely nicer.

Plus, I'd plucked and shaved and had bits and pieces of me waxed, buffed up my skin till it glowed, moisturized with mango-scented body cream. I couldn't remember making this much effort since, well, since the early days of Jack, I suppose. In the bathroom, I'd stared resentfully down at the pouchy pockets of cellulite on my thighs. It wasn't terrible, but it was there. I'd barely even noticed it before, but now I couldn't imagine anyone seeing anything else if I stood in front of them naked. Okay, so no standing. Horizontal, it looked better. 'Remember not to take your skirt off till you're lying down,' I'd said to myself like a mantra.

Anyway, as we left, he'd put his arm round me, pulled me close to him and said, 'Can we do this again?'

'Definitely. I have to pay you back.' He had insisted on paying after all, citing the fact that the restaurant was stupidly expensive and he knew that I was, as he put it, 'in a bit of a transition period'. I knew I should have protested more. I wanted us to start off on an equal footing, but the truth was my half would mean my having to do two extra days at the call centre and even my staunchest principles gave way at the thought of that.

'Exactly,' he said. 'Otherwise, there'll be compound interest and in a few weeks you'll owe me a fifteen-course banquet.'

The doorman had waved a cab over. I was just trying out the sentence, 'Do you want to come back to mine?' in my head when Simon said, 'You take this one.'

'Oh, okay.' I must have given myself away because he screwed up his face and said, 'Early start.'

'Of course! Well . . . thanks . . .'

I made to grab the handle, feeling a bit deflated. Clearly, things hadn't gone as well as I'd thought. And I had already decided I really wanted to jump him, somewhere between dessert and coffee.

'How about Thursday of next week?' he said, as I was just about to clamber in. 'I've got Ruby for a few nights before that because her mum's away so . . .'

'Oh. Um. Yes, I think. Next Thursday would be good.'

He rewarded me with a big smile. 'Great. Let's speak in a couple of days and make a plan. But Thursday, definitely.'

'Lovely. 'Night.'

As I turned away, he put his hand on my shoulder. When I turned back to face him, suddenly, somehow, he was kissing me. It was over in a second, and very soft, almost chaste. But it did things to me you don't even want to know about.

''Night,' I said again when he pulled away. Safely in the cab, I had replayed the moment over and over.

'So, what's the plan?' he says now. 'Your shout.'

I've been thinking about this. I'm broke and I love to cook, so it's a bit of a no-brainer really, but I can't decide whether it seems too much to invite him round for the evening so soon. In the end, I decide that he's been here before, even if it was during the day, with a scavenged rug under his arm, that we're both experienced adults, so we don't need to hide behind The Rules or teenage codes of etiquette, and that I have rerun that kiss in my head several times and have every intention of taking it further.

'So . . .' I start to say, and my resolve immediately falters. 'I . . . um . . . well . . .' Just spit it out. 'I was wondering if you'd like to come over to mine and I'll cook?'

'Perfect. I mean . . . if you enjoy cooking, that is . . .'

I'm gratified that he sounds as nervous as I do.

'I do! I love it. And I'm good at it. At least, people tell me I am . . .'

'We can admire the rug while we eat.'

'Exactly. And if you drop food on it, you won't even be able to tell, because, you know, that pattern . . .'

He laughs. 'Is it giving you nightmares?'

'I've started therapy, let's just say that.'

'I can always get Martin round to take it away again.'

'I love the rug. Especially now I've run the Vax on it. It's actually cream under all the dirt.'

'It's not?'

'Ha! No, of course it's not!'

'Shit. I told you I was rubbish with jokes. Not only can I not make them, I don't get them half the time. I'm a lost cause.'

I flop down on the sofa in the sun sliver. 'Okay, well, I promise I won't make any more. Ever. We can have serious conversations about quantum physics.'

'Actually, quantum physics is fascinating.'

I drape my hand over my eyes to block out the rays.

It's a beautiful day and I'm sweltering in my curtainless living room, windows firmly closed because of Oscar. Heaven forbid I would be the one who really let him escape, and he's been spending his days staring out at the street, fascinated by the traffic, ever since I brought him here, as if he's thinking it might be fun to explore. 'Did I mention I'm actually busy on Thursday?'

'Oh no, are you? . . . That was a joke, by the way. That was me joking.'

'I know. You don't need to announce it every time. Unlike you, I do get jokes. Do you think this means we're horribly incompatible?'

He sighs dramatically. 'Probably. Shall we just give up now?'

'Eat first, give up later. That's my motto.'

'That's very inspirational. So what time do you want me and what should I bring?'

'Half seven? And nothing.'

'Fantastic,' he says. 'I'll see you then.'

'What was that?'

Jack and I are FaceTiming, thankfully audio only, because the light would give away immediately that I'm not in the right time zone. I've barely talked to him since I decided I didn't care about him any more and, consequently, I've become complacent. I forgot to shut Oscar in the bedroom before I called and he's now yowling in my face because he wants my attention.

I grab him up, but he just makes even more noise so

I drop him down again, on to the sofa. I decide I'm going to have to style it out.

'That noise? Oh, I forgot to tell you. I'm looking after Mary's cat, Frank, for a few days while she's gone away. I don't suppose . . . Oscar . . .'

I might as well guilt-trip him as a distraction.

'Nothing. I'm sure someone must have taken him in. If he'd hurt himself, someone would have taken him to the vet and they'd have scanned him –'

'Poor baby,' I say, scratching Oscar under the chin. He stares up at me with his vivid green eyes and purrs contentedly.

'I still feel awful,' Jack says, and I know he's expecting me to say something soothing, but I don't.

Rather than nothing, Simon arrives on Thursday with a small but beautiful dark wood bedside cabinet in tow.

'It's gorgeous,' I say, examining it. 'But this is getting ridiculous now.'

The flat is looking its (still shoddy) best because Kat came over earlier and we spent the morning prettifying, both visually and – possibly more importantly – in the olfactory sense. She came armed with four throw cushions she claimed were only £5 each at George at Asda – although what Kat was doing trawling round the homeware department of Asda is beyond me, given the fact she won't consider anything going into her home that was made later than 1975 – and a bag full of diffusers, the kind that have sticks coming out the top.

The cushions are cute, two with a kitsch pattern of flamingos and the others a retro geometric design. They clash horribly with the rug but they liven up the sofa and the overall effect isn't too bad, so long as you try not to look at both at once. We unpacked the diffusers and put them in places like under the kitchen sink, and in the darkest corner of the bedroom, where the damp problem is worst. I insisted on paying her back and I was pleased when she let me, because I'm starting to get a complex about being a charity case.

I had finally unpacked the last of the things out of my New York suitcases – which are now stashed one on top of another in a corner of the bedroom – and uncovered some flea-market finds that I'd forgotten I'd even brought home. A dark wooden ornate panel the size of a box file that I managed to hammer to the wall between the two front windows (but which will almost certainly fall off again if touched), a set of three carved heads, also dark wood, which I lined up on the windowsill, and a flat, stern-looking silver crocodile, which I put on the coffee table. They all remind me of Sunday mornings browsing happily in Hell's Kitchen or the West Seventies before meeting friends for brunch in my fabulous former life that I can barely even relate to any more.

I've temporarily taken the grey throw down from where I'd fixed it over the curtainless bedroom window and draped it, folded, across the end of the bed. There's no launderette in walking distance so I've been hand-washing everything in the kitchen sink and hanging it over a wooden frame in the bathroom for the most part, including my sheets, which took so long to dry it necessitated a trip to buy spares. Earlier, Kat and I had loaded up her car and found somewhere that would do a service wash, so now the flat smells pleasantly of laundry under the slightly chemical diffuser smell.

'Well, it looks better than it did,' she said when we finally flopped on to the sofa, coffees in hand.

'It looks like a student lives here who hasn't got round to putting their posters up yet.'

'But at least they're a clean student,' she said, which made me laugh. 'Anyway, it's a vast improvement on the way it looked the last time he came round, and that didn't put him off, so I don't know what you're worried about.'

'I need to start cooking.' I stood up and stretched.

'Oh God, I'm getting out of here before you mess the whole place up again.'

I grabbed her in a hug. The top of her head barely grazed my chin. 'You're a really good mate. You know that, don't you?' I meant it. The way Kat was putting herself out for me was a revelation. She must have had far better and more lucrative things to do with her time, but whenever I needed anything she dropped everything to help out. Because, apparently, that's what friends did.

Kat is a bit like her namesakes. She both loves physical displays of affection and hates herself for loving them, so she let me do it for a second then squirmed in my arms.

'Okay, get off me.'

I kept a tight grip. 'No. I want to say thank you.'

'You can buy me a drink,' she said, shoving me off and laughing. 'No manhandling allowed.'

'Spoilsport.'

After she left, I spent a couple of hours happily pottering around the kitchen area. After much agonizing, I'd decided on a Thai theme, with a starter of fish cakes with a chilli dipping sauce followed by a coconutty, lemongrassy prawn curry with fluffy steamed rice and sea-bass fillets. But first I make a distinctly non-Thai cheesecake with a salted caramel sauce to drizzle over the top. I turn the radio on to eighties hits and Oscar plonks himself on the arm of the sofa opposite my work station and stares at me languidly, occasionally licking his lips as if to say, 'If you even think about turning your back on that for a second it'll be your own fault if I eat the lot.' It's a sunny day; even the tiny sun patch has expanded to fill most of the front room, and I risk opening the bottom and top of the nearest sash the tiniest fraction to let a warm breeze in. Singing along loudly to ABC, not caring who can hear, I realize I feel happy. Truly happy, for the first time in a long time.

Even though it's still light, I have gorgeous-smelling candles burning when Simon arrives (it's just as well I have a cat and not a dog, because I'm not sure a dog's sensitive nose could cope with the variety of scents I've flooded the place with today. Even Oscar looks as if his eyes are watering) and Nova Amor are playing softly on my phone.

I'm wearing a floaty floral summer dress and my feet are bare other than pristine stone-coloured polish on my brown (fake-tanned) fingers and toes.

'It's looking great in here,' he says, handing me a bag with a bottle of champagne in it, despite me insisting that I was providing everything. It's cold, so I open it straight away and pour two glasses.

'No champagne flutes, I'm afraid,' I say, handing him a large wine glass.

'Thank God. I hate those things.'

'Me, too. One swig and it's gone.'

He flashes a big smile. 'I just meant they were awkward to drink out of.'

'Oh, yes, that too.'

He's looking cute in a faded red T-shirt with some kind of inexplicable logo and jeans. I'm relieved to see that, even though it's hot out, he didn't turn up in Birkenstocks. I have a thing about men in open-toed shoes, and it's not a good thing. It's a 'run for the hills' thing.

I fuss around, making him sit on the sofa while I take the bedside table through to the other room and put it in place, wittering on with a running commentary while I do it. I don't know why I'm so nervous. Looking at the bed doesn't help, so I back straight out again into the other room. There's something about second dates that's so much more nerve-wracking than first ones. You've pretty much filled each other in on your whole life histories – what else are you going to talk about? I always find myself either tongue-tied or blathering on about nothing. I say 'always'. Obviously, the last second date I went on was with Jack, five years ago. But before him, I dated a lot. And it was usually the second time of meeting someone, once the initial excitement and anticipation had died down, that I realized I had nothing in common with them (and they with me, I'm sure, on many, many occasions). And then you'd have to get through a whole evening with long, awkward silences, knowing you had no intention of taking this any further, even if the other person wanted to.

'If you feel at any point that this isn't working and you want to bail out early, even before the food, just say so,' I blurt out as I take the fishcakes from the fridge. 'I won't be offended.'

'Whoa!' he says, laughing. 'Where did that come from?'

'I just know how these things go. There's nothing worse than being trapped on a date once you've decided there's no point being there.'

'Well, there is. Lots of things are worse than that. Most things, really, in the bigger scheme of things. I mean, no one ever died from a bad second date. Or did they?'

'Shit, that came out all wrong. I just meant . . . well, you know what I meant . . .'

'Come and sit down,' he says, patting the space on the sofa next to him.

'I need to . . .' I say, vaguely indicating the food.

He holds a hand out to me. 'This is much more important than fishcakes.'

'I've spent all afternoon making those, I'll have you know,' I say, smiling

I take my drink and go and sit next to him. He puts his arm around me and I lean back. He smells of limes and a hint of fresh sweat. I almost make myself laugh thinking I need to add those to the already too-long list of things my flat smells of.

'So,' he says, taking my glass from my hand and leaning forward to put it on the coffee table. I catch a glimpse of the smooth, tanned skin of his back above his belt where his T-shirt rides up. 'We need to find a way to relax.'

He takes my chin in his hand, looks meaningfully into my eyes. I wait for a feeling of panic, or revulsion, or even indifference, but all I feel is that I want to kiss him and I want to do it now. So I do.

Five minutes later, or it might be ten, I am definitely feeling relaxed. So relaxed that I am horizontal, Simon half on top, half beside me. The pair of us crammed on the too-small sofa with our legs hanging over the end. If I feel this good while we still have all our clothes on, I can only imagine what might happen later.

He runs his hand up my thigh, under my dress, and I shudder with pleasure.

Then he looks up, distracted. Laughs out loud.

'Is your cat supposed to be doing that?'

I wriggle around to look at what he's seeing. Oscar is sitting on the kitchen table, proudly licking his front paw and dragging it over his face in a way that says, 'Just cleaning up after a lovely dinner.'

'Oh shit. Get down!'

I push myself up, shoo my cat away from the half-eaten fishcake. 'Bad boy.'

'You might as well let him have it now,' Simon says, sitting up.

'Well, yes, that's true.' I flick the uneaten half into Oscar's bowl. 'There's one left. We can share.'

'Perfect,' he says. 'I'm starving.'

26

I've had friends who've come out of long-term relationships and they've told horror stories about sex with a new partner. The self-consciousness. The awkward clashing of two shapes that don't yet fit. I'd always thought it sounded intimidating at best, absolutely terrifying at worst.

Pia once told me a story about how she'd undressed in front of a new boyfriend – after her four-year relationship with her childhood sweetheart had ended – and he'd pulled a disgusted face and said in a voice a toddler might use when being presented with a plate of Brussels sprouts, 'What on earth are those?' 'Those' being a couple of faint stretch marks on her thigh. He was in the year below us and had, she thought, never seen a real-life naked woman before. I remember she laughed and said she thought she might have scarred him for life.

Pia was always good at laughing at herself. Not that I've heard from her in twenty years. Not that our friendship ever recovered from the tidal wave of destruction that was Mel.

Anyway, I can't lie, I was nervous before Simon arrived. All those insecurities I'd been incubating since

I found out my boyfriend had gone off with my skinnier, objectively hotter, friend. But when it happened, it was the newness that made it so exciting. There was no time to worry about sucking my stomach in because my whole body was a quivering wreck in seconds. And anyway, I didn't care any more. All that mattered was that he keep on doing what he was doing to me.

Now we are lying in a tangle of duvet on my bed and I'm fighting the urge to fall asleep. Whoever made up the cliché about it being men who just want to pass out after sex had obviously never met a woman who'd had a really good time. I allow myself to give in to it. I assume he feels the same, and what's the worst that can happen? One of us is raring to go again any minute and has to wake the other one up? Or we both sleep through until morning? I'm not working tomorrow anyway.

Later, I don't know how much later – an hour, two? It's still dark – I become aware that he's gently shaking me awake. I force open my eyes and he's sitting on the bed, jeans on.

'What time is it?'

'Only about quarter past eleven. I have to go. I've got to be on a site down in Richmond at half six in the morning so it makes more sense for me to sleep at home.'

You'd think I would be disappointed but, actually, I like the idea of waking up on my own. Being able to lie in bed for as long as I want, reliving the evening. I reach out and run my hand up his leg.

'Right now, or can you stay another five minutes?'

He gives me a smile. 'Maybe four.'

I pull him towards me. 'Four's enough. For me, anyway.'

'You old romantic, you.'

'I could probably manage it in three if you get a move on.'

Afterwards, we agree to speak in the morning and I marvel at how uncomplicated this seems, how natural. Don't get me wrong. I'm not thinking the first man I met after my relationship broke down is going to be the love of my life. It's unlikely. Statistically. We barely know each other and so I'm almost certain that at some point he'll do or say something that's a deal breaker. Or I will for him – who knows? But at the moment I'm struggling to see what that might be. I snuggle back down under the duvet, wait for Oscar to nestle in next to me and I'm asleep within minutes.

During my second and third years of college, Mel and I probably saw each other less than at any time before or since. That's not to say we didn't speak all the time, both on the phone and by email. At first, anyway. We were just so busy, both of us. Me with my studies and acting every spare minute I could muster. Her with her new course and its full schedule of classes and rehearsals and, no doubt, lessons in how to form ringlets and smile inanely.

In some ways, I envied her, being able to dedicate herself solely to her passion. I was finding it harder and harder to care about History, my chosen subject. I did just enough coursework to enable me to stay on, and no more. I knew I was heading for a third at best, but it didn't really seem to matter.

The first year we were in the house, Pia and I shared the big attic bedroom while Tom and Alistair had a much smaller room each on the floor below and Kieron nabbed the former living room for himself, because, he argued, it had been his connections that had got us the house in the first place. I didn't care. I was just happy to be there.

Pia was the polar opposite of Mel. For someone who could have just stepped off a catwalk (well, one where they were using tiny versions of models, almost child-sized), she seemed to have no ego about the way she looked. I theorized to Mel once that maybe because her looks were so obviously astonishing she didn't feel the need to draw attention to them. There was simply no arguing with the fact that, whether or not you found her attractive, she was a stunning girl.

Mel had scoffed. 'She'll grow out of them. Her eyes are too big for her face, really. And if she ever puts on any weight she's in trouble because she's so short.'

This was one of Mel's favourite games, spotting the ways in which gorgeous young women were going to age badly.

'She has the kind of looks that only work when you're young,' she would say, if anyone paid another woman a compliment in her hearing, pointing out how her chin was weak, her forehead too big or that her stunning figure meant she was destined to be apple-shaped in middle age. 'I just look at people and I can see how they're going to look in twenty years' time. It's very levelling,' she would boast. 'There are very, very few true beauties out there.'

Of course, this was usually followed by whatever sycophant she was with (often me, I'm ashamed to say) pointing out how her symmetrical features and slender build were almost certainly going to stand the test of time, while she lapped up the attention like a shelter dog on adoption day.

My friendship with Pia was uncomplicated and easy. She had no side, no sensitive blind spots that needed to be negotiated with the precision of someone crossing a minefield. She was fun, self-deprecating and sweet. Always supportive, encouraging my ambitions along-side her own. Confident enough in herself and her own abilities not to feel threatened by anyone else. Half the male population of our uni would practically swoon whenever she entered a room, but she never even seemed to notice. Compliments went over her head, except when she was giving them out, which was often.

She and Mel were never going to be a good fit. Mel was preprogrammed to dislike all my 'London friends', as she called them. In retrospect, of course, I realized she was threatened by them. Pride was making her make a hash of her own life while I was thriving. She must have worried that the more I pursued my new-found ambitions (not that she had any idea I was hoping to make a career of it. At least, I still hadn't told her. I think she just picked up bits and pieces on the rare occasions she came and stayed at the house. Pia and I, on the other hand, often talked into the night about how we were going to achieve our dreams. She had total faith in all five of us – me, especially, it seemed), the more I would come to realize that what she was doing was a bit sad. She still spoke about Centre Stage as if it were the most prestigious establishment in the world (not in front of the others, though, I'd noticed), but I could tell she didn't really believe it.

And it didn't help that, on one of her visits, Pia picked up on a passing reference to Centre Stage and, having no idea that this was where Mel now attended, let rip with:

'Oh my God! That place. The one in Maidenhead? I used to go there when I was a kid. You know they have that Saturday College thing? For the kids who can't afford to go full time, or whose parents have more sense than to send them to a stage school . . .'

We were all sitting around the grubby little kitchen table, the only communal room in the house. The breakfast things were still piled up on the side. I could totally see where this was going. Tried to signal to Pia to abandon ship, but to no avail. I looked across at Mel. Her face, always pale, was whiter than ever. And then a little pool of red flared up in each cheek.

'That's where Mel . . .' I tried to interrupt to let her know that this was the 'top drama school' Mel was always boasting about. Mel shot me a look. Pia carried on, oblivious.

'. . . They charged the parents an absolute fortune and, basically, you just hopped about to Bananarama for three hours and put on a production of something like *Annie* once a year . . .'

Even Tom had realized what was going on and tried to step in. 'I used to go to a Saturday College in Guildford! I used to think it sounded so grown up . . .'

'This one was a particular horror, though,' Pia continued, unabated. 'All the girls ended up like Bonnie Langford and all the boys like Lionel Blair. They used to bang on about being an "all-round entertainer", like that's a thing any more? I remember there was one teacher who literally – and I mean, *literally* – used to stand in front of the class shouting, "Eyes and teeth, boys and girls! Eyes and teeth."'

I could see the red spots on Mel's cheeks had spread. She flared her nostrils, a sure sign that she was furious. Pia was oblivious.

'Honestly, it was like something out of another era. And it's still going! They even do a three-year diploma now, can you imagine? It's just a complete rip-off . . . oh . . .'

Finally, she'd noticed that, behind Mel's back, Tom was pointing to her, trying to make her understand.

She tailed off. 'Shit . . . you go there, don't you?'

Mel pursed her lips, took a deep breath in. 'It's obviously very different now from when you knew it. It has a really good reputation for drama, actually. You should check your facts are up to date before you rubbish something.'

She stood up and glided imperiously out of the room. I knew it was taking all her courage not to stomp off, throwing things.

'God. I'm so sorry,' Pia said to me after Mel left. 'I really had no idea.'

'Of course you didn't,' I said. I knew she would never have said anything to deliberately demean Mel, she was way too nice a girl. Kieron and Tom, on the other hand, finally gave in to the laughter they had been suppressing once Mel had safely left the room. To give them credit, they did so quietly, and I'd be lying if I said I wasn't tempted to join in. It wasn't mean-spirited, it was just the awkwardness of the situation.

'Sorry,' Tom stage-whispered, his shoulders still shaking. 'Sorry.'

'Don't worry about it. She's just a bit sensitive. I'll go and see if she's okay.'

By the time the holidays came that year, Pia and Alistair were a couple. At least, they were admitting they were a couple. I had suspected something was going on for some time before that, from the way Pia used to blush every time he walked into the room. I couldn't imagine two more suited people getting together, and when they told me they were thinking they might like to share a room I practically cried with happiness. Alistair was as sweet as she was, but more naïve, having never really had a girlfriend before college, something the rest of us used to tease him about mercilessly. Being Pia and Alistair, they had no intention of turfing me out of the attic, Pia told me.

'It wouldn't be fair. Especially as you've already had to share for a year.'

I tried to argue that it was the much bigger room and so made more sense for two people. I really didn't mind. They were adamant, though. Pia bundled up her stuff and moved down to Alistair's tiny back bedroom and his single bed. At my insistence, she left most of her clothes up in our giant wardrobe. And she kept her little desk in the corner, piled high with her coursework. Her sleeping somewhere else was the only thing that changed. The dynamics of all our friendships remained the same. We just got used to their open displays of affection and carried on as we were.

They were the first couple any of us had known to get serious. Behind their backs, we started to call them Mum and Dad.

I had been nursing a secret crush on Tom for a while by this point. His puppyish enthusiasm for pretty much everything was infectious, but it also masked a wicked sense of humour. His gangly proportions made him a natural at physical comedy and he was a born mimic who loved to entertain us all with anecdotes about the people on his course or our mutual friends. He and I shared an encyclopaedia of in-jokes and running gags that often left the others baffled. But I'd also come to learn that he was way more kind and thoughtful than he would ever give himself credit for. I kept my feelings to myself. I was too afraid of unravelling our friendship by trying to push for something more. If it was meant to be, I decided, it would happen in time.

I got a job in a local health-food shop, stacking shelves and serving behind the till. It paid a pittance but it covered the rent and I got a huge discount on their stock, so the five of us lived on brown rice and hard chickpeas with the occasional past-its-sell-by-date head of broccoli. I remember it as always being hot and sunny, sitting up late with the kitchen door open on to the tiny backyard, drinking cheap beer and talking into the night.

Mel, stung by what she perceived as Pia making fun of her, refused to visit after that, guilt-tripping me into going home every couple of weekends to save her from boredom. I was glad that the excuse of my job made going any more frequently impossible. Relieved when she announced she was going on holiday to Portugal with her parents for three weeks. In previous summers, I would have moped like a dog waiting by its owner's grave until she came back. This year, it felt like a reprieve.

27

I'm about to have a heart attack.

I have an audition at twelve fifteen for a job I really want and it's now eleven minutes past and I can't find the place where I'm meant to be seeing them. I check the email from Sara for the fourth time: 291A Camden High Street. 'It's a little hard to find, apparently,' it says. They said to tell you it's right in the market, behind number 291. It's a separate entrance.'

I retrace my steps back over the canal, avoiding the hordes of shoppers and tourists in search of weed. The last number I can find is 285. There's a row of derelict houses on the right-hand side and then I'm in Chalk Farm Road and the numbers make no sense. My only option is to go into the market on my left, which is what the email says to do, but I've been round there three times already and there's nothing that even resembles the number 291, let alone 291A.

I'm dripping with sweat and my carefully applied make-up is sliding down my face, mingled with the tears of frustration that have decided to make an appearance. People are looking at me.

'Two nine one?' I say hopefully to a stall holder, but he just looks at me as if I'm asking him to give me his profits.

I tell myself to calm down, breathe. This must be happening to other people. I can't be the only one who's late.

I dial Sara's number, gabble at Alexis when she answers.

'It's Amy. Forrester. I'm supposed to be at an audition in less than two minutes and I can't find the building. Sara said they said it's hard to find, but this is fucking ridiculous. Sorry, I'm not swearing at you, I'm just swearing . . .'

'Hold on, Amy,' she says, as soon as she can get a word in. 'Let me talk to Sara.'

'Quickly, though,' I say, before I can stop myself, as though I think she might stop off for a loo break first. 'I'm about to be late.'

It's absolutely fucking typical that this happens the first time anything that sounds properly interesting comes up. This character has a name! Susie. I'm not sure I've ever imagined myself as a Susie, but there's a first time for everything. And it's a proper part. Not the lead, but one of the second tier, by the sound of it. A new series for the BBC called *Blood Ties*, which, apparently, is a big family saga with a murder at its centre. The blurb they sent read, 'They're a wealthy clan of feuding siblings who own a struggling country-house hotel. Susie is the family solicitor, who gets embroiled in their dirty dealings and cover-ups.' It sounds like a rip off of *Bloodlines*, which was one of my all-time favourite shows. Or maybe it's a legitimate remake, tweaked for the UK market. Either way, I want this job.

Susie is apparently in every episode of this first series of ten. And she even merits a description in the breakdown other than 'Woman'. In fact, it doesn't say the word 'woman' at all, which made me very happy. What it says is 'Susie: late thirties, trustworthy and straightforward. Takes no nonsense. Can be feisty when she needs to be. Has worked for the family for ten years. Attractive.' Trustworthy and straightforward I can do. Attractive, I'll leave up to them, but I've made an effort to look my best this morning. And I'd gone for smart. Knee-length skirt and a cap-sleeved pussy-bow shirt. Not too corporate. Not as if I was going to a fancy-dress party as a lawyer. But just enough so I looked like a professional. Obviously, that's all going to shit now.

It all happened so fast. The first episode of *Murder in Manhattan* finally went out the night before last. Greg and Kat came over and we all watched it together, even though I've already seen the finished result, obviously. Some of the cast used to get together every Thursday night, have drinks and pizza and watch the episodes air. They cheered every time they saw my face (Greg and Kat, that is, not the rest of the cast). I had a couple of really good scenes, setting up the character of my sister as a bit of a lost soul with no husband and kids of her own because she's so dedicated to the job, so she keeps turning up at my noisy family home in Queens, much to the irritation of my husband.

'I want to watch the next one,' Kat had said, once she had paused and rewound the credits three times.

'And you know she hates everything,' Greg had said. 'I mean, really.'

As soon as it ended, I got a text from Simon (looking after his daughter tonight) that basically said he fancied the pants off the lead character's sister and could she get her own spin-off series because he would definitely watch. Both Jack and Mel tried to FaceTime me, so they had obviously seen it – whether separately or together, who knew? Although the idea of them settling down to watch me together was a bit too weird a concept for me to grasp. I ignored both their calls, figuring they would just think I was filming if they compared notes.

Then Chris and Lew phoned, full of how much they'd loved it and how brilliant they thought I was (obviously, I know that this means nothing objectively, they're hardly going to call and tell me I was shit), and I filled them in on everything that had been going on since I spoke to them last, including – with loud prompting from Kat – Simon.

'Oh my God, you're a bigamist!' Lew shouted, laughing. 'Poor Jack. I almost feel sorry for him.'

'You don't,' I said indignantly.

'Of course I don't. It couldn't be happening to a nicer man.'

The next morning, my mum called to say they had watched it with their breakfast and wasn't it fantastic, particularly me, although they had no idea what was going on and they couldn't tell anyone else apart.

All the way to the call centre on the Tube, I kept looking at people, wondering whether they'd seen it. Whether, if they looked at me, there'd be a glimmer of recognition. My experience in the US was that I suddenly started being recognized after episode three went out, following a particularly well-written argument between me and my fictional husband about the fact that my sister used our house as a hotel.

And then Sara called to say someone from Sunflower Productions had got in touch to say they were in the middle of casting *Blood Ties* and they'd seen me last night and realized I'd be perfect for Susie. It was everything I'd hoped would happen (well, not everything. Everything would include me actually getting the job and kick-starting my career. But you know what I mean). And now I was about to fuck it up.

Eventually, Alexis comes back on. 'She's just on the other line to Sunflower Productions. Don't worry, Amy, we'll get it sorted out. Just hold on.'

I lean back against a wall. Now I know Sara is talking to them, I feel much calmer. They'll know I was here on time, know it wasn't my fault.

'Amy?' Sara is on the line. 'I just spoke to Carrie at Sunflower. She says go into Stables Market, walk to the back and you'll see a gate that leads round to the back of one of the buildings . . .'

I start walking. 'How can that be 291 Camden High Street?'

'She says it's an anomaly. She said no one's been able to find it.'

'And they're okay about it, right? They know I've been wandering around for ages?'

I reach the back of the market, looking around. I can feel my anxiety cranking up a notch again.

'They are and they do. The only thing is, Amy, they have to wrap up at half twelve . . .'

'What? It's twenty past now.'

'I know. She said the space is booked out after that. She's checked.'

'But if everyone's been turning up late, then surely they need to find a way to extend?'

'I think they're a new company. And none of them has ever done anything this big. Carrie said it had been quite a steep learning curve.'

'Can't they just move to a café or something? Or their offices? Where are they based?'

'I'm not sure. Out in Acton, I think. But she said the director has to rush off somewhere else anyway. Hopefully, you'll make it in time. Any sign?'

I scour the back wall. 'Nothing. No gates. Nothing that even looks like it would have an address of its own. Oh my God, this is ridiculous. Are you sure she said Stables Market? Inside?'

'That's what she said. Is there anyone you can ask?'

'No. I mean, yes, but why would they know? There's literally nothing there it could be.'

'Did you put it into Google Maps?'

'Of course. There was just a big marker over the canal, and it's definitely not in there. Anyway, you said she said it was in here.'

'Don't panic. I'm going to call her back on the other line.'

I'm all-out crying now. This is crazy. I know we can reschedule, I know they'll still see me another day, but I feel so stupid. What kind of an impression does this make? And what if, between now and then, they stumble across someone who would make a perfect Susie and don't bother auditioning me at all?

I wander up and down the back of the market space, saying, 'Two nine one?' to anyone who'll listen, which is basically nobody. There are food stalls lining the wall and I peer behind each of them, my phone still at my ear. One disgruntled falafel seller waves me away.

I head into one of the cavernous second-hand furniture spaces, although I'm sure Carrie would have mentioned if I had to go through a shop to find them. I look at my phone. Twelve twenty-six. This is hopeless.

'Sorry, Amy, it took me ages to get hold of her.' Sara is back. I sniff loudly, wipe my eyes. 'She says it's got so late they couldn't see you now even if you found them.'

'Oh my God, what? This is a nightmare.'

'She was very apologetic,' Sara says quickly. 'Really, this doesn't reflect on you at all. She says they're going to set up some more times next week and they'll book a different space. Somewhere easy to find.'

'So they definitely know this wasn't me fucking up?'

'Definitely. Go and get yourself a massage or something to make you feel better. And don't worry about it.'

I nearly say, 'I can't afford a massage because I haven't got any work,' but, thankfully, I stop myself. I need to keep her on side.

28

Simon and I are lounging in my bed. It's two in the afternoon and he's supposed to be at work but, luckily for me, because he's the boss, he can suit himself. To a certain extent. He has a meeting with a potential new client at six. A contract that, if he secures it, would take him right through the summer and beyond. And it's in Hampstead, so close enough for him to sneak off for a few hours here and there and end up at my flat.

We're looking up at the damp patch on the ceiling, where water has started dripping through. I don't possess a bucket or even a washing-up bowl, so I've put a saucepan under there to catch the drips and, every now and then, one of us jumps out of bed to check that it's not about to overflow. It's a high-class date, what can I say? Although, in truth, one that I wouldn't change a single detail of.

'You need to get someone to look at that,' he says lazily.

'I went downstairs to ask Mrs Lam in the shop, but as she doesn't speak English it's no surprise I couldn't make her understand.'

'I could take –'

I cut him off. 'No, Simon. Honestly, you've done

enough already. I'll call the woman at the letting agency. There must be a crack in the roof or something. It's their responsibility.'

He pulls me into him, kisses the top of my head, and we go back to watching it drip.

'I don't understand why I haven't heard about that audition.' I've filled him in on the whole horror. Once I got to the bit about them promising to reschedule he'd said, 'Oh, thank God. Can I laugh about it now?'

'It wasn't funny, really,' I said, a smile creeping over my face because, objectively, it actually was.

'It wouldn't have been if it had lost you the job but, now you know you're still in with a shot, it was really. Wasn't it?'

'Okay, yes it was. You have my permission to laugh.'

'Thank you.' He made an overexaggerated 'haha!' noise. 'Next time, maybe scout it out the day before.'

'Whatever time my audition is, I'm going to aim to get there three hours early.'

'Get there the day before. Take a tent.'

Now I sit up on my elbows and look down at him.

'It's stressing me out that they haven't called yet.'

'They have to find another venue. That could take a couple of days. Stop worrying.'

'I will. I have.'

He rolls over on to his side to face me, peels the duvet off my shoulders. 'I have a guaranteed method of taking your mind off things.'

'That'll work.'

He leans forward, pulls me towards him and kisses me, and I feel myself sink into it. There's an indignant yowl and something heavy lands on the bed beside me. Simon pulls away, laughs.

'Oh, good. That's not offputting at all.'

Oscar sits there staring at us. Meows plaintively.

'Get off, Osk,' I say, flapping my hand at him, but he doesn't budge.

'Aah, leave him be, he just wants company,' Simon says, leaning over and stroking him, the moment broken. And all I can think is how nice he is, which should be an insult, like damning him with faint praise. Nice isn't sexy. Nice isn't exciting. Except that, in Simon's case, it's all of those things.

'Maybe we should meet at your place next time,' I say, nestling into Simon's side. If he didn't have a meeting to go to, I'd happily stay here all afternoon.

'Too far for me in the middle of a work day,' he says. 'One evening, maybe. I like it here, though. I like the element of danger. The ceiling might cave in any moment. I might be savaged by a jealous feline. Those two in the flat downstairs could come up and finish us off. It's non-stop drama.'

'Oh God, if I get this job, I can move. Buy somewhere, even. Shit, why haven't I heard?'

'You will,' he says, kissing my forehead. 'Stop thinking about it.'

*

Once he's left, at about five, I call Sara. I already called her first thing, but I can't let the day end without checking in again.

'I've spoken to Carrie,' she says cheerfully. 'They should know tomorrow.'

'Okay. I'll stop panicking. Well, I won't, but I'll stop bothering you with it.'

'Talk tomorrow. I'll call you the second I hear, I promise.'

I remind myself it's just an audition. There will be at least twenty other actresses in the frame, possibly more. And even if they dismiss all of them, that doesn't mean they'll definitely offer the part to me. They could start another search, bring in twenty more. And then twenty more. It's perfect, though. It's the job that could save me from selling magazine subscriptions, trailing around to auditions for monosyllabic unnamed Women, living in a flat that will never feel like home, however many rugs Simon scavenges for me. It's the job that could change my life.

29

Mel

You realize that was me, right? *I'm* Carrie from Sun-flower Productions. Except that there is no Sunflower Productions, no hard-to-find building at the back of Stables Market, no *Blood Ties*. Just me with a pay-as-you-go mobile and a lot of front.

I've never been good with people assuming I'm stupid. I've always felt my lack of formal qualifications marks me out as someone they think isn't the sharpest tool in the box, especially these days, when everyone and their dog seems to have a degree and the second thing anyone asks when you meet them, after, 'What do you do?' is, invariably, 'Where did you go to uni?'

Centre Stage School of Drama and Dance in Maidenhead just does not cut it.

But Amy really should know better. Amy really shouldn't be underestimating my intelligence by thinking I haven't worked out what's going on.

I know that she's back in London, for a start. And I know that she's the one who messed with my Facebook page. What I don't know – yet – is what the fuck she's up to.

I'm sure you think I should be feeling guilty. Beating myself up about the fact that Amy has found out the truth about me and Jack. But what I actually feel is furious. Where the fuck does she get off, trying to ruin my life? Because I know it's her. Why else is she skulking about pretending to be in New York when, in actual fact, she's in London? She thinks she's being really clever, sneaking around, thinking Jack and I are stupid. Well, to be fair, he is a bit, because he's still oblivious. He's still talking about them getting married one day, for example. Like I'm interested. Like we're all in this together. Well, he's in for a bit of a shock.

I'm going to find out what she's playing at. I don't know how, because I'm fucked if I have any clue at the moment. But if she thinks she has the upper hand, she's wrong.

Very, very wrong.

Of course, I felt wretched when me and Jack first got together. Amy was my best friend. And, no matter what she might think, it wasn't pre-planned. I didn't seduce him. Tell the truth, I have no recollection of what happened. We just both got hammered and the next thing I knew we were in their bed, clothes off, having some of the best sex of my life (and, he assured me, of his).

And that's all it ever was, sex. And we had no intention of ever doing it again once we sobered up, but then, you know how it is, the first time is like the gateway drug. And then you just think, *What the hell? If she ever finds out we've even done it once, nothing will ever be the same again, so what's the difference?* Not that I ever contemplated my friendship with her being over. I always assumed that, if all went tits up, I could win her over, throw Jack under the bus and find a way to get her to forgive me. It seems, however, that I was being a bit over-optimistic.

It was pure coincidence that I saw her. Well, it was and it wasn't. Jack and I had just had a disastrous weekend. He had had to bail out of the trip to Iceland because he couldn't find his passport. I mean, what kind of a fuckwit . . . ? We'd ended up having a huge row and I'd even threatened to go without him, until he told me someone else from his firm was going to use the hotel room. And, besides, I had absolutely no interest in going to Reykjavik. It's not somewhere I've ever even thought of going. Give me Barcelona any day. Or Rome. It was the weekend with Jack I wanted.

It was our first big fight, and it was odd, but it was that that made me feel as if we were actually a couple now.

So I spent the weekend sulking, mostly, until he called me, grovelling and begging me to go over to his. But just before I left, Bella from work called. Bella never calls me. We get on okay, but we're not actually friends, but thank God for her, because she was the only person who'd seen my Facebook status and assumed it might not be a big joke or some sort of confession. I mean, you can imagine how I felt. Someone knew about me and John – not that they'd named him, but who else could they mean? Bella was all sympathy. I don't think for a minute she thought there might be any truth in what the hacker had put, she was more concerned about the fact that someone had done something that mean. She told me how to change my password and she promised she'd do damage limitation at work, if necessary.

I was petrified. Not only about people at work finding out – sleeping with the boss is not exactly encouraged, and it's even worse when he's a pudgy bully with a face like a boxing glove. And one that's just been through twelve rounds, at that. There would be no question in anyone's mind that it had been cynical self-interest, not a passion I was powerless to control. I mean, do me a favour, if I was looking for casual sex for the fun of it, I could do much better. Much, much better.

I almost didn't go in at all. I mean, to be honest, it's always hard. I hate my job. Forty years old and I process insurance claims for a living. I live in one of the most expensive cities in the world and I do a job you could do in any old provincial shithole.

But then I thought it would be better to know what the damage was. Maybe none of them apart from Bella had seen it, and I trusted her not to spread it around. And, to be absolutely truthful, I wanted to look Shaz in the eye. She was the only person I had told about me and John. She had no way of knowing my password, in so far as I knew, but, given that it was Mel123, it was hardly the height of cyber sophistication. A few lucky guesses could have got her there. And she had probably seen me enter that same password into my computer at work countless times.

Anyway, to cut a long and boring story short, I dragged myself in there. As soon as I got in, it was obvious everyone knew. You know that feeling you get that people have been talking about you because there's an awkward silence as soon as you enter the room? Well, there was that, plus John glaring at me every time he stalked past. Although that was par for the course, until he finally got lucky. I'd had a few happy work weeks since then. At one point, I went off to hide in the loo, I felt so humiliated, and Shaz came to find me.

'It'll blow over,' she said, putting her arm around me at the sink.

I looked right at her and, I have to say, she didn't flinch. 'How did anyone know, though? I only told you.'

'I don't . . . shit, Mel, you don't think this was me, do you?'

'No. I don't know. Did you tell anyone?'

'Of course not! God, I can't believe you'd think I'd do this to you.'

'I don't . . .' And actually, now she was standing in front of me, I didn't. Shaz can be a bitch but she's one of those people that, if she likes you, she's loyal to a fault. 'Fuck, Shaz, I'm not thinking straight. When did you see it?'

'Not until this morning. Otherwise, I would have told you. Obviously.' She was pissed off with me, I could tell. 'Andy took a screen shot. He's emailed it to everyone this morning. Just so you know.'

'For fuck's sake.' I thought I was going to cry, but I didn't want to give anyone the satisfaction of seeing me red-eyed. 'They don't think it's true, do they?'

'No! I don't think so. And I've spent the whole morning running around telling anyone who'll listen that it isn't.'

'Sorry, I –'

'It's okay,' she said, stroking my arm. She really can be sweet sometimes.

'Who could have done it?' I was feeling picked on. Singled out, and not in a good way.

'It's just a stupid joke. You need to try and look like you're not bothered.'

'I'll fucking kill them when I find out who it was. I mean, isn't that illegal, hacking into someone's page?'

She shrugged. 'Probably. But I imagine the police have got more important things to worry about. And I doubt they hacked. It must be someone who knew your password. Or who could guess . . . oh . . . what about Sam?'

As soon as she said it, it made sense. Not that he could know about me and John, but that could just have been a lucky guess.

'Oh my God. It is. It must be. Shit. That fucker.'

'You've changed your password now, right?'

I nodded. 'I'm still going to kill him, though.'

I felt a bit better knowing it was most probably my vengeful ex and not one of my colleagues. It's just the kind of thing that he would do. Sam was never one to let things go. My workmates would all forget about it soon enough, especially if I could bring myself to laugh it off and not give away that there was some truth in it. I took a few deep breaths and told Shaz I was ready to go back to my desk.

But, when I got there, there was a Post-it note with a message from John. 'Need a word. My office. ASAP.'

I couldn't face it. The look he had given me earlier told me he was furious that – I assume – I had told someone our secret and jeopardized both his authority and, potentially, his marriage. Although, to be fair, I'd probably have been doing his wife a favour. Imagine what it must be like waking up with that in your face every morning.

I showed it to Shaz and then screwed it up and stuffed it in my pocket. I didn't want anyone else to see it.

'Will you tell him I've gone home sick?'

I grabbed my bag from under my desk.

'Are you sure?' she said quietly.

'I can't face it. I'll feel better tomorrow.'

So that's how I found myself walking from the Tube at Belsize Park in the middle of the day, towards Jack's flat in Gospel Oak – where I knew the supplies would be better, because he did a big shop at the weekend, and, besides, he has Netflix – when I saw her. Amy. I was walking down Pond Street and there she was, coming up the hill the other way. I knew it was her instinctively, before my brain could tell me that I must be mistaken because she wasn't even in the country. Something about the way she looped her hair behind her ear and then brushed it free again. I stopped dead in my tracks for a moment I was so confused but then, mercifully, I regained my composure and ducked into the path beside the hospital where, hopefully, she wouldn't see me. She was looking down at her phone, texting, I think. I practically climbed into a bush to avoid her seeing me when she sauntered over to my side of the street. We were literally feet apart.

At this point, apart from being confused, my only real thought was that I didn't want her to ask me what I was doing so close to her and Jack's flat. And if she was coming from there, which seemed likely, she would have seen all my stuff. My clothes and my make-up, my suitcase. You'd think we would have learned a lesson after the weekend of the party but, somehow, her coming home out of the blue then had made us even more confident she wouldn't do it again. What were the chances? High, apparently.

After she'd passed, I practically ran to the flat. I wanted to grab my things and get out of there. I didn't even stop to call Jack. That could wait. With any luck, she hadn't been able to identify who the offending articles belonged to – I mentally ran through a list of what was there. Had I left anything that had my name on? I didn't think so, but if she'd gone through forensically I suppose she might have seen red hairs in the comb or worked out that I was the only person she knew who bought factor-seventy sunscreen.

In the flat — I have my own key; we resisted for a long time but then Jack got fed up of the constant need for coordination — there was no sign that she was home for a visit. That struck me as weird straight away. Her case wasn't there — and when I'd just seen her in the street she hadn't had anything with her, not even a jacket.

I started to grab my clothes, and then I remembered my laptop. I don't know what made me do it, but I checked the history. Blank. Even I know that's not normal. She must have been sleuthing to try and work out who it was Jack was seeing. And if so, I was busted. I felt like I was going to throw up. This was it. My oldest friend had found out I was screwing her boyfriend. Her fiancé. I'm not stupid. I must have known, deep down, that this would happen one day, however much Jack and I kidded ourselves, but I hadn't ever allowed myself to think what would happen then.

Something was off, though. Even through the panic and the fear, I had a nagging feeling that there was more going on. And then it hit me. Amy had looked perfectly normal. She wasn't crying or looking tormented. She wasn't shouting at Jack on the phone or rushing to find a taxi to go and confront him at work. She had been strolling along the street as if she didn't have a care in the world. I could swear I'd even seen her smile at something she saw on her phone at one point. No way had she just discovered her boyfriend was sleeping with someone.

For a second, I thought maybe she hadn't been to

the flat yet. Perhaps she had just landed and she'd decided to go for a stroll in the old neighbourhood before coming home. But she'd had nothing with her. No case. No bag.

Something wasn't right. None of the facts added up. And what was it with my computer and the blank history?

And then I clicked on Facebook. Just to be sure.

I saw the new status. 'Fucking one of my supervisors at Safeguard Insurance, even though he has a wife.'

And I knew. Not only had Amy found out about me and Jack, she must have known for a while. And she was fighting back.

30

At first, I just called the agency to try to find out what was going on. Why was Amy suddenly back in England without telling us – her fiancé and her best friend?

So I dialled Sara Cousins Associates on a whim. I said that I was calling to do some general availabilities for a list I was putting together for a new production. I had googled her client list, too, so I asked about several other actors first, for authenticity, talking quickly so she couldn't get a word in and ask me anything tricky.

When I got to Amy, I said that I knew she'd been in the US filming *Murder in Manhattan* but I wondered if she was due a break over the summer. Sara Cousins told me everything. How Amy's stint on the show had ended, how she was already back in London and looking for work.

I had to stop myself asking questions like, 'Was she sacked?' or 'Has she said anything to you about any problems in her personal life?' because it was so tantalizing to have a glimpse of the truth but not the whole story. And then Sara started asking me awkward questions like what the production was called, and what company was making it and, worst of all, what was my number, so I made an excuse that something was coming through on the other line and I would call back.

By the time I did, I had my crappy, untraceable, throwaway phone and my story straight.

Now I just have to decide what's the best outcome. And by 'best', I mean what will hurt Amy more. Because if she's coming for me now, all gloves are off. If she wants a fight, she can have one, although I never would have thought she had it in her. Do I set the whole thing up again at another, non-existent location? Let her replay the same nightmare? Do I never call back, turn off my pay as you go and leave her wondering for ever what happened? No doubt her agent would be googling Sunflower Productions, calling the BBC drama department, ringing all her agent friends and asking, 'Do you know anything about a new show called *Blood Ties*?' Although that seems like more of a punishment for her than for Amy and, in so far as I know, she has never done anything to hurt me.

Or . . . well, there is one other option. It's brilliant, if I say so myself. I just have to psych myself up for it.

31

Amy

'Are you sitting down?'

Sara is on the phone. I can tell that she's eating her lunch at her desk while she talks to me, which she has a tendency to do. It drives me crazy, the thickness of the words through a mouthful of food. I know the effect she's going for is that she's working so hard on her clients' behalf that she can't even break for a meal but, actually, all I can think of is my mum telling me not to talk with my mouth full when I was little.

'No. Why? What?'

I'm food shopping. Simon and I seem to have fallen into a routine without even realizing it, where, on the nights when, by rights, I should be paying for dinner, he comes to mine after work and I cook. Or, at least, I throw something together quickly that we pick at for a few minutes and then we end up in bed. At the moment, I'm browsing the veg aisle, dangling a basket that contains nothing but two bottles of Sancerre.

'You got it.'

I'm completely confused. I've been waiting for news

of my rescheduled audition, increasingly nervous as the days have gone by.

'*Blood Ties*. They just called . . .'

I'm aware that she's still speaking, but everything has gone a bit blurry. I look around for something to sit on. I always thought people were overreacting when they asked you to sit down before they told you big news but, suddenly, I get it.

'Hold on,' I manage to say. I put my basket down, head for the automatic doors and plonk myself down on a bench outside. 'Say that again.'

'Carrie from *Blood Ties* called. She said they were trying to reschedule all the auditions but then the director watched episode two of *Murder in Manhattan* and decided that, actually, he didn't need to see you after all. You're perfect for the part and they want you!'

'Oh my God, Sara. Oh my God.'

'All ten episodes, with the potential for future series. I asked her if they'd expect an option, and she said someone would come back to me with all the details of the deal —'

'I'll sign an option. Don't put them off me because you think I shouldn't sign an option —'

'Of course I won't, although I think you should be sure that's what you really want before —'

I interrupt her again. 'I do. I'll sign an option for three series. Five. I don't care. Ten.'

'Noted,' she says, in that slightly annoying way she has of acknowledging what you're saying while trying to get across that she thinks you're a bit of an idiot for saying it. 'So, I don't know what the fees are yet, but she said that they have a very healthy budget. She said it's going to be the big flagship show for next spring and the BBC want to make sure it has an impact, so they're spending money.'

'Who else is in it?' I've just about recovered my composure. This is it. This is my chance to get my life back on track.

'Well, she couldn't give me names because the deals aren't finalized, but she said there are a couple of big people. Do you want me to push her?'

'No. I don't care who it is. I don't care if it's starring Kim Kardashian. What are the dates?'

I hear her shuffling paper around. 'Rehearsals two weeks at the beginning of June and then it's a five-month shoot. So it's going to take up most of the year. They're sending you the first two episodes, by the way. Do you want me to wait until you've read them –'

'No! I can't fucking believe it! Sorry for swearing.'

Sara laughs. 'You swear away. It's great news. And very well deserved.'

I heave myself back up into a standing position, a big smile on my face. 'So can I tell people yet?'

'Well, technically, I should say wait, just in case they offer something insulting –'

'I don't care. I'm doing it.'

She ignores me. '. . . but I think that's very unlikely,

so I can't see the harm in giving your nearest and dearest the good news. Just don't go broadcasting it.'

'I won't. They really don't even need to meet me?'

I can hear the smile in her voice, too. 'They really don't. Now go and celebrate.'

So, I do what I'm told. I head back inside, find my abandoned basket, dump the two bottles of Sancerre and put two champagne bottles in instead.

Of course, the first thing I do is phone Kat, then Simon, then Chris and Lew and then my mum and dad. It doesn't even feel strange that I'm not phoning Jack or Mel, that's how far removed I feel from them. I allow myself a brief fantasy of Mel catching a trailer for a new show. Of her seeing my face. Realizing that, despite everything she's done to me, I'm still going to come out on top. I picture her eaten up by jealousy. I'm not going to lie: it makes me happy.

Which reminds me, I need to find myself somewhere better to live. I can afford it now and I can't stay where I am. I had finally called Fiona from the lettings agency about the roof and she had basically told me to go fuck myself.

'The deal was you took the flat as it was. That's why I agreed a lower rate,' she had said haughtily. No sign of the nice friendly woman I'd met now.

'I thought you meant full of crap and in need of decoration. Not that the place might actually be falling down.'

'It's hardly falling down,' she said. 'If you're concerned, I suggest you contact a builder.'

I couldn't be bothered to argue. Even with all my efforts at painting and prettifying, I knew this was never going to be home.

I contact an agency in Camden and one in King's Cross and explain that I'm looking for a long-term rental. Even if *Blood Ties* lasts only one series or they axe me from the second, I'm pretty sure I'm going to be earning well for at least the rest of this year. I also know that there's no way Fiona will refund my deposit, but I decide I just have to put it down to experience and move on.

Oscar is a bit of a sticking point but, eventually, both agencies come up with a couple of things for me to view and I begin the tedious process all over again, although this time at least the flats are liveable, in convenient areas, and they appear to have intact ceilings. Three days after I find out I have the job, I sign the lease on a little one-bedroom top floor above a hairdresser's in Bloomsbury. Well, more King's Cross, really, but it has pretensions. Walking distance to Kat and Greg's and the West End. It's actually a lot smaller than the place I'm leaving, and it's three hundred pounds a month more, but I tell myself I'll save a fortune on Tubes and buses. Plus, it's newly renovated and the sun was streaming through the front windows when I was there. Chris agrees to guarantee it for me, although I hated asking. Sara writes them a letter

268

telling them about my swanky new job, Kat writes a reference, and it's mine.

I call Fiona back and tell her I'm giving a month's notice. She sounds a bit put out but I don't care. It feels as if I'm shedding a skin and a new, happier, more successful me is finally about to emerge.

32

Mel

Once I've delivered the good news that Amy has the part, I ask for her home address so I can send the scripts. Because Sara Cousins is a bit antsy about wanting to see them, too (I imagine she has a whole host of other actors she wants to pitch for, once she knows what the parts are. Well, good luck with that!), I tell her I'll mail her a set, too. Why not? It's not like it's actually going to happen. All I have to do now is back away quietly, chuck my pay-as-you-go phone in the bin and leave them all wondering what happened.

I'm not done yet, though. Not knowing what Amy is up to is killing me. For all I know, she's plotting to hurt me in other ways. Christ knows what she'd be capable of when she's pushed into a corner. So, on Saturday afternoon, I head to north London, to the address her agent has given me, in the hope that I might get some clues as to what she's playing at.

I think, in my head, I was imagining there might be a café I could sit in across the road where I could while away an hour or two watching the comings and goings. Stupidly, I got a cab – although I did ask the driver twice if we really were going to the correct address, the journey was taking so long – which set me back the best part of thirty-five quid, even without a tip, which I decided not to give him because surely he must have taken me on some kind of scenic route. And, when I got here, it turned out there really was nowhere to sit other than a greasy spoon on the corner from where you can only just make out the road space in front of her building and not the actual building itself. And that's only if you sit in the window, which feels way too risky. In the end, I get myself a coffee (Jesus, would it kill Starbucks to open up a branch round here, surely the people of – wherever this is; I have no idea even what this area is called – would fall over themselves with gratitude to have something other than this lukewarm, watery stuff to drink?), pull the baseball cap I have thankfully brought with me over my much too conspicuous hair and plonk myself on a bench at a bus stop some fifty metres up the road on the other side.

I haven't spoken to her since I found out her secret. In fact, come to think of it, we have hardly spoken for a while. Amy tends to call when I'm at work these days, even though she knows I can't answer my phone then. There have been a lot of voice messages about night shoots and how hard she is to get hold of at the moment, now I come to think of it. And when I did talk to her last she claimed that she could only audio chat because her reception was so bad – something else that has been happening a lot lately. I never thought to question it.

I try to amuse myself by thinking through all our recent conversations and trying to pinpoint the moment when she found out, but after about fifteen minutes I'm dying of boredom, cold, even though it's a warm day, and pissed off. When a bus arrives heading south I get on, giving one last glance at the blank windows of what – I assume – is her flat on the top floor.

Jack is just back from the gym when I get home. (Look at me calling it home now – I never really allowed myself to before. It felt too disrespectful. Now it feels as much mine as it ever was hers). Newly showered and smelling of the coconut shower gel he takes with him because he doesn't like the stuff in the dispensers there. And he's bought dinner – pizzas and ice cream – so I pour us both a glass of wine and sit at the kitchen table while he unpacks. We're the picture of domestic bliss.

'Have you spoken to Amy lately?' I take a long sip of my wine, try to act as if everything is normal.

'Actually, not for a few days. We keep missing each other. She's been doing crazy hours by the sound of it. Do you think she's okay?'

I hate it when Jack does this. Talks to me about Amy as if we're both still the two people who care about her the most. As if he hasn't noticed what we're doing.

'I haven't spoken to her either. She sounds okay on text, though.'

'It's ridiculous how many people have seen *Murder in*

Manhattan. Everyone's talking about it. I feel quite proud when I tell them my girlfriend's in it.'

Really? He's actually saying this to *me*? I want to say, 'It's all over. She's not going to be in series two. That's her fifteen minutes of fame done. Oh, and by the way, I don't think she's your girlfriend any more.' But of course I don't.

'Right.'

'It's amazing, isn't it? When you think about it?'

'It is,' I say. 'Amazing.'

33

Amy

Every day I wait for the post like a First World War wife waiting for news from the front. That distant thud that will tell me the scripts have arrived, or a note on the door saying they've been left with a neighbour (although I doubt those two downstairs would agree to take anything in and, if they did, they'd probably use it in a ritual sacrifice). I try not to badger Sara for news of the deal and my start date. I know these things take time and they must be more concerned with confirming the leads at this point. Bored, I google '*Blood Ties* BBC' and find nothing, which doesn't surprise me, as Sara said they were keeping it under wraps till production starts.

Simon appears at my door with a ladder in tow. It's his night to cook — we've pretty much given up on restaurants altogether. What's the point? We're only going to end up here, anyway, and he works such long hours that our time together is precious. I notice at his feet he also has a bag of groceries. I pick it up.

'What's that for?' I say as he manoeuvres the ladder up the stairs.

'I'm going to have a look at your roof.'

'No. Simon, stop. You really don't have to keep doing this.'

'Doing what?' he says. 'I'm just going to have a look. See if it's something easily solved.'

'Even though I'm moving?'

'Would you stay in a hotel that had water coming through the ceiling? Even for one night? If there's an obvious crack, I might just be able to lay a tarp over it or something. They're predicting heavy rain at the weekend.'

He huffs around the last corner to my flat door.

'It's very sweet of you.'

'It makes me happy, so just let me get on with it. You can repay me later.' He waggles his eyebrows as he says this.

I've never even noticed that there's a hatch leading out to the flat roof in my little hall, but he clearly has because he wedges the ladder in there and heads on up. I take the grocery bag through to the kitchen and start unpacking. Aubergines, tomatoes, couscous.

'Jesus. I don't think anyone's opened this in years.' I hear a thump as he shoves it and then another as it must come loose and spring open. There's a welcome rush of air through the flat. It's still baking hot out, and I can never open my windows more than a crack because of Oscar.

'Be careful up there!' I call, suddenly imagining the whole thing giving way underneath him.

'Come and look at this!' he shouts. I wander out into the hall in time to see him heave himself up through the hole. His head pops back down. 'Come up.'

I hate ladders. Actually, who doesn't? Whose Tinder profile reads, 'Huge fan of ladders'? But I really hate them. I once got vertigo standing on a footstool.

'It's safe,' Simon says when he sees me hesitate. 'And it's worth it, I promise.'

I climb up slowly.

'Look at this,' he says as my head emerges.

The first thing I see is a trellis along the back and part of both the sides, where it can't be seen from the road. Along the inside are ornate planters now containing long-dead plants that clearly once covered it. Dotted around are smaller pots, their contents also shrivelled. In the middle are two painted wooden steamer chairs with a small metal table between them.

'Wow. The woman who lived here before must have done this.'

'And then presumably got too old to keep coming up to look after it. Look at the view.'

I take a look, being careful not to go too close to the edge. You can see the Wembley Arch on one side, the cars on the North Circular on another (not so scenic) and even the sparkly skyscrapers of the city in the distance. 'It's amazing. Do you think nasty Fiona knows?'

'No way. She'd have been charging you twice as much. I assume it's not really meant to be here and that's why the old lady made sure it couldn't be seen from the street. But who's going to know? The only access is from your hallway.'

None of the other houses in the row has any sign of

rooftop life. I assume, like me, the tenants have just never thought to look.

'God. It's like my own little world up here.'

'Wait here,' Simon says, and he disappears back down the hole into the flat. I peer through the trellis at the world beyond the main road. I can just make out what looks to be a few shops a few streets away, somewhere where I've never walked because I haven't exactly spent a lot of time getting to know my neighbourhood. There even seem to be some chairs out on the street there, a café, maybe.

'Ta-dah!' Simon reappears, brandishing a bottle of wine and two glasses in one hand and a damp J Cloth in the other. He proceeds to wipe the thick years of cobwebs off the chairs.

We sit down, heads up towards the sun like a pair of hothouse flowers.

'I wish I'd discovered this sooner,' I say.

A couple of days later we're walking on Primrose Hill. Now my life is getting back on track, I've started to feel guilty that I haven't told Simon the whole truth. I think, when we first met, I never imagined that this might be a relationship that would turn into something (not to mention the fact that I thought he'd run a mile if I tried to explain that I was technically still engaged to another man but holding off throwing the ring back in his face until I'd carried out some retribution, mostly on his mistress, my former best friend. That's an episode of *Jeremy Kyle* right there. *I* wouldn't have dated me). Now, though, there's no denying we are a couple, albeit one still in the early stages. I could wait it out, play my big reveal to Jack and Mel once my new job has started and I'm living in a lovely new flat with, hopefully, a shiny new boyfriend on my arm, hope Simon never hears about it – and, being rational, why would he? But that doesn't seem right. It doesn't seem fair.

'Can I tell you something?' I say as we reach the summit, me a bit out of breath. I've decided I just have to do it, throw it out there and hope he doesn't write me off as some kind of bunny-boiling loon. I don't know why I picked today, but it feels like now or never.

He puts an arm around me and we head for an unoccupied bench. 'Of course. Is everything okay?'

'It is. Definitely.' I sit down and swivel to face him. I want his full attention. He's looking so concerned, I almost back out.

I exhale loudly. 'Okay. This is going to sound crazy but bear with me . . .'

I start by reminding him about Mel and Jack. I want him to realize this is about so much more than a cheating boyfriend. I can see he wants me to cut to the chase but I need to make sure the groundwork is solid. I have to keep going, get to the end of my story. Then I babble on, about keeping what I discovered to myself, wanting to get back at them, to make them hurt like I did. This is the bit that makes me most uncomfortable. It's the part that paints me in a bad light. So I gloss over the details of what I actually did – he can ask me later if he wants to – and get to the part about realizing I didn't care any more, that the petty acts of revenge rang hollow because I'm not that kind of person.

He's looking a bit confused, and who can blame him? 'So you've told them now that you know?'

Here goes nothing. 'No. Not yet . . .'

His eyebrows shoot up, giving away how much of a shock this is. I want to reach out a hand and stroke his face, but it doesn't seem right. Now I'm in the middle of this, it's clear to me that, more than anything, I don't want this relationship to end. 'Jack still thinks you're engaged?'

'Yes. Although how he thinks that when he's doing what he's doing –'

'When were you planning on telling him?'

It's a good question. I try to explain that I needed to get my life together first. That I didn't want them – *her*, let's be honest – to think I'm a loser with no work, living in a shitty, damp-infested flat in the middle of nowhere. That, way more than Jack's, it's Mel's reaction that matters.

'She's always thought she was so superior to me,' I say, realizing as I say it that I sound about fifteen years old. 'She hates that I went into acting when she couldn't get a break but, so long as I was struggling, getting bits and pieces here and there, just enough to keep me going, it was okay. Once I got the job on *Murder in Manhattan*, it was too much for her. I mean, what kind of friend resents your successes? I couldn't bear for her to be gloating that it had all gone wrong. Not after everything else . . .'

'I have to admit she sounds lovely,' he says, and I see a glimmer of hope.

'So as soon as I'm allowed to go public about my new job, then I'm going to hit them with it. And then that's it. I'll never have to see either of them again, and I don't care. I really don't. The best revenge is living well, and all that, remember?'

He leans back and looks out over the fields to the high-rises in the distance. I've always loved this view. Today, I've hardly even noticed it.

'I know it's fucked up –'

'So, what, I'm just a part of the plan? You turn up with a new job, a new flat and a new boyfriend?'

'No! You were a surprise. To me, I mean. I wasn't looking . . . you've never been anything to do with this . . .'

'I don't know, Amy. It makes me uncomfortable.'

'Please . . .' I say. 'It's really important that you know I didn't start seeing you as part of some plan . . .'

'And you want us to carry on while Jack still thinks you're with him? I don't know . . .'

'It's just for two more weeks, max. Or I could tell them now – it just wouldn't have the impact I wanted. In fact, why don't I do that? Just get it over with . . .'

'No. I can understand why it's important to you to show that that you've moved on. That you can be successful without them in your life. I get that. I'm just not sure if I want to be a part of it . . .'

I blink back tears. I've brought this on myself, but all I want is for Simon to say we can try and get past it. I hadn't realized until today how much I like him, how much I want to keep on seeing him. But I know I have to give him time to take it all in, so I keep quiet.

'I just need to think it all through,' he says, standing. 'It's a lot . . .'

'I know.'

'I'm going to walk back to the site. Are you okay to . . . ?'

I nod.

'I'll call you soon,' he says, leaning down and planting a kiss on the top of my head. I watch as he walks back down the hill.

I'm still sitting there, gazing off into the distance, thinking about how I've fucked the whole thing up, trying to summon the energy for the long journey home, when I'm vaguely aware of hearing my name. Something about the voice sounds familiar.

'It is you, isn't it?'

I look up, squinting. It takes me a moment to recognize the face. The shaggy hair has gone, replaced by a severe short cut, and the roundness of youth has given way to a square jaw, but the puppyish smile is exactly the same.

'Tom?'

'I recognized you from miles off,' he says, out of breath. 'But that's probably because I saw you on the telly the other night. Congrats, by the way.'

'I can't believe it . . . how are you?'

'May I?' He indicates the bench and, when I nod, he sits down next to me. He's wearing a suit, a stylish one, well fitted. His brown leather shoes gleam like a pair of mirrors.

'I'm well.' He indicates his suit. 'Lawyer – can you tell?' He pulls an apologetic face.

'Around here?'

'Marylebone. I just like to walk up here when I need to clear my head. How are you?'

'I'm . . . well, you know what I'm doing by the sound of it . . .'

He nods. 'I've seen you a few times in things. This one's big, though, right?'

'Best part I've had. Definitely . . .' I tail off. I don't want to go into the details. And, thankfully, he doesn't ask.

'Marvellous,' he says, and I'm transported back twenty years to when that was his go-to word.

'So . . . what have you been up to for the past twenty years?' I say, and he laughs.

'Oh, you know. Married. Divorced. Two kids.'

'Lovely. The kids bit, I mean. How old?'

'Twelve and ten. They live with their mum most of the time. But I'm just up the road so I see a lot of them. You?'

'None of that. I would have loved to have had kids but, you know, the timing was never right. I almost got married but . . .'

'Funny how you were the only one who persevered. With the acting.'

'Kieron's a theatre director, isn't he?' I remember seeing his name once, about five years ago. He had some avant garde, experimental piece on at a festival somewhere.

'On and off,' Tom says. 'He's his own worst enemy, really. Refuses to do anything commercial.'

'You're still in touch?'

'Of course.'

'And Alistair?'

'Works in publishing. Non-fiction. Married to Siggy, three boys.'

It feels almost unreal that my friends have had whole lives since I saw them last, which I know nothing about. 'Great.'

I wonder if he's waiting for me to ask about Pia, but I'm pretty confident he'll know less than I do. She walked away from us all and never seemed to look back.

Tom stands up as quickly as he sat down. 'Meeting at two,' he says, looking at his watch. 'Would you like to catch up sometime? Lunch or something?'

'I'd love to,' I say. Who can resist the chance to get an update on their old friends' lives? Tom fishes in his inside pocket, brings out a card and hands it to me.

'What's your number?'

I tell him, he puts it into his phone and then he's lolloping off down the hill. Despite how miserable I feel, I can't help but smile as I watch him. From the back – if you substituted the suit for jeans and a baggy shirt and grew the hair – he looks exactly the same.

I tried to concentrate on work as I hurtled through my third year. We all did. Well, those of us who were still studying. But none of us was very enthusiastic. Kieron, who had graduated in the summer, had already started film school, and Alistair – like Kieron, a year ahead of me – was winging it. He had several family-friend connections in the industry and he was pretty confident he could at least get through a few doors and put himself in contention for things. Meanwhile, he was working in a fast-food restaurant and bringing home leftovers every night for the rest of us. Pia and Tom were both talking about trying to get into some kind of post-grad drama course. I couldn't afford to study any more and I had zero influential family members so I was trying to formulate a plan that would enable me to carry on doing what I loved. I had no plan B. Nothing else that interested me.

I hadn't seen Mel since the middle of the summer. She'd called me when she got back from her holiday and regaled me with stories about the horror of vacationing with your parents when all you wanted to do was go out and get wasted.

'We should totally go away together next summer,' she said, and I'd agreed, even though I knew that there was no way I would have the money or – if I was being totally honest with myself – the inclination. I was eager for my life to start. I didn't want to waste weeks of it sitting on a beach feeling as if time was slipping away.

She didn't bring up what had happened the last time we'd seen each other, and neither did I, although any mention by me of my housemates was met with a wall of stony indifference. We kept in touch mostly by email, hers full of stories of the triumphs she was having at Centre Stage, mine blandly describing a few anodyne events I thought wouldn't piss her off.

So I was surprised but delighted when, just before Christmas, she announced that she was going to come up for the weekend. It coincided with a Saturday night when we were going to have a house party. To be fair, we had these quite regularly (mostly through laziness: why go out when you could make everyone come to you?), so it wasn't a big deal. I figured she would get lost in the crowd; better that than a weekend of her pointedly avoiding spending any time with my other friends. And besides, I missed her. Of course, she could be maddening, but when she wasn't around the world felt like a duller, more ordinary place. As if all the colour had been leached away.

She arrived on the Friday night, bearing four bottles of wine to contribute to our party supplies. I was thrilled to see she was on her best behaviour, making a real effort to talk to Pia in the kitchen, asking what she could do to help before tomorrow, offering to go and find some Christmas decorations and make a big, colourful display. This offer was accepted eagerly, which sorted out any doubt about how she and I could spend most of Saturday.

I had already decided we would go out for a drink on the Friday, just the two of us. I was anxious about her not wanting to spend too much time sitting around with my housemates. But she claimed tiredness and a desire to veg out so, after a while, we took one of the bottles of wine and two glasses up to my room.

'Did Pia move out?' she said, looking around.

'Her and Alistair are a couple now, didn't I tell you? So they're sharing his room downstairs.'

'Oh, yes. He's nice but dim, right?' She flopped down on Pia's old bed, which was now dressed with cushions and a throw, while I fussed about with the wine.

I laughed, although her comment wasn't at all fair. 'Hardly dim, he's heading for a 2:1.'

'You know what I mean.'

'He's a sweetheart.'

'God knows what they see in each other,' she said. 'I mean, she's such a fucking know-all and he's, well . . . I mean, he's good-looking, but he's so . . . what's the word . . . *parochial.*'

'Mel, we come from a village outside Maidenhead with one pub, one shop and a village hall. In what way are we not parochial?'

She laughed, throwing her head back in that way that I now realize was an affectation. 'Parochial is an attitude.'

I wanted to change the subject away from Pia and Alistair before we would have to rehash Pia's whole faux pas about Centre Stage. I knew Mel was still smarting from that, even though it had been months, and I didn't want her to work herself back up into a cloud of righteous anger.

'Oh, Chris is applying to King's. Did I tell you? So if he gets in, he'll be in London as well.' Mel loves Chris. I think partly it's because, when she first knew him, he was only eight and completely smitten by her. He used to pick flowers from our garden, tie them in a posy and present them to her as if he was about to ask her to be his prom date. And Mel has always loved to be worshipped.

'I know,' she says with a smile, Pia hopefully forgotten. 'I bumped into him in the Cross Keys the other week. His exact words were, "I need to get out of this fucking shithole and into the real world."'

'Ha!'

She topped up her wine and then leaned over and topped up mine, although I'd hardly made a dent in it. She, by contrast, had swigged the whole glass in record time.

'I'm still intending to move up when I finish, obviously. I think . . . this is tricky . . . but I think I'll have to leave Sylvia's and get on the books of one of the big London agents. She's been fantastic, but she doesn't really know about big-league stuff.'

'Mmm, you're probably right.' Now would have been the time to share my own anxiety about finding an agent. I knew from watching my fellow Dram Soc members over the past couple of years that the thing to do was to try and interest them in coming to see a final-year show.

Easier said than done, of course, when they were going to be using what precious time they had to scout out the talent leaving all the prestigious drama schools. But one person had been picked up that way last year (though not Alistair), two the year before, so it wasn't hopeless. Since Mel came to my first-year performance in *The Deep Blue Sea*, though, we had still never discussed my ambitions. As elephants in rooms go, this one was more like a woolly mammoth. I opted to let it go.

She stretched her long, jean-clad legs out in front of her. 'I'll probably try Fraser Michaels first,' she said, mentioning one of the oldest and biggest. 'Have you heard of them?'

Who hasn't? 'I think so,' I said.

In typical Mel fashion, she suddenly sat up and changed tack. 'You are coming home for Christmas, aren't you?'

'Of course. Not until Christmas Eve, though. I'm working.'

'Thank God,' she said dramatically. 'You have no idea how shit it is without you around.'

On Saturday, we hit the shops. That is to say, we went to Poundland. Mel had her credit card, which allowed her access to her mum and dad's account, and was all for heading to the Harrods Christmas department, but I didn't think expensive baubles would go down half so well as kitsch, and I managed to persuade her that we could have more fun with quantity, not quality. Over breakfast, she had been friendly with Pia and Alistair as they pottered around in a cloud of domestic bliss, making toast and tea. I could tell that Pia was terrified of saying the wrong thing again, but Mel seemed to be on a charm offensive and she made a real effort.

We came back with so much tinsel and bags full of paper chains and shiny stars and huge crêpe Santa masks that it took us the whole afternoon to decorate. You couldn't walk two feet without something festive hitting you in the face. We found a radio station playing Christmas hits and cranked up the volume. By five o'clock, we were almost hysterical with anticipation, as if we were ten rather than twenty years old.

'Fucking hell.' I heard the front door close and, somewhere through the fog of silver and red, Kieron's voice. 'Santa came.'

'Good, huh?' I said, peering through two strands of angel hair.

'Fab.'

He wrapped me up in a hug. Kieron was famed for his hugs. 'Oh, hi, Mel.'

She gave him a mega-watt smile. 'Hi. Happy Christmas.'

He leaned over and kissed her on the cheek. The front door opened again almost immediately and Alistair burst in, triumphantly holding aloft a bag of burgers and fries that had sat on the counter for more than their permitted time.

'The hunter has brought the spoils!' he shouted, to no one in particular. We always fell on him like a starving pack of wolves when he came home from a shift. Then he stopped in his tracks. 'Jesus. It looks amazing in here.'

'Let's have a drink to celebrate before we start getting ready,' I heard Pia say from the direction of the kitchen, although I couldn't see her through the tinsel.

We all fought our way through. Tom was lovingly stirring something that could only be described as lethal. He loosely described it as 'punch' but, really, we all knew it was a mixture of whatever random alcohol he had managed to find at a knockdown price and a bit of fruit juice. Every student's answer to the question of how to get wasted as quickly as possible on limited resources. Alistair laid out his booty like a banquet – three beef burgers, a veggie burger, a fish sandwich and two portions of fries – for us all to share. I looked around, toasting the five people I felt closest to in the world, Chris aside.

'I love all you guys,' I said, halfway through my tumbler-sized glassful.

'Oh God. You know she does this,' Mel said affectionately, and I remember thinking how beautiful she looked, standing in our shoddy kitchen with ratty bits of tinsel framing her like a halo. 'She's going to get all maudlin. Christmas, booze and Amy don't mix.'

'Well, we love you, too,' someone – either Alistair or Kieron – said, and the next thing I knew we were all in a big group hug and I felt an overwhelming wave of happiness.

It didn't last.

34

Mel

There's a man ringing Amy's doorbell with a big plant in a pot. Something flowery. Geraniums, maybe? I've never been any good with plants. At least, I assume it's her doorbell. I've seen a miserable-looking couple coming and going so I'm guessing they live in the other flat. And they don't look like anyone would bring them a half-dead dandelion, let alone this riot of yellow and orange beauties.

I can't overestimate how big a piece of news this is. I've sat watching from my car for days now. Literally, days. Well, after work, obviously, because I'm not trying to get sacked. Jack thinks I'm working late, which I've never done in my life, but I started using that as an excuse when me and John first . . . you know . . . so he just accepts it. That's still going on, by the way. Me and John. Just a quickie in his office at the end of the day, a couple of times a week. I can't work out how to end it now without making things worse, but I had to do damage limitation after the whole Facebook thing, so now he's convinced I find him irresistible. And, once he realized he seemed to have got away with it, he returned to his usual cocky form. It's so grim I can't even think about it.

Anyway, I head straight up here as soon as I can get away – I have to sneak back to Jack's and retrieve my car first because, after that first bus-stop experience, I decided I was way too visible in the street – and then I sit there for a couple of hours until I decide she's in or out for the evening, when I give up and go home. I have no idea what I'm expecting to see – just something, *anything*, that will give me a clue what she's up to. Thus far I've seen her twice – once coming home with a couple of Tesco bags, and once arriving home with Kat – Katty – Mackenzie. So *she* knows. Which makes me think that whole thing about helping sell my flat was bullshit. I always knew she was a silly cow.

Last night, I even spoke to Amy while she was in the flat, presumably concocting something from whatever she had bought in Tesco, and I was sat outside it. We chatted as if everything was normal. As if she were in New York and at work and hadn't found out a thing. She was telling me some story about something that had happened on set. 'Surreal' doesn't even cover it.

I was about to give up, I'll be honest. Tonight is the fifth evening. I was bored stiff. I was thinking I was just going to tell Jack what I knew and let it play out from there. And then a smart van pulled up along the road and a good-looking bloke got out with this big, flowery display. At first, I thought he must be a delivery guy until I noticed that the van had 'Simon Rigby Interior

Design' written on the side. I watched as he walked confidently up to Amy's door. Rang the top bell.

Now I'm sitting here holding my breath. I have no idea if she's in or not. I haven't caught sight of her today. I slide down in my seat, pull my baseball cap over my hair, tilt down the visor and watch.

After what seems like an age, the front door flings open. Handsome guy proffers the plant. There's a tiny pause and then they're in a clinch. Right on the doorstep. Then she ushers him in, face beaming, and that's it. I wait for a moment, just to make sure he's not about to come out again, snap a quick picture of the logo on the side of the van on my phone and get out of Dodge. My work here is done.

35

Amy

I waited twenty-four agonizing hours, and no word from Simon. I hadn't expected to hear, really; I knew he needed time to process what I'd told him. Or to run away to somewhere where he'd never have to see me again, change his name and his appearance and hide from the crazy lady. I decided to put it down to experience. I liked him, but I'd fucked up. I hadn't been expecting to get into a new relationship and I was just going to have to accept that this one hadn't worked out. It was probably for the best. I already had too many complications in my life.

The problem was that I didn't just like him, I *really* liked him. Ridiculous as it seemed so soon after Jack, I thought we might actually have a future. Okay, so we'd never even spent a whole night together and I had never even been down to his place in Barnes – there were a whole litany of 'never's – but we felt so comfortable together. (Oh God, if my twenty-year-old self could see me thinking 'comfortable' was a good thing! But it is. I don't need drama or hysterics. I've had enough of both.) I knew I had to leave this one up to him, though.

Meanwhile, I distracted myself by alternately getting hysterical with excitement about *Blood Ties* and panicking because I still hadn't heard any more about it. It had been a week since I'd heard I'd got the job, which doesn't seem long in the scheme of things but feels like an age when you want to announce your good news to anyone who'll listen.

I hadn't heard from Sara at all but I decided to give it one more day and then call her. Maybe she was in the middle of a frenzied negotiation on my behalf (although not too frenzied, I found myself hoping, for the hundredth time. I'd heard horror stories of agents losing clients jobs by being too combative). But my hand kept reaching for my phone, despite all my good intentions.

I tried to keep myself busy sweeping the roof and giving the chairs and little table a proper going-over. Even though I was only going to be here for another couple of weeks, the heatwave showed no signs of abating so I told myself I might as well enjoy my outdoor haven while I could, but my heart wasn't really in it.

'I wish you were a dog,' I said to Oscar, about the worst thing I could ever say to him, I imagine. 'At least we could go for a walk.'

I was just trying to convince myself to clear a space in the living room and do a bit of yoga before my body just gave up through underuse when my phone rang. Simon. The way my heart started to pound told me just how much I wanted to hear from him. I took a big breath in then exhaled slowly to try and calm myself down.

'Hi?' It came out as a question.

'Hey,' he said, and from the tone of his voice I knew he wasn't calling to tell me I was a terrible person.

'How's things?'

'Good,' he said. 'I'm feeling like an idiot for over-reacting the other day.'

I sat down on one of the kitchen chairs.

'It's understandable.'

'I'm not going to lie. It makes me uncomfortable. I'm not good with deception —'

I interrupt. 'Me neither. I hate it.'

'But I just wanted to say I understand why you're doing it. And it's nothing to do with me, anyway. I don't have the right to judge what you're doing.'

'I know it must seem ridiculous —'

He laughed, and I thought, *All right, this might be going to be okay.* 'A little.'

'— but it'll all be over in a week or so. I just need to do it this way for my self-esteem.'

'If I'm being honest, it's a bit weird thinking you'd still happily be with him if you hadn't found out.'

I think about this for a second. 'You're right. I would. But you have to believe me when I say I can literally not see what I ever saw in him.' It's true: I can't. When I see him on FaceTime now it's like I'm talking to a pleasant-looking ex-work acquaintance who I don't have anything in common with since he took a job somewhere else.

'But you still care what he thinks of you?'

'Not him. Mel. She's the one I care about. I know what she's like. This whole thing will have become a competition for her. She always has to win. And you've got to understand she's been my best friend since I was eleven . . . was –'

'You're better off without her.'

'I know.'

'Listen, are you around later? I want to come over and make up for stomping off like a stroppy teenager the other day.'

Yes! 'I am. And there's no need. To apologize, I mean. Not to come over. There is a need for that.'

'I assume that's a yes. I got a bit lost.'

'That's a yes.'

Which is how come he's on my doorstep now with a gorgeous pot full of nasturtiums in his hand and a big smile on his face. ('They're for the roof,' he says, as he hands them to me. 'They'll grow up the trellis.') I'm so pleased to see him, for it all to be okay, that I don't bother to remind him I won't be here long enough to see that happen, I just go in for a hug that somehow turns into a bit of a snog. I pull him inside, shut the front door. That's enough entertainment for the neighbours for one evening.

36

Mel

Simon Rigby Interior Design

Lucky for me, Simon Rigby has thoroughly embraced the modern age and has a state-of-the-art website for his business. It even has a photo of said Simon Rigby on it, as if seeing that he has a face might convince potential clients that he's one of the good guys.

And that face is the face of the man I saw rocking up at Amy's new place with a pot plant. The man I saw with his tongue down her throat on the doorstep.

Hello, Simon Rigby.

There's precious little else about him online. He has a Facebook page, but I can hardly ask to be his friend out of nowhere and all that I can see is his profile picture and the company logo – an artsy but tasteful representation of his initials in duck-egg blue on a cream background. The only thing I can do is call him and tell him I'm thinking of completely remodelling my flat and would he like to take a look.

From the testimonials on his website, it looks as if he mainly takes on huge projects on mansion-sized houses, usually in north London. I remind myself that my flat is in a prestigious block, that it might not be worth a fortune but the square footage is decent and the situation very desirable. I can make myself sound more impressive by implying that this is my pied-à-terre and that, most of the time, I reside in a country pile somewhere. What's the worst that can happen? He tells me it's not worth his while?

So I gather up all my courage and all my acting skills and I phone Simon Rigby Interior Design. I'm a bit nervous I might get palmed off on some underling but, when the charming secretary hears that I am interested in a consultation because I'm thinking of giving my home an overhaul, she tells me Simon will call me to talk over the details. It's obviously a small operation he has.

I give her my number. My name: Annabel Phillips. No idea where I got that one from, but it sounds posh. And then I wait.

Not for long, as it turns out. I'm heating up a Waitrose ready meal of Thai green curry when my phone rings. I grab it up from the kitchen counter, take a moment to steady myself.

'Hello.'

A pleasant male voice, warm-sounding, bog-standard London-stroke-Home-Counties accent, neither posh nor not posh, greets me. 'Hi. Is that Annabel Phillips?'

Apparently so. 'It is.'

'Simon Rigby. Of Simon Rigby Interior Design,' he adds, as if I might not recognize the name otherwise.

I channel a smile through my voice. 'Simon! Hi! Thanks for calling me back. So, in a nutshell, I'm looking to do a complete refurb on my flat and, well, I wondered if you'd like to come and take a look?'

I imagine he hears the word 'flat' and not much else because he says, 'We're quite busy at the moment, I'm afraid. When were you thinking of getting the work done?'

You don't get away that easily, mate.

'I'm completely flexible. It can be next month, next year, at short notice if you suddenly realize you've got a gap, I don't care. All I'd ask is that you could come and view it now so I can get a better idea of what can be achieved and the cost. Not that money is an issue here.'

'Sounds good,' he says and I think, *Yes! I've got him.* 'Tell me a bit about the property.'

'Well, it's a twelve-hundred-square feet with one large terrace and a small balcony. Floor-to-ceiling windows. Two bedrooms. Modern. As in nineties. What else?'

'And what are you hoping to achieve?'

I laugh a flirty, girly laugh. 'That's where you come in. It all just feels a bit tired. A bit dated.' I look around guiltily at my state-of-the-art kitchen. 'Actually, that's not fair. It's not dated, it's just conventional. It's the same as everyone else's and that's just a bit . . . dull . . . isn't it?'

How can he resist? 'So you're looking for a radical change?'

'"Radical". I like it. And I need inspiration.'

'Where are you again?'

'Kingston. Near the river.'

'Perfect. I don't live far. I could come over to you before I head over to the site I'm working on now one morning?'

'You're talking about stupidly early, aren't you? Eight o'clock or something like that?'

'I was hoping more for six thirty,' he laughs. 'Or I could come one evening if that suits better?'

'That definitely suits better.'

He takes my details and we work out that actually this evening would be perfect because he's on his way home now, as luck would have it, so he could make a detour and be with me in forty minutes, and I'm spending a rare evening at home while Jack's mum and dad visit their little boy. I can't believe my good fortune.

37

Amy

So that was our first tiff. Not even an argument. Not even a tiff, really, if truth be told, but enough of one that it justified make-up sex, and you know what they say about that. There's no doubt that a moment like that, laying everything out and clearing the air, moves a relationship on. It's as if you unlock another door and step boldly through. Anyway, enough of that, I never said I was a philosopher. Let's just say we had a really good time and I felt closer to him than ever.

And . . . drum roll . . . he stayed the night. It got to about ten o'clock and I was waiting for him to say he had to go, looking forward to it almost, so that I could luxuriate in my own space, playing the evening over and over in my head, when he propped himself up on one elbow, looked and me and said:

'I was thinking I could stay. If . . . I mean . . .' He leaves it hanging out there. I'm touched that he doesn't just assume it's fine. That he has his own insecurities.

'Of course,' I say, deciding that I can have a lie-in after he goes to work at the crack of dawn and do my mental debrief then. 'Oscar likes to sleep in the bed, just so you know.'

'Are you kidding? That's the main reason I'm staying.'

'You made a joke,' I say, smiling at him like a proud parent on sports day.

'I was being serious. I can't have a cat at home because Ruby's allergic, so I need to get my fix some-how.' He raises an eyebrow at me as if to say, 'Am I doing well?'

'Two jokes! If you carry on like this, you could have a whole new career.'

'That's it, that's my whole repertoire.'

'Oh,' I say. I'd forgotten about this, the awkward practicalities. 'I don't have a spare toothbrush.'

He gives me a lazy smile. 'I brought one. Just in case.'

I can't decide whether to be impressed that he had the forethought to plan ahead or offended that he had assumed I would want him to stay. I decide, on bal-ance, I'm impressed.

Apart from the night of Mel's party, when I woke up to find a comatose, fully dressed Jack had climbed in beside me, I haven't spent the night in the same bed as anyone since Jack came to New York for a visit in Feb-ruary. It's weird to think that he was months into his affair with Mel by then because we'd had what I thought was an idyllic three days. We went to a stargazing night on the High Line and I remember thinking it was the most stupidly romantic date ever, up on the train tracks in the middle of the city, holding hands, sipping a glass of wine and looking up at the clear sky. And then a couple started having sex up against the window of one of the smart hotels that's popped up along the way – apparently, this happens often; exhibitionists book particular rooms for this very purpose – and the whole group of us strangers, about ten in all, whooped like a bunch of eight-year-olds until the expert, who had been trying to point out Saturn at the time, shooed us along grumpily. He'd cried when he left the next after-noon. Jack, that is, not the astronomer. Guilt, probably.

Which reminds me. When I spoke to him last (the day before yesterday), he'd been making noises about coming out again, taking a long weekend in June. I imagine it's as much about the pull of the Big Apple as a desire to see me. He loves New York. I'd tried to sound enthusiastic while not actually agreeing to any-thing date-wise.

'The thing is, I've got a couple of big episodes com-ing up,' I'd said. I'd been in the middle of emptying the saucepan under the leak when he'd called – Simon had identified a small crack in the roof where the parapet joined the floor but had yet to have the chance to fix it. 'I should wait for the schedule.'

'We'd still see each other in the evenings, whatever it's like. And I can amuse myself in the daytime.'

'Not if it's night shoots or split days. And . . . you know . . . if it was, then I'd need to sleep . . . it wouldn't be much fun for you.'

'I don't know when I'll get another chance to take time off,' he'd said sulkily.

I replaced the now-empty saucepan. 'Let me at least ask Production if they have any clue what might be happening then.'

If he shelled out for a ticket, that would be his own fault. Although, as he'd probably take the money out of our joint account, I'd be losing out, too, so, hopefully, I can stall him for as long as it takes.

He was down when I spoke to him. Fed up with work. Another of his rivals is being promoted over him – fallout from his no-show at the Icelandic pitch, he has no doubt – and he feels as if his glittering career is faltering. And I actually felt bad. Now I just look on him like a distant elderly relative who I have promised the family I'll keep in touch with I get no pleasure from knowing it's all down to me.

When we're ready to sleep, I'm nervous to see how well Simon and I will fit together. I think about warning him that I hate feeling crowded, can't stand someone draping themselves over me so I can't move and I start to sweat from the heat of the covers and their body, but I decide that might come under the category of TMI, so I wait it out.

I turn on my side away from him and he leans over and kisses the back of my head then settles down behind me, but with just enough of a gap between us. Then he puts a hand on my hip, but lightly, not flopped over like a drunk python, the way Jack used to. I feel the dull thud of a determined cat at the end of the bed and then Oscar settles down in front of me. Simon reaches out a hand and tickles his head and he sighs contentedly. Oscar, not Simon. Or maybe it was both of them.

I have the best sleep of my life. By which I mean I'm out cold for a couple of hours and then one of us wakes the other. It's hard to tell who, because the first thing I know is we're in a clinch. Then we repeat the whole sequence. Twice. After the final time, Simon whispers to me that he has to get up. He had already warned me that he needed to leave the house before seven to get to the site in St John's Wood, and I'd told him in no uncertain terms that he would be fending for himself. Fifteen minutes or so later, after I've heard him creeping around in the bathroom and getting dressed in yesterday's clothes, he sits down beside me to say goodbye. He smells of toothpaste and my citrusy shower gel.

'I've brought you a cup of tea,' he says.

I reach up and circle my arms around his neck.

'Thank you.'

'And I fed Oscar so, hopefully, he'll let you go back to sleep.'

'Oh my God,' I say, flopping back down. 'You might be perfect.'

He smiles and reaches down, pushing the hair back from my face. I'm sure it's sticking up in all directions, that I have yesterday's mascara smeared under my eyes and questionable breath, but I don't care. 'Only "might be"? What else do I need to do? Hoover up before I go?'

'Too noisy. And, besides, I don't have a Hoover. Maybe go round on your hands and knees with a dustpan and brush. Actually, I don't have one of those either. That's why the rug's so great – crumbs just blend in.'

'You are taking that rug with you when you move, aren't you? I mean, I sweated blood for that thing. It's a symbol of my devotion.'

I laugh. 'Of course. That was my main priority: "living room must be big enough to accommodate the rug".'

He leans down and plants his lips on mine. 'I really have to go,' he says when we finally break apart. 'See you tomorrow night.'

'Lovely.'

'Ring me if you get any news.'

'Mmmm,' I say, already feeling the pull of sleep. 'I will.'

I think about how sweet he is to bring me a cup of tea that we both know I'm never going to get round to drinking. By the time I hear the front door close behind him, Oscar is back on the bed, full of breakfast and ready for a nap, so I settle back and start to run through the night in my head, but I'm too tired, too relaxed, too content to stay awake for longer than a couple of minutes. As I drift off, I allow myself to think that, finally, for once, everything is going to be okay. I allow myself to feel happy.

38

Mel

Oh, Simon Rigby, what are you doing?

I don't quite know what I was expecting to happen when I – that is, Annabel Phillips – arranged an appointment to discuss the refurbishment, but it seemed important to find out as much as I could about this man Amy has moved on to. For example, how long it's been going on. Does it predate her finding out about me and Jack? In which case, she's every bit as bad as the pair of us.

It's going to be quite apparent to Simon Rigby that this is a bit of a non-starter of a job as soon as he walks in, because my flat is already pretty perfect, if you ask me. I just need to keep him here long enough to get him talking, find a way to bring up his girlfriend, see where that leads.

I get changed into an outfit that I think says, 'Posh bird'. Floral-print pencil skirt, a cream, short-sleeved cashmere top that I once bought in an effort to look more grown-up but then quickly realized that cream makes me look like a barely warmed-up corpse. But I'm not trying to seduce him (at least, not yet, although that's something to consider), I just need him to believe

I'm who I say I am and feel at ease in my company. I slip on a pair of heeled sandals to finish the outfit off, then I do that thing they tell you to do when you're trying to sell your flat (it is now on the books of two agents, by the way, after Kat singularly failed to get me an offer. Four viewings so far, no bites) and brew up an aromatic pot of coffee. Then I sit at the kitchen island, drinking a glass of red wine for courage, and wait.

Eventually, just when I'm thinking of calling him to see if he's having trouble finding the place, the entry phone buzzes and he's here.

Simon Rigby, on first meeting, is as good-looking as he seemed to be from across the road. Just enough, but not too much. You wouldn't feel as if you had to compete with him for mirror space or that every woman you met was going to throw herself in his direction. He's dressed down in work clothes, but you can tell he's got a bit of style. Firm handshake.

'Would you like a drink? There's wine, or I've got coffee on the go, if you'd prefer . . .'

I lead him through to the kitchen. He looks around, taking the place in.

'Just water would be great,' he says, so I get a bottle out of the fridge and pour him a glassful. 'Nice place.'

'Let me level with you,' I say, intending to do no such thing. 'My husband and I just split up and, to be honest, I don't want to live in the place we decorated together. I want to change everything. Maybe take a couple of walls down, open it up.'

'That makes sense.' He walks around, tapping here and there. 'Do you mind . . . ?'

'Help yourself,' I say. So far, he seems professional and pleasant. I can see why Amy finds him attractive. I wrack my brain for a way to get him on to the subject of her.

'This one could probably come down,' he says, peering through the doorway to the adjoining living room.

'That's what I was thinking. Make it one big space. And I was thinking of maybe making the bathroom bigger by knocking into the hall cupboard.' I take him over and show him where I mean. This would in fact be a great idea if I was staying.

'You'd need to put some more storage in somewhere else, though, probably. How about a wall of cupboards along here?' He indicates the hallway. 'But with invisible fixings, so you can't see them. If you did the whole wall, they'd only need to be about thirty deep and they'd still hold masses of stuff. It's wide enough.'

'I like that idea,' I say, and I do.

'Then you could turn the cupboard into a walk-in shower opening off the bathroom and use the space where the old shower was to maybe put a unit in.'

'Or a bath,' I say, getting into my role. 'I'd really like a claw-foot bath.'

'That would probably work. If you tiled throughout, you wouldn't need to put a door on the shower, and that'd make it feel bigger. What else?'

'The terrace,' I say, knowing I need to keep him there for a bit longer. 'I've always wanted to do something radical with it. Build in a load of seating and maybe a cooking area. Turn it into an oasis.'

We head out to have a look. I have to get him talking about more personal stuff. 'Where do you live yourself?'

'Teddington,' he says. 'So just up the road. Although I seem to spend most of my working life in north London.'

'Word of mouth, I suppose? You do one person's place and they recommend you to a neighbour.'

'Exactly. To be honest, the projects I do are usually on a bigger scale than you're looking for but, if you really are flexible about the timescale, it would be a joy to be doing something a bit closer to home.'

'Keep the other half happy,' I say, and I can't believe I'm coming out with something so cringeworthy. 'Or does she not live out this way, too?'

I'm just thinking what a stupid and intrusive question that must have seemed. If I didn't already know better, why wouldn't I assume he and his girlfriend lived together? Or, indeed, that he didn't have a boyfriend?

Thankfully, Simon Rigby doesn't seem to be bothered. He's happy to indulge me in small talk. And just as well, because the next thing he says blows my mind.

'Wife,' he says, smiling. He has a big, open, honest smile. The smile of a man who has nothing to hide. 'I'm married. And yes, she'd be thrilled to have me home from work before nine occasionally.'

39

Amy

Kat, Greg and I are celebrating. Partly my own good fortune (for about the third time), but mostly because Kat has pulled off a big deal seemingly out of nowhere, by persuading a client they wanted to live in Highgate rather than Notting Hill.

We're in the pub that will be my local when I move. In fairness, it's pretty awful. The music is too loud, the staff snarling and unfriendly. But it has a little, sunny garden out the back, so we park ourselves there, ignoring the other drinkers, who are looking at Kat in her thick batwing glasses and Greg with his quiff as if they've just been transported in on a space ship. I'm looking forward to it going dark just to dim the spotlight on us.

The client exchanged on the thirteen-million-pound house of their dreams today so Kat is due a payday that will be a more than decent salary for the whole year. And the clients are happy, she tells us, because she managed to negotiate the price down from fourteen million, so it's win–win for everyone.

'They just knocked a million pounds off the price?' I say, incredulous.

Kat shrugs. 'At that level, the prices really aren't based on anything except what they think someone might pay.'

I can tell she's pleased with herself, though. This is the biggest deal she's ever made and, naturally, she's hoping the contented purchasers might tell their friends about what a good job she did.

'What if you found someone their perfect house on day one and you made an offer and it was accepted immediately? Would you still earn the same amount?'

'It's never worked out like that yet but, in theory, yes. But I'd still see it through to completion, like I always do, and help them organize moving in or builders or whatever. And, you know, with this lot, it's taken the best part of a year for them to see something they wanted to buy . . .'

'I am very proud of my lovely wife,' Greg says, slightly tipsy. We all chink glasses and a couple at a nearby table glare at us like they want to kill us. I refuse to let it dampen my mood.

'Here's to everything going well for once. It must be karma.'

'I'm also very proud of you, my lovely friend,' Greg adds, and Kat beams at me. I bask in their affection and my own good fortune for all of – what? – ninety seconds? And then my phone rings. Sara.

'It's my agent,' I say. 'I'd better take it.'

'Amy?' she says, the second I answer. Something about her sounds off.

'Hi . . . Is everything –'

'Sorry for calling you so late,' she interrupts. I look at my phone. It's twenty to eight. 'But . . . I don't know how to say this . . . I don't know what's going on . . .'

I feel the blood drain from my face. I put my drink down and press my phone against my ear to drown out the chatter.

'What? What's happened?'

Kat and Greg must have realized something is wrong because they're staring at me, concerned looks on their faces. I indicate that I'm going to go and stand out on the street. I don't think I can hear whatever it is she has to say with an audience.

'It's . . . God, I don't even know where to start. It's *Blood Ties*. It's . . . well, I've been trying to get hold of them, obviously, because you're meant to be starting in a week and I'd heard nothing. Nothing. I assume the scripts haven't arrived?'

'No. I would have told you.' I sit down on someone's front doorstep. I'm worried I might just fall over otherwise.

'Shit. So I've been calling that Carrie. At Sunflower. Because hers was the only number I had. But I just left message after message and she didn't return my call, and then, a couple of days ago, the number went dead.'

I hear myself let out a yelp. I know exactly where this is going.

'So I started trying to find another number for Sunflower and there's just no record of them anywhere. I know they're supposed to be a new company and everything but . . . Then I started asking around. No one's even heard of them, Amy. And I just got off the phone with a friend of mine who works at the BBC. I asked her to check the drama-commissioning slate, just in case it had changed title or they were making it under an umbrella company or something, but she said there's nothing that could possibly be it. Not even anything in the early stages of development, let alone something that's about to go into production . . .'

I feel numb. I have no idea what to say, how to react. An image of Mel's wedding to Sam flashes into my head. The church decked out in a riot of sunflowers. I remember her saying, *They just make you feel so happy, don't they?*

'Are you still there?' Sara says eventually.

I manage to say, 'Yes, I am.'

'I'm so sorry. I have no idea what's going on or who this Carrie is, but it's as if this is some kind of a hoax . . .'

'That's why they hired me without meeting me,' I say. It's all becoming clear. 'That's why I couldn't find fucking 291A Camden High Street. Because it isn't there.'

'It doesn't make sense,' she says. 'Why would someone do this?'

I know why. Mel must be on to me. Somehow, she's found out I'm back. That I know about her and Jack. She's decided to fight fire with fire, and she knows exactly what will hurt me most.

I ignore her question. 'So that's definitely it? There is no *Blood Ties*?'

I hear her inhale slowly. 'I don't think so, no. Does someone have it in for you, do you think?'

'I have no idea,' I say. Despite everything, I don't know Sara well enough to begin to tell her even the half of it. And I don't want her to start thinking I'm a liability to have as a client.

'Or me, maybe. Nothing like this has ever happened before . . . I really am sorry, Amy. Something else will come along, I promise.'

'It's okay,' I say, but the traffic is so loud I doubt she can hear me.

On autopilot, I go back to where Kat and Greg are sitting. Their concerned expressions are too much for me. I slam my phone down on the table so hard the glass cracks.

40

I'm back at the call centre. Yesterday, I phoned the property company and told them I could no longer take the flat. At first, I thought they were going to refuse to return my deposit and first month's rent (as is their policy) so I cried and pleaded and begged and, in the end, the very sweet woman on the other end of the phone promised to try to sort it out somehow, although she did say she would at the very least have to offer the landlord a couple of weeks' money so that he didn't lose out completely. Then I called not-so-nice Fiona and asked if I could change my mind about moving out and she, thankfully, said, 'Fine,' mainly, I think, because finding someone new would be too much hassle. So I'm back where I started.

Oh, and I told the supervisor at Huntley Media Marketing I'll do as many days as she can give me.

The rest of yesterday was spent alternately crying and throwing things across the room. How could Mel be this cruel? Okay, so I had let slip to all her friends, family and colleagues on Facebook about her affair with John and I'd ruined her prospect of a romantic weekend in Reykjavik WITH MY BOYFRIEND, but that was it. Nothing she couldn't get past. So, maybe

I'd made her job a bit uncomfortable for a while. But no one would have actually thought the rumour was true. And she hated her job, anyway. She was always saying she needed an excuse to leave. And let's not forget I only did any of that in the first place because I found out she was sleeping WITH MY BOYFRIEND.

Did Jack know? Were they doing this together? I can't imagine it somehow. Whatever I now think of him, I believe that guilt would be his overriding emotion if he knew I was on to them. He's not a malicious person. Weak, disloyal, sneaky, maybe, but not sadistic. And I think Mel knows that.

Plus, there's no way in hell she would want him to find out about her and John.

I went back to Kat and Greg's when we left the pub shortly after I got Sara's call. Both of them were steaming on my behalf.

'See,' Kat said, clicking down the street on the way home through King's Cross. Her face was red with indignation. 'I told you we shouldn't have let her off so easily.'

'How would doing more stuff to her have helped?' I said, still through a veil of tears. 'I should have just confronted them both when I found out and then never had to deal with either of them again.'

'Because then she would have got exactly what she wanted,' Kat said. I looked around and Greg, a full foot taller than her and eight inches on me, was struggling to keep up with the pair of us. It was as if we were powered by rage.

'Jack?'

She looked as me as if I was crazy. 'Your life. Or, at least, if she can't actually have your life, then she doesn't want you to be having it either. Sam left her, so why should you be planning your wedding? Her job sucks, so why should you be doing everything she's ever dreamed of?'

'She's right,' Greg piped up from behind us. He sounded out of breath. 'I mean, it's not as if she hasn't got form.'

As the first of our guests arrived for our Christmas party, we were all already half cut. We'd hit that happy 'I love you so much, you're my best friends ever' place, overcome by warm, fuzzy, sentimental happiness. Except for Mel. Not that she wasn't happy, she just wasn't drinking after that first glass of punch. She told me she wanted to make sure she was on her best behaviour. She wanted to try and make a better impression on my friends. She had realized how important they were to me and that she needed to make an effort. I threw my arms around her and hugged her.

'I'm so glad you're here.'

'Me, too,' she'd said, hugging me back. 'I miss you.'

What I remember of the party itself was noise, chaos, singing, dancing, drinking. Lights and tinsel everywhere. One of our neighbours knocking and asking us to turn the music down, then accepting the offer of a drink. Last seen wearing reindeer antlers and singing along to 'Barbie Girl'. Every now and then, the five of us residents would find ourselves in the same space and another group hug would materialize out of nowhere. Whenever I looked for Mel, I found her easily. She always stood out but, tonight, she was especially radiant. I remember her glowing in the light from the candles we had lit. Skin luminous, hair on fire, smiling, smiling, smiling.

Some of us were drunker than others. I realized I'd hit my limit early on and loaded up on water while I waited for the spirits to kick in, before I carried on. Kieron, Tom and Pia must have done the same, or else they all had a far greater tolerance than me, because none of them ever tipped over from happy drunk to car crash. Alistair, on the other hand, who had always been a lightweight where alcohol was concerned, was slurring by ten o'clock, but we were all so used to seeing him like that by this point that we just rolled our eyes affectionately and left him to it. He was also, bizarrely, the only one of us who never suffered from hangovers, getting up bright-eyed at the crack of dawn the morning after and clearing up the detritus while the rest of us pulled the covers over our heads, groaning.

I remember seeing Mel chatting to him and them both laughing. I remember being so thankful that she'd let her guard down with him and given him a chance. Privately, she might still refer to him as 'nice but dim', but I remember hoping she'd come to realize what a good bloke he was – they all were, but Alistair especially. He had only ever been friendly towards her. This was the boy who picked up worms or beetles from the pavement and moved them out of harm's way before anyone trod on them, for God's sake. He helped old ladies across roads and once travelled halfway across London to return a wallet he'd found in the street. He was incapable of maliciousness.

And then it was later and the numbers were starting to thin out a bit as people headed off to find night buses. A few had already crashed out on the floor in Kieron's room. The stragglers were crammed into the kitchen or on the stairs.

'Have you seen Al?' Pia was leaning against the sink. I was hunting through open cans of lager for one that might contain some liquid.

'He's probably passed out.'

'He's such a lightweight,' she said affectionately.

'I'm knackered,' I said. 'Do you think this lot are staying?'

'God knows. I'm just going to leave them to it in a minute.'

'Me, too.' I looked around. 'Where's Mel?'

Pia shrugged. 'I haven't seen her for ages.'

'Maybe she got lucky,' I said, laughing. It felt as if life was going to be so much easier now the ice wall between my friends had thawed.

Pia pulled a face. 'I hope for your sake they're not in your room.'

'Oh God. If they are, I'm getting in with you.'

She followed me as I mounted the stairs, happy to leave the few remaining revellers to it. We stopped as we got to the door to her and Alistair's room. 'Really,' she said. 'Come back down if Mel's got someone in there. Al's such a gent I'm sure he wouldn't mind moving on to the floor.'

She leaned forward unsteadily, gave me a hug. 'Hopefully, she's just passed out as well. Although she wasn't drinking –'

I stopped dead as Pia opened the door to the bedroom and I saw a flash of copper, a lightning strike of ghostly white skin. Mel, stark naked, was sitting astride Alistair, his hands enthusiastically grabbing at her boobs. She knew we were there, I had no doubt about it. She hesitated just enough to make it obvious she had heard the door opening. But she made no effort to cover up. She just threw herself into the task even more enthusiastically, head back, eyes closed. I stood there, rooted to the spot. My first thought was that Pia shouldn't be seeing this. I went to shut the door again but she stuck out an arm and stopped me.

'No,' she said. And she must have said it just loudly enough for it to penetrate Alistair's fug of booze and bliss because he opened his eyes wide and then sat bolt upright, half throwing Mel across the bed.

'Shit, no!' he said, as if he'd only just realized what he was doing. He grabbed the covers and pulled them up over himself. Mel, on the other hand, sat up and stretched like a contented cat then smiled a beatific smile directly at Pia.

'Awkward,' she said, with a fake little laugh. I hated her in that moment.

'Pia . . .' Alistair said pleadingly, but she turned on her heels and walked back down the stairs.

'Put some clothes on, Mel, for fuck's sake,' I hissed before I followed.

41

Mel

So, what to do with my shiny new piece of information?

Obviously, I need to let Amy know. She's always had a rule for herself: no married men. She stuck to it, too. So I'm pretty sure she's clueless about the lovely Mrs Rigby. Georgie, she's called, by the way.

I remember there was this bloke once. A couple of years after I'd moved up to London. Amy was in a play with him at some tiny community theatre in Stoke Newington or somewhere. One of those things that no one goes to see but the actor hopes they might get a decent review in the local paper which they can quote on their CV. I can't remember what he was called but I do know that he wasn't even married, he just lived with his girlfriend, and he did a lot of that 'It'll bring more intensity to our performance' kind of crap, which Amy lapped up, as if she were a thirsty camel who'd found an oasis in a desert. She wouldn't cross the line, though, however much he pushed. Even when I encouraged her just to go for it, to think of it like a holiday romance. What happens in Stoke Newington stays in Stoke Newington, and all that.

'It's the worst thing you can do to another woman,' she'd said to me haughtily.

I'd just shrugged and said, 'You don't even know her, what do you care?'

'God, Mel,' she'd said, with a roll of her eyes. 'Imagine if every woman thought like that. We have to look out for each other.'

She'd announced this in the full knowledge that I had far fewer scruples where things like that were concerned, by the way. Got up on her high horse and gave me a lecture about how, if no woman ever knowingly slept with a married man, then no other woman would ever have to go through finding out her husband was cheating on her or something. It didn't quite make sense to me, because isn't the whole point that attached people don't usually announce that they are when they're trying to cop off with someone?

So, I'm one hundred million per cent certain that, when she finds out, she'll dump him. But it'd be great if she was *really* into him first. If she'd started to think this was the man who was going to save her from her heartbreak over Jack. On the other hand, I don't want to wait so long that he develops a conscience or, more likely, starts to worry about getting caught and bails. It's only fun if she thinks he's the one. If it really puts her principles to the test.

Other things I found out about Simon Rigby and his lovely family are: wife Georgie makes ceramics (that sounds like a made-up career to me. Something someone does as a hobby but tries to fool the rest of us into thinking they actually make a living from it, not just that they dabble a bit and sell one pot every three years); his daughter is twelve and called Ruby; and Georgie is really keen to leave London and move down to the West Country for a gentler pace of life.

'What would you do, then?' I asked sweetly. 'Move your business down there?'

'Not sure,' he'd said. 'It's got momentum here. Half of my work is recommendations. More, probably. It would take me a long time to build that up again.'

'How would that work, though?' I knew that was far too personal a question to ask someone I'd known for fifteen minutes, but I had nothing to lose. And he didn't seem to mind.

'No idea. Split my time? Employ more people and delegate? There'd be a way, if we definitely decided to do it.'

Nothing in the way he spoke about his situation implied that he wasn't happy with his wife, that he thought she was a pain in the arse for wanting to move them halfway across the country. And he didn't flirt with me. Not a bit. The image he projected was that of a happily married man. Which probably meant he was experienced at what he was doing. That he'd done it more than once.

He left after about half an hour, promising that he would come back to me with some ideas and an approximation of how much various options might cost.

Annabel Phillips thanked him very much for his time and told him she was looking forward to seeing what he came up with. When he left, I started shaking. I'd pulled it off. It gave me a buzz I haven't had in years. Stage fright mixed with adrenaline mixed with euphoria.

As soon as he was out of the door, I googled Georgie Rigby Ceramics, obviously, and came up with one Georgie Rigby-Taylor who makes godawful misshapen-looking vases that are available to buy – according to her website – for hundreds of pounds each. Of course, there's no evidence any of them have ever actually sold. There's a picture of her, though, her face clay-streaked, tendrils of hair falling into her eyes, and she's attractive in that blonde, fragile, artsy kind of way. Nothing like Amy, so Simon clearly doesn't have a type. I felt an unprecedented pang of pity for beautiful, wan Georgie, immersed in her ugly art, oblivious to her husband's betrayal. For now, that is. Sadly, I'm not sure how long her delusion can last.

42

Amy

Simon is burning with anger on my behalf. I've never really seen him cross before and it somehow takes the edge off my own rage, as if I've handed over the baton. He wants me to take him to Mel. He wants to tell her what he thinks of her.

And, I'm not going to lie, it's tempting. I like imagining the shock on her face when I turn up, new boyfriend in tow. Someone who cares about me. Someone who'll fight my corner. But I'm not going to let it happen. I don't want him involved in that other, messy side of my life. Instead, I allow him to make a fuss of me, bringing me a takeaway from the local Lebanese restaurant and making soothing noises about how something else will come along and blow the fake job out of the water. I don't for a minute believe him but I appreciate the effort.

He'd turned up with two huge outdoor candles, as pleased with himself as a five-year-old bringing home the cake he's made in school. Each was inside an intricate crimson metal lantern. The smell was heavenly – jasmine or honeysuckle – even before they were lit.

'Where did you find those?' I asked, as he lined up the ladder and started his ascent. 'How dare you? I bought them,' he said, mock-indignant. 'Selfridges' finest.'

'I love them.'

I followed him up with the takeaway and a bottle of wine.

'Nice,' he said, indicating the nasturtiums that were now planted up in one of the long planters. That was a hard day's work, lugging the bag of soil up the ladder, but I wanted to show willing.

'Well, I'm stuck here now. I thought I might as well. Maybe I should stay at yours tomorrow night?' I say now, as we lean back, looking up at the sky, stuffed from the meal and two glasses of wine down. 'Just for a change.'

'My sister and her kid are coming to stay tomorrow night,' he says, pulling an apologetic face. 'I forgot to tell you. So I won't be around at all.'

'Doesn't matter.'

My mobile rings. Usually, I turn the volume down whenever Simon and I are together. It's easier to ignore my other life if it's not shouting in my face. But tonight, I forgot. I pick it up.

'It's her.'

'Answer it,' he says, and then immediately follows up with 'Don't! I was joking!'

'Yeah, don't give up the day job.' I let the phone ring out.

'God, you really know how to crush a man's dreams.'

I nuzzle back on my chair and he reaches a hand out and takes one of mine.

'What time do you have to go?' I know he has a meeting much nearer to his home first thing. He looks at his watch. 'Half an hour?'

'Sex or dessert? There's half a cheesecake in the fridge from when Kat and Greg came over.'

He smiles a lascivious smile. 'What flavour?'

'Popcorn and something. God knows. She made it from some seventies American recipe. It's unbelievably good.'

He raises an eyebrow. 'That, then. We can have sex any time.'

'My thoughts exactly.'

As I spoon the creamy dessert into bowls, I try not to get too excited about the fact that Simon and I seem to have reached the 'couple' stage. Not the 'been together for years, barely even notice the other person any more' phase, or even the 'secure enough to break wind loudly in their presence' phase, thankfully, but we've started to feel like a pair, not just two people who fancy the pants off each other. I like it.

On Friday, Kat takes the day off and we mooch around the Courtauld Institute in an attempt, in her words, to 'take my mind off things'.

'How come I'm back at square one again?'

'Is there something else you could do other than the

call centre?' she says, pushing her glasses up her nose. 'Something that pays better?'

'Nothing that would let me go off and audition at a moment's notice. Or where I could just call them up in the morning and say I had another job for a few days and they wouldn't care. Maybe this is it. Maybe now's the time I have to acknowledge defeat and give up.'

'No!' she shouts, and I jump. As do two American tourists who were gazing intently at a Van Gogh a second ago. 'Not yet. Not while *Murder in Manhattan* is still going out and you're still in it! Anything could happen. You can come back and stay with us for free for as long as you want if it all gets too much.'

I lean over and give her a hug. As usual, she squirms away. 'You're a really good friend,' I say. 'I love you to bits, I really do.'

Kat, never one for compliments or sentimentality, blushes a deep red. 'Shut up. You, too. Whatever.'

'It has to stop,' I say, sinking down on to one of the benches. 'Whatever's going on between me and Mel, I should never have started it.'

Kat snorts. '*She* started it. Her and Jack. Don't ever forget that.'

'Who cares? It doesn't matter who started it. In the greater scheme of things.'

Kat's not giving up that easily. 'Well, you have to finish it. Once and for all. We just have to think of how.'

*

There was no big row. No *Jeremy Kyle*-style accusations and recriminations. But everything changed. Mel, possibly realizing that she had gone too far even for her, left to go home early in the morning. I had feigned sleep when she'd come upstairs a few minutes after me, and again in the morning when I heard her get up, even though, at one point, she had shaken my shoulder. What was she going to do?

'I know you can hear me, Amy,' she had said, sitting on the bed beside me. 'It wasn't all my fault. He was all over me like a fucking octopus. He's the one that made promises to Pia, not me.'

I ignored her. Stifled my desire to say what I knew to be true, that she'd gone into overdrive to seduce him. That Pia was his first real girlfriend, he had zero experience with casual sex and the drink had clouded his judgement. Of course, he'd thought all his Christmases had come at once when someone like her had basically offered him a quick one with no strings attached. Yes, he'd behaved appallingly, yes, he was the one with the girlfriend, but I knew, without a doubt, that Mel had been the driving force. That this was her way of getting back at Pia for her Centre Stage comment. That her whole weekend – the charm offensive, the not drinking while the rest of us partied – had been building up to it. It was a side of her I'd never seen. A truly vindictive side. And, I won't lie, I was shocked by the cold calculation behind it.

I crossed my fingers under the covers and hoped she would just leave. I had no idea how I was going to face my friends and having Mel there would make it ten times harder.

'Okay, I'm going,' I heard Mel say. 'I'll call you tomorrow.'

I waited until I heard her clumping down the stairs and only then did I open my eyes to check she had taken her bag with her.

There was no Alistair already downstairs cleaning the house and no sign of Pia either. I threw myself into tidying the kitchen instead, a kind of penance. After about half an hour of my shifting half-full cans of lager from one spot to another without achieving anything, Kieron shuffled in, bleary-eyed.

'You okay?' he said, putting his arms around me from behind.

'You heard what happened, then?'

'Pia crashed on my floor.'

I wiped my hands down the front of my T-shirt, turned around and buried my face in his chest.

'It's not your fault,' he said gently. For all his front, Kieron could be very sweet sometimes.

'But she's my friend. She wouldn't have even been here if it wasn't for me,' I snivelled.

He stroked my hair. 'Al's an adult. She might have hit on him, but he went along with it.'

'He never would have, though, not in a million years, unless she had made all the running.'

'She's a complete bitch, don't get me wrong. I'm just saying, don't blame yourself.'

'I know.'

He broke away, weighed the water in the kettle. 'I'm making tea for everyone. There were nine people in my room at the last count. Want one?'

'Thanks.' I sat down at the kitchen table. I knew I wasn't to blame but I felt wretched. I made a decision there and then. Mel and I were done. We might have a long history, but history wasn't everything. In the past two years, I'd found a family. A bunch of people for whom someone else's success was a thing to be celebrated, not a threat. Who supported and encouraged each other. I felt happier and more confident than I'd ever felt – well, not this morning, obviously, but in general. I didn't need Mel belittling me. I didn't need to always play the role of wing girl to her life. I had my own to get on with.

And then Pia walked into the kitchen, eyes red raw. She stopped dead when she saw me.

'She's gone,' I said. I felt as if I needed to let her know that right away.

Pia just stared at me, a look of absolute loathing on her face. Then she turned and walked out again without saying a word.

43

'What does Mel care most about?' Kat is sitting on the sofa, knees curled under her, baby-blue-and-white polka-dot pyjamas on. I'm staying at theirs because I can't go blowing all my non-existent money on cabs up to north London from Bloomsbury every time we have an evening out and I'd really rather not negotiate the night buses on my own.

'Herself,' Greg says. He puts a cup of peppermint tea in front of me, and one in front of Kat. We're revisiting our favourite topic, although I'm struggling to care. I just want to move on, forget about her.

'Status, money, being better than everyone else,' Kat counts off on her fingers.

'Okay, maybe we should look at it like this. What do we have on her?' Greg sets his tea down and flops on to the armchair. Because it's an austere G-Plan design with seemingly no give, he more or less bounces straight up again. On a happier evening, I'd laugh. 'We know about her and Jack, and she obviously now knows we know . . .'

Kat pushes her glasses up her nose. 'There's her and John. We could make her work life very miserable . . .'

'Her work life already is miserable,' I say unenthusiastically. 'She hates her job. She'd probably just leave and live off the cash she's going to get when the flat sells.'

'And Jack would dump her, let's not forget that.'

'I don't honestly think she'd care that much,' I say, warming to my theme. 'She only wanted him because I had him.'

'We have a copy of the email she sent Shaz telling her about John,' Kat says. 'And the cringy DMs between her and Jack. I still have a set of keys to her flat. It doesn't add up to much.'

My mobile suddenly bursts into life. I grab it. 'Fuck, it's her again.'

Kat and Greg both look at me, wide-eyed. 'I still haven't called her back since the other day.'

'We could . . .' Kat waves at the door, as if to say, 'We could leave you to it.' I can't face talking to her, though. What's the point? Why go through with the charade when we both know that's what it is?

'No.'

So we all sit there, staring at my phone until it rings out. A few seconds later, it beeps to say I have a message. I assume it's just Mel leaving a voicemail but then I glance at the screen and see she's sent me a photo. I pick it up.

'Hi, hun, I'm thinking about getting some work done on the flat before I sell,' it says. 'I thought about using this guy.'

I jab at the screen to see the large version of the picture. It's a business card. Simon's business card. Simon Rigby Interior Design.

'What the . . . ?'

I hand my mobile over to Greg, who's sitting nearest to me. He peers at the screen.

'Fucking hell, what's she up to now?'

'She just wants me to know she knows about him,' I say, although I feel there must be more to it than that. 'Maybe she's going to tell Jack, but she must know I wouldn't care about that any more.'

'Or she's going to try and seduce him herself,' Kat pipes up. 'That's her style, right?'

I let out a half-laugh. It's so childish. So teenage. 'Well, good luck to her. There's no way –'

'Of course not,' Greg says. 'Simon would never . . .' He doesn't seem able to finish the sentence.

'He already knows she's a psycho. I just need to tell him she might be getting in touch with him. He'll avoid her like the plague.' Even as I'm saying it, I feel uneasy. Thrown back to my insecure self at fifteen, at twenty. I've seen the power of Mel in action when she's decided she wants someone. It was one of the things I first loved about Jack, I remember now. That he seemed immune to her charms. At least, for a few years. I remember the first time I introduced them, nervous because I wanted her to like him but also because I knew she'd go into flirt overdrive, as she always did whenever she met one of my boyfriends. And she did. Jack, though, had seemed oblivious. He'd been friendly and polite but he'd kept all his attention on me. Later, when we were having a debrief about how the evening had gone, he'd said, 'I know she's your best mate, but she's a bit full on,' and I'd realized that he hadn't been oblivious at all, he'd just chosen not to acknowledge what she was doing.

And Simon is a grown-up. He's not about to have his head turned by some woman throwing herself at him.

Kat must catch the expression on my face. 'He would never,' she echoes emphatically.

'Why don't you ring him and warn him?' Greg says, as if Mel were a crazed knife woman skulking about in the bushes outside his house.

'He'll be with his sister and her kid.'

'So? Just so he can give his office the heads-up.'

'You're right,' I say. I hit Simon's number, but it rings and rings. Eventually, voicemail kicks in. I don't want to leave a message because I don't really know what to say. Watch out, Mel's after you? Don't let your office book you any appointments with strange women? Run away!!!?

'I'll talk to him in the morning.'

'If it wasn't for the fact she's clearly barking, this would actually be funny,' Kat says as we say goodnight. 'The fact that she still thinks making a play for someone's boyfriend is the ultimate revenge.'

'No one could accuse her of being emotionally mature,' Greg says, knocking back the last of his tea.

'How can she do this, though? How can she hate me so much? Do you think she always did?'

Kat leans over and hugs me, a very unKatlike

gesture. 'She doesn't hate you. She just knows she's been caught out so she's using every weapon in her arsenal to defend herself.'

Later, in Kat and Greg's spare bed, I think about the perfect flat I had been about to move into, the job I thought I was just about to begin that wouldn't just have sorted out my financial woes but would have jumpstarted my career back into life, about the fact that I can't even enjoy the tiny bit of success I've just had with *Murder in Manhattan*, because Mel has made sure of that. About how my life since I first met her in form 1A has been all about showing her off to her best advantage, dimming any light that might accidentally come my way and retraining it towards her.

And about how, now, she's trying to mess with my new relationship.

And I decide that's it. Enough is enough. It's time for me to be the grown-up.

44

Pia moved out within days. Alistair moped about, look-ing haunted, trying and failing to make contact with her, hanging around outside her lectures and then, when he found out where she'd moved to, her new shared flat. She wanted nothing to do with him. With any of us. She stopped coming to rehearsals and, on the rare occasion when our paths crossed, she would nod a terse hello and walk off quickly before I could say any more. I tried to speak to her several times but she made it clear she wasn't interested.

I offered to go, too, but the others wouldn't hear of it. They made it very clear that Mel wasn't welcome, though, and I didn't argue. For the first time since I first met her, I had no interest in seeing her.

But the conversations about our collective future, about keeping the house on and staying together, ended abruptly. I knew that they were still planning on sharing, the three of them – Kieron, Tom and Alistair – because I would walk in on them talking about who they might ask to move in to make up the numbers. On the surface, everything between us was fine but their hushed silence spoke volumes.

Eventually, as the Easter holidays loomed and so

did my finals, they plucked up the courage to tell me. Tom was the nominated spokesman and, over a cup of tea at our kitchen table, he broke it to me gently that two of the first year Dram Soc members, a couple, were going to be joining them in the house in July. When I say he broke it to me gently, what he actually said was:

'So, Johnny and Caroline are moving in. Sorry. You can stay until the end of June, though.'

I was grateful for his honesty. It was easier than trying to pussyfoot about, throwing around platitudes about how we'd all stay friends and nothing would change. I already knew how much it had.

I knew I had to let any fantasies I'd been harbouring about him and me die a natural death.

I had the lead in the end-of-term production of *Hedda Gabler* – the last one I would be eligible to appear in, as summer-term shows were traditionally for first and second years only. The rest of us were supposed to be concentrating on our finals. Tom had a part, too, which could have been awkward but, in actual fact, was fine. Because they were nice people. They didn't bear a grudge. They just didn't want to live with me any more in case I invited my vindictive loose-cannon mate up again.

I mostly stayed in my room, studying for my exams and going over my lines. I arranged to move into a tiny box room in a house in Cricklewood with four girls from my course I had barely exchanged two words with in three years. I wrote countless letters to agents, asking them to come and watch my final performance, followed them up with phone calls, got nowhere.

In the end, not one came to see me, but someone who Tom had persuaded to watch him offered to sign me up instead. They were a tiny company and Christian was only just starting out, having worked there as an assistant for three years, but I didn't care. They were a bona fide theatrical agency and Christian was a bona fide agent. I happily agreed to pay them twelve per cent of the fee for any acting job they ever got me – which, as it turned out, added up to a big fat nothing in the four years they represented me, because everything they found me was either unpaid or a split of a profit so pitiful they couldn't bring themselves to ask for any of it. Not that it mattered. It was experience, and I could, and did, earn a basic living in other ways.

Elated as I was, I realized I had no one to celebrate with. Kieron, Alistair and Tom congratulated me in a way that seemed heartfelt (and also slightly awkward, because Christian had not extended his offer of representation to Tom and neither had anyone else), but they didn't suggest we throw a party or even all get drunk in the Student Union together. I mentioned my stroke of luck to one of my soon-to-be new housemates and she just looked at me blankly and said, 'What does an agent do?' and then, when I explained, she looked as interested as if I'd just read her the specifications from the back of a manual for a fridge freezer. I felt horribly alone.

I hadn't seen Mel since Christmas and had avoided all her calls and emails for months now, except for the most perfunctory responses here and there. I'd sent her a card on her birthday and received a gushing response. It was obvious she wanted to make it up with me and I started to think that maybe she had learned her lesson. I needed a friend and, with Pia gone and my college days about to be over any second, it was suddenly clear to me that I had no one. That is, I had lots of friends, but no soulmate. I started to remember all the good stuff about Mel and, gradually, to forget the bad. In her absence, I rewrote her into the friend I had always wished she was.

I started to panic about my new, square, neat room with square, neat Karen, Ann, Jenny and Sue. Their names were as dull as they were. They had already tried to engage me in conversations about cooking rotas and drawing up a schedule for household chores. I seemed to spend half my life abruptly turning corners when I saw them approaching from the other direction, and that was before we'd even moved in together. I could feel my exciting new bohemian life – a budding actress in one of the coolest cities in the world – slipping out of my grasp. Karen, Ann, Jenny and Sue would wear me down, chipping away at my soul until the next thing I knew I'd be working in a bank, wearing court shoes and engaged to a middle manager named Ian.

I needed an antidote. I needed a Mel in my life. So, when she sent me an email saying she thought Centre

Stage had taught her everything it could and she was thinking of leaving a year early, I found myself suggesting she move up to London and we live together, just like we'd always planned, before I'd even thought about what I was doing. She sent me a reply within seconds.

'Yes! Me and you against the world! I love it!'

And that was it. We were best friends again.

45

'She actually sent you a photo of my card?' Simon says, picking up on what, to me, is the least important point in the whole scenario. I have to admit I'm a bit irritated. We should just be able to laugh off the fact that Mel has more or less announced she's going to make a play for him. If he's taking it seriously, then I'm going to start to feel as if I should.

'Well, yeah, but she could have got hold of that easily if she's been watching what I've been doing –'

'She's not a redhead, is she? Skinny? Lives in Kingston?'

I put the latte I've just bought – from a little coffee shop that I've found in the row of shops I can see from the roof, an oasis of civilization that also includes an organic grocer's and what must be one of the last independent bookshops known to man – on the wall in front of a house to give him my full attention. 'You've *met* her?'

'She got me round last week. Said she wanted to give her flat a radical makeover.'

'You didn't end up in bed with her, did you?' I say, attempting a joke. He doesn't laugh.

'Of course I didn't.'

'I know. Jesus, lighten up.'

I hear him sigh down the phone and I imagine him pressing the heel of his hand into his forehead, the way he does when he's stressing about something. 'Sorry,' he says. 'It's just . . . I mean, I'm not being unsympathetic, but I don't really want to be dragged into your feud.'

'You won't be. I was only telling you so you could avoid her if she called.'

'Bit late for that,' he says, but thankfully with a laugh.

'But . . . if she gets in touch again, you'll know. I don't think she will. She's just trying to freak me out.'

A day later, and I'm standing outside Jack's office on Paul Street, trying to pluck up the courage to go in. It's time. This whole thing has gone on long enough and I need to bring it all to an end. Starting with Jack.

Lately, I've almost forgotten all about Jack, in the face of Hurricane Melissa. I certainly can't find it in me to be angry with him any more because I just don't care enough. What he did – is doing – is disloyal, mean, thoughtless, but I can't even say it's hurtful because I don't feel hurt by him. He's just a man I never should have stayed with for so long, I never should have agreed to marry. I can't even imagine what I was thinking.

I've been here so many times before, the tall, pale stone building with the big cartoonish sculptures of brightly coloured fish in the foyer windows. It screams

'We're creative, we don't take ourselves too seriously!' Jack's office is on the fifth floor, but I'm hoping I don't have to go up. I don't want to have to play this scene out in front of his colleagues.

As I'm standing outside, plucking up courage, a young couple walk past and do a double take. I see them talking excitedly to one another, looking back, and I remember again that I'm temporarily a tiny bit famous. Among a certain, very small demographic. It's bizarre, to say the least. I'm about to head into the building when I see they've turned around and they're now heading towards me. I have to make that split-second decision: do I carry on going where I was going and leave them hanging (and possibly look rude), or do I wait, thus looking as if I expect them to be on their way to ask me for a selfie (and therefore full of myself), or, even worse, like an idiot when they walk straight past me with no idea who I am. Luckily, I'm spared when the girl says:

'Are you her? You are, aren't you?' I should point out that this happened to me once in New York and I said, 'Yes,' and it turned out they thought I was someone off *Game of Thrones*. They were quite pissed off with me when they realized, as if it had been me who'd stopped them and demanded we all take a picture together. So this time I go with, 'Maybe.'

'You are. You're Yvon from *Murder in Manhattan*. Oh my God, we love that show . . .'

She burbles on while her boyfriend fumbles with his phone, and then they wrestle me into position between

347

them and he holds his hand out and snaps a shot of the three of us. It's all over in a few seconds and then I'm dumped back down in the middle of my real life.

A middle-aged woman with two big bags of groceries and a tired look of resignation on her face is standing at the bus stop a few metres away.

'Are you famous or something?' she calls over. I imagine if I thought I really was I'd be mortified.

'No. It's, um . . . not really.'

I turn on my heels and head inside before she can quiz me any more.

Jack swoops into reception, looking around impatiently to see who it is who's dragged him from his desk. Luckily, the receptionist is new since I was last here, and she clearly isn't a *Murder in Manhattan* aficionado because when I tell her I'm an old friend of his from uni and I want to surprise him, she doesn't bat an eyelid.

His face when he spots that it's me is a picture. Or more like a short film. Shock. Pleasure. Realization. Guilt. Terror. I'm actually touched that there was a moment in there when he was happy to see me.

'What . . . ?' he says.

'Surprise!'

'I . . . what on earth are you doing here?' I see him reach into his pocket for, I presume, his phone, and then stop himself. The main reason I didn't announce my arrival was because I didn't want to give him the chance to call Mel before I've said what I have to say.

'I need to talk to you. It's important.'

'Is everything okay? When did you get here? Can I just . . .' He indicates upstairs. 'I should . . .'

'Just get Reception to phone up and tell whoever you need to tell. I know you weren't in a meeting. I got her to check.'

He flusters a bit, realizes he has no option. 'They won't miss me for a minute.'

'Let's go and sit in the park.' I don't wait for him to agree, just walk out, and he follows a few paces behind. Neither of us says anything until we reach Finsbury Square and I sit down on one of the benches.

'I know about you and Mel,' I say, once he's sat down beside me. I look right at him and he colours up, looks away.

'What? It's not . . . I mean . . . it wasn't meant to . . . we're not . . .'

I decide to put him out of his misery. 'I've known for months, so don't even try and bullshit me. I know it's been going on since way before Christmas. I know she's been living at the flat.'

Jack looks like a toddler who's been caught with his hand in the biscuit jar. I actually think he might cry. I almost feel sorry for him.

'Shit, Ames . . . I don't know what to say.'

'How about "Sorry, I've behaved like an absolute bastard?" How about "I'm a despicable person?"'

He nods, looks down at the ground. 'It got out of hand.'

'It never should have started in the first place.'

He looks right at me, his wolf-blue eyes watery. I have to make myself look away. 'I don't want her, though, that's the thing. I never have. It was just that you went off and I was terrified you might never come back or you'd meet some flash director and that'd be it –'

Unbelievable. 'So it's all my fault?'

'No! That's not what I mean. It's not an excuse –'

'When did it actually start? Be truthful. You owe me that much.'

He puffs out his cheeks, exhales noisily. 'About a week after you left –'

'A week? Fuck's sake, Jack.'

'I told you, I was all over the place –'

'So you fucked my best friend?'

'No. Yes. But I didn't set out to. It just happened.'

'And then it happened again and again for – what? – nine, ten months now? Hold on, she was still married to Sam, then.'

He looks at the floor, always a giveaway with Jack. 'You're the reason Sam left her? It wasn't him who went off with someone else?'

Jack swallows. 'He didn't know it was me. He just found out she'd been seeing someone.'

'So all those hours I spent on the phone to her, comforting her about her marriage breaking up, I was actually making her feel better about sleeping with you? All those fucking times I told her she was worth more and she should just go out there and find someone

350

fabulous, she was already shacked up with you? Jesus Christ.'

'I told her she shouldn't make up that stuff about Sam –'

'You didn't tell her the two of you shouldn't be sleeping together in the first place, though, did you?'

'I did, actually. Several times.'

'Oh, spare me. If you'd felt bad about it, if you'd wanted it to end, you would have ended it.'

'I'll tell her now. I'll call her and tell her that's it for ever.'

'You are kidding me? You think we're going to carry on, me and you? That – what? – we're going to go ahead and set a date for the wedding?'

He wipes his eyes. I have no idea whether he's actually shedding a tear or not. I don't care. 'Please, Amy –'

'Why would you even want to? We barely talk to each other these days.'

'Because you're always too busy with your new life –'

'Oh, do me a favour, Jack. We could both have made more of an effort if we'd wanted to. It's finished, by the way, the job. I've moved back.'

To say he looks confused would be like saying Hitler looked a little bit miffed sometimes. He can't compute. 'You've . . . already? Where are you living?'

'A few months ago, actually. I've got a flat.'

Jack opens and shuts his mouth like a beached goldfish. 'But . . .'

I take him through the basics. The weekend of the

party. The fact that Mel knows I know. I don't, obviously, mention the fact that I lost him the job at Colby Sachs. That's probably the one thing I really regret in this whole saga.

'Mel's known you were back all this time?'

'For a while, definitely.' I'm not going to tell him about *Blood Ties*. There's no point. I don't want his sympathy. Or his help. I just want to let him know he's free to run off into the sunset with Mel, if that's what he decides to do.

'Oh,' I say. 'And I'm seeing someone. It's only fair that you know. It started way after I found out about the two of you.'

He looks crestfallen, which almost makes me laugh. Did he think we were somehow all going to go back to the way we were?

'Who . . . I mean . . . I guess I don't have the right to ask –'

'You don't. Just be happy for me. What you and Mel did could have crushed me. I just want to move on.'

I reach into my pocket and pull out the engagement ring he bought me what seems like a lifetime ago. I haven't worn it since I returned and, in fact, I rarely wore it while I was away because I was so scared I would leave it in the costume trailer (my character had her own bling). I just used to leave it in its box in my apartment. Maybe that was symbolic.

'Here . . .'

He takes it, turns it over in his hand. 'I don't want it back. What am I meant to do with it?'

'I have no idea. I'm going to withdraw exactly half of what's in our joint account this afternoon, okay?'

He nods. 'Sure.'

'And I'm going to the flat now to take whatever's mine. Do me a favour and don't tell Mel you've seen me until later. I don't want her coming there to try and talk to me. I just want to get my stuff and go.'

'I won't,' he says. 'I won't tell her until tonight. Are you sure this is what you want?'

'I'm sure.' I stand up to leave.

'I'm really sorry, Ames,' he says, and he reaches for my hand. 'It all got out of control.'

I take it back gently. 'Let's just move on. For the record, though, remember that Mel is Mel. She's never going to change.'

He breathes out noisily. 'I know.'

And I think, *No, you don't know the half of it, but it's not up to me to tell you.*

'Bye, Jack.' I start to walk off, remember something and turn back. 'Oh. I have Oscar, by the way. He's fine.'

'You . . . ?' He looks more confused than ever.

'Long story,' I say.

'I have no idea what's going on, but that's the best news I've had in ages.'

He looks as if he's going to cry again, and then he does, but he's smiling, too, and laughing. I resist the knee-jerk, hard-wired, comfort-a-crying-child urge to hug him.

'Mel always hated him,' I say.

He wipes his eyes with the cuff of his shirt. 'She did. I'm glad you've got him.'

At the flat – Jack's and mine – Kat and Greg are waiting for me with the car. I spot them almost from the Tube station, leaning on the bonnet. Her with a mouse-ear polka-dot bow in her black bob, him a foot taller in a mustard-yellow polo shirt, quiff adding another three inches to his height. A couple of people look back as they pass, probably wondering where the fancy-dress party is. Kat and Greg are oblivious. I adore them.

'How did it go?' Kat spots me first.

'Grim,' I say. 'But not as bad as it could have been.'

They've brought a couple of big suitcases that we fill with all my clothes and books, papers and bits and pieces. I'm scrupulously fair, taking nothing that doesn't belong at least fifty-one per cent to me. Then I retrieve Mel's gold necklace from my pocket and leave it on the bedside table I assume is now hers.

'Oh, Sam left her because of Jack,' I say, as we start to bump the cases down the communal stairs. I watch as both their mouths fall open. 'So that was nice. All those times Sam tried to call me and I rejected the calls. I even sent him a text telling him to fuck off.'

Once we're done, I push the keys back through the door. I don't even look around as we drive away.

On the way back, I scroll through the contacts on my phone and find Sam's mobile. I don't even know what I'm going to say, so it's a shock when he answers, my name a question.

'Amy?'

I launch straight in.

'Hi. Sam, listen, I'm sure I'm the last person you want to hear from. Well, one of them. I just wanted to say it was Jack Mel was seeing. I only just found out. And that I had no idea she was cheating on you with anyone. I wouldn't want you to think . . . she told me you'd left her for someone else . . .'

'Shit,' he says. 'I'm sorry, Amy.'

'I'm fine,' I say. 'I'm over it. But I'm sorry I wasn't supportive when the two of you split up. I'm sorry I just believed her version of things.'

'I appreciate it. I do,' he says. 'But I never held it against you. You're her mate . . .'

'Was,' I say. 'No more. Be happy, Sam. I intend to be.'

'Well done,' Greg says when I end the call. 'That was a nice thing to do.'

Mel, I have decided, does not deserve a confrontation. She'd probably relish the drama. And besides, we both know exactly where we stand already. Mel's worst nightmare is to be ignored, so back at home, I block her on Facebook and Twitter and change my email address, making sure to let anyone I might ever want to hear from know the new one. Then I head down to the Vodafone shop along the street and sign myself up for a brand-new account with a brand-new phone number even though I can't really afford it. I get them to transfer all my contacts from my American mobile and then I delete Mel's numbers. I make one last call on my old phone – to the US, to cancel the contract – and then I take the battery out and throw the whole lot in the back of a drawer.

And that's it. Mel is ghosted and I'm moving on with my life.

46

Mel

I can't decide which is worse. Or, should I say, better? Let Amy know that her new boyfriend has a wife at home, who, I assume, knows nothing about his bit on the side, or leave it for her to discover the awful truth herself?

Both options have their plusses. But, ultimately, I decide there's no fun for me in just leaving things to fate. It could be months, or even years, before she finds out. Or worse, it could just fizzle out naturally (or he could get cold feet) and she would never know. She'd just be left with a bittersweet memory of the transitional relationship that helped her get over Jack.

And speaking of Jack, she's been to see him. Told him the truth, in so far as I can work out. I arrived home from work to find him slumped on the sofa. He feels terrible, he said. It all went too far, he said. Bit late for that now.

Anyway, her stuff has gone. All trace of her eliminated, leaving me and Jack to get on with our lives. Separately or together, I have no idea. I never even considered that, one day, it might just be me and him and, clearly, neither did he, because he can't stop telling me how it wasn't supposed to end like this.

'Too fucking right!' I shout at him. He's doing my head in, lying there, feeling sorry for himself, as if none of this was his fault. Okay, so she was my best friend but she was his girlfriend, too. *Fiancée.* We're as bad as each other.

I'm actually furious that Amy's just moved on. That she's found herself a whole new life and she can't even be bothered to fight for the one she had. As if it was never important to her anyway.

There are so many ways to do it, though, how's a girl to choose? Do I send Amy a note 'from a concerned friend'? Do I let Simon know I know so he has no choice but to tell her? Or is there another more drastic – for which read "more fun" – way? One that would cause maximum carnage?

47

Amy

I'm not back at Huntley Media Marketing until tomorrow, so I take my time trying to work out what to do with my day. Making a cup of tea and reading the papers online seems like as good an idea as any so, even though I know I should be trying to be more proactive about my flailing career, that's what I do.

I'm still browsing idly when an email pops up from Sara.

'Why is your phone dead? Trying to call you. Don't get too excited.'

I still haven't got round to doing the big group text message telling everyone my mobile number has changed. I've been finding it quite peaceful, to be honest, knowing that, if anyone calls, it's either going to be Kat, Greg or Simon. No nasty surprises. If anyone needs me, they can email. Although I probably should let Huntley Media Marketing know, in case they decide to cancel my shift for any reason. And Chris and Lew, in case they start to worry about me. And everyone else. Eventually.

I call Sara back, aware she probably just wants to

check I haven't topped myself after her bombshell on Friday night.

'Amy!' she shouts, almost rupturing my eardrum. 'Where have you been? I've been worried about you.'

Ah, so I was right. My heart sinks just a little bit, as it always does when there's no prospect of any acting work on the horizon.

'I'm fine. I got a new phone.' I give her the number.

'Right. Good. And I can't say sorry enough again for what happened. Still' – she carries on, not waiting for a response – 'do you want some better news?'

'Definitely.'

'*Murder in Manhattan* is obviously selling well, because we got a big fat royalty cheque for you this morning. It'll take a few days to process but I thought you'd want to know.'

I'd forgotten all about royalties. One of the reasons why a part in a series is the Holy Grail is because of the royalty cheques. If it's popular and sells well around the world, it can practically be a pension fund. Actors who appear in seven or eight seasons of twenty-odd episodes can more or less live off that for a good few years after it's all ended, depending, of course, on how high their fee was in the first place and how many other countries want to snap it up. Obviously, I only appear in twelve episodes and my fee was a pittance compared to everyone else's and already included a UK showing, but, still, the sum Sara tells me is on its way, along with my share of Jack's and my savings, will soften the blow of my lost two weeks' rent.

'That's amazing,' I say. 'Thanks for letting me know.'

'And there might well be more in the future. The more seasons they end up doing, the more sellable the whole thing becomes, but don't, you know, rely on it.'

'I won't go straight out and spend it all on sweeties, if that's what you mean.'

She laughs. Or should I say she brays. 'Exactly. Well, that's it. Putting you up for everything.'

'Thanks, Sara,' I say, but she's already hung up, on to the next.

I think about celebrating by going out and buying myself a vacuum cleaner from Argos (£59) and paying for a taxi to lug it home. I know how to live large. But then I think maybe I should see if Tom is free for lunch. He's texted me a couple of times suggesting dates that never worked out for one reason or another, so it feels as if it would be the polite thing to do to return the favour.

Simon has a theory that trying to connect with my old friends might help expunge the ghost of Mel. So I've already tried, and failed to track down Pia. I've had no contact with her in nearly twenty years; I've never even searched for her because I always thought, *What's the point?* To throw myself back into my friendship with Mel, I had to pretty much put all thoughts of my old gang out of my head. It was too painful thinking about what she did to them, to Pia and Alistair. Easier just to move on.

Googling Pia threw up nothing so I spend a couple of hours going into the wormhole that is Facebook. Pia Daribar is an unusual enough name, although I have no idea, of course, if she still uses her own surname. There were a few Pia Daribars on there (is there any name in the world so unique that there's only one owner? I wonder) so I worked my way through them, but none of them looked promising, mostly for no other reason than that I couldn't imagine her ending up looking like any of these women. I couldn't see her elfin sweetness in any of their faces.

So I decide Tom is next best. I text him, asking if by any chance he's free today, and he answers almost straightaway, in typical Tom fashion, saying he is but is it really bad to expect me to travel all the way into the West End to meet him at his office, because he can't get away until one and then he has another meeting at two thirty and, if not, let's do another day, when he could maybe meet me halfway, although it would be lovely to see me. I laugh as I read it because it's just like having a conversation with him. I text him back saying it'll do me good to drag myself into town for once and that I'll meet him in reception.

'How's the law?' I ask him as we walk through Gordon Square towards a pub that he tells me does fantastic sandwiches but also, more importantly, usually has space outside.

He grimaces. 'Loathsome.'

'Really?' I wasn't expecting that. I assumed he'd found his calling.

He nods. 'I hate it. Don't tell them that.' He jerks his head back in the direction of his office.

'You've been doing something you hate for twenty years?'

'Pretty much. Well, if you don't count the extra year of college I had to do to convert. Seventeen years. And eight months.'

'At the same place?'

'Yep. And three and a half days.'

'Ha! Not that you're counting.'

'It's not that bad,' he says, striding along. I'd forgotten how fast he always walked, long legs flying out in front of him.

'Slow down,' I say.

'Oh, sorry.' He does. The tiniest fraction. 'It could be worse, of course it could, so I try not to moan on about it.'

He comes to an abrupt halt as we turn a corner and arrive at the pub. I almost bang straight into him, manage to stop myself just in time.

'Here okay?' he says.

'Lovely.'

'You can't tell me you've hated it for the whole seventeen years and eight months?'

'And three and a half days. No, of course not. I think I was quite excited for a week.'

'So why not change and do something else?'

He shrugs. 'Responsibilities. Once the kids came along, you know. And it's okay, really. It's just a bit dull. The job, not the kids. The kids are marvellous.'

The waiter comes along and we order a turkey-and-cranberry sandwich (Tom) and a blue-cheese ploughman's (me), along with two fizzy waters.

'Anyway,' he says, once our order has been taken. 'Enough about my boring career, let me live vicariously through you. Tell me everything.'

'You don't want to know,' I say.

'No, I really do, that's the thing. Every job you've had since you left college.'

I laugh. 'Every single one? Most of them only lasted a day, didn't pay anything and no one ever saw them.'

'I love it,' he says. 'Tell me about the really awful ones before we get on to *Murder in Manhattan*. Which, by the way, I'm completely hooked on. Is it Courtney? The murderer? It is, isn't it?'

So I tell him a couple of funny stories about the more outlandish jobs I took in the early days (one playing an owl in a children's community theatre, which just involved me hooting a lot and looking stern, and another about the time I appeared in a film student's graduation film and he talked to me for two hours about my back story and motivation, then it turned out all my part required was for me to walk into a shop and ask for a packet of Nurofen). Tom lapped them up, laughing in all the right places.

'I love it. Remember how pretentious we all were

when we were at college? Sitting around discussing Pinter like it was the most important thing in the world?'

'And Kieron would always bring up Brecht, because he was the only one who'd ever read any.'

'He's still the same,' Tom laughed. 'Honestly, I swear the last time I saw him he started on about the Theatre of Noh like I was meant to know what he was on about.'

'So, he's still directing. Alistair's teaching . . . what does he teach?'

'English. Seems quite happy.'

'And Pia? I don't suppose any of you kept in touch with her?'

He raises an eyebrow at me. 'Hardly. I mean, I would have, obviously, but I guess she didn't want anything to do with any of us. Last I heard, she'd gone to work in Spain. She had family there.'

I wait for the waiter to put down our drinks and fuss around with knives and forks.

'I've always felt guilty. I should have known what Mel was capable of.'

'Hardly your fault. Alistair was the one who betrayed Pia, not you. Not that it matters, not that I ever would have brought it up at the time, but you know Mel told him she'd seen Pia with someone else that night.'

'It doesn't surprise me. Mel, I mean –'

'God, Mel was a nightmare. I wonder what ever happened to her.'

I put my head in my hands. 'Oh God, Tom, you can't even imagine –'

'You're not still in touch with her?'

So I tell him the whole story, and he sits there, open-mouthed, taking it all in.

'Poor you,' he says when I get to the end. 'Shit.'

'It's all my own fault,' I say. 'I should never have let her back in my life.'

'We should have stood by you more. I always felt bad about that. The way we all just dropped you.'

'We were kids,' I say. 'I've missed you all, though.'

We settle up and I stroll back in the direction of his office with him. That is to say, I trot along beside him, trying to keep up.

'We have to do this again,' he says. 'Or we could meet up one evening. You could bring Simon, and I could see if I could persuade Alistair out with Siggy. She's scary. In a nice way. Impressive, I think I mean, really.'

'Only if you promise to go a bit slower if there's any walking involved.'

'Shit. Sorry.' He changes pace, slows right down so now we're walking too slowly, but I don't say anything.

As we reach the corner of Tottenham Court Road, my phone starts to ring. Sara.

'I'd better take it. I'm going to head for the Tube anyway.'

We have a quick hug and he strides off, turning to say, 'Next week, maybe?' as I press to take the call.

'Lovely!' I shout back, feeling a warm glow that it's gone so well, that Simon might be right and reconnecting with my old friends might be just what I need. 'Hi, Sara.'

'Can you make an audition tomorrow?' she barks, leaving out the pleasantries. 'One episode? Five lines?'

'Sure,' I say. 'Give me the details.'

'New comedy drama for ITV called *Sisters*. About – well, you've guessed it – sisters. Made by Framework Productions – and yes, before you ask, they're definitely legit. They're in Percy Street. They could see you pretty much anytime between two and four.'

'And what's the part?'

I hear the usual shuffle as she finds her notes. 'Woman with Dog. You pass the time of day with one of the sisters waiting in a queue for a coffee in the park.'

'Fine,' I say. 'Later is better, I can do a half-shift.'

She promises to call me back to let me know the time. Before I head down into the Tube station I ring the call centre, tell them I'll only be in for the morning. I'm gratified to find that I still get a little jolt of excitement when I say the words, 'I've got an audition.'

48

Mel

Amy has cut me off, vanished into thin air. I know this because I tried to look at her Facebook page but I was denied access, so then I tried Twitter and it told me I was blocked. I rang her phone out of curiosity – I knew she wouldn't answer if she saw it was me, and I didn't want to speak to her, in all honesty. But the number is dead.

Which is a shame, because I was hoping to hand it over to Georgie Rigby once I'd told her exactly what her husband was up to. What better way for Amy to find out Simon is married than the poor wronged wife calling up, looking for answers?

I could give her Amy's address, obviously. I assume she's still living there. Although, as she now knows the whole *Blood Ties* thing was fake, she must also realize that it was me her agent gave her address to so I could send her the non-existent scripts. Would she do something as drastic as move because of me? It only looked like a shitty little rented flat to me, so maybe she would. And I don't really want to send Georgie Rigby all the way up there to try and catch her husband in the act, only for it to be a wild-goose chase.

Of course, this is assuming Georgie will bite. Maybe she's such a drip she'll just accept whatever he's doing. Refuse even to confront him in case he leaves her. Maybe she knows already. Maybe she's actually got a man on the side herself and it'll be a relief. I doubt it, somehow. She doesn't look the type.

I've got a few days to think how best to handle things. My appointment to view Georgie Rigby's ugly ceramics isn't until Friday.

'I can't decide which one I want,' I told her on the phone. 'They're all breathtakingly beautiful.'

She was so flattered she agreed that I could visit her at home and check out the whole collection. She didn't usually deal with people in person, she told me, but I sounded nice and it was obvious how much I loved her work (self-effacing little laugh).

'I do!' I told her. (I almost choked at this point.) 'It's so . . . unique, so . . . personal.'

How could she refuse?

49

Amy

Woman with Dog, it turns out, has a lot in common with Woman in Pub and Woman in Park, in that she has absolutely no distinct personality. She's just a woman saying lines to facilitate the plot. Only, this time, she has a dog. That's her USP.

It's the same old same old. I show up ten minutes early, having been home to change after my shift (only one sale; they would have sent me home at lunchtime, anyway). I wear jeans, a T-shirt and a gilet, which feels to me like something a woman walking a dog might wear. If she was a massive cliché. I nod hello to the other Woman with Dogs, chat briefly to the casting director's assistant about the weather, and then I'm in. I answer politely when the casting director (who I've met before) and the director and producer (who I haven't) ask me about *Murder in Manhattan*, and then I read my five lines with the producer reading the responses.

'Great,' Joy, the casting director, says when I've finished. 'Thanks, Amy.'

I'm about to get up and leave when Nick, the director, mutters to the producer something about Catherine.

With a question mark afterwards. I hesitate, unsure what to do.

'Good idea,' the producer, whose name I've already forgotten, says.

'Oh . . . yes . . . why not?' Joy says. She's wearing the casting director's uniform of a floaty, oversize top, baggy trousers and large clunky jewellery that rattles when you're in the middle of your reading.

'Are you okay to hang on a sec, Amy?' She shuffles bits of script around and it's like being trapped in a room with Evelyn Glennie. I wonder how the other two can sit in here with her all day without wearing earplugs. Finally, she locates what she's looking for.

'Here it is.' She thrusts a piece of paper at me. 'Nick was just saying maybe you should have a read of Catherine.'

Nick chips in. 'It's a bit of a bigger part. Single mum. Feisty. If you want to pop outside and have a read through, we'll call you back in in a bit.'

'Sure. Great. See you in a minute.' I'm gratified that my Woman with Dog must have gone down well, not to mention delighted to be able to have a go at something a bit more meaty. I manage my excitement, though. This has happened to me before and has never yet amounted to anything. I wonder if, as soon as I leave the room, they're all going to decide this is a big waste of everyone's time and why did anyone suggest it?

Joy shows me out and tells her assistant to send me back in in about ten minutes, whenever there's a gap.

The three other women waiting look at me with expressions ranging from curiosity to out-and-out loathing.

I sit in the corner and look at the scene. It's two sides of papers stapled together and it's a two-hander between feisty Catherine and someone called Miranda, so there are a fair few lines to get my head around. Feisty Catherine doesn't seem to be being at all feisty, in fact she's crying by the end, which is a challenge in itself, as I don't really know anything about her or what might have happened to make her so upset.

It's always weird, being given a disembodied scene with no context. I don't even know what relation these two women are to each other, let alone what they might have argued about, but this is obviously some kind of post-argument make-up. Catherine thinks the Miranda woman never takes her seriously seems to be the bottom line.

I read it through a few times in my head, trying out different ways of approaching it. And then I sit and think about sad things to get me in the mood for crying. I'm spoilt for choice when I consider my own life. The danger is that I'll be bawling before they call me back in.

'Have you had enough time?' Joy's voice snaps me back to reality. I hadn't even noticed her appear. Which, given the jangly bracelets, is a miracle in itself.

'Yes. Fine. Thanks.'

I follow her back in, say hi all over again, and then I'm reading, with Joy playing Miranda. The first read is a bit awkward, not helped by the fact Joy has all the acting ability and enthusiasm of a robot. She plonks out line after line in the same flat intonation, so we sound like two people playing different songs on one piano.

'Okay, let's go again,' Nick, the director, says. 'This time, think that Catherine has held this resentment for years but she's never really verbalized it. When she cries, they're tears of frustration, not sadness.'

I resist the urge to say, 'You could have told me that before,' and throw myself into it. I try to ignore Joy and imagine Miranda's lines said in a way that would provoke me – the truth is, I imagine Joy is Mel, that I'm saying the lines to her – and, somehow, I manage to get lost in the moment and, at the end, produce a couple of real tears. So, all in all, I'm pleased I've done as well as I can.

'Great,' Nick says. He looks at Joy and she stands up.

'Thanks, Amy. Good to see you again.'

And that's my cue to leave.

I haven't seen Simon since the weekend. He's been up against it, finishing the St John's Wood job, and he's just, he says, been too knackered when he finally finishes late in the evenings. It was a relief to be able to tell him I'd been to see Jack when we talked on the phone yesterday. It felt as if I'd finally removed a barrier that had gone up when he'd found out I was still 'officially' engaged to someone else. It felt like a new start.

'Oh, and I had lunch with Tom.'

'Good for you. How was it?'

'It was great,' I said. 'You were right, it felt almost cathartic.'

'See? I should be a life coach.'

'What? You'd give people old rugs and tell them to meet up with long-lost friends?'

'Exactly. Can I come over tomorrow? I've missed you.'

'Definitely.'

I had already decided I was going to get him a set of keys cut for my flat. I felt as if I wanted to make a gesture, something that told him how I was starting to feel without me having to actually say it.

Last night, Kat and Greg came over and we sat on the roof with gin and tonics, watching the sun go down.

'God, you'd pay a fortune for this view if it was officially yours,' Kat said at one point. They had arrived clutching a tray of little geraniums and a couple of bags of soil and we'd spent twenty minutes planting up a few of the nicer pots.

'You could do a whole herb garden up here.'

'I'd spend the rest of my life watering it all. I'd never be able to take another job again.'

'Let's toast the end of a very unpleasant era,' Greg said, and we all clinked our glasses, them on the two recliners, me sitting on the wall. I felt as if I'd finally reconnected with the world.

'Well, you obviously did something right because they want to see you again.'

'For Woman with Dog?' I'm half asleep. After Kat and Greg left, at about quarter to ten, I polished off the rest of the wine from the second bottle we'd opened and fell into a deep, contented sleep on the sofa, from which I woke at about three this morning, no idea where I was, hangover already kicking in. When I finally found the bed (via the best part of a pint of water), Oscar was sprawled right across the top, snoring away, so I sort of shuffled on, curled around him as best I could and consequently have a stiff neck to add to my headache.

Sara laughs. I hold the phone away from my ear. 'No! For the other part you read for. Catherine. They want you to go in and read with the actress playing Miranda.'

'Really?' Suddenly, I'm wide awake. 'That's good, isn't it?'

'Of course it is. Although it's by no means a done deal.'

'No. Of course. I know that.'

'It'll all depend on the chemistry. Miranda's cast already – she's one of the sisters – and Catherine is her life-long friend. It's a decent part, I think. Not one of the leads, but second level. They're bringing six people back, apparently.'

'Who's playing Miranda?'

Sara names an actress of the down-to-earth, woman-next-door variety who I have always admired.

'She's great. I could imagine being her friend.'

'Well, that helps,' Sara says. 'They're seeing people Monday, if that works?'

'It does. It works. Any time.'

'Okay. Well, I'll let you know the details later.'

'Thank you,' I say, and then, before I can stop myself, I add, 'And it definitely is real, isn't it? Definitely?'

'Definitely,' she says and, to be fair to her, there's no sense of irritation at being asked this again. 'Don't worry, Amy, I'm double checking everything from here on in.'

I know nothing is guaranteed. I've been down to the last two for a part before and the director has more or less told me I'm their favourite and they're looking forward to working with me and then I've found out I haven't got it. Anything can happen. One piece of the jigsaw moves and the rest has to shift to accommodate it. But it's been so long since I had a proper audition for a proper part – since *Murder in Manhattan*, nearly a year ago, in fact – and that's all I ask. That I'm given the chance to show what I can do, even if I end up being too old or too young or too fat or not fat enough or just not right for one of a million reasons. If I can do that, then I'm allowed to think of myself as an actress and not someone whose career is working in a shitty call centre.

50

Mel

Georgie and Simon Rigby's house is picture-postcard pretty, with flowers climbing around the door and stylish black window boxes full of lavender. It's only small – part of a terrace of narrow, yellow-brick, two-storey-and-an-excavated-basement cottages on a quiet road, but you can tell from the outside that it's both homey and chic. I'll be honest, I'd die of boredom living in a place like this. Give me lateral living, roof terraces and big windows any time. But I can appreciate its appeal to families. Even ones where the husband is playing away.

She opens the door, all hesitant smiles. Big man's shirt streaked with paint over some kind of leggings. Blonde hair just past her shoulders, side parted and tucked behind her ears. Skinny in a way that screams an excess of nerves rather than concern for how she looks. Freckles on her nose. She's beautiful in a kind of sixties-waif way. You can imagine some randy old artist using her as a muse. Despite everything I'm about to do, I feel protective of her. She's fragile. It wouldn't take much to break her.

'Alison?' she says, in a posh but sweet voice.

That's me. I'm Alison for the day. Alison Butler. It's ironic that, the past few weeks, I've been doing more acting than I've done in years.

'Yes! Hi, Georgie. I'm so grateful for this.' I feel I need to get inside before I let off my bomb. Although, inside, she could stab me with some kind of implement for cutting clay and no one would see, I suppose. I'm also banking on Simon not having taken the day off; I've checked the whole road and his van is nowhere to be seen. It's handy when you're trying to avoid someone if they drive a vehicle with their name plastered on the side.

'Come on in,' Georgie says, and she leads me into the hall and down the stairs. The basement is basically a large kitchen that takes up the whole floor, with doors open at the back on to a patio leading up to the small garden. It's beautifully done as, of course, it would be, given what Simon does for a living.

'My studio's out the back,' she says, indicating a pale yellow wooden summer-house-type thing.

'How cute,' I say, which probably sounds patronizing but isn't actually meant to. It looks as if – with one huge exception – she has an idyllic life.

'Would you like a drink of something, and then we can . . .' She wafts a hand at the shed.

'No. I'm fine . . . well, just water, maybe . . .' My mouth suddenly feels dry. Am I really going to do this? Ruin this woman's life? Assuming she doesn't already know, which seems unlikely.

378

'Did you have to come far?' She runs one of those fancy taps that basically do everything. I make a note to myself: must get one of those when I find a new place. Speaking of which, still no firm offer on my beautiful flat, which makes no sense to me. I might have to drop the price. Just as well, probably, because I haven't even started thinking where I might move to. I was going to head north to be closer to Jack and Amy, but that doesn't seem like such a great idea any more. I have no idea how long he and I are going to last now we can be out in the open. The deception was half the thrill.

'Notting Hill,' I say, making it up on the spot.

She smiles. 'I love it up there.'

I try to compose myself, steel myself for my big moment. I've been rehearsing this in my head for days.

'The thing is, Georgie, I . . .' I start, just as I hear a noise on the stairs, and my heart thuds alarmingly. I stop what I'm saying and stand there frozen, desperately trying to work out how I'm going to explain myself to Simon Rigby. What is Annabel Phillips doing in his kitchen and calling herself Alison Butler?

'It's just Ruby,' Georgie says, as a girl – dressed in PJs and big, fluffy slippers – shuffles down into the kitchen. She's fair-haired – how could she not be, with these two as parents – but with none of Georgie's ethereal qualities. She's a grumpy-looking, robust but pretty soon-to-be teenager and I would put money on her just having woken up.

Georgie hands me a glass of water.

'Hi,' I say to Ruby, and she grunts in my direction, then slumps at the kitchen table, phone in hand.

'Alison has come to look at some of my pots,' Georgie says with her nervous 'look at little old me' laugh, as if this were an everyday occurrence. Clearly, Ruby knows differently, because she looks at her mum in confusion, as if to say, 'What pots?'

'Sorry, what were you about to say?' Georgie says to me as she gets Ruby a glass of pink juice from the American fridge.

'Oh . . . I don't remember . . . is it school holidays already, Ruby? They come round so quickly now, don't they?' I'm boring myself. Ruby looks at me with barely disguised disdain.

'No.'

'Ruby's been off for a couple of days with a bad tummy,' Georgie tells me. 'They don't break up for another couple of weeks.'

I give Ruby a look that I hope says, 'You'd better not have anything catching and come anywhere near me,' but she just sits there, slurping her juice.

'Well,' Georgie says brightly. 'Shall we . . .'

She heads towards the garden and I follow. The summer house is deceptively big when you get close and, to be honest, absolutely adorable. There are window boxes stuffed with cheerful flowers both on the sills and on the steps and two wooden rocking chairs side by side. The whole front is opened up, I assume in honour of my visit, and I can see a potter's wheel and pots of paints and glazes and tools laid out. There are shelves full of Georgie's shapeless creations lining the walls on two sides. If she had any talent, this place would be inspirational.

I wait until we're inside and I know Ruby won't be able to hear what's being said.

Georgie waves an arm around expansively. 'So . . . here we are . . .'

It's now or never. I have a brief moment of panic when I wonder if she might be unhinged and come at me with a scalpel. I mentally run through my escape route, through the patio doors and back up the stairs. Try to remind myself why I didn't just do this by phone or in a letter. I think I thought she would be more likely to believe me if I was standing in front of her, willing to come all this way just to make sure she knew the truth about her husband. I have to just spit it out and get out of there. What happens then is out of my hands.

'The thing is, Georgie, I'm not really here to buy ceramics. Lovely though they are . . .'

She looks at me with utter confusion. I imagine she's scared for a moment, as if I might have come to rob her and her family. Which, in a way, I have.

'Right . . .' she says, and I can see she's trying to work out what's going on.

'It's Simon.' I don't even stop to let her take that in. I just blunder on with my prepared speech. 'A friend of mine . . . well, she's not a friend, she's just someone I know . . . she's been seeing someone . . . Simon . . . and then I found out he was married and it seemed so wrong, so awful, that they could be doing that when he has a wife at home . . . and I just felt you had the right to know, that's all. I'm sorry.'

Georgie reaches out a hand and steadies herself on the work bench. 'I don't understand. Who are you again . . . ?'

'Alison. Butler. There's no reason why you'd know my name. This friend. Acquaintance, really. She's been bragging about her new boyfriend for ages and how he's married but she doesn't care, and then I met him and he mentioned how he has a daughter and everything . . . Ruby . . . and, you know, I just . . . I tried saying to her that it was wrong but she just said she couldn't give a fuck. I know it's nothing to do with me and I probably should have kept out of it, but I feel really strongly about these things. I've been on the other end, you know . . . my husband – ex-husband . . . so I know what it's like and I know I wish someone had told me what he was up to rather than just all laughing behind my back . . .'

I'm doing well, I can tell. She one million per cent believes me.

'No. You're sure that it's my Simon?' Georgie says in a small voice. 'Could you have mixed him up with someone else?'

'Simon Rigby Interior Design,' I say. 'I've seen them in his van.'

I expect Georgie's face to crumple, but she holds it together and I realize she's stronger than I gave her credit for. It dawns on me who she reminds me of. Mia Farrow. Looks like a fawn, but I bet she's got lion-like qualities underneath if you threaten her family.

I put a hand on her arm. 'I'm really, really sorry to have to be the one to break it to you. I hope you don't think . . .'

'No,' she says. 'You've done the right thing. Thank you.'

'I should go, really, before he comes back and sees me here . . .' I really can't get out of there fast enough. Not just because I'm scared of being caught but because the look on Georgie's face is heartbreaking. I'm relieved that at least what I'm telling her is mostly true. I'm not lying about the essential fact at the core, that her husband is cheating on her.

'Yes, of course.'

I wait for her to ask me details, who this woman is – something. That'd be the first thing I'd want to know. And I need to let her know how to get in contact with Amy, otherwise this is all for nothing. She doesn't, though. She just stands there, looking shell-shocked.

'Her name is Amy Forrester, by the way. She's an actress. I think, you know, maybe if she saw you, spoke to you, it might sink in what she's doing . . .'

'Oh . . .' Georgie just stands there, not biting, looking blank, as if the Quaaludes have just kicked in.

'I don't have a number for her but she's with the Sara Cousins Theatrical Agency. If, I mean, if you wanted to get in touch with her.'

I can't force her to confront Amy. Even though I'm relieved for myself that Georgie doesn't seem the type to be openly aggressive, I just have to hope she has some balls under there somewhere. I grab a pencil from one of the shelves and a scrap of paper. I write down Amy Forrester and the name of the agent and put it down in front of her. What else can I do? It's out of my hands now.

51

Amy

I'm back in the same place in Percy Street: same producer, same director, same casting director. This time, though, there's also Charlotte, the actress who has been cast as Miranda and who will be reading with all six of us re-calls. I'm the only one in the waiting area when I get there. Joy's assistant fills me in a bit on the relationship between Miranda and Catherine – friends since their first day of secondary school, more like frenemies at times, but they're joined at the hip. It's a bit of a toxic friendship, she tells me, and I almost laugh.

'I know all about those,' I say.

She rolls her eyes. 'God, me, too.'

She gives me five scenes to study from three different episodes (I only know this from the numbering at the top). They cover a range of emotions – in one we're having fun, possibly a bit drunk; there's one that's a heart-to-heart, with Miranda confiding in me; one that's a bit of everyday nothing – or maybe there's a huge subtext you would only get if you'd seen the build-up; one where Catherine is being very passive aggressive to get her own way; and a full-blown row. It's a lot to take in, and I have a moment of panic that they're going to call me before I'm prepared.

'They're not running early, are they?' I say to Joy's assistant.

She laughs. 'You're the second person to ask me that. They're not, and they won't see you before your allotted time even if they suddenly are. They know you need the time to get your head around that lot. They'll just take a break.'

'Okay. Phew.' I take a few deep breaths. Try and calm myself. Start from the beginning.

Even though it's probably the longest audition I've ever had (Twenty-five minutes! Unheard of!), it's over in a flash. Charlotte is friendly and offers up helpful bits of back story in between our readings. I give it my all. Nick, the director, suggests different interpretations and has us read all the scenes at least three times, and then we're all saying goodbye. It's gone as well as it can go but, as I know all too well, that means nothing. On the way out, there's another woman about my age sitting in the waiting area, superficially similar to me, and we exchange nervous smiles.

I'm walking home from the bus stop an hour or so later when my phone rings. At the sight of Sara's name, my heart starts pounding. Surely they can't have made a decision already? Maybe someone stormed the audition. Walked in and blew them away to the extent that they don't even need to take time to consider. Maybe that someone was me? All that goes through my head in the few seconds it takes to yank my phone out of my bag and hit the green button. I stop in a shop doorway, finger in my ear so I can concentrate.

'Hi!'

It's actually Alexis, Sara's assistant-stroke-receptionist. 'Amy. How did it go?'

Of course. She's just being conscientious and calling to ask me how it went.

'Good. I think. It's hard to know –'

'Great.' She cuts me off. 'I'm actually calling because I've had a woman on the phone who says she needs to get hold of you urgently.'

I break out in a cold sweat. Mel. It must be. She has no other way to track me down, short of turning up on my doorstep, but she wants me to know she's not giving up. She can still get to me whenever she wants.

'She sounded a bit . . . well, I hope everything's okay. I thought I'd better let you know asap, in case . . . you know . . . and she did say it was urgent . . .'

'Melissa Moynahan, right? Mel?'

'What? No. Her name was Georgie Rigby.'

Rigby? Simon's sister? I can't remember what her name is, although I'm sure he must have told me. Shit. Something's happened to Simon and this is the only way she could work out how to get hold of me to let me know. An accident on site? A car crash?

I can hardly hear myself think for the blood pounding in my ears. 'Oh my God, what exactly did she say?'

'I wrote it down. Just that she needs to get hold of you urgently and that her name was Georgie Rigby. Oh, and that she's Simon's wife, but you obviously know that already. She sounded a bit hysterical, though, Amy. That's why I thought I should call you straight-away, in case something's happened. Is she family?'

The blood that was thundering around my head floods to my feet and I have to reach out a hand to the wall to steady myself. Simon's wife? Alexis must have got it wrong. She must have said 'ex-wife'. That must be it. Although I thought his ex-wife was called Amanda and that they didn't really speak unless there's a change to Ruby's regular arrangement to stay with him. Maybe Alexis got muddled up. She's not known for her efficiency. That must be it.

'Did she leave a number?' I say, ignoring her question.

'Yes. Can you write it down, or shall I text it to you?'

'Text,' I say, trying to keep my voice steady. My mind is running away with all the awful accidents that might have befallen Simon. Badly supported joists falling from ceilings, scaffolding collapsing, half-finished staircases giving way. Even though I know his job only really starts once the serious construction is more or less over, I know that building sites at any stage can be death traps.

In the time it takes for Alexis's text to reach me, I manage to get around the corner to a quieter street with a bench I can sit on. I fumble at the number she's sent me, manage to hit call.

It feels like an age before a woman answers, although it's probably only three rings.

'Hello.' She sounds hesitant.

'Is that Georgie? It's Amy. Forrester. My agent . . . has something happened to Simon?' I wait anxiously for her to say whatever it is she has to say. My left hand grips the edge of the bench and my knuckles glow white.

'Do you mind if I ask you how you know my husband?' Her voice is tremulous. Maybe she can't accept that it's over between them. Or maybe it's all a bit more recent than he led me to believe and the wounds haven't healed.

'He's my . . .' I hesitate. What do I say? 'Boyfriend' sounds like we're sixteen and we're going to the prom together, 'partner' as if we've gone into business. 'Lover'? No. Way too cringy.

'We're friends,' I settle on in the end. 'That is . . .' I hope the implication will be obvious. 'Is he okay?'

'Are you sleeping with him?'

Okay. This isn't right. You don't call someone to break the news that there's been a terrible accident and ask that.

'Georgie, sorry, I don't know if you've got a problem with me, but I assume you called me to tell me something. Is Simon okay?'

'Oh my God. You don't know, do you?'

No. I definitely don't. Whatever it is. 'Have I done something to upset you?'

'Simon's my husband –'

'Ex-husband.' I can't help myself.

She laughs a weird little nervous laugh. 'Who told you that? Did he?'

'Aren't you . . . ? I mean, I know I thought your name was Amanda . . .' I'm rambling, like I tend to do when I get rattled.

When Georgie speaks again, she sounds almost gentle. 'Amy, I hate to break this to you but Simon and I are very much still married. I was calling to tell you I know about you and him and to ask you to please consider what you're potentially doing to our daughter, our family. Please . . .'

I find myself trying to work out if I can hear Mel in her voice as she speaks. Could this be her? Another nasty joke to try and fuck with my life? But there's nothing. Not a trace. Could she have roped someone else in? Shaz, or some friend I've never met? It's not impossible. Or, and this is the conclusion I really don't want to have to come to, could Georgie really be who she says she is? Could it be true that Simon has been married all this time?

'I . . .' I start to say, but I don't know how to continue. 'I need to talk to him, Georgie. I'll call you straight back, I promise.'

I hang up before she can say anything else, which I know is rude, but I have to find out if she's telling the truth and I'll know as soon as I hear his voice.

'Hey,' he says when he answers, pleased to hear from me. Clearly, Georgie hasn't shared her suspicions with him yet. Maybe, like me, she wanted to know if it was true before blowing everything up. 'How did it go?'

I can't think what he's talking about for a moment, and then I remember. The audition. It feels like a lifetime ago.

'Fine. Simon, who's Georgie?'

I hold my breath so I don't miss a millisecond of his reaction. I wait for him to say, 'Georgie?' or 'Who?', in genuine confusion, to laugh and say, 'What are you on about?' But none of those things happen. Instead, he pauses. And that gives away everything.

'Amy . . .' he says after a second, his tone serious.

'I don't want to speak to you,' I say, and I cut him off.

I sit there on the bench, shaking. My teeth knocking together as if I'm freezing, as if it's not seventy-five degrees and a beautiful day. How could he do this to me? How could he do this to the woman he's married to? And their kid? Suddenly, the fact that he's only stayed the night once makes sense. And that I've never been to his place.

Georgie answers on the first ring this time. I speak before she has a chance.

'I am so, so sorry. I had no idea – you have to believe me. I would never . . . I mean, I wouldn't even have given him the time of day . . .'

'I believe you,' she says quietly.

'I'm ending it, obviously. Immediately. I don't want you to worry that, you know, we're going to be sneaking around meeting up behind your back, because it's over. Completely. I only wish I could undo the last few months. Not put you through this . . .'

'Thank you,' she says, with a resigned sadness that makes me want to cry.

'He's a bastard,' I say loudly. A woman passing with a tiny dog on a lead starts and crosses the road abruptly to get away from the crazy woman. 'You'd be better off without him.'

To be fair to her, she doesn't say, 'You don't even know me' or 'Who do you think you are, telling me what I should and shouldn't do?' She just says, 'No. I can't . . .'

'I really am sorry,' I say again, because I have no idea what else there is to say.

'Your friend said you knew,' Georgie says. 'She made it sound as if you didn't care –'

I interrupt her, already knowing the answer. 'What friend?'

'Alison Butler. She's the one who came to the house and told me.'

I don't even bother saying that I don't know and have never met, in so far as I'm aware, anyone by that name. Georgie has enough to worry about without having to factor in my crazed ex-best friend. I just say, 'Red hair, skinny?' And she says yes. And that tells me all I need to know.

52

Ten minutes after I get home, my doorbell starts ringing over and over again, insistently. I don't even have to look out of the window to see who it is. I know. Then my phone starts, too, and I pick it up and see Simon's name. He must be using one hand for each. Either that, or there's a very angry postman on my doorstep who won't take no for an answer.

I open the window and hurl the keys down to him/ at him. I see him flinch so, hopefully, I hit my target. By the time he's reached my top-floor flat, I've made myself take a few deep breaths and checked I haven't left any sharp objects lying around.

'Amy, I can explain,' he says, as he half falls through the door. The familiar sight of him – the kind eyes, the rogue piece of hair that flops across his forehead, the stubble – almost makes me lose my resolve.

'You can explain being married? You can explain having a wife?'

'I should have told you.'

He reaches out a hand towards me and I take a step back.

'Yes, that might have been an idea. Somewhere

between the first time we met and when we slept together maybe?'

'I was going to. I knew I had to. But I was scared I wouldn't stand a chance if I did –'

'You wouldn't have!' I yell over him. 'Of course you wouldn't have, and that's exactly why you should have been truthful.'

'I know. It was just, it was too late by then. I didn't want to risk losing you.'

He gives me an intense stare. I turn away, not wanting to get drawn in. It would be so easy to go along with what he's saying, to believe that, when we met, he was so besotted by me that, more than anything, he couldn't bear not to follow his heart. But it doesn't change the facts.

'That's bollocks, and you know it. You pursued me right from the beginning, when you didn't even know me. You engineered that whole trip up with the rug and then us being left on our own together. If you'd mentioned then that you had a wife, it would just have been a failed pick-up attempt, hardly the greatest love story ever told.'

He exhales loudly, changes tack. 'I fucked up not telling you. I know that. Maybe it was just a temporary madness, I don't know. Maybe I had the world's shortest mid-life crisis. But I accept there was a moment at the beginning when I should have been honest and I wasn't. You must see that, then, it was too late, though? That I had too much to lose if you found out?'

'The point is that it shouldn't have been about you. It should have been about me being armed with all the facts before I threw myself headlong into something. And about Georgie. Mostly about her, let's face it. If this is bad for me, imagine what it's doing to her.'

'How did you find out, by the way?'

'From her. From Georgie.'

'Shit. Who told her?'

'Does it really matter?' It's not that I don't want to tell him it was Mel, I just don't think we need to get sidetracked by that at the moment. It's not how Georgie and I know what we know, it's the fact that we do.

'You knew how I felt about cheaters,' I say. 'You knew how upset I was about what had happened to me.'

'You didn't tell me Jack thought you were still together, though, did you? Not for weeks, anyway.'

Really? 'Jesus, Simon, there's no comparison. I should have been more honest with you, too, yes. But it was over with Jack.'

'He didn't know that, though, did he?'

Now it must be dawning on Simon that he's fighting a losing battle, he's clearly decided that belligerence is the way to go. It won't work. Devastated as I am, there's no going back, so we just have to move forward.

'This is ridiculous. I don't know why I'm even arguing with you. Obviously, we can't carry on. Let's just end it like adults. Go and try and sort things out with your wife.'

'I'll leave her,' he says, reaching out for me again and

putting a hand on my arm. 'It's been over for years, anyway.'

'I don't think she's sees it like that.' I sidestep his hand and it falls to his side as if he has no control over it.

'We just stayed together for Ruby.'

'So Ruby is real.' I say. 'What else? How about Amanda, your ex?'

He looks at the floor. 'No. That was just –'

I interrupt. 'And do you really have a sister? Did she come and stay that night I wanted to come to yours? In fact, do you even live in Barnes?'

He sighs. 'No. And no. Amy –'

'Go home and talk to Georgie.'

'Please . . .'

I make the mistake of looking right at him and, for a moment, I almost falter. I feel so comfortable with him. So safe. I'd never have got through these last few months without him. I know who I am, though, and who I am is not a woman who is okay about shacking up with someone else's husband.

'No. That's it, okay? Done.'

All the wind seems to go out of his sails. He slumps. 'Fine.'

Only when the flat door bangs shut behind him do I finally burst into tears.

You could argue that I should thank Mel for exposing the truth about Simon. That it was far better for me to find out now than further down the line. And you'd be right. Well, about the second part, anyway. For the record, if you ever see me out with a married man again, assume I definitely have no idea that he is married and that you should tell me asap so I can extricate myself before too many lives are ruined. Don't, though, go to his unsuspecting wife and blow her world apart. She's in for enough heartache and trauma already, without her having to deal with some vengeful bitch who probably thinks the whole thing is funny.

And if you decide to do it anyway, to drag an innocent party into your petty rivalry, then you'd better be prepared for what comes next.

53

Mel

Mondays always drag. For everyone, obviously. I firmly believe that, even if you're doing your dream job and every night you lie in bed thanking all the gods that you can think of for making you so lucky, you still have a little bit of a feeling on a Monday afternoon that the day will never end.

And I am not doing my dream job. Not by any stretch of anyone's imagination.

What I am doing is a job that is bearable, with mostly okay people, some of whom have become casual friends, and which allows me to pretend I have a purpose in life while being mindless enough that I never have to think about it outside the hours of nine thirty to five thirty. The plan always was that I'd hang on until Sam and I got pregnant, get paid maternity leave and then quit as soon as I was allowed. Sam thought that, as I'd been there so long, I might as well get that out of them. But it never happened. And now, of course, with him and his big old City boy salary gone, I need to stay here to get by.

It's hardly the life I had planned out for myself.

I don't think Jack is going to be able to keep me in the style I think I deserve to be kept in. Don't get me wrong, it's not that I think that's the man's role, it's just that I've not managed to organize myself well enough that I can pay for my own glamorous existence so I need someone else to step in. I need someone to come and take me away from all this.

And, just when I'm thinking that, my mobile rings. Unknown. Ordinarily, I wouldn't answer. I hate not knowing who's going to be on the other end when I pick up the phone. But any distraction from the boredom of work seems like a good idea at the moment.

'Hello.'

'Is that Annabel Phillips?' a man's voice says. Shit. 'Or is it Alison Butler? Oh, wait, isn't it Mel?'

'I don't know what you're talking about,' I say. I know I should hang up but I'm too curious about what Simon Rigby has to say to me.

'You must be really proud of yourself.'

'I am,' I say facetiously. 'I mean, you had no idea who I was, right? And if you hadn't brought up your wife, then I would probably never have found out about her.'

'Not that it's any of your business, but I really liked her. Amy. I was going to tell her –'

'Yeah, right. That would have gone down well.'

'– once I'd told Georgie. I wanted to try and make it as painless for my wife as possible.'

'For God's sake, Simon!' I realize at least two of my colleagues are listening in, doing that thing where they

399

look as if they're reading something but really they're just staring at a piece of paper with their ears cocked in your direction, so I stand up and walk out into the corridor. 'You really think I believe that crap?'

'I don't really care if you do or you don't. I just wanted you to hear it. This is the first time I've ever done anything like this, and it'll be the last.'

'Of course it will. Hey, we should go for a drink. Compare notes.' It strikes me that Simon Rigby is attractive and has a very good job. I could do worse.

He laughs, but it's not a nice, friendly laugh. 'I don't think so. I'm not like you, Mel, that's the thing. I fucked up, but I've learned from it. I'm going to try and make it up to my wife.'

'Well, good for you,' I say. 'Be happy up there on the moral high ground.'

Back at my desk, I count slowly in my head and, when I get to three hundred, I look at my watch. I swear only two minutes have gone past, which proves to me that this place operates in some kind of weird time warp. I put my head down on the desk for a second, will the day to be over.

I'm aware of one of my colleagues laughing. I can't be bothered to look up and see what the joke is. Then there's a flurry of muttering voices, followed by more laughter. Clearly, I'm missing something hilarious. I lift my head up and look over just as someone – Adrian, I think – says, 'Oh, my days!' in that annoying patois he puts on, despite being from Windsor. They're all sitting at their own computers so I can only assume someone's sent round one of those viral videos of people falling over or getting some kind of almost lethal prank played on them. Anything that helps pass the time is welcome.

'What's so funny?' I say. And, to a man, they all fall silent and stare at their desks as if I've caught them watching porn.

I check my inbox but whatever it is doesn't seem to have come through yet.

'What?' I say. I can't bear to be left out of a joke.

No one says anything, but I catch Adrian sharing a furtive smirk with Martin. Just as I'm about to tell them to all go fuck themselves, Shaz breezes in, comes over, takes me by the arm and says:

'I need you for a minute.'

I get up and follow her out and along the corridor towards the accounts office she shares with two others. A loud burst of laughter follows us.

'That lot are driving me mental,' I say, struggling to keep up. She's motoring along, which is very unlike Shaz, and I'm wearing wedges that are a bit too big and therefore not very stable.

Neither of her roommates is there, which is odd, as it's past lunchtime. Shaz pushes the door shut.

'Don't freak out,' she says, words guaranteed to make even the most stable person do just that.

'What?'

She hauls me over to her desk, sits me down, then leans over me and brings up her email. She clicks on one from someone called KarmaBitch@hotmail.com. As she does, I see it's titled 'Melissa Moynahan Urgent. Watch immediately'.

'What the fuck?' I look around at Shaz. There's no text in the email, just what looks to be a movie clip. It's called 'Melissa Moynahan, This Is Your Life'.

54

Amy

Kat, Greg and I all sit staring at my computer, waiting for the clock to tick over to two and the noise that tells us the email has been delivered to the forty-odd appointed recipients.

I stand up, walk to the window. 'Shit.'

'Nothing we can do about it now,' Greg says, and he leans over and switches on the kettle.

On Friday night, Chris and Lew drove all the way up after I finally filled them in on everything from *Blood Ties* to my bombshell about Simon. They tried to pretend they just fancied a weekend in London, but I knew it was a mercy mission. A moral-support intervention. They arrived tired and crotchety (they always argue on long drives, whoever isn't driving providing a running commentary on the other's shortcomings. It brings out the worst in both of them) at about eleven and we sat up half the night picking over the ashes of my life.

And that's when operation Humiliate Melissa was born.

I'd had enough. That was the gist. I wanted it all to

end. And her dragging an innocent party into our very personal fight was the final straw. Don't get me wrong, it wasn't a bad thing that Georgie now knew what Simon was capable of. Or maybe it was. Maybe her life would have been much happier keeping her head buried in the sand, believing that her husband loved her. It wasn't for Mel to decide.

I needed to do something that would hit her where it hurt. A final death blow.

After Chris and Lew had passed out (they were in my bed and I was on the sofa), I dug out my box of old photos and newspaper cuttings, which I'd retrieved from Jack's flat (as I now thought of it), and flicked through them, trying not to get distracted. I knew what I was looking for but pictures of me and Jack in matching ironic Christmas sweaters, or arms draped around each other on a weekend to Prague, kept getting in the way. I put them to one side, not sure what the etiquette was with the remnants of a failed relationship. I had no photographs of me and Simon, I realized. None. I remember taking a selfie of us one night and he laughingly deleted it because he said he looked like a gnome. Which he didn't, obviously. Either look like one or think he did, that is. He just wanted to destroy the evidence, I realize now.

Chris's job involves making (hopefully) viral videos for an Exeter-based radio station. He's in charge of 'extra content', whatever that means. It mostly seems to require him to film wacky scenes with unfunny DJs, which the station then puts online and boasts about a lot. It's destroying his soul one hard-fought-for 'like' at a time but it means he knows his way around a computer, so on Saturday morning I arm him with everything he needs and leave him to play around while Lew and I take their car to the nearest big Sainsbury's and push a trolley around, squabbling about what we should all have for dinner like an old married couple.

If both Shaz's and Mel's email addresses are anything to go by, the company they work for has a standard format for contacting employees. First initial, last name @ safeguardinsurance.co.uk. All we need is a list of all the people who work there, which proves easy to find when we spend a few moments online.

By mid-afternoon, we have something we all think is about as good as it can be. I email it over to Kat and Greg and, two minutes later, receive a reply: Perfect.

All that needs to happen now is for Chris to set up a group email via some program called Boomerang that he's installed, timed to send at 2 p.m. on Monday. We picked two o'clock because we decided that was prime slump time. The hour everyone would welcome a distraction.

'Shall I?' he says, finger poised over the enter button.

'Hold on,' I say. I want to make sure this is what I want to do before it's too late. It's probably the meanest thing I've ever done (well, with the exception of losing Jack the Colby Sachs job but, this time, I think mean is called for. I need to hit Mel in a place where I know it will hurt).

I take a deep, slow breath.

'Go on.'

55

Mel

I'm completely torn between wanting to watch it again and insisting that Shaz delete it. Now! But I need to relive the horror. To take in every last detail. To know what's come back to haunt me.

I lean over and click on the icon and the music – 'Fake' by Alexander O'Neill – even I have to admit that is inspired – starts up again.

'Melissa Moynahan, This is your life . . .'

The words fade in over black.

'Remember how Mel told you she used to be an actress? How she once starred in a regional stage production of My Fair Lady?'

A photo pops up. Me on stage, face covered in soot, arm full of flowers to sell.

'Well, what she didn't tell you is that she was TWELVE and the production was at the Flackwell Heath Girl Guides hut. There were two performances. Sixteen people watched the matinee and a whole nineteen saw the evening show.'

I give a sidelong glance at Shaz to see if there's even the hint of a smirk, but I'm relieved to see she has her serious face on.

A new black card pops up bearing the words:

'Remember how Mel told you she used to be a model?'

This time, there's a newspaper cutting. You can tell it's old and yellowing even in the picture. At the top, you can clearly read that it's an edition of the *Bucks Free Press*. The headline screams out: 'New girls' fashion at Spicer's!'

It leaves the screen for a merciful second while the words, *'This is the sum total of her modelling experience. Aged thirteen. Unpaid. Posing with half of the rest of the girls in her class at a show for mums at the village hall, put on by Spicer's, the local children's clothing store.'*

The cutting is back. This time, zoomed in on the photo. My blurred face is ringed at the back of the group.

'She didn't even get a name check ☹'

'Everyone exaggerates stuff,' Shaz says kindly. I ignore her.

'Or a pay cheque. In fact, Mel has never been paid for any acting or modelling work. Ever.'

If that was bad, I know there's worse to come.

'In 2008, Mel married Sam . . .'

Up jumps an email exchange between Sam and me.

Are you telling me you only married me because I had money?

Too fucking right I did. It was hardly because you were Man of the Year. LOL.

'But in 2016 he left her. Not for someone else, as Mel likes to

407

tell people. But because she was having an affair with her best friend's fiancé.'

There's a montage of pictures of Amy and me together, starting with one of the two of us aged eleven, arms around each other, grinning. It ends with a snap of Amy and Jack.

I have to look away as a screengrab of the Twitter DMs between me and Jack flashes up on the screen. Not quickly enough that I don't see the word 'minky' in all its glory.

'Oh God,' I say, and rub my hand over my eyes.

'Never one to worry about the emotional wellbeing of her sisters, Mel has also been sleeping with her married boss, John. (Sorry, John, you're busted!!)'

I know this is the one that will sink me with my colleagues. I can see from the email that it seems to have gone to everyone in the company. After the Facebook incident, I went into denial mode, backed up by Shaz and – probably because the truth was so unthinkable, that ex-model, ex-shining star Mel would stoop so low as to have sex with the overweight, vertically challenged bully-boy boss – had basically got away with it. Now an email exchange between me and Shaz, rearranged into chronological order, is there on the screen for all to see.

It just happened! Me and John!! Shit, what have I done?? Goes without saying, don't tell ANYONE!!!

Whoa! That came out of nowhere (no pun intended!!!). John as in . . . JOHN WELLER??? You fucked him???? I need you to tell me all. Ring me NOW!!!

'Where did she even get those from?' I groan, turning to Shaz.

Shaz grimaces. 'Nothing to do with me, I swear.'

The final card is up, fixed in place as the music fades.

'Melissa Moynahan: Model (this has a line through it), Actress (ditto), Friend (and again), Absolute bitch.'

56

'Who cares?' Shaz says. 'Fuck 'em all.'

We're still sitting in her office but I can see Shaz's two roommates looking anxiously through the little square window in the door every now and then, clearly wondering when they can get on with their work. Shaz shakes her head at them every time they come near, but it's been an hour now and I imagine she's not sure how much longer she can keep them at bay. At one point, one of them, Hayley, manages to keep Shaz's attention for long enough to indicate frantically that she needs her mobile phone and Shaz opens the door just wide enough to hand it to her.

'Can you work at Mel's desk?' she says in a stage whisper. I can distinctly hear the strains of Alexander O'Neill coming from somewhere in the building.

'Not for long,' Hayley says. 'I need my computer.'

Shaz comes back to her spot sitting beside me. 'Why don't you take the afternoon off?'

'I can't work here any more,' I say, for at least the third time.

'Don't be stupid.' Shaz rubs my back in what she hopes is a comforting manner. 'It'll all blow over.'

'It won't, though, will it?' I snap. 'How can it?'

I don't know which is worse, the fact that they all now

know for certain about me and John or the fact that they all now think I'm some kind of fantasist who made up all the past glories that, in my eyes, make me who I am. So, I may have exaggerated them a little, left out key details like the fact that I have never had a paid job in the fields of either acting or modelling in my life, but the essence was still true. Without that, who am I? An ordinary woman with a failed marriage behind me, a boyfriend who cost me the closest friendship I've ever had and a married lover who I wouldn't find attractive if he was the last man left on earth but whose wife probably loves him and doesn't deserve to have me steal him away from her when I don't even want him. I'm sad. Pathetic.

I stand up. Stretch. I check the email on my phone. There are three from John, building up from 'What the fuck?' to 'I need to see you NOW!!!!', and one from the big boss, suggesting I come in for a chat. Soon.

'Do me a favour,' I say, turning to Shaz. 'Go and get my bag from my desk.'

'Of course,' Shaz says, although I imagine she's not really looking forward to the barrage of questions she'll face either about why she kept the fact that I've been screwing one of the bosses – the most hated one at that – a secret. 'Are you going home, then?'

I sniff, nod my head. What I don't say is that I have no intention of ever coming back.

57

Amy

I thought guilt might kick in once I knew the email had found its way to its forty-four destinations. At least, I could only assume it had. There was no way of knowing unless Mel tracked me down, and I somehow didn't think she would bother. But all I feel is a sense of relief. I've fired the biggest shot I have. I have nothing left.

I sent a long text to Georgie Rigby confirming that everything between me and Simon was over – completely and for ever – and reiterating again that it never would have started if I'd known he had a wife at home. 'I can only apologize again, but never enough,' I said. 'I really am sorry and I hope you can be happy, whatever you decide to do.' I don't tell her that I've already had three begging messages from Simon and a host of other missed calls. I have no intention of calling him back.

Later, she sends back, 'Thank you,' so I'm none the wiser about what she might do but at least I feel as if I've done everything I can to make amends. I think about putting a block on Simon's number so he can't leave me any more messages, but there's no point. It's not as if he doesn't know where I live.

I spend the rest of the day furiously sanding down the windowsills of my flat, having decided that physical activity was the only way to keep my mind from wandering. I might as well finally paint the woodwork. I turn the radio up loud and sing along to eighties hits. Of course, I regret the whole thing as soon as I start, because it's way harder than it should be to scratch away the old gloss evenly, but I try to do that thing where I imagine I'm trying to scrub away the remnants of my relationship with Simon (I read about this in a magazine once) and, when that doesn't work, I imagine it's his face and that makes me laugh, which doesn't make the job any easier but does make it more fun.

I eventually finish one whole window, and my right arm feels as if it's gone ten rounds with Floyd Mayweather. So I decide to take a break, make myself a cup of tea and then manoeuvre the ladder into position (this is Simon's ladder, I realize. Do I need to offer to give it back? I decide that he'll ask me if he wants it. That ladders are ten a penny in his line of work) and climb up, placing my mug and an old bottle of water I've filled from the tap one step higher as I go. Oscar sits at the bottom, watching me. I imagine, if he could roll his eyes, he would. I push the hatch open and the sun streams in. Outside, the heat bounces off the concrete and there's a melted-tarry smell coming off the repair that Simon did to the small crack he found that was causing my leaky roof, but my little plants are flourishing, so I empty the water on to them, then

413

go back down the ladder twice more and refill the bottle.

I sit down in one of the steamer chairs, face in the sun. Remember I don't have any suncream on and turn around the other way. Remember I left my phone downstairs and decide I can't be bothered to go and get it. Ditto my sunglasses. I force myself to close my eyes. Relax.

A few minutes later – at least, I assume it's only a few because my tea is still hot when I spill it all over myself – I jerk awake when I hear the distant sound of my phone ringing in a break between songs. Despite the fact that I know I have no chance of getting to it before whoever it is is put through to voicemail, I decide to give it a go and half throw myself back down the ladder, landing with a thud just as the ringing stops. I snatch up the phone, cursing whoever is calling as if it's somehow their fault, and then see I have three missed calls from Sara, all in the past hour.

I try not to think what it might be about as I hit the number to call her back. Maybe Georgie has called again to tell her the whole sordid story. Or Mel has sent her the video. It doesn't even occur to me that it might actually be work-related until I'm put through to her and the first thing she says is:

'You got it.'

So it takes me a second to work out what she means, which she must realize because, just as it's starting to sink in, she says, '*Sisters*. You got the part.'

'Woman with Dog?' I say, and I can't keep the relief and happiness out of my voice.

'No. Catherine. The friend.'

I scream so loudly that Oscar leaps about a foot in the air and then races off, knocking over a stack of books as he goes.

'No! Really?'

'It's a hundred per cent real. Ten days of rehearsals starting the week after next – they'll only need you for a couple of them. You're in all ten episodes, so it's a twenty-week shoot with a production break over Christmas. Option on series two and three, if you're okay with that. I'll make sure they build in a pay hike –'

'Definitely. Don't ask for too much. Don't put them off me.'

She laughs. 'I will definitely ask for too much, because that's my job. And when they say no, it won't affect how they feel about you at all. It's ITV. It'll be good money. The bad news is they're filming most of it down in Tooting so you probably couldn't be further away and still be in London, but I'll make sure they get you cars.'

'I don't care,' I say. 'I don't care if I have to leave home at four in the morning and get the bus –'

'Yes, well, hopefully, it won't come to that. The finished scripts aren't available yet, but I imagine that's not a deal breaker?'

She doesn't even wait for me to answer because she knows exactly what my response will be.

'Costume fittings will be during the rehearsal period.

I think that's everything. I'll let you know what the deal is, but I'm assuming you're happy with whatever I think their best offer is?'

'You know me so well,' I say through my huge smile. 'It's fantastic news, it really is. I couldn't be happier.'

'And I can tell people?'

'They didn't say you couldn't.'

'I'm telling everyone,' I say. 'I'm taking an ad out in the paper.'

I head back up to the roof and phone Kat and Greg, Chris and Lew, and my mum and dad, in quick succession. Each time I say the words, their genuine happiness and excitement for me boosts my own until I'm practically in a state of hysteria. I ignore the tug on my insides that's reminding me how much Simon would have loved to have heard my news. His loss.

It strikes me that maybe Tom would be pleased for me. I check myself to see if I'm just looking for a boasting opportunity and I think I probably am but, on balance, I'm allowed, just this once. It's not every day you land a shiny new job, particularly when things have been going so spectacularly badly. So I call him on his mobile, expecting him not to answer, but he does, almost straight away.

'Amy, hi!'

'I'm not disturbing you, am I? Are you at work?'

'Walking between appointments,' he says. 'How's things?'

'I got a part,' I tell him, and then I worry that perhaps I'm not just being boastful, I'm being insensitive, given his youthful ambitions. Although I hardly think the Tom I've been back in touch with lately has any regrets about giving up.

'Marvellous,' he says, and I can hear his old puppyish self in there. 'Tell me all about it.'

I give him the lowdown and he laughs when I get to the bit about Catherine and Miranda's toxic friendship.

'You'd know all about that.'

'You don't know the half of it,' I say. I'm pacing up and down, looking over the rooftops.

'Want to have lunch before you start?'

'Lovely,' I say. 'I'm basically free. That's how sad I am.'

Later, Kat and Greg join me up on the rooftop – me on a third steamer chair, one of a pair they brought with them as a present to celebrate my new job and also because they didn't want one of us to have to sit on the wall all evening. I've stopped asking why everyone feels the need to bring me furniture whenever they come over – with glasses of wine and a pizza. I've dotted some more candles around because it's such a still evening and, even though they'll probably all burn out before it gets dark, the effect is still good.

'Have you heard from Simon?' Kat asks, picking a dead leaf off one of the geraniums.

'Not for a few days. And I don't want to.'

'I wonder if he and Georgie will stay together.'

I can't decide what I feel about this. On the one hand, I don't want to think I was responsible for the break-up of Georgie's marriage. On the other, I don't want her just to lie down and let him get away with it.

'I don't care.'

I had a slight dilemma earlier, where I thought maybe I should throw out all the things in my flat that came from him. Weren't you supposed to throw people's gifts back in their faces when something like this happened? And then I looked around at how nice the flat was starting to look and thought, *Sod it*.

'And, obviously, nothing from Madam?' Greg says, leaning back, legs dangling over the end of his seat.

'Nothing. At least, not yet.'

'It's over,' Kat says. 'We found her kryptonite.'

Three Months Later

58

I got picked up at just before six this morning, sat in the car for an hour going over my lines, arrived at the unit base half an hour early for my call, as I almost always do, such is the second assistant's paranoia that there will be some kind of early-morning bottleneck on my cross-London journey. I'm exhausted, but I don't care. I've never been happier.

Not-so-nice Fiona called me to tell me that Mrs Lam's family had decided not to sell the shop. She was going to retire and the younger generation were thinking about taking it in a different direction, aiming less at trade and more at the home market who might have been inspired to make their own clothes by *The Great British Sewing Bee*. One of her daughters-in-law was hoping to run classes teaching people how to put in zips or do darts. So my lease was up for renewal, if I wanted it. This time, for a year. At a ten per cent rent hike as, she said, was usual.

I told her I was in the middle of something and then called Kat.

'I might stay. What do you think? I can't face moving again.'

'Are you happy staying up there? I mean, you could afford to move a bit further in now.'

I thought about it. 'I think I am. I've got to like it. And you know what it's like, Catherine might die in series two and at least I know I can stay afloat here.'

'And that roof terrace is worth another – what? – a hundred, hundred and fifty a week, easily. I mean, if they knew about it and included it in the price.'

'Really?'

'Put it this way, I would never take you to see a flat with a roof terrace like that, because they would charge too much. Just don't mention it to her. Or let her see the ladder, if she ever comes round.'

I thought about it. Even though it had rained more or less non-stop for the past month, I still liked knowing I had my secret rooftop garden up there (and, to be honest, it was a bonus, because I was so busy I wouldn't have had time to go up there and water every day). And if I stayed, I could maybe splash out on some new kitchen cupboards from Ikea or on tiling the bathroom. I knew Fiona was never going to stump up for any improvements but if I knew I was going to be somewhere where I could afford to pay the rent for a whole year, maybe I could.

'Ten per cent is way too much, though,' Kat was saying. 'Tell her you'll stay if it's five.'

'What if she says no?'

'She won't. She doesn't want the hassle of having to find someone new.'

'Oh God, I don't know, Kat . . .' Now I'd decided to stay, I really wanted it to work out.

'Jesus Christ,' Kat said. 'Let me call her.'

In the end, Kat managed to get Fiona to agree to a four per cent rent increase and that the landlord would pay for any future structural repairs. I have no idea how. Some kind of Jedi powers or secret estate-agent code of honour, I assume.

'Oh, and those two downstairs are moving out,' she told me when she called back. 'She let slip that the new tenant is paying more than she's asking you for.'

Knowing I'm staying put for another year has galvanized me into action. On my days off, I have finished sanding and painting the woodwork and put up curtains. I've whitewashed the ceilings and tiled the bathroom. Oh, and I invested in some inexpensive wooden flooring for the whole flat and threw away the rug. It reminded me too much of Simon every time I looked at it and, the truth is, I'd never even liked it, it had just been a running joke between us that I no longer found funny. We put it in Kat and Greg's car, hanging out of both back windows, across my lap, and drove around looking for a skip to put it in. Last seen in Hampstead Garden Suburb.

A woman called Celia has moved in downstairs. Forties, I would guess. Quiet. She seems nice. Friendly.

I'm home from work early today. I wasn't in the final scene so I finished just after four and got back here just in time to make it to the little organic grocer's around the corner before they close. It's unexpectedly cold, the first nip of autumn in the air, even though it's only August. I'm letting myself in through the street door, with my bag of asparagus and blackberries, when someone says, 'Amy,' right behind me and I jerk back and drop my keys. I know that voice. I'd know it anywhere.

I'm tempted not to turn around. To barge into the hall and slam the door behind me. But then she says, 'Please . . .' and, before I know it, I'm looking right at her.

She looks even thinner than usual. Her faded jean jacket swamps her. Underneath it, the bright neon-pink top confirms that this is definitely Mel.

'What do you want?' I bend down to pick up my keys.

'To talk to you. Please.'

'I don't think we've got anything to talk about. I don't know what you're doing up here, but I don't appreciate you hanging around outside my house.'

'I've got no other way of getting in touch. Just let me come in for ten minutes. Please. I've been freezing my tits off for hours out here.'

There's no way I'm going to let her into my flat. It's become my sanctuary. 'Ten minutes,' I say, walking off. I don't even wait to see if she follows. The café on the corner will be closing any minute now, but I head in and sit at a table by the window before they can tell me I'm too late.

'Just a water, please,' I say as the waitress heads over. 'We won't be long.'

'Two,' Mel says, as she sits down. 'Thanks'.

She looks at me. I'm finding it hard to make eye contact. I'm still furious but, also, I'm terrified I might get sucked back into her world.

'How are you?'

'I'm fine. We don't have time for the niceties. Why are you here?'

The waitress plonks two small bottles of water and two glasses on the table. She flips the sign on the door to 'Closed' and gives me a look as if to say, 'You saw that, right?' I give her a weak smile.

'To apologize. I know you won't believe a word of it, but I'm really sorry. For Jack. For the whole thing.'

I look up, finally, and I'm met with the full force of her green eyes. She wipes away an escaping tear.

'Okay. Well, I appreciate that. Thank you.'

'Amy, please,' she says, too loudly. The waitress looks up from the counter she's wiping down. 'I need to know you forgive me. I'm not expecting you to want to be friends –'

I snort. 'Huh.'

'– but I need you to know I'm sorry. That I took you for granted. That I behaved like a bitch.'

'Fine,' I say. I just want her to finish saying her piece and go.

'It's not fine, though, is it? Of course it's not fine.'

'Mel, we don't ever need to see each other again. We

can just get on with our lives. It doesn't matter what I think of you.'

'It does, though,' she says, and now she's all-out crying. I glance over at the waitress, aware that she wants us out of there, and her expression has softened. She waves a hand as if to say, 'It's okay, take your time,' and goes back to covering the food in the display case.

The thing is, I can't just sit there and watch Mel cry. Despite everything, it's still always going to tug at my heartstrings to see her upset.

'Okay,' I say, more gently. 'I accept your apology. And I apologize, too, for the stuff that I did. I'm not proud of it –'

'It was nothing compared to what I did to you. I'm a horrible person. I've always been a horrible person.'

I don't contradict her. She's right. We sit there in silence for a moment.

'But I'm trying to be better,' she says.

There are so many questions I want to ask her, but I force myself not to. I pour the last of my water into the glass. As if she can sense my curiosity, she says, 'Jack says hello.'

I'm so taken aback I don't know what to say.

'We're still together,' she says, through tears. 'We're trying to make it work. It seemed as if that was impor-tant after . . . you know . . . that at least I didn't just give up and move on to the next, as usual. I don't know how long it'll last – I think he still misses you, in all honesty – but I'm giving it a go. He knows I'm here. No more sneaking around.'

'No,' I say. I wait for a residual pang of jealousy or regret, and there's nothing.

'And I left my job. I couldn't . . . after . . . not that I'm having a go at you for that, because I know I did a million times worse . . . and you know I hated it anyway and needed a kick up the arse to do something else. And I don't think Jack would have even considered trying if I'd still been seeing John every day. Anyway, I'm going to use some of the money from the flat to train to be a massage therapist. Something completely different, you know.'

'Good for you,' I say. I down the last of my water as if to say, 'It's time to go.' But Mel's not finished.

'Oh, and Jack got a new job. Colby Sachs. They called and asked if he wanted to apply because they suddenly had a position vacant and they'd met him before or something. Anyway, he got it.'

I'm surprised by how pleased I am. Pleased and relieved. I was never comfortable with the idea of ruining someone's career.

'Great. Tell him congratulations. I mean it. We should go.'

'Oh. But I wanted to ask you how Chris was. And Kat. I'm sure they must both hate me –'

'They're fine. Everyone's fine. We've all moved on.' I don't say, 'Kat's a really good friend, a proper friend who's pleased when things go well for me and always there when they don't,' even though I'm tempted to. I put a fiver on the table. The waitress picks it up and goes off to retrieve change.

'Could we . . . I mean, do you want to go and have something to eat, or a proper drink or something?' She looks at me pleadingly. I almost accept. Almost.

'I don't think so, Mel. I appreciate you coming all this way to apologize. I really do. And I accept. No hard feelings. I'm happy you're sorting your life out. Happy for you and Jack. But let's leave it there.' I stand up, take the change and hand the waitress back a fifty-pence piece. 'Thanks.'

'And you've got this great new part, haven't you?' Mel says. 'I was reading about the series somewhere and I saw your name. I'm so pleased for you. Genuinely. I hope it really takes off. I mean that, Amy. You have to believe me.'

'I do. Really. It's okay,' I say, heading for the door. Outside, it's cold and drizzly, far darker than it should be for the time of day.

Mel walks beside me in silence. I don't know if she's hoping I'll change my mind and go out with her or invite her in. I stop when we reach my front door.

'Bye, then. Don't stress yourself about it. It's all forgotten, I promise.'

She looks at me for a moment, mascara streaked down her cheeks. 'I miss you.'

'Mel, do me a favour. Don't come up here again.

Don't get in touch. If you really want to show me you care about me, you'll give me that.'

She nods, blinking back tears. Puffs her cheeks out and exhales slowly. 'Of course. Okay.'

I lean forward, give her a quick hug. 'I hope things work out.'

I wait for her to turn away and head across the road, presumably towards her car, before I let myself in.

59

By the beginning of July, we had moved in together. Me, Mel, Kat and Liz. I'd found the house in an ad in *Loot* and I'd taken it before Mel could see it and object to how shoddy it was and the fact that I'd had to conjure up two complete strangers to make up the rent. I wanted to live a real life, not one where her parents would rent a beautiful two-bedroom apartment in a nice part of London and let us both live there for free.

I did make sure she had the best bedroom though. I was afraid, otherwise, she'd take one look and walk straight out again. With the landlord's permission, I painted both her and my bedrooms, and the communal kitchen and hallway, too. Not knowing Kat or Liz from Adam, I decided they were on their own with their little rooms.

Mel wanted to explore London while she waited for all the agents she'd contacted to snap her up. She had finally binned off Sylvia, telling her that her move to the city was the reason, and she'd sent out headshots, along with a letter listing her achievements. When she realized I wasn't about to drop everything to keep her company, she went into a major sulk.

'You've basically abandoned me,' she whined when I came in late one afternoon after a shift at a local café.

'I've got two jobs, Mel,' I said, flopping down on to one of the kitchen chairs. 'I can't just bunk off.'

To be honest, if I could have, I would have. I hated knowing she was pissed off with me, but I also knew I had no indulgent parents waiting in the wings to pay my rent if I couldn't afford it. And I was avoiding signing on, for fear they'd make me take a full-time job I didn't want and which would prevent me from going to auditions.

I remember so clearly Kat coming in from her job in the office of a building firm – this was long before she decided what she really wanted to do with her life – just as Mel was saying:

'I'm so bored all day.' In a voice that would work well on a four-year-old.

'What do you do, Mel?' she asked innocently. Mel hadn't exactly spent a lot of time making small talk with her by this point, despite Kat's efforts to be friendly, and Kat was out at work all day, so I guess she just assumed Mel was, too.

Mel had looked at her imperiously 'I'm an actress.'

'Oh, like Amy,' Kat had said, taking off her glasses and cleaning one lens on the hem of her skirt.

There was no way she could have known this was the wrong thing to say. I wanted to throw myself in front of her like a fire blanket to protect her from what was about to come.

Mel sniffed. 'I actually went to drama school. And I model and sing as well.'

'Oh, right.' Kat said. 'Which one are you doing at the moment?'

'I'm in between jobs,' Mel said. 'I'm waiting for the right thing to come along.'

I looked between them like a dog watching a game of catch.

'So, like Amy, then?' Kat said. I couldn't tell if she was trying to wind Mel up or not. Later, I realized that she was just getting the facts straight in a very Kat-like way.

'Oh, I'd take anything at this point,' I said, deciding to defuse the situation. 'I don't care if it's the right thing or not.'

After a few weeks, Mel had heard nothing from any of the agents she'd written to and so she started ringing round, checking whether they'd received her details. One by one, they told her their books were full.

'Will you introduce me to your agent?' she said one night when we were sitting in my room, sharing a bottle of wine.

'Of course,' I said, although I didn't really want to. I felt my own connection with them was hanging by a thread – I was sure they would suddenly realize they'd made an awful mistake taking me on and drop me at the first opportunity – and I knew what a wrecking ball Mel could be. But I couldn't say no to her. I wanted her to be happy and I knew that she wouldn't be until she could get her career underway. So I plucked up the courage and asked Christian to do me a favour and, probably because he wasn't very experienced and had hardly any clients, he said yes.

Mel came back from the meeting beaming. She was sure he was going to offer to represent her; he had more or less said so. He just wanted to see her in action, so she was going to drop off a VHS she'd had made when she was with Sylvia, a compilation of some of her finest moments. And even though it made me uneasy, I was relieved.

And then two things happened on the same day. I got my first job (a new play in a tiny theatre above a pub in Shepherd's Bush. It was a profit share, and I soon realized that ten per cent of nothing was nothing, but I didn't care. It was a real part and, even though we played to only a handful of people a night and I still had to do my shifts in the café during the day, it was work) and Mel got a call from Christian saying that he was sorry but he didn't think they had room for her on their books after all.

And then a week later, Mel's mum rang in tears to say her father had been made redundant. They were going to be fine but they weren't going to be able to pay her rent any more. For the first time in her life, Mel was going to have to stand on her own two feet. I expected her to pack up and move back home where she could live for free and keep on pursuing her dream and I was proud of her when she decided to stick it out in London. She took the first (decently paid) position that would have her, courtesy of a contact of her family's. I wasn't expecting her to give everything up so completely, but the life I was living – scrabbling around doing several badly paid jobs and performing to six people in a shithole – held no appeal for her. But she was never going to be content just being someone who worked in an office. She'd clung on to her gilded past, telling anyone who'd listen her exaggerated version of her many achievements.

I learned to play down any successes I had – even though most of them were things she wouldn't have considered doing in a million years herself anyway, like Theatre in Education or unpaid roles in student films. To me, it was all experience in the bank. To her, it was a big waste of time – and she rarely asked for details about anything I was doing.

She never once came to see me perform after that first time at college. Not once in twenty years. But if I think back now, I can picture Kat sitting in tiny pub theatres or community centres or Soho basements, face beaming, hands clapping, gushing afterwards about how amazing I had been, even when I knew, on many occasions, that simply wasn't true.

It's taken me a long time to realize it, but I think I finally understand what a true friend is.

60

Who would have thought that my flat in the middle of nowhere would become the place we'd all agree to meet up, but it turns out Alistair and Siggy live in West Hampstead and Kieron and his other half, Jim, in Muswell Hill. Neither couple has a garden and the muggy late summer that's emerged after all the rain makes sitting outside a huge plus, so Tom has volunteered my roof.

The summer of extreme sun and rain means that my plants are thriving, and I've filled the rest of the planters with lavender and honeysuckle, with a copious amount of ivy thrown in. I've strung coloured fairy lights across the three fenced sides and replaced the candles. I've even splashed out on two Adirondack chairs, painted sky blue, and Tom has agreed to help me lug the two kitchen chairs (now also sanded and painted by me, in white, with a stencilled flowery motif across the backs) up the ladder, so everyone has a seat. There will be eight of us. Kat and Greg are coming over. My best friends meeting my (now) oldest friends for the first time.

They get here early, helping me finish off the last bits and pieces to the pizzas I've made (everything from vegan to gluten-free, because I have no idea what anybody's preference is). I'm so nervous I don't know what to do with myself. What if they don't like me? What if I don't like them? I changed clothes at least three times until Kat finally told me to get a grip.

'If they decide they don't like you because you're wearing khaki trousers instead of grey, then they really aren't people you want to be friends with.'

'I know. Love you,' I say, making a grab for her and landing a kiss on the top of her head. She pushes me off. This has become my new favourite game. Hug Kat, tell her how much I love her and watch her squirm.

Tom arrives first, as he's been instructed to. He's been here once before, for a lazy evening of binge-watching *Narcos* on Netflix, because we discovered we were both obsessed and each had four episodes of the latest season left to watch. He greets Kat and Greg with a big grin and wraps his arms around them each in turn.

'Thank God Amy had you two,' he says. 'She's told me she never would have coped with the whole thing without you.'

Greg slaps him on the back. I almost expect him to start calling Tom 'mate', like he did Simon when he first met him. Greg has always been more at ease with women than with men, as if he's not sure how to be one of them. Kat, of course, huffs and turns red and mutters something that sounds like, 'Shut up.'

'For God's sake, don't pay Kat a compliment,' I say, laughing. 'Not if you value your life.'

The doorbell rings again and I almost have a coronary. I don't know why I'm so nervous.

As if he reads my mind, Tom says, 'Do you want me to go and let them in?' and I accept gracefully.

'He's nice,' Kat says when he's gone.

'Oh no you don't,' I say. 'It's nothing like that.'

'What? I just said he was nice.' She looks at me, owl-eyed.

'It was the way you said it.'

We're saved from ourselves by the sound of voices in the hallway. I recognize Kieron's immediately. He's first in, followed by a blur of others.

'There she is,' he says, making a beeline for me. He looks so exactly the same but not the same that I get a lump in my throat. He's still as striking looking as ever, but his once shaggy hair is now a number one, a casualty of impending baldness, by the looks of it. It suits him.

He swoops in for a kiss and then introduces me to Jim, who is behind him. I'm surprised that he's on the short side and not in the slightest bit classically handsome, but then he smiles and it's as if someone has turned on a light.

'I'm going to say literally the worst thing you can ever say to someone you've just met,' he says, as we shake hands. 'I've heard a lot about you.'

Alistair is next. I'd recognize him anywhere from the haircut alone.

'You haven't changed a bit,' I say, as he kisses me on the cheek.

'You can talk,' he says. 'This is Siggy.'

A tall, blonde woman emerges from behind him. 'I've also heard a lot about you,' she says, in a clipped accent I take to be Scandinavian. 'Good, I should say! All good.'

She hands me a fancy box that contains some kind of delicious-looking chocolate truffles.

'They look amazing. Thank you.'

'I made them,' she says, rolling her eyes. 'Our youngest just started nursery and I don't know what to do with myself until I find a job.'

'She's basically superwoman,' Kieron says affectionately.

Tom has clearly filled them all in on who Kat and Greg are because, one by one, they greet them like old friends. The sheer amount of warmth I feel coming from all seven of them could heat a sauna.

Kieron and Jim have brought a couple of bottles of fizz, so I put them in the fridge and Greg opens a cold one.

'The bad news is you all have to climb a ladder now,' I say, and four of them look at me as if I'm mental.

The next thing I know, it's three hours later and I haven't stopped talking and laughing all evening. There hasn't been a lull in the conversation, no one has been left out. Both Kieron and Alistair have quietly told me that they're sorry we lost touch, sorry they iced me out because of Mel.

'Oh,' Siggy says out of nowhere. 'Did you tell her?' She looks at Alistair. 'We found Pia. Alistair tracked her down through a mutual friend. She's living in Spain, very happily married, three kids and a job in a drama school.' She beams happily, the bearer of good news.

'She sent everyone her love,' Alistair says. He looks at me. 'Especially you. She told me she watched *Murder in Manhattan* religiously. She says, next time we all meet up, she'll try and come over.'

I can feel I'm smiling from ear to ear, and it's not just the wine. I'm feeling warm and fuzzy and melancholy all at the same time. I look over and see Kat happily chatting to Kieron and Siggy while Greg, Alistair and Jim all laugh heartily at something one of them has said. The evening is still warm and lights are twinkling all over London.

'Are you having a nice time?' Tom says from the seat next to me.

'Lovely,' I say.

He gives me a big, Tom-sized smile. 'Marvellous,' he says, and he reaches out and takes my hand. 'Is that okay? Tell me if I've overstepped the mark.'

I look over and see Kat watching. She raises her eyebrows as if to say, 'I told you so.'

I smile and look away. Leave my hand where it is, in Tom's. 'It's definitely okay.'

Even if nothing more happens between us, I don't care. So long as he's my friend. Because I've realized that, once you find your real friends, you have to hang on to them. And so long as I have him and Kat and Greg, and all the other people currently partying on my roof in my life, nothing else matters. I'll be fine.

Acknowledgements

As usual an army of people helped make this book happen and I can't thank them all enough. Or individually, because that would be a whole other book in itself. Special mention though to Maxine Hitchcock at Michael Joseph, Jonny Geller at Curtis Brown, Charlotte Willow Edwards for her research and Elsie Fallon for actor-friendly call centre intel.

Also by
Jane Fallon . . .

'A deliciously devious plot'
Daily Express

 JaneFallon

 JaneFallonOfficial